D1388050

JUDE

By the same author

Women are Bloody Marvellous!

JUDE

Betty Burton

GUILD PUBLISHING LONDON

Grafton Books
A Division of the Collins Publishing Group
8 Grafton Street, London W1X 3LA

Published by Grafton Books 1986
Reprinted 1986, 1987, 1990

British Library Cataloguing in Publication Data

Burton, Betty
Jude.
I. Title
823'.914(F)   PR6052.U69/

ISBN 0-246-12801-1

Photoset in North Wales by
Derek Doyle & Associates, Mold, Clwyd
Printed in Great Britain by
Robert Hartnoll Ltd., Bodmin, Cornwall

For Russ, Brendan,
Simon and Tania

Contents

THE VILLAGE OF
CANTLE

To Motte (1 hour)
and Blackbrook (2 hours)

WINCHESTER HILL

Standing Stone

OLD MARL

RIFT

Ruined
Fortifications

Bell Tump

Mill

Willow
farm

Bellpitt Lane

THE DOWNS

Dunnock Brook

Track to Motte — when dry

Manor
farm

Meadow farm

Park manor

Dragon and Fount
Inn

Annie
Bassett's
House

THE DOWNS

Raike Bottom

green

pond

ford

church

Eastfield
farm

Chard
Lepe
Pond

Howgate Path

Curt

rectory

TRAPPER'S RAIKE

Croud Cantle

Church farm

RIFT

Beacon Point

BEACON HILL

Part One

———

FARMGIRL

JUDE NUGENT, small, strong, with square practical hands, rough from work and weather, sits on Tradden Raike.

Judeth Nugent: her pale red hair – the legacy of her mother's family, the Estovers, who had come into Hampshire from Devon a couple of generations ago – complements the green of the chalk-hill.

Jude kicks rabbit-droppings from a well-grassed molehill and sits looking. An image of her sister Jaen, as she had seen her earlier that morning, tries to thrust itself upon her. Jude resists it, not allowing herself to cry, and concentrates upon the far side of the valley.

People used to live there. Gilly Gilson had said that it had been a fortress. He knew such a lot that Jude thought that it must be true, though it wasn't easy to believe when you were actually there, scrambling for sloes or blackberries. But from Tradden Raike it was possible to see squares and lines, which you could imagine were the outlines of dwellings of some kind. And the skyline there was straight for about a mile, where there were the walls of the old stone fortifications which, apart from lichens and moss and the occasional gap where stone had been filched, were much the same as when they had been erected.

In spite of her misery Jude wondered if there were places that were better than here. There probably were, but she could not imagine what they might be like. Behind her the county sloped slowly away. On clear days in early summer it was possible to see the glitter of the sea, Portchester or Portsmouth, Gilly said. Jude would love to go to the sea. Gilly said that in one day's walk you could be standing on Portsmouth mudflats and looking at the Isle of Wight, close enough to see roofs and trees on the island. Jude had a great desire to look at most places she heard of, except Winchester City, which looked as though it must be grey and dull from what she had seen of it from an engraving in the rectory hallway.

Thoughts of the rectory close in the shadow of the church brought Jaen flickering into Jude's mind. She poked a finger into the ground and hooked out a knob of chalk using it to whiten her short work-roughened fingernails. She never tired of Tradden Raike. Just now, larks were spilling out ribbons of notes, clear as the air and sky, into which the birds seemed to dissolve.

Later would come the chalk-hill butterflies and moths flittering crazy paths from blue scabious to purple, stunted thistles, bee-orchids and ox-eye daisies. From March, through high summer and on into the time of old man's beard and wayfarer-berries, there was always scent, colour and movement on the chalk hills.

Small bits at a time, Jude let Jaen in, remembering when they were here together.

Almost as soon as Jude could walk, Jaen, six years older, had taken her on to Tradden. As they grew more capable of climbing they went higher and higher to places where there were nuts and berries. But as they grew older, there wasn't so much time to spare. There was always work to be done.

"There an't time to be always off up there, messing about, not doing nothing." Bella Nugent's words – their mother's words. Mother could not do with people who messed about, doing nothing.

Yet there had been a time when their mother had been indulgent if they played on Old Marl or Tradden – but that was when they were very young.

As soon as they could walk, the girls had chores for which they were responsible: carrying wood, collecting eggs, feeding the chickens. As they grew older, the work they had to do became harder and more important to their livelihood, although some people thought that some of the work the girls had to do was just Bella Nugent making a rod for their backs.

Bella had some queer standards, especially about keeping things clean. In matters of scrubbing and laundering and dairy work nobody ever matched her standards. Most of her criticisms of work that was not up to scratch were prefaced by, "I know I'm a bit particular, but ... " So as, over the years, Jaen and Jude slotted into the routine of the work, it was Bella who scoured floor-tiles and the soft pine of the table, it was Bella who boiled and pounded and scrubbed clothes, and it was she who drew water from the deeper of their two wells. A yoke with its two dragging pails seemed sometimes to be part of Bella's frame, but she seldom let them get the better of her and draw her shoulders down and her head forward.

The caring of the animals, the planting and harvesting, ditching and hedge-laying on their small acres were done for the most part by Dicken and Rob, and by casual and travelling workers who sold their skill or strong backs to Croud Cantle.

Bella worked them hard. She liked order and routine and things to be done when they needed to be done.

Thoughts of Jaen would not be repressed any longer.

"Jaen," Jude said aloud, releasing the pent up stress of the last few months and the unhappiness of the morning; obliterating the ancient, ruined settlement across the valley, the larks, wild-strawberry flowers and Cantle village in a grey cloud of misery.

Dan Hazelhurst. Why did she go with him? Why couldn't Jaen have gone with somebody else? But Jude could not think who. There wasn't a man in any of the four parishes who had brains enough to love Jaen properly.

Jaen had always been the one who started things, had ideas and schemes, had dreams and imaginings that Jude adored listening to. Even an ordinary job like collecting blackberries, Jaen could turn into an event that stayed with you.

Jude remembered, when they were still very young, climbing up Tradden or Old Marl with sticks and bowls and Jaen saying, "We shan't go blackberrying today, Ju. We shall go after some special fruits that nobody has ever found before. You have to walk a long way to get them, and witches have put tiny, sharp knives to stop people getting them. That's what we got sticks for. We can hook them over and the witch-thorns on the sharp stems can't get us; then we can rescue the special fruit that the witches want to keep in prison on the bushes."

"What shall we do with the fruits, Jaen?"

"When we have filled our bowls, we shall take them home and hide them in the big black pot on the fire-back where the witches won't be able to find them. In the morning the fruits will have let out all their sweet selves. Then we shall take a great lump of special rock, that looks like ice but isn't cold, and crack it into pieces and pound it up. That has to be mixed with what the fruits have give up, and then put to the fire. And the fire works magic. When the special fruit and the ice have been fired and it gets cold, it turns into the only food that will make sick fairies better."

Jaen. Only Jaen could make a magic out of bramble jelly.

And she had gone with Dan Hazelhurst.

The image of Jaen close to the great work-horse body of Dan Hazelhurst was too painful for Jude even to think about. It was like when the great prancing black cockerel went after one of the little red bantam hens; if Jude saw him she would brave him to rescue the hen. But Jude hadn't even known about Dan Hazelhurst going after Jaen.

That was what some of her misery was about. Pain that Jaen had not shared the greatest secret of all, and anger at Dan Hazelhurst. For the first time Jaen had excluded Jude, had not told her that when she had gone over to Rathley for a few days she had met Dan Hazelhurst. When it all came out two months later, Jude withdrew into wretchedness and would speak to no one.

And this morning Jaen Nugent had gone into the church with Dan Hazelhurst and had never come out. In her stead had come Dan Hazelhurst's wife with a baby inside her.

This morning, Jaen had taken not only herself and belongings over to the Hazelhursts, she had taken ... Jude did not know the word to put to it ... Jaen had taken her presence. Jaen had gone – total.

Jude rose and began walking downhill. Around her, deep within the jungle of brambles and dog-roses, and more openly among the new bread-and-cheese shoots of hawthorn, thrushes and blackbirds and dunnocks – mostly the dunnocks – were noisy at making this year's broods. She saw a sparrow-hawk almost motionless before it plummeted and soared in one curve of movement. Watching it, her spirit rose. The grey cloud began to dissolve.

She wondered whether the white violets had come yet: Jaen used to say that the white ones had given up their colour to put into a cloak for God, and were blessed – like palm leaves on Easter Sunday. They had come every spring to pick white violets. You could never rely on the time they bloomed, which added to their mystery.

She found a clump of them, blooming in the usual place. She picked some and made a posy with new ivy leaves as Jaen did. As Jaen used to do. The tears that had trickled out as Jude sat on the sparse grass at the top of Tradden Raike, drained from her the pain that had grown around Jaen like pus released from a boil. The wound was still tender but would heal. She could think about her again.

She and Jaen had picked white violets here. She and Jaen had looked after the house-cow between them. She and Jaen had slept curled around one another. Now Jaen was married. Soon Jaen would have a baby.

The baby.

At last the smooth mound that was the cause of the metamorphosis of Jaen into Dan Hazelhurst's wife stopped being a malignant growth inflicted upon her by him – it was Jaen's baby.

By the time she reached the lower slope of the hill, she was lighter-hearted than she had been for months. She had not noticed the passage of time on Tradden, but now saw that the April sun was beginning to slide down to where Winchester and Beacon hills merged, and was reflecting off the Croud Cantle duck-pond.

The Croud Cantle holding was a good walk from Cantle village; past the triangle of green which was bordered by the Dragon and Fount, past the church and the common pond, along Howgaite Path, or take the cut across Manor Farm fields. The holding was small – a marshy meadow, some cultivated land for vegetables, and grassland at the foot of Tradden Raike.

The cottage, barn, cow-shed, piggery, latrine and dairy formed an "L" around a yard. There were a number of rickety-looking hen-houses, and some pens for geese and ducks. Goats and three donkeys grazed a small orchard. There was a shallow well and a deep well; the deep one being a fair distance from the house, but nearer to the cattle-troughs in the meadow. The Dunnock Brook ran close by but, being downstream of Cantle village, Bella never fancied it.

There was no cohesion in the buildings, but they were so old that there was an air of satisfying degeneracy about them. The outhouses were shingle-roofed and the cottage had a quite good but shaggy thatch. The cottage had, in earlier times, been a single room in which people and animals had lived communally, but now, in the latter half of the eighteenth century, the ground floor had a separate scullery with a stone trough, and the upstairs was divided into two rooms.

When Jude reached Croud Cantle, Bella, pail-carrying as always, was crossing the yard.

"Well, Miss? Nice of you to honour us with your company. Don't you worry, the cows have milked theirselves into the pails and the milk have had a good jump about and made itself into butter, so all you got to do now is tell the logs to set on fire and it'll all be done."

It's a wonder Bella Nugent's tongue don't cut her lip!

[13]

Jude's quiet, "I'm sorry," caused Bella to give her a sharp look. That wasn't like Jude.

"Here." Jude tucked the violets into Bella's cleavage.

They both knew that the violets were intended to take the place of words – less frightening, no involvement, you could pretend that they were just flowers – but words? They were something else.

Bella had never been good at accepting even their childish offerings.

"Ah, all right then," off-handedly, was all that she could ever bring herself to say when they brought her a few primroses, but later she would arrange the flowers in a pretty pot; or if they brought in some interesting stone or shell, Bella would wash and shine it and place it on the mantelpiece.

Bella looked down at the violets. "Better take them indoors, case they falls down the well."

On her way into the house, Jude collected a basket of logs from the pile. Although the yard was dry that day, Jude automatically hooked off her boots at the door, as she had been taught from the day she first had boots. Most of the time she went barefoot, or in pattens when the mud was deep. A good many people thought Bella Nugent a bit on the queer side, but Bella seldom made rules without, what was to her, good reason. Once made, she enforced them, not caring what anyone thought.

Most of Cantle's cottages had pounded earth floors strewn with reeds or bracken, but in Croud Cantle red clay tiles had been laid. Bella had few comforts or pleasures, but one of the few was to see her kitchen when the tiles were still wet. The men, when they came in for their food, came in their muck as any would – but not in the living end of the kitchen. At the end where they all sat at the long table, the tiles were reed-covered, and fresh reeds brought in frequently, but the house-place end was clean according to Bella Nugent's rules.

Bella was quite strong about mud and muck indoors.

"Haven't you never seen dust-motes floating about in the sun? Stands to reason, that an't nothing but dried up muck and dung. Anybody who wants that flying around when they'm eating is welcome."

Some people might have wanted to retort that a bit of good clean muck never done no harm, but Bella Nugent had bright eyes and foxy, flaring hair and a sharp tongue. People said that Bella Nugent was a queer piece of goods, always washing and scrubbing and on about dirt – but not so that she could overhear. Bella Nugent was a real Tartar.

Jude made a neat pile of the logs on the hearth. By evening they would become warm, filling the room with a mellow scent, bits of moss would shrivel and the bark make small cracking sounds as it dried. There were times when Jude would sit for a whole evening and think of little else but those things.

What was a smell? How did noses work to smell anything? Was there something in the skin? Once, at a pig-killing, she had offered to make the brawn so that she could minutely examine the pig's nostrils, but found nothing that accounted for the sense of smell.

She had asked Gilly Gilson, who had done the pig. Sharpening his jointing knives in preparation for the resurrection of the pig as pork, bacon and ham.

"How do noses smell things?"

Gilly had raised his head for a few seconds whilst looking around in his mind for an answer.

"Blowed if I know." He thought on. "Now that's interesting, Young Jude, cause come to think about it, how do smells theirselves come about? There's nothing there to see."

Gilly – full of knowledge picked up on his travels doing pigs, on farms and holdings where an extra pair of hands were needed to do a pig.

"Oh Gilly!" Ten-year-old Jude had said with exasperation. "Why do you always wind up my brain so when I ask you something?"

"Better wound up than letting him run down slow. I heard people say too much looking wears out your eyes, and too much thinking wears out your brain. And I asks if they don't think jawing wears out your mouth. And they got no answer to that one."

"Don't you know how noses work?"

Gilly had started up slicing away at the belly-pork. "I never know anybody so full a questions as thee's, young Jude – ah ... not unless it was me."

"How do you find out all the things you know? About Africa and the men who never cut their fingernails? And about trees that are wide as a house, and the sun being a fire?"

"I listens. Sometimes I asks. I reckon between all of us in the world we got the answer to everything. It's just getting it all together."

[15]

"Couldn't it all be put down in a book? A big book like the church bible?"

"I reckon it'd need a sight bigger book than that."

Young Jude's imagination couldn't conjure up anything larger than the church bible.

"Two then. Big as the church bible."

"I reckon that'd do it," Gilly had agreed.

Jude placed a couple of logs on the thick bed of charcoal, careful, as had been drummed into her, not to disturb the white ash.

The room felt empty.

The whole cottage felt empty.

Jaen had gone.

But work and routine soon took over. Bella rattled a scoop of wheat into a pan and Jude fetched milk to pour over it, then set the grains to sprout for tomorrow's fermity. She took down two plates, aware that the third remained on the dresser. A pity it wasn't dinner-time when the boy and the yard-men would have been at the table with them.

"There's enough rabbit stew, or shall I get cheese?"

Bella didn't answer. Jude peered into the scullery through the round window-light in the door.

"I said 'cheese'?"

Bella was sitting drying tears with her apron corner. Discovering her mother like this was quite a shock, and Jude felt guilty. It had not occurred to her that her mother would miss Jaen. She had tried hard enough to get her married.

"Don't cry. We shall see her all the time."

Her mother pushed her hair back and let out a sigh.

"Ah well, that's my howling over and done for this little lot. Every birthen, marriage and death is due for one good cry – then be done with it."

Jude had never seen her mother show such emotion, and although she was embarrassed, she felt as she occasionally did when a ewe nudged its dead lamb, she wanted to offer comfort, but did not know how.

"Did you cry when I was born then?"

"Ah, twice. You wouldn't wait till the hay was in, and we had a thunderstorm and it got beat down."

She brisked herself to her feet. The show of self-pity over Jaen was done with.

That evening they sat late, talking over the rearrangement of farm-work and chores. When they had settled everything Bella said, "It's not been a bad year taken all in all. There hasn't been a bad day at Blackbrook market this eighteen-month, but we been lucky."

She talked on about the cow, the butter and cheese-making, about eggs, hens and geese, chutney, and the pickled walnuts for which Bella Nugent had a good local reputation. It was small enough business talk, but to Jude it was important. Talking about Croud Cantle on an equal basis, woman to woman. Jude was already a worker on the farm, now she had taken over Jaen's place as partner.

Nothing that Bella said was new to Jude. She had sat on the hearth throughout her childhood listening to Bella mulling over the pros and cons of buying, selling, barter and exchange. Whether to make more apple wine and less cider or whether to put down a glut of eggs in preserve, or to pickle them in vinegar. Croud Cantle was, and would always be, Bella's main preoccupation. Now Jude's turn had come to have a say in how they kept their head above water.

Jude was at the undefeated age, when crocks of gold may be found in the roots of trees, ambitions achieved; a wish needed only to be made at the right moment for it to be fulfilled.

As they were going to bed, Jude took the bull by the horns.

"Mother?"

"Jude, you're as clear as Dunnock Brook. When you say 'Mother?' like that, you're after something."

"All right then – Bella."

Bella gave her a that's-enough-of-that-cheek! look.

"I want to learn to read and write. Gilly went to school till he was eight ... If I could a done that ... " Bella's unresponsive expression made her trail off.

"I don't mean for me to go, but there might be somebody who could tell me how to do it."

Bella's non-committal, "Oh yes?" followed by silence, was her stock response to any question needing more thought.

"I want to write things down."

"Oh yes?"

"In a book."

Bella sat gazing into the fire. Without realising that she was doing so, Jude breathed shallowly and intermittently, her hopes hibernating until the spring of Bella's answer.

If I could write. If I could write. And read! She did not know

[17]

exactly what she would do when she could write, the answer to that would come. The most important thing was to learn how to do it.

It is like everything you want to know being a prize at the centre of a huge ball of cord that is all tangles and knots. You can see the prize, but you don't know what it is, and you can't get it because of the tangle. You work at undoing the knots by asking people things. Every question answered is a bit of the tangle straightened out, and a pin-hole glimpse at the prize. But the ball of cord is so enormous and the tangles are so great!

Jude saw the ability to read and write as the knife to slice through the tangle, and she had been thinking about it since she was about five years old, when Bella had taken them to Rathley.

It was the first journey that Jude had ever been on. It was extraordinary and out of routine, but even so the memory of it was hazy, except for two clear impressions. One was the awful soreness of her feet. The other was a picture.

Bella had got them clean and dressed early in the day. They wore gaitered boots. Bella had done a deal over the boots with a packman a few months before they were needed, and Jude's feet had grown. The boots rubbed her toes and the backs of her ankles. Just as they were about to leave, the little studs around which the laces were wound had popped off one by one. Bella had got cross because the studs would not have popped off if Jude hadn't gone kicking at stones in the yard. Bella had got some twine and Jude had gone to Rathley with the gaiters bound to her legs like corn-stooks.

Jude never knew why they went to Rathley. Bella took a roll of papers with her, she remembered that, and they had gone into a big place full of shelves with more rolls of paper. Jaen had held her hand and said they must be good. Jude was, her small feet and legs wanting nothing better than to be left alone, dangling from the high bench on which she and Jaen had been placed.

The only thing to see was a painting hanging on the wall opposite to where they sat. It was of a life-size group, and seemed enormous to the small Jude.

At first she could think of nothing but her feet, but as they cooled she began to see the picture. She became interested because there was a woman with red hair, like her mother's, holding the hand of a small child whose hair was the same colour as Jude's own. They were standing behind a man. The mother and the little girl had obviously come in to look at him. The woman held her head on one side and looked at the man with admiration. The child was looking cross. The man was in the middle of the canvas, seated at a table with a board resting upon it. He wore dark-blue, strange clothes and was holding a piece of chalk. The entire board was covered with marks, letters and numbers. The man had a pleased look in his eyes, and his mouth was turned up in a smile. He had been captured in the act of looking up, and he looked directly at Jude. He was pleased and excited; he had been searching for the answer to something and had at last discovered it. He must be saying, "Ah yes! Of course!"

When the soreness in her feet subsided a bit, Jude slid from the bench and moved closer to the picture. The man's gaze followed her. "Ah yes! Of course!" She walked up and down, until Jaen had hissed at her to sit down. Wherever she moved the man looked at Jude and said "Ah yes!"

Of course, none of this actually presented itself as immediate inspiration to the five-year-old Jude – only the impression that the man had found something wonderful in what he had written on the board.

There were some people, like the man in the picture, who got at the prize within the tangle.

After a long silence, Bella said, "Why d'you want to do that?"

"I don't know. But sometimes I find things out that seems important, and I want to keep them, and then I get afraid that I shall forget and they a be lost for ever."

Bella fell silent again and Jude was afraid that her mother would dismiss it, suddenly jump to her feet and say, "This won't do," and the right moment would never come again.

She was eleven, and she hadn't much time.

What she really wanted to say was, "I don't want to just work like we do now. I don't want to grow up grumbling about dust motes getting on things, and cleaning floors so they can be walked on, and spinning and making clothes that wear out, and drawing pails and pails of water. Nor making food which goes as soon as it's made so you have to make some more, and as soon as that's made you have to make more and more and more." She really wanted to say, "I don't want to be like you, Mother, where everything you do has to be done over and over again, for ever. I want to find out things and put them in books so they will be there, for ever."

But she just said, "I know that there's books about all different things, and I should like to have a read of them. I want to find it all out."

"You'll get over it. When I was about your age, I was always drawing things and making figures. I used to make people out of anything – scrape away with a knife at lumps of chalk, any lump of old clay – used to draw things everywhere. I used to be just like that. I wanted to make little figures, or make pictures. I made a pig once, with a whole litter on her teats. I remember my father putting it on the top shelf. He said, 'We shan't get a lot of ham out of they, but they'll give us another pleasure.' He seemed quite proud of my pig. It stayed on the shelf for years. Never knew what happened to it. You'd a liked my father."

She returned her attention to the present and looked at Jude as though she had forgotten something. "He could write, you know," Bella said.

Then, rubbing the small of her back, she stretched and said, "This won't do!"

"Please Mother. Let me learn writing."

"It's no good Jude. I told you, I know how young people feels, but you'll get over it. Just ask yourself, what good would it be? If you learnt to read, where would you get books and that? Any case, there an't anybody round here as could show you how it's done."

"But your father could. Somebody must have taught him."

"That was a long time ago."

It was useless arguing about it. There was not a single school in the four parishes, and they knew no one who would be able to teach her. But that would not stop her trying.

She had expected to feel desolate without Jaen, this first night without her, but the wedding-morning seemed now to be much further in the past than just those few actual hours. When she got into bed, her mind was so much given over to how she was going to find somebody to show her how to write, that she fell asleep before she became aware of the empty place at her back.

NEXT MORNING was bright, clear April. When Jude awoke, less than a day after the grey misery on Tradden Raike, and so soon after her disappointment of the previous evening, she felt almost guilty that she should feel cheerful.

The sky was just lightening. Jude loved to be first up. She quickly dressed, went to the rain-water butt and splashed her face and arms. She blew up the fire. Added milk to the wheat-grain that had been standing overnight, making a thick fermity which she put on the side to heat up.

As the little well still had plenty, she drew water from there. Bella would almost always go to the deep well, swearing that its water had special properties – she never seemed to be able to bring herself to make her life easier. Perhaps Mother was right and the water in the deep well was better. Jude would have liked to know.

She went to let the hens out, just as a red eyelash of rising sun showed above Tradden. It spread a flush on the blackthorn that was in bloom on Winchester Hill and down Bellpitt Lane. From within the hen-house she saw the great sweep of the hill, its ancient ruined fortifications framed by the open hatch.

"When I was your age, I was always drawing things ... You'll get over it ... Just ask yourself, what good would it be?"

What good was anything then? Why did people have to get over it? Gentry didn't. She had seen ladies and gentlemen who stayed with Old Sir Henry sitting in the park with paints. Not just children; ladies and gentlemen as old as Mother. They went about drawing and painting: why did her mother have to get over it?

Her answer came in the heavy tread of the men's boots as they came in at the gate, and a clatter from the dairy as her mother started the scouring of milk-pails.

There being nobody else to confide in, she silently told the hens, "I an't never going to get over it. I shall learn to read and write."

The hens pecked around, nodding their jerky heads in agreement. Jude laughed aloud. "I'm glad you agree," she said.

"Glad somebody's got summit to laugh about. I thought you'd be ready for market, Miss."

"Am I coming?"

"I thought we settled all that last night. I thought you was so keen taking over Jaen's ... "

"Oh yes, yes. I just never thought about going to market."

"Then you'd best begin thinking now."

"Who is going to see to ... "

"Johnny-twoey. You was seeing to the beasts and that on market-day when you was seven. He an't no stupider than you."

Jude rushed everywhere at once in her enthusiasm. It was seldom that she had taken part in going to market. Bella saw no fun in it – the heavy loads; wondering whether there would be better stuff than hers on sale; worried when the weather was warm in case the cream might turn or the butter go rancid or oily – but to Jude it was next to Fair Day for excitement.

For all the interruption of routine by yesterday's wedding and the evening spent talking, Bella was ready for market, and half an hour after sunrise was waiting with the donkeys harnessed and packed.

She called, "Ready!" in the voice that Dicken always reckoned could rattle the bones in Rathley graveyard.

Jude flew from the house. She had changed from her rough dress and put on a cotton-print skirt, clean white apron and bodice, and the shoes with a buckle that had been bought for the wedding. As they walked down Howgaite Path, Bella leading both donkeys, Jude finished pinning her hair and put on a muslin cap that had been Jaen's.

Bella looked down at Jude's feet.

"What you think you got on your feet then?"

Jude looked down at the shiny buckles.

"Go on, back and put your boots on. They shoes a be in shreds before we gets as far as Motte."

Jude ran back, put on her boots and brought her new shiny shoes for Blackbrook market to see her in.

The Dunnock was low for April, the clear water flowing gently round the stepping-stones at the ford. Cantle women there, scooping and carrying water, exchanged a brief nod of greeting. Jude would have liked it if they had uncurled their backs, smiled and waved, put down the heavy pails and asked what she was doing going to Blackbrook. She wanted to share her prospect of pleasure. At least she carried her shiny buckles in full view.

As they crossed from Howgaite on to the Dunnock track, they passed The Reverend Mr Tripp, incumbent of St. Peter's, Cantle. As the Living was in the gift of the Goodenstone family, Tripp was returning from the Big House, Park Manor, where he went each morning to kneel with the servants to ask God to look favourably on Old "Sir" Henry Goodenstone, and to plead that they, Tripp and the servants, be worthy to serve Sir Harry dutifully – and God, of course.

He was now on his way back to St. Peter's to give thanks that he had been called to be a theological, rather than a practical, shepherd in Sir Henry's employ, because the Reverend Tripp loved comfort. Every day he was grateful that, when God shared out wealth, privilege, power and ability, he had not overlooked Archbold Tripp: not that God had been profligate, but He had at least looked after His own by giving Archbold Tripp a better living than he had ever expected – after intercession by a Bishop friend of Rev. Tripp Senior's.

Jude and Bella bobbed a curtsey which Tripp acknowledged with a nod.

"Mother!" Jude gripped Bella's arm and whispered urgently. "Mr Tripp can read and write."

"Oh Jude, be sensible."

"We could ask."

"No we couldn't."

"I will."

By now they had crossed the ford and were losing sight of Mr Tripp.

"Please, mother. Let me just ask. You go on, I'll run fast to catch up," and, without waiting for her mother to answer, Jude ran back to Mr Tripp and caught him up outside the church.

He turned to see the cause of the running breathlessness.

"Mr Tripp?"

He stopped.

Jude had no idea what to say.

"Mr Tripp, I want to learn how to write." Sudden, subconscious inspiration: "And read, so I can read the bible for myself."

[23]

"Do you not listen at morning service?"

"Yes, Mr Tripp."

"Well? There is no more in the bible than what you hear from me. The Lord's words are the same whether heard by the ear or seen by the eye."

Jude knew that it was no good – it was in his voice – but she pressed on, hoping that something might happen.

"And I should like to be able to write."

"Girl, there are many things that we should all 'like'. Had God wished you to read and write, then he would not have made you ... " He did not wish to say, "made you one of the lower orders", for he prided himself on having a certain sensitivity in some matters. We are all God's children, created in His image, and Tripp himself would not have liked to be called "lower" anything. "Had God wished you to read and write, then He would not have made you such a strong right hand to your mother. We each must use what He has given us."

Jude ran faster than necessary to catch up with Bella. She wanted to rush away from the anger that was rising within her. She snapped off a hazel switch; slashed at the bitter-sweet which grew self-satisfied along the hedge; whipped at the smug celandines: serve them right!

All Bella said was, "One of these days your temper's going to get the better of you," which made Jude want to give her mother a slash with the hazel-switch too.

For five or six months of the year, the journey from Cantle through Motte and on to Blackbrook had to be made up the dragging incline of Bellpitt Lane and over Winchester Hill. But early spring had been dry this year, so that they were able to follow the track that ran north beside the Dunnock and around the back of Winchester Hill.

Walking steadily and quite fast beside the donkeys, they were through Motte and on the outskirts of Blackbrook in good time. As they neared the market-town, they became part of a stream of carts, women with hugely laden baskets, girls with small flocks of geese, and drovers who had perhaps come fifty miles or more with their herds, spending the night in some hired meadow, and now completing their journey. Villagers and townspeople, who wanted to get in early for the best and freshest produce, swelled the stream on its way to the market.

Bella and Jude exchanged very few words on the first miles of the journey, but after Jude had rid herself of Mr Tripp, she tried to get her mother talking about the market.

"You'll know when we gets there," or, "Don't you never stop talking Jude?" soon shut Jude up, leaving her to speculate and wonder about the day.

BLACKBROOK, LIKE CANTLE, was in a valley, though the enclosing hills had gentler slopes. People had lived there in small settlements from the earliest times, building their huts and wooden churches close to the river; but it was not until the building of the great stone abbey, after the Normans came, that it grew in size and importance. By the eighteenth century, it was the centre for the buying and selling of all livestock in that part of Hampshire.

The cattle-market was away from the main square, and on market-day anyone using the side-streets was liable to find droves of cattle or flocks of sheep racing towards them. Occasionally the call, "Bull loose", would be heard, when the streets would clear in seconds. Close to the market was a slaughterhouse, where the shrill of pigs and the smell of blood and dung caused unexpected adrenalin to flow momentarily through passers-by.

The produce-market was held close to the abbey in the open square, which from centuries of practice had been divided into specialist areas. The hutches and baskets of fowls in-lay in one place, those for the pot in another, sellers of iron pans and skillets further along, and so on.

The Nugent stand was outside the Star Inn, which was just right. It was inside the market-square, yet close to the Motte Road. Jude helped Bella unpack and lay out their stand. Bella knew that what she offered was as good as any and better than most. A few people tried haggling, but those who knew Croud Cantle produce knew what they were getting; pretty good value. Bella was good at her job. She could smile, banter or confide to suit a particular customer, and from the moment they arrived they were kept busy.

By the time the abbey clock struck eleven ponderous times, the bulk of their stuff had been sold.

[26]

"If you want to go up the Star yard, you'd best go now," said Bella.

"Will it be all right if I have a walk round?"

"You make sure you'm back here be the time it strikes the half-hour then. We don't want to hang about no longer than we got to. It an't holiday."

Was that enough time to find somebody? Then, hearing the shriek of a pig being stuck, she thought of Gilly Gilson. He worked at slaughtering on market-days. He would be sure to know where she could start asking.

She found the butchers' shambles and pushed her way into the chaos. Animals in a frenzy from the smell of blood; men with hazel-switches shouted, whipping at cattle for no better reason than that they held hazel-switches, forcing the herds through small gates; the sound of clubbing; animals shrieking and lowing, and more men shouting. Raising her voice above the noise she asked one or two men for Gilly, but received only shrugs in reply, until a man who was slithering mounds of pig-entrails into a trough shouted, "Wickham", which Jude took to mean that Gilly was over at Wickham market.

Back in the street, Jude saw that she had used up ten minutes already. Blackbrook must surely be full of people who could read and write. But then it occurred to her that a Blackbrook person wasn't any good. It was too far. She thought that if she walked up and down the side-streets something would come to her. She walked, noting places where book-work and letters appeared to be daily business.

Did she dare to go in one and ask? If she didn't ask ... What could she say? "Have you got anybody lives near Cantle who can write?" "I want to learn ... " It sounded silly. What would people think of a girl ..? Before she thought twice and her courage failed her, she plunged into the lobby of a place where she saw people at desks and knocked on one of the doors.

She waited, her mouth dry. The door was ranted open by a red-faced man in an old-fashioned wig that was askew. He, seeing that it was just a village child, wiped from his mouth the smile that he had ready for the client he was expecting.

"Yes?" He breathed alcoholic, market-day breath over her.

Before the man's aggressive stare, she capitulated. "Oh," she said, and went quickly away. The solicitor's door slammed. A clock chimed out midday. She raced back to the Star corner.

[27]

"Half an hour means half an hour!"

"I'm sorry Mother, I was just ... "

"No 'just' anything. We an't here for pleasure. We shall be finished up in about an hour. I'm going up the Star yard and on round to see Fred Warren about the seed he was supposed to get for me."

Jude began loading things into panniers. She was furious with herself for being such a great, stupid lump. What do it matter looking a fool? What do it matter if they get cross with me asking stupid questions? What counts is finding somebody.

Next time I shall find out what all the other places are.

One or two people came to make purchases, but the rush of market-day was over. Jude was sitting staring into space when a man came and asked for Bella. He was not all that old, not as old as her mother. He wore a rough woollen coat and breeches and a loose worsted waistcoat. His hair was unpowdered and bobbed to collar-length, like a joiner or some other craftsman. He had a thin, nice face.

"She won't be long. Can't I get what you want?"

"Are you Judeth?"

"Yes sir, I am."

"Not necessary to ask, you look so much like Mrs Nugent."

Jude did not know the man and was not sure how to answer. His speech was lovely, not broad, a bit like Rev. Tripp's. He was pale and tired-looking.

"It's about the seed. Mrs Nugent made an order and ... "

"Are you Fred Warren ... Mister Warren? The seed man?"

"Yes, that's who I am." He had a nice, friendly smile, not at all like Rev. Tripp's.

"She has gone to find you."

"Ah! I wondered if I might miss her if I left the yard. I tell you what Judeth, I will leave the seed with you and put it on the Croud Cantle account. I know Mrs Nugent does always like to pay coin, but just this once ... " He took a little book from his pocket and made an entry.

"Well, Judeth, no doubt we shall meet most market-days now you have taken over from Miss Jaen." He gave a little bow and turned to go.

"Mr Warren?"

He raised his eyebrows enquiringly.

"Where do you live?"

He closed his eyes and wagged his head and said in a joking tone, "For my sins, at Motte. There also live Mrs Warren and our four children."

"Mr Warren, could you teach me to write?"

"Write?"

"And to read too."

Fred Warren's eye scanned Jude's anxious and eager face, his expression slowly taking on something of a hungry and penniless person who, having found a piece of gold, wants to shout their good fortune, whilst at the same time holding back for fear someone claims the find.

A man of vision. An idealist crushed into the mould of a low-waged grain-merchant's assistant for two-thirds of his day, and a poverty-stricken family man for the other third. Fred Warren felt elated. A girl from the back of beyond, from Cantle! A girl who had not even been to Blackbrook market more than a couple of times. Who lived the harsh, barefoot life of a farmgirl. She wanted to write!

He seemed to take so long in answering that Jude felt a flush creep up her throat and into her face.

"How old are you, Judeth? Do you know how old you are?"

"A course I know. I shall be twelve come this June."

"What does Mrs Nugent say to it?"

"About me wanting to learn? She says it will pass."

And it would. It would indeed pass. Fred Warren knew that it happened, often. That, frequently, seeds of interest are sown in the minds of children who are then sent into fields to throw stones at crows. Everywhere, little children scratch and scrawl wherever they find a lump of chalk and a bare surface, yet what ploughboy, what cottager milk-maid or woman yoked to pails ever did more than perhaps trace something on a steamed or frosted window-pane?

If Fred Warren did not protect this child's tender shoot of enthusiasm then the frost of apathy, resignation and fatigue from labour would blast and stunt it. However difficult it might be, Fred Warren was determined to feed and tend that shoot until it could safely be left to grow and blossom into whatever it was that had just germinated.

Fred Warren's own tender plant had been an enthusiasm for Liberty, Equality, Fraternity, though at the time he had not heard that cry. His was not blasted by frost, but had been wilted by a youthful heat of desire and consequential mouths to feed.

"If I got your mother to agree, you would still have to do your same work at home."

"A course I would."

"And most of the time you would have to get on by yourself."

"A course, I shouldn't mind that. Just as long as somebody told me what to do."

"I'm not promising. Depends on what your mother says."

"Oh yes, Fred Warren, and what depends on me?"

Fred was one of the few people Bella trusted in business; consequently she liked him. Not that it showed much in her manner, but it showed there in her eyes, and in the time she was willing to spend standing there gossiping when there's work to be done.

"Judeth was asking me about learning."

"I dare say she was. I dare say she been asking half Blackbrook. She got a bee in her hair. She always been the same. Won't never take no for an answer." Bella began clearing up and indicated to Jude to do the same.

"I shouldn't mind giving her a hand."

"I'd a thought you got enough on your plate."

"It would only be the odd hour or two."

"You can't afford to work for nothing."

"It would not be work to me."

"Maybe not, but it'd be taking time you ought to be spending planting your vegetable plot or something. You got a lot of mouths to feed."

Jude kept quiet. She saw that Bella could be persuaded by Mr Warren, and if she put a word wrong her mother would squash the idea, and it would be no good raising it again ... For goodness sake, Jude, you an't on about that again? I told you I didn't want to hear no more.

"What about a couple of hours on a Sunday afternoon?" Fred suggested.

"And what about Mrs Warren?"

"Ah." He had not thought that far.

The panniers packed and the donkeys harnessed, Bella was ready to start for home.

"And you coming to Croud Cantle regular. And on a Sunday."

Jude could see it all slipping away.

"Couldn't I go over to Motte, Mother?"

"Inviting yourself are you?"

"That'd be all right. I'm sure Molly would not mind at all."

Bella clicked her tongue at the donkey.

"You better find out."

Fred Warren walked beside them as they left the market-square, not wanting to leave the idea to shrivel.

"If Molly does not mind, will you agree that Judeth can come? Just to give it a try? Just for a couple of hours. Perhaps you would let her have the donkey so she wouldn't be away too long?"

Jude saw that it was possible. Mother could be persuaded.

"I couldn't let you do it for nothing. You would have to take something. And your wife'd have to say it'd be all right."

Jude found the week till next market-day endless, but she had sense enough not to bring up the subject. By the time they next saw Fred Warren, Bella had worked out in her mind what would be fair payment in produce for his time, and what extra to give so that Molly Warren would have no cause to complain, it being Sunday and all.

[31]

SURPRISINGLY, Jude found that the places Jaen had occupied in the routine of Croud Cantle were quickly filled. Jude became more reliable. Perhaps it was that she felt her responsibilities more, now that she was Miss Nugent, or that she did not want Bella to regret having agreed to the lessons.

Next market-day, Fred Warren said that Mrs Warren was quite agreeable to Jude coming early on Sunday afternoons, when she took a bit of a rest anyhow, and would no doubt be delighted when she heard of the barter arrangement that Bella suggested.

It was a good many years before Jude realised how fortunate that, of all people, it was Fred Warren who had taken her under his wing: what if Rev. Tripp had known a moment of generosity or conscience!

Fred's only family, when he was a child, was a reclusive aunt so set in her ways that when she found herself, at the age of forty, sole guardian of her dead widowed sister's eight-year-old boy, she got him a place at Blunt's charity school where she was sure he would be better off. And in many ways he was. The crabbiness of Blunt's schoolmasters was little different from that which he would have found in his aunt's home, but at least he received an education, and a good one at that.

At the age of sixteen his aunt gave him one hundred pounds and not at all a bad piece of advice – to look for work in any business that dealt with food, but not to grow it. People always had to eat, but the growing of food, animal or vegetable, was governed by weather, disease and infestation. Buying and selling had a different set of problems, but as these were not so much in the hands of nature, they were more readily coped with. She had not taken Governments into account, but the main tenet of her argument – people always have to eat – made sense to the sixteen-year-old Fred Warren.

In Blackbrook, Barnabas White, a corn chandler and general dealer in anything that grew and would turn a farthing, was looking for a clerk. On discovering that young Warren was not only able to keep books and that kind of thing, but also had one hundred pounds, Barnabas White offered to accept Fred's hundred pounds and make him a junior partner. Young Fred was impressed by the title, Junior Partner, and satisfied with his good luck at being taken into a business dealing in grain, the most basic of foods. He took the job, handed over his fortune and became an overworked clerk, sleeping behind White's little office for three years, until he married Molly Tarrant, the youngest and jolliest of nine of a Blackbrook grocer's nine children.

Fred Warren was generally known for being as decent a fellow as ever stepped foot in pair of boots. He was a catholic and voracious reader, which led him into an interest in politics, religion and philosophy. He never had time to study deeply, but read every pamphlet and attended every meeting that he could.

When he asked Molly Tarrant to marry him, he did so partly because she was good company and he was lonely, and partly because he thought that life would be more comfortable for him, even if only in a couple of tiny rooms. He had not bargained for the overwhelming desires in both himself and Molly, and very quickly they found themselves with a family which, in spite of Fred's slow betterment, kept them poor. At the age of twenty-six, with four small Warrens to feed, the barter of lessons for generous produce was therefore welcome.

The payment, though, had little to do with Fred taking on the young, ignorant farmgirl, whose desperation to feed her mind had shown so clearly in her intelligent face on that first encounter in Blackbrook market.

JUDE STARTED straight away on the following Sunday, and kept her bargain with Bella that she would work earlier and later to make up for some of the lost time.

After her first lesson she could recite the alphabet, and returned home with it written on a slate. By the next Sunday she could put a name to every letter. After each lesson, Fred Warren gave her work to do during the week. Jude was serious and enthusiastic. She wanted to learn everything at once.

The frantic spring planting was over and the hay was not ready, so occasionally there was an hour when Jude could get away on the Downs, usually Tradden Raike. On a June afternoon, just before her twelfth birthday, she took her slate with her and climbed the steep raike, intending to write from memory some of the words she had been taught.

It was just the weather she loved, hot and steady. When it was like this she never complained, even when the butter would not come, or the flints in the soil burned the soles of her feet as she hoed between the bean rows, or the water-pails had to be dropped ever lower in the wells. Hot, steady weather meant clear sky, where the blue of it changed subtly throughout the day. What she liked was to lie on the slope of one of the hills and do nothing but look.

She reached one of her favourite places, close to where she had wept on Jaen's wedding-day, but lower down the slope. The layer of soil that covered the hills surrounding Cantle was thin and did not cushion or spring lushly; its thinness pleased Jude. She liked to sit here rather than in the soft meadows in the valley bottom. You can feel their muscles and bones, Jaen had once said. Jude scratched the hill like the back of an animal.

"I can feel your bones," she said aloud.

Now that it was June, the leaves of the different grasses had become glossier. Some had grown and shed seed, some were at the stage of hanging out tiny tongues of pollen and others, like wiggle-waggle grass, still purple. The chalk-hill flowers of early summer were open. Fragile blue campanula, pale blue scabious, blue, blue speedwell, yellow vetch, yellow toadflax, cornflowers, cranesbill, a few spider orchids and the low, flat thistle that thrived on Tradden.

This was the first time she had come to the hills as a woman; her first flow had come about six weeks ago. Today was her second. It seemed to Jude to be more important than the first, which had been a bit bewildering and restricting, for all Bella's common sense advice. This time Jude was poised and tranquil; she was a woman and could never be a child again. She would have been quite pleased to have gone about telling people. She wanted them to know. "I am a woman now," she would have liked to say. "This isn't a child's body, you know, it is a woman's."

Why did it all have to be so secret? She had known what happened to change girls – she had always shared a bed with Jaen – and had not thought it much different from the seasonal changes in the animals. But now she knew that it was different. It was mysterious and beautiful, the way it had all been designed.

Why was there never a sermon about how wonderful it was for a child to suddenly turn into a woman? They went on so much in church about God's gifts, the good earth; they talked about death; there were celebrations for marriages and baptisms. There should be a special day for becoming a woman, or at least a place in the service, same as speaking banns or taking communion. She imagined her own dignity as she stepped forward. I should have my hair parted and drawn up on top and wear a plain dress with a dark corset bodice, a fichu, white stockings and my shoes with the buckles. And I would not have my head covered.

"If there be new women here, let them come forward and be blessed."

"I am a woman."

"Let us praise the Lord for this new woman, Judeth Nugent."

"Amen."

"There are meats and wine and dancing to celebrate this new woman."

And every year there would be a celebration on the anniversary of A Woman Day. The only thing was, you couldn't picture Mr Tripp calling forward new women.

She picked up her slate to write "woman". The "w" she knew, but the next was a puzzle. Mr Warren had shown her which were vowels, but there did not seem to be one to fit "woman". She put the slate aside. Her mother had said, "You don't have to dwell on it Jude. Just go on the same." But Jude liked to think about it. It was the most important thing that had ever happened to her. Even her lessons were not as important. "You'll get used to it," her mother had said, and perhaps she would. But she was not used to it yet.

Bella had shown her how to use the cloths and tapes, speaking in a low voice. They were alone in the house, mother and daughter, yet mother had spoken as though the miracle that made the daughter become a woman held the stigma of a shameful disease.

"You don't have to go telling anybody mind, Jude. Don't never get caught out. You a get used to it in time, you a get to know."

And Bella had given her twenty-eight beans to be transferred, one each morning, until she got used to it – so that the new woman would not get caught out.

Jude stayed on the hill longer than she had intended. When she wandered back home, Bella was taking it easy on the porch.

"I'm sorry I was gone so long."

"I'd a thought you'd a been a bit more careful going off like that – until you're more used to it."

Jude was a woman, and revelled in it.

Quite soon the hay turned and they were busy from the early dawn to the late dusk. The weather stayed steady for weeks. Jude became twelve, and when they went to Blackbrook that week, Bella gave Jude an empty book of plain paper in which she wrote, with Fred Warren's help, "This book was given to Judeth Nugent by Bella Nugent. June 1780."

When Jude showed her and read it out, Bella nodded and looked pleased.

"You ought to have wrote 'Isabell', though."

"I never knew that was your name, Mother."

"I shouldn't wonder that there's a lot you don't know yet, Jude, nor never won't."

"I hope not. I want to find out everything there is."

Fred Warren was quite overwhelmed at the speed at which Jude absorbed his instruction, to say nothing of her intuition and intelligence.

"That is really quite good, Judeth," was about all he would say by way of a compliment on her work. He was afraid that she would somehow be spoilt if, as he would have liked, he said, "That is an astounding week's work!"

On the Sunday when she was twelve, he gave her a brass-handled magnifying-glass that had been his father's.

ONE MOMENT Jude had been there in the church porch, the next she had vanished from Jaen's sight. Jaen felt a moment of panic. She had been abandoned, left to the Hazelhursts, who had turned out in force as they always did when there was a family event occasioning eating or drinking and preferably both.

The Hazelhursts always appeared to be in greater numbers than they actually were. They were a family famous for "heighth and breadth" and, even though the men always appeared to favour very small women for wives, the Hazelhurst heighth and breadth came out generation after generation, particularly in its men. "Big as Ben Hazelhurst" and "A voice like a Hazelhurst" were local standards.

Dan, at five feet eleven and twelve stones in weight, was a slip of a lad amongst his older brothers. When, at the church door, Dan said to Jaen, "Come on then, Mrs Hazelhurst," a roar went up from the family and Jude slipped away.

Jaen, at not yet eighteen, was the pretty one. Her hair, although Estover red, was not as wild and frizzed as Jude's, but soft and easier to control. Winds did not whip up her cheeks to redness like Jude's and her hands, though weather-worn, sinewy and strong from farm and dairy work, were as elegant in shape as Jude's were practical. She had an open look, a kind of wide-eyed innocence that made it seem inevitable that, if it had not been Dan Hazelhurst, it would have been some other hearty young man would want to prove his masculinity and dominance. Jaen was a doe that made young stags want to clash antlers: to take, to possess, to own.

All the Hazelhurst men had married small women, so that when they all got settled in the back room of the Dragon and Fount for a wedding breakfast, Jaen stood eye to eye with Dan's mother and her sisters-in-law, and eye to mid-chest with the menfolk. Bella, in a new

[38]

skirt and wearing gloves for the occasion, stood with the men talking market prices and good seasons.

At eleven o'clock, the assembly broke up. As Jaen kissed her mother she said, close to her ear, "Ju will be all right, won't she?"

"Don't you worry about Jude. By tomorrow she'll be kicking herself she didn't have none of this." Bella indicated the remnants of the celebrations.

"I should have told her what happened straight away. She was very cut up about it; we never had no secrets from each other before. Poor little Ju, I hurt her bad not telling her."

Bella, panicking at the possibility of her emotions coming to the surface, resorted as always to a straight back and a stern voice.

"You got enough on your plate now. You have to leave Jude to sort herself out. There an't nothing you can do."

Jaen, knowing her mother's dread of anybody making a show of theirselves, smiled cheerfully and said, "She'll like the baby."

"Ah, she'll be like a mother hen, you'll see."

Bella did not look at Jaen's eyes, but concentrated on her own mouth, which she was trying to shape like a smile. Her panic subsided, she was safe from her dreadful, soft emotions. She waved gaily as Jaen mounted the wagon with her boisterous new family.

For the few miles drive to the other side of the Tradden and Marl hills, the Hazelhursts kept up an exchange of banter and good-natured argument. They talked about Parliament as though there was a Hazelhurst seat there. Most of what they said was above Jaen's head, but one thing obvious was that they were a family full of themselves, with a poor opinion of anyone who held different beliefs from their own.

They got down from the wagon a few at a time; sometimes still disputing, raising their voices ever louder to make a point as the wagon drove away. For the last quarter-mile only Jaen, Dan and his mother and father were left.

Nance Hazelhurst nodded forty-winks and old Baxter clicked his tongue at the horses and jiggled the reins, for want of something better to do now that there was no chance of an argument left. Dan sat upright in an unexpectedly stiff neck-cloth.

Jaen still had the feel of Bella's brushing kiss on her cheek. It had flustered her with its unexpectedness. Her mother had felt soft and warm. So many years had passed since they had touched, except

[39]

accidentally whilst working, that Jaen had grown up imagining that her mother's cheek would feel like a ham or a flitch. Instead it had felt like warm, risen dough.

Suddenly, panic rose.

It had been something like that that had started it all. The unexpected warmth of the palm of Dan's hand on her face that had landed her here. The months between then and now – the time she had no choice but to tell Bella, the meeting with Dan's parents to see what was to be done, the eventual arrangements – seemed almost unreal, as though it was something somebody told her about, a dream from which she was awakening. She shivered.

"Don't worry," said Dan. "We shall be all right when we gets going on our own."

And with those few words of assurance, Jaen started her life as a Hazelhurst wife.

The Hazelhurst's place, Up Teg, was much more of a farm than the Nugent holding and the house was bigger. There was a separate cooking fire in a room off the living place, a pump close to the house and a large upper floor that was sectioned off into several rooms, with tarred timbers and wattle and daub partitions which had been smoothed and whitened. Outside there were barns with napped-flint walls and good roofs. Jaen had come up in the world.

Nance Hazelhurst was a bustling woman used to ordering about Baxter and The Boys; six sons, all with a great amount of heighth and breadth. Nance Hazelhurst knew that although they kept bringing these swollen-bellied wives into the family, there wasn't really any of them that was good enough for The Boys.

All The Boys had got away with it for a time, but eventually there was always some girl, some determined mother like Bella Nugent, who forced a wife upon them. And perhaps it was as well for Dan to get settled down; he did seem to go a bit wild over girls.

Baxter used to say, "If you puts a young bull in a field with heifers, they a bound to get a hoof round the ear'ole if they plays'n up." But really, Dan had been in one too many bits of trouble, and now he might settle down and leave the maids alone.

She was good-natured, disorganized and not house-proud, which was just as well, for at times there were ten or more pairs of muck-heavy boots tramping in and out.

"I've put your bits and pieces in the Yard Room up above," she told Jaen. "You'll be all right in there till you've birthen, then you can go down yonder when the boys have put down the new thatch."

She was no less outwardly tough than Bella, but she did, on family occasions when there was wine about, become a bit sentimental. In the Yard Room she put her arms about Jaen.

"They're all right if you handle them right. There isn't a lot of harm in them, not really. They got a lot of energy, being so big and all that. As long as you'm a good wife, you a be all right. The Hazelhursts have never gone short of much; even when times is hard they always seem to do all right. There's always that to think of."

FOUR MONTHS after coming into the Yard Room Jaen – much to the Hazelhursts' surprise because she was such a slip of a thing – easily, quickly, getting it over with no fuss, gave Hanna a push into Nance's waiting hands. Nance, eyeing the neat child covered with faintly-red down, said, "Only her mouth is Hazelhurst."

By the time Bella and Jude received the message about Jaen's confinement, the child was well on the way. Bella quickly organized work with the yard-men, then she and Jude rode over to Up Teg.

Nance greeted them at the door with, "She'm one of yours, a red one, won't hardly make five foot nothing fully grown."

Bella and Jude did not let her see that they were pleased that Jaen had not had the Hazelhurst heighth and breadth fathered upon her.

Jaen allowed herself to be petted, admired and fussed about, and listened seriously to Bella's advice. Suddenly she had become initiated and accepted as one who had the full knowledge of womanhood. Jude was left to consider what it felt like to be Aunt Jude and to marvel at the baby. During a pause in the exchange of confinement experience, Jaen and Bella's gaze fell upon Jude. Together they let out a scandalized, "Jude!" – not loud, because Nance Hazelhurst was below.

Jude had uncovered the child's hands and was absorbed in examining them through her magnifying glass.

She jumped guiltily, and hastily put the glass back into her pocket. "I'm not doing anything. I just wanted to see."

"For goodness' sake put that thing away."

"I have, I have." Jude responded to the obvious, patting her pocket.

"What would the Hazelhursts say if they came in now?" Bella

swaddled the baby's hands, as though Jude had left some invisible evidence of her strange behaviour.

"There's only Missis and she's in the yard. I can see her."

"It's all right," said Jaen, picking up the baby and looking at its hands herself. "What were you looking for, Ju?"

"Take no notice," Bella interjected. "You know Jude, she just don't know where to draw the line."

"It don't hurt anything, Jaen, just to look. This is the first chance I've had to see human skin that's unused. I've watched rose-buds open. You should see ... "

"Jude!" Bella took her "I've just about had enough" stance.

Reasonably, Jude went on. "Before Jaen left home, she would a wanted to look too. There are tiny creases you can't see with your eyes." She capitulated before Bella's gaze and sat humbly on a hard stool.

Apart from Dan and being Mrs Hazelhurst and now the baby, Jaen should still be the same as she had been for the eighteen years she had been a Nugent, Jude reasoned. Jaen had always been interesting and interested. Jaen was the one who had ideas, thought up good guessing games, climbed trees to throw down conkers and who, even when quite grown up, would say, "Dare you!" or swim naked in Chard Lepe Pond on warm nights, even when Mother had forbid them to go near. Mother never knew about the secrets of Chard Lepe. They were doing something forbidden without really knowing why.

And now Jaen wasn't the same any more.

Jaen watched Jude. She was growing up, growing up, and they were growing apart. And for what? It was all such a mess. So awful and miserable. She longed achingly for home, Tradden, for her mother's wet, bright-red tiles. She missed the order, the regularity, the stability. Mother was always a bit of a Tartar, but there wasn't nothing degrading about being told what to do by her. Not like Dan.

When Mother told you to do something, she'd say, "An't it about time you got that there pig fed?" But now it was, "Here!" and a bucket of swill was shoved at you. And he was so rough. She hadn't thought he was rough when she met him, but now ...

That time when she first went with him, he said he'd never met a girl so carefree and lively; then when she behaved the same after they were married, he said that wasn't no way for a married woman to behave. Then when they was in the bedroom, he'd get on to her saying, "You wasn't like this that time in Rathley; you was just trying to catch me."

Dear Lord, nobody had to try hard with the Hazelhurst boys.

Jaen wished she could run home and take her lessons with her. She wouldn't a got caught a second time. And she would look after Ju, see she didn't get herself into that kind of trouble.

You'd a thought anybody would love their baby more than their sister; but I don't. I'd change it for Ju.

"Hold baby, Jude. Whisper in her ear, like I used to in yours."

Jude took the baby peace-offering and Jaen asked, wanting to understand, "What were you looking for, Jude?"

"Not anything, really. Just looking ... to see. You never know what will be there when it gets magnified. If you ever saw a bit of cheese ... "

"Jude!" Bella warned, and Nance Hazelhurst came into the room.

"Well then, Judeth, it won't be long before it's your turn. You got better hips than Jaen there."

Bella stepped forward as though to protect Jude.

"Plenty of time yet."

"Get it over when you're young and got your health and strength is what I always reckon."

ELLA WAS QUIET on their drive home. Jude, knowing her mother's moods, made no attempt to talk. Bella was not so much angry with Jude as nonplussed at the feeling that Jude was getting a sight too difficult to handle.

She was quite proud of Jude, the way she had learned to write. Fred Warren always came to see Bella at Blackbrook market to give progress reports on his pupil's extraordinary learning ability. "Like rain on a parched field," he would say, "soaks up everything. She's thirsty for knowledge, Mrs Nugent, thirsty."

At first Bella was unimpressed. Interested, it is true, as she watched, teeth on edge, while Jude scraped letters on to her slate. "That says 'Isabell Nugent', and this is 'Judeth'. Mr Warren showed me how to look it up. Mother, did you know that everybody is written up in a book in their church? Mr Warren says that my name and Jaen's is not spelled in the usual way. He says the Parish Clerk was bad at his letters and half the village has their names put in wrong."

"It's not against the Law? I can't see that it is. Jaen got married. I only hope they got it right on her marriage lines."

"Mr Warren says ... "

"Mr Warren says, Mr Warren says ... "

"Well Mother, he does know a lot."

When Fred Warren had taken Jude to show her the Parish records, it was as a practical primary lesson in history.

"When you start reading properly, Judeth, you will discover that all the books are concerned with kings and barons and battles. But they were just a tiny, few people. These are the real history books."

"Then I'm somebody in history?"

"You and me and Mrs Nugent and Mrs Warren and all of us."

Once she had discovered that there was a kind of equality in the writing down of events in the parish records ("Even Bishops and even the king," as Mr Warren had said), she spent much time laboriously copying down bits of information in her unformed writing.

One day she had rushed into Cantle. "Mother, Mother, I found father. It says, 'Nugent, Tomas Chester Bertram. Mother, Alice Mary; Father, George Chester, Farmer.' And the entry was put down in the year 1744."

Bella Nugent's face had been a picture as she'd looked out from the hen-house.

And now on their silent ride between Up Teg and Croud Cantle, Bella wondered whether this learning hadn't gone a bit too far, going into history and examining things.

Knowing that Bella never let the sun go down on her wrath, or anything else that could be settled, Jude guessed that her mother would say something over supper.

"Jude, you're twelve. You're not a child no more. People make allowances when you're growing up, but not once you're a woman. You are a good girl at your work, and I haven't got no complaints on that score. And I'm glad to see you happy. And I like you to have interests and I like listening to you and all that."

She paused, hoping Jude would say something so that she could jump to the point she was trying to reach, and say, "That's just what I mean." But Jude wasn't having it. If Bella was going to tell her off, she wasn't going to make it any easier for her.

"It's time you thought a bit more about what you're doing and got a bit more serious."

"Serious about what?"

"Like ... well, like today. Looking at babies through glasses!"

"I don't see why not. It doesn't do anything to the baby."

"And it don't do much for you neither."

"It does. I can see things I never dreamt was there. There wasn't much on the baby's hand, but there might have been. That's why you have got to just keep looking at everything, everywhere. You never know what you are going to see."

"Don't twist what I'm saying. I mean it don't do much towards what people will think about you. You're twelve now, but next year you'll be thirteen. What's people going to think? A man's going to run a mile if you suddenly take it into your head that you want to see what his whiskers look like under that glass. Or what if somebody catches you looking at maggots ... I saw what you was doing with that bit of blowed-meat."

Jude held her apron to her face. For a moment Bella thought that Jude was going to weep. She couldn't stand tears. Jude could hold it in no longer; suddenly she burst into explosive laughter. Bella held her face straight. At last Jude subsided with a sigh.

"I'm sorry. Truly I am. I wasn't laughing at you. It was just I remembered seeing Jed Parker and Polly Allen courting and you know how close Polly has got to get to see, and when you said ... " She trailed off, suppressing the desire to start giggling again.

"I don't want people to think I'm queer, but I don't see that it's any different from people who uses eyeglasses."

"I'm not saying that, and you know it. It's about proper behaviour for a girl. It's about what is expected. It's bad enough as it is in our position."

Bella stirred the fire and a log fell.

"What position?"

Bella carefully placed the log where it would flare up again. "How many other holdings or farms in these parts do you know of as is run by women and girls?"

"We've got Dicken, and there's Bob and Rob and Johnny-twoey, and Gilly comes."

"They don't run it."

"They work it."

It had never occurred to Jude before. She had grown up with Bella always working, doing the same jobs as any wife of a farmer or smallholder; going to market and selling produce, with the hired men doing the rest. The fact that it was Bella who made the decisions and gave the orders had entirely escaped Jude.

"You mean because you're a widow?"

Bella did not respond, but gazed at the log that had burst into flame.

Jude continued. "I can't see why I have to be specially behaved because you are a widow."

"Jude, there are times when I just can't make you out. You can talk the hind leg off a donkey; you can read and write; you aren't anybody's fool. People talk! Women don't run places on their own. People have been waiting years for me to come a cropper, to see the place go to rack and ruin."

Amazed, Jude saw that her mother was vulnerable.

Bella's self-assurance was like a coat of thick pitch on timbers. The dry rot of neighbour's disapproval and the worm-holes of her own doubt were hidden.

"Oh mother," was all that Jude could say.

Staring at the flames, Bella went on: "When Jaen ... when she and Dan ... You don't know the half of it. Jaen wasn't no worse ... and anyway I blame Dan Hazelhurst, ten years older ... but then I blame myself."

Through the half-sentences, Jude realised Bella's anguish. Anguish concealed during the months before Jaen got married. The worry about whether the Hazelhursts would agree to their Dan marrying Bella Nugent's girl. And for those months she had continued the day to day work at Croud Cantle.

"I never thought."

Bella sat, withdrawn, her bottom lip thrust up.

"Jude, there's a thousand things you have to watch when you're a woman on your own."

BY THE AUGUST when baby Hanna was a year old, Bella and Jude were well settled in their routine without Jaen.

The Hazelhurst Boys had mended the thatch on a cottage, and Dan had taken Jaen and Hanna to live there. By Christmas Jaen was pregnant. At first she did not see how she could have fallen again, because she was still suckling Hanna. Like many another woman, she soon discovered that there were a good many tales about that kind of thing. Her milk disappeared almost overnight.

Next Christmas there would be a second child.

Dan was pleased and said that next time it was sure to be a son – a Hazelhurst with heighth and breadth, and no red hair.

Old Baxter Hazelhurst had developed farmer's chest and was obliged to delegate much of the running of Up Teg to The Boys. For years now he had been buying up little parcels of land adjoining his, so that when Dan moved down to the farm at Ham Ford, Up Teg had a sizeable acreage; enough to provide all the Hazelhursts with some security and comfort in return for early mornings and long hard hours of labour.

Ever since that evening when Bella had talked about her position, Jude's admiration for her mother had grown. She could hardly believe how naïve and thoughtless she had been hitherto. Bella's reputation as a lone woman with two daughters – what with vigorous men coming and going, eating at the same table, working in the same dim barns and outhouses – must have come under close scrutiny from their neighbours. But never a word could be said against Bella. When Dan Hazelhurst got Jaen pregnant, it must have been a blow to Bella.

In the room that she and Jaen used to share, Jude put up some rough plank shelves on which she kept the great variety of things that she was either watching or thinking about or wondering what to do with. It had the makings of a kind of laboratory, and what Bella called, "fiddling about", was simple research and experiment.

Every day they rose early and ate a good breakfast of bread, creamy fermity and a piece of fruit or a carrot. Recently, Bella had allowed Jude to discuss the day's work with the men, and to give some of the orders to them. All of them except Johnny-twoey, the small boy, had been at Croud Cantle for years. Although at first they were a bit resentful at having to discuss fence-mending and ditching with young Jude, who not long since had been begging shoulder-rides from them, they soon began to respect her knowledge and serious approach to work. She was interested in their skills and they responded by taking pains to see that she didn't neglect any job that needed attention. Jude was making a good little farm manager.

"A chip off the old block," said Rob.

And they all agreed that Jude was an Estover to her very fingertips.

On Christmas Day of that year, Bella and Jude went over to the cottage at Ham Ford. The daylight hours were short and the ride took a good part of them, so it was a flying visit. Dan was proud of his cottage, his furniture, and of being recognised as a man with a family. Jaen was suffering sickness and young Hanna was a handful; grizzling with red-gum and teething.

"Will you let me take Hanna out round the field-edge a bit, Jaen?" asked Jude.

"I could show her the ... " She realised it wouldn't be wise to be specific. "The sun is out and you could wrap her up and I'll have her inside my shawl."

And so Jude was allowed to have Hanna to herself. She walked for an hour, talking to Hanna as though the child understood, which – if the intent gaze she bestowed upon Jude was anything to go by – she did.

Bella, in a roundabout way so as not to appear to be interfering, asked Dan if he didn't think that Jaen looked a bit peaked.

"Mother says she's got thin blood," Dan said. "She's told her to take raw liver."

Raw liver was a popular and well thought of treatment for any anaemic condition. The only problem was getting women in Jaen's condition to accept it.

"Have you been taking any?" Bella asked Jaen. Jaen glanced at Dan before replying. "I tried, Mother, I tried really hard. I can't bear the stuff; it just won't stay down."

"You an't supposed to like it. You just have to get it down," Dan said.

The dinner Jaen provided was beautifully cooked and plentiful. She and Dan appeared to be happy enough: it was just the look of frailty about Jaen that concerned Bella. During the meal, when Hanna started grizzling again, a look of hatred at the child flashed across Jaen's face. It was gone again in a second, but Bella had seen it and remembered what it was like. Hatred, guilt, resentment, love. Immediately Jaen picked up the baby, kissed and fondled it and rubbed salve on its sore gums.

There were times when Jude's intuition or mature perception surprised Bella. She wouldn't have dared ask herself for fear of interfering.

"Dan, do you think you would let Hanna come with me and mother for a few days? You and Jaen" – she was going to say something about having a chance to be alone or getting a good night's rest, but she thought twice before speaking these days – "You and Jaen could then go and visit Mr and Mrs Hazelhurst and not have to bother too much about taking baby out after sundown. And a change of water is supposed to be good for red-gum."

She had said exactly the right thing. Nobody asked how Jude knew about red-gum and its possible cures; it was the reason they were all looking for to get the baby away from Jaen, to give her a rest from the child's grizzle.

Jaen protested as much as she thought proper for a mother to do, and she would probably experience pangs of guilt, but both Bella and Jude could see that she was relieved and pleased at the thought of being free of the baby.

The decision to take Hanna over to Croud Cantle for a few days cut the visit short. Jaen and Bella collected a bundle of the baby's necessaries. Soon the donkey-cart containing Hanna, her Aunt Jude and Grandmother Nugent was creaking over the downs: Jude holding the reins, Bella revelling in the feel of a child asleep on her bosom again, and Hanna sweetly peaceful with never a suggestion of the grizzles, and the red-gum not troubling her at all.

They arrived back at Croud Cantle just as the first snow-flakes of the year fluttered down.

"Bank up the fire, Jude. Empty the dresser drawer. Put some new milk to warm. Skim it a bit so as it's not too rich."

[51]

It being Christmas Day, work was cut to only that necessary for the animals. Little Johnny-twoey had been minding the place all day. As the snow started, Dicken and Rob trudged in to feed and water the beasts in the barns. Before they went back down the lane, Bella had tucked Hanna up in the dresser drawer and had a red-hot poker ready to mull some ale to keep out the night air.

Proudly, Bella drew aside the wrap so that the men could look at Hanna.

"My eye Master! but she'm a Estover, and that's a fact." Dicken would have said that even had it not been true. He did not think Bella would have been pleased to say she was a Nugent, or yet a Hazelhurst.

"They reckon she's got the Hazelhurst mouth. What do you think? asked Bella, cocking her head to one side.

"Never!" said Rob. "Hazelhursts' mouths is a lot nearer their ear'oles."

And the men agreed that the peaceful child was the spit and image of an Estover, and just as well, seeing she was a girl-child and all that, for "what 'ooman in her right mind would want the heighth and breadth of a Hazelhurst?"

O N CHRISTMAS NIGHT there was a blizzard.

In that easy, mild southern county where Croud Cantle and Up Teg were tucked in, one on each side of the downs, there had not been such weather in living memory. Snow drifted up to hedge-tops. Sheep on some exposed hillsides astounded people by surviving beneath layers of snow, but many died of cold and starvation.

There were tales of bravery – or foolhardiness, according to how you looked at it – on the part of some shepherds, who risked their own necks to bring down some of their flock. It was the weather of Yorkshire moors rather than of Hampshire downlands.

The Croud Cantle men shovelled their way from the village and Johnny-twoey, having been shoulder-carried through the worst drifts, curled up in the barn beside the house-cow. He had spent the first seven years of his life sharing a dilapidated estate-cottage with his mother, father and seven siblings: presumably finding the barn more pleasant, he stayed on there.

On looking out next morning, Jude saw almost unbroken snowfields stretching as far as Winchester Hill. Small streams were frozen and snow-covered and only The Dunnock, fast-flowing from the chalk-hills, marked the white plains. No question about it, Hanna's stay would have to be prolonged. Of course it was terrible weather, terrible, but it's an ill wind that doesn't blow some good.

"The babe will be here for a while yet."

"Ah, I reckon she will."

"Jaen will know she'll be all right with us."

"Even if we can't get over there for weeks."

They smiled at one another at the prospect of having the baby in the house.

It was four weeks before any road was fit to walk. The tracks melted a bit during the days, became surface mire and froze again at night, until it was impossible for even a donkey to make the journey.

In January, one of Baxter's men came over with a message.

"Master Dan'l's missis have lost the child. Miz Dan'l says she's not bed-rid but will you see to the little one till the weather is better?"

He was sent back with messages of reassurance.

Just to be sure that all was well with Jaen, Bella sent Dicken over a few days later to the cottage at Ham Ford.

"I rely on you Dicken. You know Jaen well enough ... Don't say I'm worried, because I'm not, and don't say anything that might worry her, because there isn't anything. But you take a good look and see if she's all right."

Dicken returned with a full appraisal of Missis Daniel's high spirits and good health.

"She's as fine as I ever have seen her, Master."

Bella and Jude didn't quite know what to make of it, but accepted Dicken's shrewd opinion.

So with messages being carried back and forth over the downs, Hanna stayed on until Easter Sunday and was tottering about when she saw her parents again.

Easter 1782

Went to Jaens. Jaen will have a new baby it will come November. Hana will stop with muther and me (I)

Judeth Nugent

This time Jaen was neither sickly nor fragile but they agreed, to be on the safe side, it would be as well if Hanna stayed on for a bit at Croud Cantle.

At first it was only until the new baby came: he was Daniel, a Hazelhurst to the last hair. Then a bit longer, in case the introduction of Hanna back into the family disturbed Jaen's milk-supply for young Daniel; then Hanna had thrush followed by chicken-pox; and so on, until there was some kind of understanding that Hanna was best off at Croud Cantle.

And she was. She had Bella and Jude.

THE YEARS BETWEEN the coming of Hanna to Croud
Cantle and Jude's seventeenth birthday were not uneventful,
but the events were minor, and personal to the family and the
freeholding.

Jude took Hanna everywhere with her. She held her on a donkey
even before she could walk, and grasped the small hands beneath her
own as she milked the house-cow. Talked to her endlessly, humping
her up into the loft to look at bats and nests of barn-owls. She scolded
her, chided her, taught her and loved her.

Hanna's Estover legacy of red hair, like Jude's, was less foxy than
Bella's, and when Jude carried Hanna slung in a shawl about her, the
two russet heads close, it was not surprising that neighbours remarked
that, "Anybody would think twadden Jaen Nugent's babe but Jude's,
if you didn't know like."

All the while Jude was learning. She had a few books, mostly
picked up for her by Gilly Gilson at some fair, or by Fred Warren.
Jude had finished with her Sunday lessons, but still visited Fred and
Molly. He continued to be absorbed in Jude's progress and often went
up to Croud Cantle to give her some paper or pamphlet he thought
would interest her. The book which was most important to Jude was
the one Bella had given to her: ruled, white, unused, inviting pages for
Jude to write in.

An idea that was formed from the conversation that she and Gilly
Gilson had when she was a child, about collecting all the knowledge in
the world, never left her. As soon as she got the book she started to
enter information. At first she wrote haphazardly, but soon realised
that her entries would be difficult to retrieve, so she created her own
system of indexing. As far as Jude was concerned it was just "putting
the right things together so you knew where they were". By the time

she was seventeen she had perfected her system, which was intelligent and workable.

"Whatever you find to write down, I shall never know," was Bella's attitude.

"I wrote how Gilly does a pig and about talking to bees, and I write down the words of songs, and that sermon when Mrs Dunnaway ran out of church shouting, 'For shame! for shame!' "

"Pour soul! I don't think you should put down things of that nature."

"It happened, and I always put down interesting things that happen. In a hundred years, nobody will know things like that unless they get put down. Things that get told by word of mouth can get changed, but written things can't."

Bella shook her head. "But still ... "

"I put the Croud Cantle pickle receipt in."

Bella's expression!

"That's our secret thing. Supposing somebody else should get a hold on it? Folks could make their own and they shouldn't want to buy ourn no more. There's many that'd like to know our receipt."

"Oh mother! And supposing the chimney should come down on us and we should be killed, Hanna would never know how to do Croud Cantle walnuts."

Bella could see the logic of this, but her authority rested in always having the last word.

"Well just you see you keep the cupboard locked on it."

When Jude was eighteen, Ben Hannable called upon Bella.

In the area of the four parishes, and in the village of Motte and Cantle in particular, Hannable was well-known and respected. His father had been the local elliman, dealing only in oil. When Ben joined his father in the tuppeny-ha'penny little business he saw its potential for expanding into other areas, so that by the time he was forty-five he was virtually the only retailer of hardwares in the area. At forty-five he looked about him for a wife and he decided to honour Bella Nugent's younger daughter and take her to his large, new house in Blackbrook.

Ben Hannable and Bella, being much of an age, had known one another since childhood. In those days, the Estover's social status was somewhat above the Hannable's, but by the time he was ready to marry their positions were about equal. Long ago he had known a fancy for Bella, but it was at a time when he was just the elliman's boy and then she married Tomas Nugent.

His search for a wife had not been directed towards Croud Cantle until he saw Jude in Blackbrook market: she was Bella Estover all over again.

He rode to Cantle and called at the farm.

"You done pretty well, Bella, seeing as you been a woman on your own all these years."

"You come up in the world yourself, Ben. I'm glad to see it. You've worked hard."

Ben didn't let on at that time that he had his eye on Jude.

"I seed your girl in the market, reading a notice. She been learning?"

"Ah, she's taken to it. Took it into her head when Jaen left home. Something to keep her mind off Jaen: they was always in each other's pockets up till then. I didn't know she would get so keen on it though."

Ben laughed his jolly laugh that had helped him in many a deal.

"A husband and house to keep and she'll forget all them fancies."

It was one thing for Bella to deride Jude's skill, but quite another for a man like Ben Hannable – he wasn't nothing to write home about.

"Not so much of the fancies; neither you nor me can't do no better than make our marks."

Ben Hannable looked smug.

"I learnt to write ten years back, Bella. Not a lot, mind you, but enough to keep my business in order. Men in business needs it."

Bella was impressed.

After he had broken the ice with his first visit, he called more often.

"Mother, I think he's courting you."

"My dear girl, I'm a grandmother."

That summer Ben Hannable called formally to ask Bella for Jude. Formally Bella said that she would give him her answer on his next visit.

"You'll never get a better offer than Ben Hannable."

"If I had a hundred better, I shouldn't take none of them."

The threads of veins on Bella's cheeks and the fox-red hair seemed brighter in her worry and anger.

"He's a bit rough, but he has tried. If you had seen the start he had, and look now at what he's made of himself. He's good at making a living, and that's security in later years."

"You're good at making a living. What has he got that we want for?"

"Gold coin, that's what!"

"Whatever do I want with money like that?"

"And whatever will you do without it?"

"Same as you."

Jude adopted her mother's stance and they stood facing one another, Jude grinning until Bella capitulated and sank on to the hearthside stool.

"Jude girl, you haven't got the brains of a louse. Haven't you seen enough of me to know what it's like for a woman to keep going on her own?"

"I've seen you. And I've seen Jaen. And I've seen Mary and Catherine and Cilla and all the rest of them I used to play with. I shall never do it. Never! I shan't be bound to any man, not Ben Hannable nor nobody else. Coming here flaunting a watch-chain on his belly and thinking I'd be fool enough to settle for a slave-chain. I should rather be like you any day than tied down like the rest."

Bella opened her mouth to protest, to put again the arguments for security, respectability, comfort in old age, children, but closed it again. She hadn't got much, but she was as much her own mistress as a woman could be. And she always had to keep going in any argument.

"You're headstrong and foolish."

"I'm like you."

Ben Hannable tried once more before he gave up: he tried Bella. Bella knew that she was second choice – perhaps not even second, for it took him two years before he got round to asking her – and she told him not to be such a damned old fool, and he said, "Hang it, Bella, we'd a made a good pair."

Mister Warren has given to me a pamphlet which is very interesting about common people, and this is why I record it here.

[58]

It concerns some people of Norfolk county who had poor treatment and tried to get certain things changed. Their leaders put forward twenty-nine complaints. Anyone reading them can see it, that these were just. Such as, Lords should not freely use commons, that rivers be free to all men and that rabbits not be kept unless they be paled in. The people got together in the town of Norfolk where, on order of the government the earl of Warwick with thousands of soldiers cut down the reformers.

It is two hundred years since this was done, and still things are not changed. The poor people of these four parishes would find no difficulty in finding the same number of grievances, and many more. I think that they would be set upon in the same manner by the lords and earls.

One of the reforms was amusing to me today because Mr Benjamin Hannable, an old man who has made money from selling dear oil to poor people, has made a proposal of marriage to me. The reform was that a child "if he live to his full age shall be at his own chosen concerning his marriage".

I was at my own chosen and did not choose Mister Hannable.

J. Nugent 1786

AFTER BEN HANNABLE there were one or two other men who thought they might like to capture Jude Nugent's interest. One of the Hazelhurst Boys, Edwin, rode over from Up Teg for weeks. Jaen hoped that Jude might take to him. Then it would be like when they were girls. She did not think too deeply about it because of the complications to do with Hanna, who now seemed settled with her aunt and grandmother, but she would give a lot to have Ju living near.

As it was, Jude would have no more to do with Edwin Hazelhurst than any of the others.

People said that Jude Nugent wants a man tailored from her own pattern, and Jude would have agreed. Not only her own pattern, her own special cloth and all.

They made changes at Croud Cantle. Gradually Jude persuaded Bella that they would do better making products than selling their stuff fresh. These days, Bella took serious note of any suggestion from Jude.

They continued selling their staple products – milk, cheese, butter and eggs – but Jude's interest in making notes about anything and everything, then observing and comparing, resulted in her discovery that their most profitable sales were their preserves and pickles and, to Bella's amazement, a savoury tart of Jude's own invention. It was a buttermilk tart.

Jude experimented. She thickened buttermilk with corn, put in curd-cheese, herbs and onion and baked it as an open tart. Locally, Croud Tarts became well-known as a savoury that would not disturb even the most delicate digestion. So instead of the hard outdoor work of their previous livelihood from small crops and a few animals, they worked more and more in the kitchen. They had a large cooking-range installed in the scullery and in ever-increasing numbers produced buttermilk tarts and preserves.

With the changes, their work patterns altered. Bella was a bit concerned about the men who had worked at Croud Cantle for years, hired and re-hired time and again. Things sorted themselves out.

Bob left to go in with his brother some miles away at Fordingbridge. Dicken took over the livestock, and although he grumbled that chickens was 'ooman's work, knew, when he was honest with himself, that he was a lot better off than many another man of his age who had got the screws in his joints. Rob, though still attached to Croud Cantle by casual arrangement, took on more and more fencing, hedge-laying and unskilled repairs in and around Cantle and Motte, working further and further afield until he met an Andover woman and moved there to live.

Johnny-twoey, since his defection from the rest of the Toose family, had become indispensable to life at Croud Cantle, and at about eleven years of age was a healthy lad. He turned the soil of the vegetable plot in November to catch the winter frosts, then he broke it down in spring; planted brassicas, beans, peas, potatoes and salads and brought on fruit and rhubarb.

What he was really good at was the ever-expanding herb garden that he had started when Jude made her first experimental buttermilk tarts. He was good at taking cuttings, cross-pollinating and developing new varieties. His collection of mint appeared at one time to be taking over the kitchen garden. But Jude liked his way of working and would not let Bella make him dig it up.

Mr Warren has brought me recently a great many broadsheets and pamphlets from his travelling in the north of the county. Many of them deal with the great riches and great poverty in the country and what should be done to make things fairer. Some were not very well written and I think I could write better myself, except that I do not know anything of the arguments about such as tithes and taxes.

I have invented a good pie which sells very well at the cost of a loaf. Poor people cannot buy Croud Cantle pies, which causes me much argument with myself, for if we should give them away, then we should not make a living, yet it does not seem too great a thing that all people should have such a small treat as a pie.

Judeth Nugent 1787

[61]

WITH THIS slightly less hard-wearing life-style, Jude and Bella had a bit of leisure and more time to spend with Hanna.

They took her regularly to Newton Clare so that no one could ever suggest that they kept her from the Hazelhursts. As Jaen and Dan's family grew in number and size, the cottage appeared to grow smaller. Young Dan'l now had brothers: Baxter, Francis, Richard and Gregory. Eventually The Boys built an extension, which ruined the proportions of the original place. Jaen was pleased, but only because it gave them room to breathe: she found little else in life pleasing. Only Ju's occasional visits.

Hanna didn't mind spending a day with her mother and father, nor did she mind taking a look at each new brother when it was just a day or so old, but when it was time to return to Croud Cantle she was always ready to go.

"Why don't you have another girl baby?" she once asked Jaen, and Jaen had looked at Hanna slightly puzzled, for she had got into the habit of not really counting Hanna.

"We do seem to get all boys, don't we?" she said.

When she was quite little and they had not visited Jaen and Dan for several weeks, Hanna had asked Jude: "Why haven't I got a mother too?"

"Jaen's your mother."

"Jaen's Dan'l's mother, and Baxter's."

For a while, Bella and Jude were concerned, so took turns in going more frequently to the Ham Ford cottage with Hanna.

Bella once, straight out, not beating about the bush, brought it up with Dan.

"What about Hanna?"

"What's wrong with her?"

"She has been over Cantle near on three years."

"Is it so long?" Dan asked.

"Is she to come back?"

Bella, having taken the bull by the horns, was at once filled with a dread, and Dan's reply seemed long in coming. What if they said Hanna should go back to them? The hole in her life without Hanna would be too enormous to fill.

Dan said, "Is she too much for you?"

"Oh no, no, she isn't the slightest trouble. We hardly know she's there." Bella forgave herself this untruth, for she knew that Hanna was there every moment of the day. A baby to care for with all the experience and maturity that made it a pleasure.

"She seems to be happy enough, if you wants to let her stay on a bit," said Dan.

Bella never knew whether Dan could have taken to any child that was not all Hazelhurst and he was never tested, for he never fathered another at all resembling Jaen's family. And she never wholly knew what Jaen felt, but suspected that she would have preferred to be entirely childless. The misery that Bella had seen that Christmas when she and Jude had brought Hanna over to Cantle never entirely left Jaen's eyes.

Nance Hazelhurst's comment to Bella that, "She's one of yourn," was a lot to do with why the child was better suited to life at Croud Cantle rather than at Ham Ford. By the time that she was seven, even the Hazelhurst mouth had altered. Like Jude and Jaen she was an Estover to her fingertips. Nugents were never mentioned.

During these years, Jude read everything that she could get hold of. If a subject caught her interest, then she followed it as far as resources and resourcefulness allowed. Her room had shelves on every available bit of wall-space and each shelf was gradually filled with piles of papers, pamphlets, tracts and a few books.

Fred Warren had moved off his high clerk's stool and had become indispensable to his gouty senior partner. He spent much of his working life travelling round the southern counties of England, looking at fields of standing cereal and estimating their worth, or perhaps handling threshed grain, trickling it from hand to hand, biting into it to test the quality. Over the years he expanded his knowledge and area of trade, dealing in barley and hops for brewing, even malt and honey.

Fred Warren had become a man of substance in more ways than one; he put on a bit of weight. Beneath his more substantial exterior and under his superficial appearance as a man of business, the poverty-stricken clerk remained always at his core: the radical idealist who had taught Jude to write in exchange for the luxury of cream and butter for his family. The hard early years had left him looking older than he was, but his enthusiasm and passion for living made him seem far more youthful than his peers.

To Jude, a luxury meant a book. At Croud Cantle they never went short of food and had a change of clothes, but there was never a penny to spare, certainly not for such inessentials as books. Jude was so hungry for reading matter that she read the same things over and over again.

Here are two maps which are of the village of Cantle. The top one is the village when the land was shared by all. It is clear how, except for the Manor and Manor Farm, the land was all open. The bottom one shows that it has all been taken by enclosure. The Goodenstones have now got everything west of the Dunnock, and the church holdings are large. The cross shows Croud Cantle which is but a flea-bite of land. Fred has told me about how people got the land taken from them legal, but it was hard to take in. A map such as this makes it clear to me. I have put it in this book, because my promise to myself was to put down my thoughts and things that may be of interest to people who come after.

J. Nugent 1787

THE OPEN FIELDS of Cantle, which had once spread into surrounding wastelands and commons had, by the late eighteenth century, largely disappeared: much of the land had been hedged, ditched, enclosed and claimed. There was still some common land, but most of the great acreage was now safely out of the reach of the villagers behind the high walls and iron gates of Goodenstone Manor.

The lands of Goodenstone had been enclosed quite legally. A Commissioner was appointed by Parliament. He visited Cantle, surveyed and valued the land and checked legal claims. Claimants were then free to hedge, ditch and build walls around their land. That is to say, they were free to do so if they could afford the labour and materials. The Goodenstones could afford to enclose every acre they could lay claim to; practically every other Claimant could not.

When the re-allocation of village land was complete, the Goodenstone family found that it now owned most of Cantle, while other Claimants discovered that they were left with meagre acres on which they could not keep body and soul together. People became hired labour on land they considered their own.

One of the few exceptions to the absorption into the Goodenstone estates was Croud Cantle. Croud Cantle retained its identity, not because of foresight by the Nugents or any ability to enclose, but because the land had always needed draining ditches. When the time came to fulfil the requirements of the Commissioner, it was found that most of the common land sharing the Croud Cantle boundary had been hedged and ditched, and was considered to be part of the farm.

Three other holdings remained outside the Goodenstone enclosure: Willow, Meadow and Eastfield farms. A fourth, Church farm, was too closely connected by patronage to the Goodenstones' estate to be anything but Goodenstone land in the minds of the villagers.

At the lodge gates, Harry Goodenstone stuck his head out of the carriage window and called to his driver.

"Maytes, let me down here. I will walk up to the house."

He jumped down and strode off through the trees towards the house. Striding did something to enhance Harry Goodenstone's gait, for he was a small man, greatly encumbered by clothes of the latest London fashion: cords, toggles, buttons, tabs, fobs, frills, braid, lace and a cut-away coat and tricorn hat trimmed with fur.

For much of the time Manor House was occupied only by servants. In the past, it had awoken once or twice a year like a creature from hibernation. Smoke from kitchen ranges and log fires drifted over the cedar trees. Lamps and candles made prisms flash from crystal drops on chandeliers and glitter on polished window-panes. The house breathed out odours of spices and roasting meats, of toilet water, yellow soap, metal polish and boot-black. Doors opened and closed, releasing sounds of silver clinking on fine china; of music, laughter and dancing.

Now, though, the house awoke only on rare occasions.

Harry Goodenstone had not been home for a year and felt pleased at the prospect. His father had died. The funeral would take place in a day or so. There had been no love lost between Old "Sir" Henry and his sole heir. Young Harry had quite a spring in his step. As he approached the house, he became aware that he had changed in the last year. He had at last come into his own. Harry Goodenstone had inherited.

Young Harry Goodenstone, at thirty, now had in his charge the well-being of most of the villagers of Cantle. Land, property, wealth, investments, plantations and people who had no choice but to see that he retained it all. People such as the Cantle villagers, who would labour on Goodenstone land from dawn to dusk, year in year out, for the whole of their lives. It was they who kept him in braid and toggles.

Maytes, with the baggage, alerted the servants to Master Harry's arrival, so that they were assembled, a humble guard of honour for him. They bobbed and curtseyed in a manner suited to a house in which lay the corpse of its late master.

"Thank you. Thank you," was the only response from the new master to the expressions of sympathy.

The day of the burial of Henry George Goodenstone JP was wild. The wind blustered up and around the downs, rattling the empty shells of last year's beech mast, and making little waves on dew-ponds and horse-troughs.

"Do we have to go?" Jude asked.

"Of course we have to go," Bella answered.

"Why?"

"Why! Jude, there wasn't ever anybody like you for 'why?' Out of respect."

"You never had a good word to say for him."

"Respect for the dead."

Jude was not serious in her argument. In such matters she lost to Bella even before they began.

"The dead don't need respect – especially one like him. He never had any respect for a soul around here."

"Respect for the family then."

"Young master Goodenstone – touch your forelock and bow your knee and say Sir! He never liked his father any more than anybody else in Cantle."

"You don't have to like people you do your duty to. It'd be a sad day when people forget their duties," was Bella's last word.

All the while she was protesting, Jude was pinning on a bit of black crape to a straw hat with a large brim. At the last moment, too late to do anything about it, she found that the ribbon needed replacing and rather than have Bella chide her again about her laxity in caring for her clothing, she tucked the ribbon up into her hair behind her ear.

But Bella saw everything.

"Oh Jude. You are worse than Hanna. When will you get to be a bit more ... " She had intended saying "ladylike", but Jude would have laughed. "And it's that windy, you'll have to hold on to it all the while."

They left Hanna in the care of Johnny-twoey and went off to see the last of Henry Goodenstone JP, MP. Jude idly talking, to counter the prospect of the dismal ceremony.

"In some countries they wear white at burials."

"Oh Jude, you do say some things."

"It is true. And they put the bodies on platforms and set them alight, and everybody watches to see the soul fly up to heaven."

"Then pray the Lord that good Christians may save them."

Jude laughed aloud and was shushed by her mother as they approached the solemn and grand occasion.

Jude lowered her voice. "I think it's a lot better than rotting in the ground."

Bella glowered. "If you let us down, Jude ... "

They joined the procession of villagers and followed the cortège up to the church.

Quietly Jude said in Bella's ear, "When the fire is well alight, all the wives leap into the flames."

They walked solemnly on, Bella pretending to be deep in prayer.

"Imagine if widows here had to do it. Imagine flinging yourself into a grave."

As Bella could not close her ears, she closed her eyes.

The prayers said for the late magistrate by the visiting Canon of the Abbey of St Mary and Ethelflaeda, Blackbrook, were many and ponderous, but eventually the sexton unlatched the door to allow the passage of the coffin and its attendants. Suddenly the wind gusted through the little chapel and whipped the door from his hands, sending it thundering back against the porch.

"The devil has come to claim the soul," said Jude.

When Jude was in this sort of mood she would make jest of anything. Bella forced out between goffered lips and latched front teeth a "Jude!"

When they were free of the gloomy church, Jude took Bella's elbow.

"I'm sorry."

"And so you should be."

"It's just that I cannot bear all this, so I have to say silly things."

Jude indicated the dark spread of the yew trees; the cold, dead, grey stone cross with its green slime and yellow lichens; the heavy tombs of other Goodenstones.

"All the black. Look at it. Crows."

Bella looked about her. The wind dragged and flipped at black crape and fine wool; it flittered black satin bonnet-strings and black lace trimmings and plucked at threadbare shawls. The canon's full skirt and cloak sounded like sails and flapped like wings. Shiny black jerky movement. Crows. How did such things come into Jude's head? But she was right when you looked at it.

At the graveside, the fashionably expensive chief mourner was watching the expensive coffin slide into the tomb, when suddenly he was hit directly in the face by a flying straw bonnet with a broken string.

In many cottages, in the milking-sheds, barns and alehouses of Cantle and Motte on the evening after the funeral, there was a great deal of close-lipped merriment. Any joke that could be bent around the word, "bonnet", received unstinted appreciation. Old men who had picked stones from the Goodenstone fields when they were children had long, sore memories: a story like that was cool self-heal balm.

Like the time lightning struck the house and brought the bounty of work to masons and bricklayers. Or when Old Sir Henry's collection of rare plants took blight and died. And best of all when he got his shoulder all ready for the touch of the king's sword and it didn't fall. There was not a great amount of malice in them, but thereafter he was always referred to as "Sir" Henry – behind his back.

Ah, the satisfaction of saying, "Serves 'm right," about a Goodenstone – very quietly, out of the corner of the mouth.

On their walk home, Bella was torn between feeling that she should chide Jude for making a spectacle of herself, and wanting to tell her the joke: "Well, that was a slap in the face for Harry Goodenstone, and no mistake." In the end, like the rest of Cantle, she had her laugh at The Estate, and she and Jude arrived home in good spirits.

ABOUT A MONTH later, Jude was working on the Parish Records in the church vestry, when she heard the deformed accent of Harry Goodenstone. He and the Reverend Mr Tripp were walking down the side aisle towards where she was, discussing a suitable site for a plaque to commemorate the old squire, the church's late benefactor. Jude stopped rustling papers and hoped that they would not come into the vestry. She had apologised briefly on retrieving her bonnet and hoped that finished the matter.

They came into the vestry.

Tripp had forgotten that Jude was there.

"Ah, so it's you here, girl," was all that he could think of saying.

The girl had caused a muddle on a solemn occasion, an important solemn occasion. Under the eyes of the Abbey of Saint Mary and Ethelflaeda. There was something very unsatisfactory about the Nugent girl: he had thought so ever since the day she had raced up to him and asked to be taught reading, and she had been only a child. The mother was an honest and hard-working enough woman, but any family without the authority of a man was bound to suffer. This girl lacked proper humility. The vicar was annoyed and embarrassed to find her there.

Not so Harry Goodenstone.

"Ah, the far-flung bonnet," he said.

"I was sorry if it appeared disrespectful. But I have learnt a lesson: I shall not neglect to secure ribbons again," said Jude with a humility that the vicar could not fault, except in its sincerity.

"I cannot see that you are wholly to blame, for the wind was very strong." He appeared very gracious, seeing that Jude was a village girl.

Bright, red-gold hair shone through with sun, coloured by the church window: discovering a village girl studying old documents in a dusty vestry was considerably more interesting than a dutiful plaque.

[70]

On their entry into the vestry, Jude had collected her belongings and put away the records she had been using. She was now ready to leave.

To Reverend Tripp she said: "Thank you, could I use them again next week?"

"What are you doing here?" asked Young Harry.

"Everything, really."

He raised his eyebrows.

"Well, I don't ever know what I'm looking for until I found it. There's such a lot in these old books."

Tripp nervously fingered the pages of a Parish Register, wondering, perhaps too late, whether it was wise to let a girl loose with such documents. They were public documents, true, but nobody had ever asked to see them before. Where would they all be if The Estate removed their patronage? Perhaps there was information here about past Goodenstones that The Estate would not want to see the light of day. The old squire had been generous, but this young man was an unknown quantity.

Harry Goodenstone did not seem perturbed. In fact he smiled at Jude. "Well it is no doubt a good thing, but I must say it looks somewhat dreary – births, marriages, burials."

"It's people's lives," said Jude, "How can that be dreary?"

Well now, thought Harry Goodenstone, a villager who speaks up! And that hair. To Tripp he said, "The position near the porch will be quite suitable. White marble, gold lettering, simple name and date. No eulogising. He was not a saint."

The vicar knew this to be true, but he would not allow a disloyal comment. Old Sir Henry had been prepared to put almost as much money into the repair of God's house as he was into the stabling of his hunters.

The fabric of estate-workers' cottages had come very low on his list, but that was not Tripp's concern.

Jude quickly put away the Parish Register and left. She had gone about a quarter of a mile on her way home, when Harry Goodenstone, on horseback, caught up with her.

"Tripp says you spend a lot of time there."

"Not a lot, just the odd hour when I can get away."

"I don't see what interest you can have in them."

"Them?"

[71]

"Villagers, the common people."

"They aren't them to me – they're us. I'm a common person."

He gave a Bath Assembly Room laugh, automatically, as when a very pretty young woman declares that, really, she has no looks at all.

"I see nothing common in you."

Jude had reached a gap in the hawthorn and bramble which led on to the short-cut. "Good day Mister Harry."

Jude squeezed through the space too small for a horse and rider.

When she reached home from the vestry, Jude immediately started on preparations for the big baking next day. Bella was draining honey from combs and Hanna had already started her part of the operation, which was chopping lard into small pieces and breaking open eggs to see if they were good. Good eggs went into a jug, bad ones into the pig bucket.

At coming seven, Hanna was a smaller version of both Bella and Jude. Bella – no nonsense, hard-labouring, sharp-tongued Bella – had gone quite soft where Hanna was concerned. Naturally the child had her chores and duties, as was proper and necessary: their living was not generous enough to allow for idle moments or idle hands. The hour or two that Jude spent in the vestry or reading some tract or pamphlet was worked for at some other time. Jude's good fortune was that in spite of all the hours of physical hard work she put in, she seldom needed to sleep for more than five hours. When she did sleep she slept deep and awoke refreshed.

Jude tied on an apron and immediately began making pastry for the plate-tarts. Hanna chattered, pausing from time to time whenever Bella popped a morsel of honeycomb into her mouth.

"What was you doing there today?" Bella asked. She was not particularly interested, but liked to keep track of things and people.

"I didn't get much of a chance. The vicar and Fancy Harry came in."

Bella gathered up her lips and frowned at Jude, nodding with great meaning across Hanna, who was intent on her lard chopping.

"You might think it's clever to talk like that, but we do quite well out of The Estate one way and another, so you mind yourself."

"Oh mother, this is our own kitchen. If we can't talk free here, where can we talk?"

"Little brooks babble," said Bella.

"And little donkeys have got big ears. I know," said Jude with a "heard it all before" expression.

"I won't tell what Jude said," said Hanna.

Jude laughed and Bella wagged her head with her you-will-all-be-the-death-of-me-yet look.

They worked quietly for a few minutes, then Bella said, "Well?"

"He wanted to know what I was doing."

"And?"

"I just said I was going through some old records."

"Didn't he say anything about," she looked at Hanna, "the burial?"

"No. Well, only something about bonnet-strings."

"What about?"

"Nothing. When I left, he came after me up Howgaite."

"Came after you? What d'you mean came after you?"

"He came after me on his horse."

"On his horse? What did he ..?"

"Lord, Mother! In the vestry he looked at me like men do. I'm nearly twenty; lots of men look at young women. They have to, even if they are not serious about it, they have to ... well, keep going, chasing, hunting, whatever it is they do."

Bella gave another signal over Hanna's head and sent Hanna to collect the day's eggs.

Jude went on. "I don't know why you're making such a to-do."

"It's not a to-do. But things you say sometimes ... "

"Oh mother! He is fancy. With his buttons and his curls over his ears. He was wearing a cloak with a collar touching his ears and a high black hat with a buckle in front. Why, mother, the hat was near as tall as he was. Nobody can take him serious, not like old Sir Henry. You had to take him serious: you knew he'd a soon ride you down as go round you. Harry Goodenstone is only a man like all the rest. He didn't have anything better to do, so he rode down Howgaite just to give himself the pleasure of looking down on me from his high horse, then ride away showing off his tight bum-bags."

Close-lipped, Bella kneaded dough.

"He isn't coming courting," said Jude drily.

"There's times when you behave like a five-year-old, Jude. You seem to have this idea that you can say anything you like and one of

[73]

these days it's going to land you in trouble. Harry Goodenstone and his sort can make or break the likes of us."

Knowing that when Bella was in full flight it was useless making any comment, Jude continued rolling and cutting the pastry for the plates.

"Just because we aren't bound hand and foot to The Estate, don't mean that we are a deal more independent than the rest of Cantle. They got money, and that's power. Harry Goodenstone could finish up in Parliament and make up some law to take over people like us. They took over most everything else. It's only with God's grace we're here. I tried to bring you up strong, but you're a sight too strong if you ask me. You seem to think that just because people is fools, you can treat them like fools. Well you can't if they'm called Goodenstone."

She was running down, but Jude knew that she was not quite finished. Eventually she said, "Tight bum-bags!"

Hanna came back with the egg-pail and Bella set her to preparing vegetables and herbs. Hanna didn't at all like the sore eyes the onions caused, but Bella made her persevere, saying that in a couple of years she would be able to chop onions dry-eyed like a proper little woman.

The irritation that had begun in the vestry when Harry Goodenstone began to intrude upon her – impertinently as she saw it – had been exacerbated by Bella's homily.

"We don't owe the Goodenstones anything. They don't buy anything from us, and we don't get anything from them."

"Where do our wood come from?"

"Why, the common mostly."

"And what if The Estate claims it and encloses it?"

"They can't!"

"But suppose they did?"

"It wouldn't be any good to them."

"I'm not saying it would. What I'm saying is that they got the money to do it if they took it into their heads, and then we should have to look about us for fuel, shouldn't we? So we are dependent on them."

The argument did not slow down the production of the plate-pies and tarts, and gradually the cold slab became covered with rows of them. For quite long periods they worked silently, Hanna quietly absorbed in making little dough people from the scraps Bella always passed to her at the end of the process. Jude prodded Bella, but Bella wasn't having any. She'd had her say and did not rise.

Jude said, "We aren't here by God's grace either. This place is yours and we work it very well."

Bella scoured the flour from crevices in the soft pine of the table.

Jude went on, "And you're wrong: I don't treat everybody I think's a fool like a fool. There's a lot of them can't help it. It's fools who wear big black hats and tight bum-bags and think they have the right to ask people anything they like that I treats as fools."

AFTER THE DEATH of Old Sir Henry, the lives of the working people of Cantle, Motte and The Estate were unaltered with the exception of two beneficiaries under the will, who had the millstone of rent lifted from them.

Harry Goodenstone was no new broom.

He looked briefly at books put before him by bailiffs, stewards and head gardeners and at more length at the cellar records. He entertained a great deal and rode about The Estate doing his duty, taking an interest in his land and his people.

" 'Morning to you Ned", "Salmon running yet, Dawkins?" "Good crop of fruit, eh?" in his high voice, and with inflections and tortured vowels that were understood in places like Bath and London, but not in rural Hampshire. He had been made into a gentleman, and was vaguely aware that the men who tended stock, grew cereal and fattened cattle, and the women who milked and churned and stooked, had something to do with his personal comfort. Harry Goodenstone behaved as a gentleman ought, and was gracious to those who served – his workers.

His workers – they would touch their brow and feel irritable for the rest of the day.

From the day his new tailor mentioned how seldom it was that he had the pleasure of dressing such a good figure, Harry Goodenstone took care to live up to the good figure. He held his head well clear of his shoulders, whatever the occasion; his back was straight; he stood whenever he could. When riding, he kept his backside thrust out, moulding the fine cloth of his breeches about his buttocks and thighs. "The Master sits a horse like a button-hook," as one stable-lad commented. He kept his long chin and short upper lip clean-shaven of

[76]

the hair that hardly grew there, and allowed mouse-brown curls to show beneath fashionable headgear.

Fred Warren often had business with The Estate. One day, there being a Bill that needed signing, Goodenstone took him into the library.

"Don't reckon I've seen any finer library than this, Master Harry."

"Interested in books?"

"Indeed, when I have the time."

"Look nice in a room, but I have never discovered a great deal of pleasure in reading. Like to see books on a wall, though. I'm about to clear this lot out. Going to make it into a room for performing arts and the like.

"You can take some books if you care, Warren. The new library shall be on a good deal smaller scale than this. Be a fine room though, having in one of the best London architects to design it ... along with my other room. I will arrange it ... the books. Come when it suits you."

"That's extraordinarily generous of you, Sir. Any books in particular you want to be rid of?"

"Don't take those." He indicated a wall full of red morocco, raised bands and silk headers. Jolly nice colour."

To Fred Warren, the prospect of the pleasure of selecting books was enormous. The offer was made so casually that, with the exception of the red calf, he was unsure which and how many it was appropriate to choose. On his first visit he took six.

When Warren visited The Estate office again, Harry Goodenstone asked him when he was going to come in for the books. On hearing that Fred had taken only an armful, he said, "Good God Warren, I want a whole wall cleared." Fred offered to make an inventory of what was there before anything was removed, as obviously Master Harry would want to keep the best of the books.

"Good fellow, Warren. You do what you like. I never got on well with that kind of thing. Never did learn a word of Latin. Tried to cram it in – fell out again." Young Harry Goodenstone laughed at himself.

"Would you mind if I brought someone with me? A village girl. I've taken an interest in her, taught her to read and write. She's a rare one for reading, but never gets enough to keep her going."

"Do you mean the girl from over yon? The one with the hair? I saw her in the vestry one day. Odd girl. Writing a history of farm-hands or some such. Extraordinary hair. Like russety hair."

Fred Warren had never thought much about Jude's hair.

"Judeth Nugent. I never met anybody who could pick up things as quick as Judeth." As always when he talked of Jude, he felt the pride that he would like to have felt about his own children. "She has such a brain under that hair. She would love to come to your library, I'm sure of it."

"Tell her to come to the house. Come when she wants."

April 1787. It is seven years today that Jaen got married to Dan Hazelhurst.

Sometimes I can scarce bear to look her straight in the eyes, she is so full of misery. She keeps her face in the shape of a smile, but it is all false.

It is natural for women to give birth, we are made to do so, yet why is there such pain? Some animals will not suckle their young. It seems to be a natural thing.

I wish that I was not so ignorant. I want to ask about such things, but who to ask? I hardly care to write them secret, let alone talk. In any case I do not even know how to say the things that come to me. Most it is feelings that a thing is wrong yet I do not know what it is that makes it wrong. Like Jaen who, I believe, is in terror of giving birth, even suckling and holding the children. Yet she is a woman and our bodies are made for this.

J. Nugent

What I wrote above about animals. I stopped myself putting it down because I was afraid to admit my thoughts, but what is the use of thoughts if we run from them.

Animals couple, it seems without being able to help it. If Jaen went with him in that way then that is natural and good. Most animals give birth and feed their young, and if you hear a cow lowing for a dead calf you know that it wants that calf very much. However, there are some creatures that do not accept their young. They will not suckle them and will often devour them. Perhaps there are women who cannot abide their own young, but have no choice.

J. Nugent 1787

May 1787. Further thoughts on this subject.

It would be better if we were to be more open and say that there are women who find it hard to take to the children they gave birth to. And men who are the same, for Dan is pleased that Hanna is away from them. There is nothing wrong in that, yet I know that it must never be talked of.

It seems that even women, who ought to give tender support to one another, join in the hurt of women like Jaen. If Jaen does not want her children, then it must be natural to her. If it is natural to her, then she should not be blamed.

Jude Nugent

THE MORNING WAS bright and fine when Fred Warren at last found time to call at the holding and tell Jude about the books.

Jude, in her rough dress, head uncovered, hair straggling from its string, was leading the old donkey with Hanna seated upon its back. Hanna was giggling and trying not to fall off as Jude jumped and tickled her.

As always, Jude was delighted to see her old tutor. He looked as though he had become quite the gentleman. His hair was cut fashionably to the collar and was still powdered, although he wore no false queues or curls. His coat was elegantly cut away and his neck-cloth was of fine lawn. His black leather boots with turn-down cuffs looked far too shiny for country wear.

"Mr Warren, you do look fine."

He looked pleased at the compliment. "Well, it's nice to be some people, playing games in the sun with little fidgets like this." He picked up Hanna and gave her a toss in the air. "I been up and on the road since sunrise."

"Then you lazy thing Mr Warren," said Jude. "I was up even before the sun."

"I'll believe you there, Judeth, knowing how you can't bear to waste time sleeping."

"It do seem a bit of a waste when we haven't got much time on this world. Come into the house. It's all right," she laughed at the question in Warren's raised eyebrows. "Mother's finished her scrubbing down. She's gone down to tether the new kid in the orchard."

"I've got somebody with me. Showing him the ropes. We are getting so much business, Mr White decided to get me an assistant."

"Well he can come too, can't he? Where is he?"

"Round the front, holding the horses. Jude, I got the best news for you. Books, Jude!"

Jude loved Fred Warren's enthusiasm whenever he had some tract or pamphlet to bring her, or news of a meeting he had heard of. She returned the grin he gave her when he said, "Books!"

Jude and Hanna went in through the back door and cut some tart and fetched a jug of cider. Then Fred came in, followed by a young man of about twenty-five.

"Jude, this is Will Vickery."

That Will Vickery was of middle height and had brown, unpowdered hair was all Jude took in of him. They each made polite acknowledgement of the other, he accepted refreshment and sat quietly eating.

Fred Warren was exuberant. "What would you say to having free rein in a library full of books? I know what you're thinking – what else would a library be full of? Except this one won't be full of anything much longer, apart from play-acting. There's books to read and to bring away by the armful, Judeth."

He held his knees together like a child in anticipation of Jude's response.

"There's never going to be an open library in Blackbrook like the one you saw in Southampton?"

"No, nearer than that. Here in Cantle. Up at Park Manor. You can use the library there, and have what books they don't want. In return we shall make a catalogue for him."

Fred Warren waited for the effect he expected from her.

"There! I knew it'd knock the wind out of you."

"I don't know that I could do that," she said.

"Lord girl, why not? Old Sir Henry bought the books by the yard to make an elegant room to be up with his friends. Harry Goodenstone isn't one bit interested in books. He's taken up with theatres and plays and is going to have a stage built in the library and wants a good many of them gone."

"Well, I don't know what to say."

"I could come over with you a time or two till you got used to it."

"I haven't got time. I can't be always off on such things when Mother's got so much to do."

Fred Warren looked quite crestfallen.

"Jude, you cannot possibly turn down this opportunity. There's

[81]

books there ... I can't tell you ... poetry, bound engravings, plays – William Shakespeare, imagine that, everything that he wrote. Jude there's books in that library that has never seen the light of day."

There was a clatter outside and Jude was saved from answering as Bella came in and Jude remembered she was supposed to be preparing food for the men. She busied herself swinging the stew-pot over the fire, then putting out cheese and cutting bread into large hunks.

After she and Fred had exchanged the time of day and the young Mr Vickery introduced, Bella sat with bread in one hand, cheese in the other, as she always sat at this time of day, unrelaxed and ready to spring at the next job, as though she had not a second to spare.

Fred Warren knew that the best approach to Bella was always the direct one. "Could Jude be spared for the odd half a day, to do some reading?" he said.

Bella shrugged her shoulders. "As well as writing down the whole world?"

"Why," said Mr Warren, "I had quite forgot that." He turned to where his new assistant sat unobtrusive and quiet, Hanna at a distance, weighing him up with the solemn expression of an old lady.

"D'you know, Will, the first time I met Judeth – you were coming up twelve, isn't that right?"

Jude nodded.

"She asked me to teach her to write so that she could put down everything in one big book."

"Two," said Jude.

"Well, if that's not just the best kind of ambition I ever heard say of."

Until now Vickery had said no more than a quiet "Good morning", but the words he now uttered caused both Jude and Bella to turn in his direction. His voice was quiet but clear and he put stress on words quite unlike anything they had ever heard.

"You're not from round these parts then," said Bella.

"I was born in Motte. My father was a groom on the Estate there. He got taken to Ireland by his master – I was two at the time – and lived there ever since."

"Ireland! Oh, Ireland," said Jude, with just as great an interest as though he had said Iceland or India. "I have always wondered what it was like there. Is it all so green? I've heard it said that it is all green."

"It is green. There's a lot of grass, and surely plenty of rain."

Fred Warren looked enormously pleased. "That's a bit of information for your book, eh?"

Will Vickery asked, "Do you really do that?"

Jude laughed. "I only just put down some things that people may forget, things that might be worth knowing in a hundred years."

"Judeth's got brains," said Fred Warren.

"They don't remind her to see to the broth though," said Bella, jumping up to clatter the iron spoon against the soup-kettle.

Immediately, Fred Warren sprang to his feet.

"Mrs Nugent. I have overstayed my welcome. The men will be in soon."

Jude began collecting the mugs they had used.

"What do you say then? Half a day? It's a chance too good to be missed."

"She'd have to stop all that in the vestry," said Bella.

"I don't know that I can go up there," said Jude.

"But why, Judeth?" asked Fred Warren.

Jude hesitated; she was not wholly sure why. It was, of course, partly to do with her recent encounters with Goodenstone. It was also partly that she was not sure what she was getting into. Not that she thought that there was anything amiss in being allowed access to the Manor library, but it was, to say the least, extraordinarily unusual for a village girl to go up to the Manor in any capacity other than servant. Perhaps that was it, it was not being able to place herself. You were safe when you knew who you were and what you were.

"I thought you would jump at the chance," said Fred Warren.

"Well, it's being May and all that. There's all the bean planting, the carrots and beets; the fruit has to be thinned. This time of year ..." She trailed off.

"You don't work every hour God sends?"

"Mostly."

Fred Warren looked at Jude with mild concern. "Come Judeth, why? All the times you've wailed and moaned about not having enough books. He's giving away books."

Jude felt unhappy. She had great affection for her tutor.

Had it not been for him, she would not know the excitement she felt every evening when she took out her books with the blank pages.

"I don't know. I think I should feel beholden to people I don't want to be beholden to."

There was a moment's silence and into it the younger man said: "It seems to me that if there's anybody should feel beholden, it's for the likes of them. Is there a one who ever did a day's work in their whole life. Where did the books come from? Where else except from the sweat of the brows of the people round here. Books don't get bought by riding to hounds, nor by entertaining and dinner-parties, nor by sitting in theatres and the like. Those books got bought by the sweat of people who have worked all their lives and ... "

He stopped mid-sentence. Bella had stopped stirring and Jude looked at him as though his words were pictures streaming from his mouth.

He looked down at his own hand, which had slapped the table for emphasis, as though it did not belong to him. "I'm sorry," he said. "My tongue has always been quicker than my brains."

Bella was leaning slightly forward, as though something quite new and strange had caught her interest. She squinted her eyes and compressed her lips in case they should smile too much.

"No," she said, "you'm right. That kind of thing have been in my mind all my life. My father used to talk like that, but I never heard it put in such words before."

She did not look at any of them as she spoke, but her eyes raked the whole room as though gathering in thoughts that had been waiting there for her to collect. Bella looked as though the entire mystery of the universe had been revealed.

"Why, Mister Vickery, a course the books is ourn." She smiled broadly at the young man. "And I reckon Jude ought to get a read of them."

THAT EVENING, the days having lengthened towards summer, Jude and Bella worked late. Hanna had traipsed about after them all day, Bella petting and praising her, indulging her as she had never done Jaen and Jude.

"Goodness, what a hard little worker you are my lovely."

"Look Jude, see how many potatoes Hanna have put in their holes."

"Well, my Lord! Did you pick all that lot of snails off they cabbages? Tell Jude you shall have that bit of ginger-bread that was left." And so on.

Now late on the warm May evening, Hanna had fallen asleep curled up on some sacks. Jude carried her into the house and put her to bed as she was.

Right from the beginning there had always been a bit of competition for putting Hanna to bed and an unspoken agreement had grown up between Bella and Jude that they would do it turn and turn about. In winter they would sit on the hearthside, perhaps rocking and singing, taking time washing her face and hands, counting fingers and toes. In warm weather Jude enjoyed carrying the little girl upstairs, and then sitting squeezed up on the sill of the dormer window.

The upper floor of the Croud Cantle house was really one large room divided with hurdles and laths that had been daubed and whitened. The part that Jaen and Jude had once shared was now Jude's. Hanna was in with Bella. The three of them shared a space that the vast majority of Cantle families would have considered great luxury. Not only that, they had a good roof and the walls were dry.

Tonight it was too dark outside to sit in the window, and as Hanna had not been disturbed when being transferred from sacks to bed, Jude went back down without lingering. The light had faded, and it was too dark to see to work any longer. Jude brought some food out on to

[85]

the porch for the two of them, and left Johnny-twoey's bit of bacon and some bread ready in the scullery. He was an odd boy: eating – like a wild creature – when his body told him, rather than at regular intervals. They left his food ready and he took it when it suited him.

What Jude had said about all the May planting to be done was true. However hard and long you worked, there was always something else waiting. Every green haze of germinated carrot seed had its accompanying haze of groundsel. As beans appeared overnight, so did slugs and blackfly. Traps baited with ale had to be sunk along the rows, and solutions of hard, yellow soap were in constant need to deal with aphids.

The soil was warm now and dry enough for sowing a succession of the vegetables that would be needed to keep them going for the rest of the year. Like every villager who had muscles and joints that worked, Bella and Jude dug and raked and hoed; planted, weeded and thinned; carted muck, pulled rhubarb, thinned carrots and earthed up the potatoes for their own table – all done after a good day's work.

The loud birdsong of spring had dwindled now that territory claims and nesting were done, so that only short bursts from thrushes and blackbirds were heard. But cuckoos still called, on and on, whilst there was daylight.

They sat in the dark porch.

"Hark at him," said Jude.

"Ah, I suppose he got the strength to keep on like that because he don't have to work to feed his own young."

"You can't really blame them. I don't reckon they can help laying in other nests. It is their nature. Perhaps they wasn't ever given the remembrance of how to do it like all the other birds."

"Always takes me back when I hears his May song. It was that hot the year I was carrying you, and you seemed heavy enough to have been a calf. Then he changed to his 'cuk-cukoo' and it near drove me mad when I was in labour. I lay there hating him for being out there flying free, making his silly song."

Bella talked and talked. Jude could not remember such animation in her mother for ages, probably since Jaen left. To keep her talking, Jude said: "I never knew you had such ideas as those you spoke of this morning to Fred and Mr Vickery."

"It's funny how you change. I can remember when I was young my father was always talking of such things. But it all seemed so old

[86]

and dry. I can remember one of his stories. It was about some people who banded together and tried to take over land. I don't even know whether it was some he knew when he was young or long in the past, but he was always on about it. About how they dug up the commons and planted them."

"There was a group that Fred got me a paper on. Shall I tell you some?"

"Can you just say it off?"

" 'Thou has many bags of money, and behold I the Lord come as a thief in the night, with my sword drawn in my hand, and like a thief I say deliver.

" 'The plague of God is in your purses, barns, houses, horses.

" 'Your gold and silver is cankered ... the rust of your silver shall eat your flesh as it were fire ...

" 'Have all things common or else the plague of God will rot and consume all that you have.' " Jude knew the whole pamphlet by heart, having read it so often, and spoke it like poetry.

"Why Jude, that's beautiful. Not that I see why there must be a plague on horses."

"I think it only means he is saying it to people who keep horses to themselves, separate, when the rest haven't got a horse. It's something like that. And that's what that group who dug up commons thought was right."

Although she knew that Jude wrote and read most nights before going to sleep, Bella had never been interested except on those occasions when Jude said, on hearing some old song or cure, "I'll put that down."

"And is that what all them books and papers you got are about?" she asked.

"Some of them. There's poetry and songs, and a play by William Shakespeare. It's just a mixture of things."

"And do you write that kind of thing down yourself?"

"Not anything that sounds as good as that. Really I just argues with myself on paper."

Neither of them said anything for a while, then Bella, safe in the darkness, said: "Jude, I think you'm a clever girl."

It was the first direct compliment that Jude had ever received from her mother, and it would not do to make anything of it.

"Oh," she said. "I'm glad."

[87]

They sat on until stars showed in the darkness. Eventually Bella said, "I'm going on up," then, almost as though she had just thought of it, added, "See if you can't get to read them books Fred Warren was on about. Hanna's big enough now to see to things after market. Perhaps you might go there on your way back."

Part Two

WOMAN

THERE WAS BAD WEATHER in the first days of July in the year when Jude became twenty. Some mornings mists hung over the downs so that the ruins on Old Winchester and the beeches on Tradden Raike were invisible, giving the impression Cantle was not deep in a valley.

There was a feeling of insecurity, living in a place that was not enfolded, surrounded and protected by the great, swelling chalk-hills. People became fratchety. Labourers passed one another, trudging their miles to work with hardly more than a nod – not that they were ever given to jolly greetings – and women, scooping water from Dunnock Brook, slammed their pails about.

At Croud Cantle, Hanna was under Bella's feet and Bella got cross with Jude because of it. Bella had been argumentative all the way back from Blackbrook market. When they reached the crossroads at Cantle, Bella said: "For goodness sake, Jude, get on up there. Fred Warren told you all you got to do is tell the housekeeper who you are."

"All right then!" said Jude, committing herself simply to get away from Bella's irritable mood, and she was on her way up Farm Lane to Park Manor House almost before she realised what she was doing.

They're the ones who should be beholden, Mr Vickery had said; but the fact remained that the park was hundreds of acres, and Park Manor House was big enough to hold every house and cottage in Cantle, including the rectory. It was intimidating, even for a girl whose character had been strengthened and back stiffened by Bella Nugent.

The Farm Lane was about a mile long, well-drained and surfaced with local red hoggin. The hoggin crunched loudly, making Jude conscious of her steady tread. This part of the estate was at the foot of Old Marl, but the steep rise was not visible because of the mists and the dripping, full-grown oaks Jude was walking under. She skirted the farmhouse, going on up to the big house.

Jude had never been further than the farmhouse before, and had to guess that she was going in the right direction. She was surprised when, suddenly, she found that she was going down through a garden with a summer-house. There were a few worn steps with ferns and periwinkle growing at the joints, which led on to a small circular terrace made of bricks laid in a pattern. A sundial on a carved plinth stood at its centre. Surrounding the circular terrace was a high yew hedge which, because it was clipped into castellations at the top, looked like a dark-green fortress wall into which an archway had been cut. Jude went through the archway. She found herself on the main terrace at the back of Park Manor House and was stopped in her tracks by what she saw.

She had heard about the place, which was not surprising considering the number of sons and daughters of Cantle and Motte people who served there, but the fragments of description had put together for Jude an entirely different picture from the reality and did not prepare her for her first sight of the terrace of Park Manor House.

The original house had been quite small, built of local blue and red bricks laid in the orderly pattern of English bond. Over generations, as the Goodenstones reaped their harvest of other people's land and crops, they had extended and built wings on, until the early part was swamped by grandness. What remained of the original house could be seen only from the back, where Jude was standing.

For all its alterations and additions, it was a very beautiful building. There were many sparkling windows with roses and clematis blooming round them. A golden-leaved ivy climbed the walls and pinks, mimulus and stocks had been planted below the windows, where they would waft evening scent into the rooms. The terrace was of a faintly pink stone, and wherever there was an angle a spreading shrub had been planted to soften the line. In four large marble bowls grew fuchsias and trailing vines.

Jude was entranced. She advanced a few steps, feeling that there must be people watching her, wondering what she was doing standing there, staring. There did not appear to be a door, not a proper door, although some of the windows reached the ground and looked as though they could be walked through, but not knocked on.

As Jude was hesitating, somebody opened a window and said, "What you want?" Jude advanced towards the voice.

"I was looking for the Housekeeper."

"You won't find her there. Come round the side."

A side-door was opened by an elderly servant wearing a cross-over bodice dress and apron, and a round-eared cap of a style worn fifty years before.

"I'm Judeth Nugent. The Housekeeper knows I am to come."

Indicating that Jude should follow, the servant led the way through the house. Jude's eyes were everywhere; on the panelling, the glossy floor, the carpets, the lamps.

"You're Bella Nugent's an't you? Bella Nugent that was Bella Estover?"

"Yes."

"No mistaken. You looks just the same as she did when she was your age. Dare say she have changed, she's a good six years older than me."

Jude looked again at the woman. Sunken cheeks through loss of most of her teeth, thick skin, and a stooped walk of an elderly woman. Bella's hard life and worries showed in her face, but the way she held herself, her bright, clean skin and the red hair, still gave her the appearance of a younger woman. This woman, at something over forty, looked ten or fifteen years older than Bella.

The woman led the way through a grand door where the panelling, carpets and decorated lamps ended, along a short passage, then through an ordinary painted door.

"You wanting to be taken on?"

"No," said Jude, and before she had time to say more, the servant woman had stopped outside a door.

"Tell your mother it was Mary Holly. I dare say she a remember."

Mary Holly knocked at the door and opened it.

"Mrs Cutts? Judeth Nugent. Says you know about her. You didn't say anything," said Mary Holly in a tone of voice that was almost insolent.

The Housekeeper was younger than the servant. Her dress, of grey striped cotton with a close-fitting over-bodice, was much less dated than the other servant's. She was inspecting a pile of linen.

"Yes." Then to the hovering Mary Holly: "You need not stop." Mary went. "Is it you that's supposed to be sorting out the library?" She looked Jude up and down.

Jude said yes, was it all right, she had been told to come whenever it suited.

[93]

The woman gave a small shake of her head – whatever next!
"This way."

Jude tried to get some idea of direction so that she would not get lost in the maze of passageways and doors. Mrs Cutts strode ahead, her dress whisking and keys jingling.

She stopped abruptly and opened a double door.

Mrs Cutts showed Jude into the room and shut the door. It was probably six times larger than any room Jude had been in and the number of books was hundreds of times more than Jude's own few.

At first she stood and looked around. The room was hexagonal and shelved from floor to ceiling on five walls, the sixth being a window. There were some deep easy chairs, a sloping desk with an upright chair, several tables and some curious little circular steps which Jude assumed were for reaching the topmost books.

She read some of the names: Butler, Swift, then two under 'D' whose names she had heard of – Defoe and Dryden. Most of the works were entirely new to her. On one table was a pile of plays. She was like a hungry person given free choice in a bakehouse, tempted by the confection of bound prints, yet wanting to feed upon the nutritious literature. In the end, she took something at random and stood reading, not liking to use a chair; intimidated by the size of the room and air of solemn luxury.

"What's all this about, then?"

Totally absorbed, Jude had not heard Mary Holly come into the library. A false smile, aggressive, sneering.

"What you got to do with this place?"

"Nothing, only that Mister Goodenstone says I can have some books and borrow some if I want."

"Is that all?"

"I don't see what it's got to do with you." Jude was irritated by the woman's unfriendly manner, as well as feeling uneasy about the way she seemed to do as she pleased, although she was obviously a servant. You'd think she owned the place, thought Jude.

She made no attempt to leave Jude alone, but sat on an upright chair and took some darning from her apron pocket; quiet except for a heavy breath from time to time, as though she might be hoping that she could attract Jude's attention. She appeared to be quite at home in the huge library, like any cottager sitting darning.

The mist outside became very dense, making the room too dark to continue reading. It was impossible to concentrate with Mary Holly there, obviously wanting a chance to gossip.

"Want me to fetch some light?"

"I think I should go now," said Jude. "It's getting thick and I don't know the back road."

"You don't want to take no notice of her." She jerked her thumb in the direction of Mrs Cutts. "I'll let you out. You can go down the front drive if you wants."

Mary Holly let Jude out and then walked with her as far as the main drive. The older woman had an odd expression, savouring something, almost malicious – a trouble-maker. Jude did not want to be involved. She was the kind of woman who loved to insinuate half-truths and appear confiding, but was treacherous. The way she had said, "Tell her its Mary Holly – she a remember." The suggestion that the remembering would not be pleasant and Mary Holly savoured it.

The more Jude quickened her pace, the more Mrs Holly hurried.

"You had better not come any further, Mrs Holly," said Jude. "It's fair dripping off the trees."

Jude hurried on down the wide drive.

"Here," Mary Holly called after her, "Here, don't you forget to tell Bella you met Mary Holly."

Jude felt chilled in the still, white mist.

Jude had often been on the downs on days like today. When you were up there, where the sun shone in a clear sky, you could look down upon the Cantle valley which became a lake of chalky water. All along the broad, mile-long drive from the house and on up Howgaite Path, trees dripped upon Jude. Cows and people loomed up and were swallowed up again. When she reached home, her hair was drenched and the hem of her skirt sodden.

There was a winter-fire on the hearth. Bella and Hanna, the child's stocky little legs dangling, the grandmother upright and solid, sat one on either side of the ingle-nook. Bella had obviously got over her irritable mood. She made Jude a thick piece of toasted bread spread with dripping, whilst Jude took off her wet skirt before the fire.

Bella was dying to know how Jude got on, but it was not in her nature to show interest in things other people did. She had an idea that it made children and young people feel too important by half. Jude had half a mind not to say anything, knowing very well that her

[95]

mother would try not to show any interest. But knowing also that it might cause a return of the earlier irritability she said, "Well, that wasn't so bad."

"Why should it be bad?"

"I didn't mean bad really, just that it was quite all right once I made up my mind to go."

Hanna, eager to know all about the house, asked, "Was it very big?" Granma says you can put our cottage into one room."

"Easy, and there are ever so many rooms."

"And are there lamps with glass raindrops?"

Hanna asked the questions, Bella was content to listen. Hanna was not quite as interested in curtains and carpets as she was in ladies with wide dresses and feathered hats. "What should you have done if you had met a grand lady?" she asked. Jude, giving a recognisable imitation of Dicken, said, "E'venen Missis, 'ow be 'ee then?" and Hanna went off into fits of giggles.

Bella, thinking that some sort of admonition was due, simply said, "Jude!"

Presently, Jude began to collect up the mugs before starting the evening's chores. She did not want to make too much of her encounter with the unpleasant woman but felt that she must mention something, give a hint of warning perhaps. Off-handedly, she said, "I met a Mrs Holly."

The name came out of the past like a blow on the breast to Bella, but she took it with hardly any outward sign of shock.

"Did you?" Bella, pretending to be preoccupied with pounding some cheese-cloth in cold water, waited for a possible second blow.

"Mary Holly. She said you would know."

Mary Holly! Bad enough. But not the other one, thank goodness.

"Mary Holly?"

"She said she was younger than you. She don't look it."

"She was one of them born old."

"She reminded me of Fish Mary. D'you know what I mean?"

"Ah."

Fish Mary was notorious at Blackbrook market for the kind of insinuation and half-truth that starts trouble. Yes, but there was this difference. Fish Mary had never been anything of a threat to Bella. But Mary Holly!

Bella had thought that the wood beetles that had once bitten into the timbers of her life had been killed off, but they had been there all the time: chewing away, invisible, destroying the fabric to the point of collapse.

Hanna went off into the mists of early evening to try to find the eggs of hens that had been laying in odd places and to throw bits to the pigs and goats, whilst the two women worked in the cow-shed and the dairy.

They called Hanna back in. With nightfall, the valley mist thickened and became unmoving, so that she could not see a hand in front of her, let alone find hidden eggs. Normally one could hear animals bleating and lowing right across the valley, but tonight even the sound of their own beasts close by was muffled. It was as though the farm cottage of Croud Cantle was cut off from the entire universe and time had halted. It reminded Jude of the time when they had first brought Hanna here and it had snowed.

When it was bedtime for Hanna, Bella said, "Don't be long up there Jude," and to Hanna, "Now lovey, let Jude come straight down, then we shall have a long bit of joking tomorrow."

It was obvious that Bella had something on her mind, and she began as soon as Jude was back downstairs again.

"Jude. Now Mary Holly's come back to Cantle, there's things I shall have to say that had better been left buried and forgot."

"It's about my father, isn't it?"

Bella flushed. "What did she say?"

"Nothing. I just had a feeling. The way she spoke – something – but I did not give her a chance to say anything."

"It is about your father. And it is about me, and other people, and it is things I would not ever have said but for Mary Holly coming back to Cantle."

"I don't know much about him, do I? Only that bit in the church records. I know he was lost at sea and that's how Croud Cantle comes to be yours."

"There's more to it than that." She paused, wondering where to start. "The Estovers is related to the Nugents you know. Quite distant, but we always thought of them as family. Well, I was about twenty and was going to marry a Rathley lad, but that don't matter. Anyway, an old uncle was dying and I was sent to come over here as a family duty and nurse him to his death.

"It wasn't much different then than it is now, except for the close barn was more part of the house. I was here about a month before he died." She paused, looking about her and clasping and unclasping her fingers. "Jude, I find this very hard. Anyway, I started and there's no going back, no matter what you thinks after this.

"Tomas, the son, your father, was quite broke when the old man died. He begged me to stop on till he was on his feet again. I have to tell you, Jude, and I've never spoke of it before, that your father was about the most beautiful looking man that I have ever seen and had a way of asking things that nobody could deny. Well, to cut a long story short, I stayed on. Before long, Jaen was on the way. He was only eighteen – and I was a woman. I have to say that I was responsible for some part of it. At that time, if he'd a told me to jump off Beacon Hill I'd a done it. But I was the older one."

Bella's mouth tightened and she shut her eyes in an effort to control herself.

Jude would have given anything to spare Bella tearing into herself like this. Her mother's whole being was concerned with her straight-backed dignity: never letting your emotions get the better of you, never making a show of yourself. She moved across, sat close to Bella on the ingle-nook bench and put an arm round her. It was years since they had touched. Jude was taken aback at how soft and warm her mother was. It was like feeling the bones of little birds through their feathers. Having made the move to touch, she gently hugged Bella, who seemed to collapse like a puppet when a string snaps.

Jude said in the gentle voice she used with Hanna when she was distressed: "You know you can tell me anything you like about yourself, mother. I will never, never think any less of you. I don't know anybody else who comes close to comparing."

Bella braced herself, her hand hovering. Then, affected by the strangeness of the white blanks of the windows, the silence outdoors and the soft female touch of Jude, she allowed the hand to pat Jude's.

"He said we should be married and we was. No doubt you have found that out up the vestry. Two months later, Jaen was born. He was the kind of man who wanted – not just wanted – needed all of anybody's attention to himself. He didn't like seeing me with the baby near. If he came in and found me with Jaen at the breast, he would go straight out.

"Anyway, it was only about three weeks after I was Churched that he came and said he was going away. I think I knew he would. I'll say

[98]

this for him, he came straight out and said it to me. I think by that time I was glad. That seems a terrible thing to say, but he was such a youth I felt sorry he had been tied down like he was.

"He said he would sell off a bit of the land, which he did. You know that bit of land, corner of Raike bottom and Howgaite? That used to be Croud Cantle. He said I was a good farm-wife and I should have the farm. You see, Jude? He was quite decent then."

"Where did he go?"

"I never really knew at the time. He said he would head for Bristol and would seek his fortune, which do seem like a boy's adventure, don't it?"

"But he must have come back or you wouldn't have had me."

"He came back. Oh, my eye. You should a seen him. He'd a been gone about five years. He'd a become a man. He'd grown even more handsome than before. He'd a been to some place – Jamaica or summit like that I think it was – and he came back with a pretty penny in his pocket. I never really fathomed out why he came back. Perhaps it was he wanted to see what Jaen looked like. It wasn't for money, he had plenty. And I doubt it was for me."

Bella paused, assembling her story before going on. Jude waited quietly, not wanting to break the spell of this history that she had never suspected.

"Be that as it may, by the time he went off again I had fallen for you. That was before I found out ... " She paused momentarily before going on. "Jude, that money and his fine and beautiful clothes he turned up in was got from the trading of human beings. All right, they was blacks, but they was people nonetheless, and that was what he had done the years he had been gone." Her voice was affected by an old anger. "That have always seemed to me to be the trade of the devil. It puts people as low as beasts to trade them like sheep and cattle ... and Tomas Nugent, what had been the son of Croud Cantle, did trade of that sort.

"I told him as much. He called me some things I don't like to recall, for I tell you he wasn't nothing of the weak youth that I married. But generally he was a weak character, with no backbone, and whether he's your father or no I have to say it. And off he went again."

"What's Mary Holly got to do with it?"

"This is the bit I don't like saying, but you have to know so as Mary Holly can't say nothing to you as you don't know already. She thinks she had one up on you – and maybe she did – but when you knows the whole story there an't nothing she can say that a give her satisfaction.

"When I first came to Croud Cantle to nurse the old man – your Grandfather – Mary Holly was working here as a milk-maid. She wasn't more than fifteen, but she looked a deal older. She was always a real hard worker, so when your father went off I was glad to keep her on. I hadn't hardly been here a year, and I had Jaen and I didn't know how to run a place. I could do a lot of the work, but I didn't know anything about buying and selling or anything like that, so I was glad of any help I could get.

"She had a young sister, oh, about seven years younger, and she asked if I would take her on. I did, seeing how good Mary was, and she came as milk-maid and dairy help, like Mary. Well, you never saw two sisters as different. Charlotte was like a little china fairy. Her hair was straight as straight and as white as the driven snow – not old woman white but, you know, fair, like some babies. And she was light on her feet, like she was always going to skip or dance. She just stood out from everybody.

"I have to go on to the bitter end. After I found out about the trading in black people, he said whatever I thought about it didn't make no difference to him and he was going back to it. He went off and he took young Charlotte Holly with him. Mary Holly went after them straight off. And that's the last I ever heard of Mary Holly. And the other one.

"Only thing I could find out was that your father sailed out of Bristol on some ship called the Farmouth and it went down with all hands."

She heaved a great sigh.

"What Mary Holly is doing up at the House ... Your guess is as good as mine.

"Well there you are Jude, there's a box of bones to shake about. Shall you put that down in your book of histories?"

"Would it matter?"

Bella had no ready answer, so she thought it over for quite a minute or so.

"I don't suppose not. It happened didn't it? Not writing it down don't rub it out. Though what them people you say is going to read it in a hundred years is going to make of it ... "

She stretched and went to the window.

"The mist have lifted. It'll be hot tomorrow. The greenfly a be all over everything."

As Bella had foretold, the next morning was as bright and clear in the Cantle valley as on the downs. It heralded a long run of summer weather and a season of long hard hours on Croud Cantle.

Unspoken and unacknowledged, there was nevertheless an agreement between Jude and Bella not to talk about the intimacy of that evening. It seemed, though, to mark the beginning of Bella's drop down into elderliness. She worked no less hard and she was as firm in her business, but she occasionally allowed Jude to do something for her without protesting: "Thank you very much, I an't dead yet!"

Although it was a busy season on Croud Cantle, things at this time were slower for Fred Warren. Farmers and growers had long since bought their seed and the deals to be done with hops and cereal crops and next year's seed had not begun. He rode around looking at the growing fields and had time to take things a bit slowly. So he rode over to Croud Cantle, simply for the pleasure of talking to Jude.

He saw her as he rode up the Howgaite Path, weeding the beets that would soon be ready to put down in spiced vinegar for the market. She was wearing a thin cotton dress with puffed sleeves, low, round neck and high waistline. Her hair was tied loosely back, her face was shaded by a wide straw hat and her feet were bare. The sun was shining through the thin cotton skirt revealing the faint shape of her figure below the high waist.

As Fred watched her working, he saw her for the first time as a woman, and a flicker of desire for the combination of intelligence and a soft body ran through him. He suppressed the thought. It had a suggestion of incest about it. Their earlier relationship of tutor and student had developed into a friendship that he valued and would not spoil. He still felt a bit at odds with himself when he reached the vegetable field.

"I haven't got time to stop," Jude said. "You'll have to talk to me while I hoe this patch."

"I'll give you a hand." As he took off his jacket, he took from it a book. "Here you are – a nice, easy story. No philosophy, nothing to bend your mind. A nice story by Mr Goldsmith." He started hoeing the next row.

[101]

"I've been up to the House. Mrs Cutts said you had called there. I'm glad you did. What do you think, Judeth?"

"I've never seen anything like it. What does he want to get rid of books for? You wouldn't get me giving any away."

They worked silently for a while. Fred's maverick thoughts had gone and their old state – tutor and pupil who had now become friends – returned. Presently he said: "Have you ever given thought to where it is all leading, Judeth?"

"What is leading?"

"Judeth, for somebody with a head on their shoulders there are times when I think you are just obtuse. When you asked me to teach you, I was pleased ... this farm girl who was wild to learn. I had been thinking for years how things could be changed if people were to have some learning in them, and I thought that with you I was making a start."

Jude went on steadily cutting through the weeds but did not answer.

"What are you going to do now? Are you going to keep on doing this? Being neither fish nor fowl? Are you going to waste your brains?"

"I've got my writing."

"And that satisfies you? The hour or two you spend at night filling up a book with receipts and old stories? And the rest of your time with mud halfway up your legs and your face pressed against the side of a cow."

"Fred. You do exaggerate. Some of the work here is boring, but then where's work that isn't?"

"All I wondered is, are you going to just keep on doing this?" Making his point by chopping at the weeds in the baked soil.

"Fred, don't push me."

For a moment he saw anxiety in her expression. He was as unprepared for it as he had been for the sudden sexual arousal, for his vision of his pupil as a woman. He changed the subject back again to the library at Park Manor, both agreeing that, though it was terrible having all those books shut away, it did seem a shame that Young Harry should want to be rid of them and demote the library.

When the sun reached midday, Jude went into the house to slice up some fat bacon and bread. Hanna had been scrambling about in the walnut trees, throwing down to Bella any that were ready for pickling. Dicken, now bent and full of rheumatics, was working in the far field, so Hanna was sent out with his food. Johnny-twoey, now a big, silent youth, took his dinner and went off to sit alone.

"Well, Fred?" said Bella, eating her bread whilst perched on the edge of a stool, as though she had not a minute to spare.

"Well Mrs Nugent?"

"Didn't see you at Blackbrook yesterday. Been roisting about on that new horse I reckon. What do Mrs Warren think of you these days, now you become a gentleman businessman?"

"It suits her very well. In this new house in Blackbrook she's got a room especially for entertaining ladies to tea; she has lace and flounces and gives little card parties. The children have got food inside them and boots on their feet. It is all she ever wanted. I reckon Molly's as happy as anybody can be."

"I heard all about this here house from Hanna. Well, it's nice seeing somebody going up in the world, for there's many going down in these parts."

"Not only in these parts. All over the South. This last four or five years, since I left my desk and took over from Mr White, there have been more and more men tramping the roads. Not just men, neither. I've seen plenty of whole families who haven't got a roof to their heads, humping the few things they have with them, sleeping on the roadsides. Most of them look starven, but they all think when they get to some cotton or iron town gold coin will shower upon them."

"More fool they," said Bella.

"What else can they do?" said Jude sharply. "What else can people do? People like the Dunstans, when they get put off the farm and out of their cottage?"

"That family wasn't never much for hard work."

"It hasn't got to do with what they were like. He got thrown out of his job and they got nowhere to go. There's work in the coal towns so he's got to go there. There's precious few labourers wanted in these parts is there?"

Bella shrugged. It was all perfectly clear to her. If people buckled down and got on with things, everything would work out. If you found yourself on the roads, then it must be your own fault.

Hanna came back and started on her own food.

Her affections for her aunt and grandmother fluctuated between the two. Sometimes she would follow Jude everywhere; at others she was always under Bella's feet. Physically she looked like both women but her nature was more like Bella's than Jude's.

She was a solid, plodding child who got on with her work: scaring birds from the crops along with other children; feeding animals; collecting eggs and helping with the baking and preserving. They often took her to market, except when the weather was particularly bad. She still saw Jaen and Dan. Up Teg had been roughly divided into separate parts, worked by The Boys. The visits were all one way: Dan could never spare time to take his family to Cantle.

Today Hanna favoured Jude and sat close beside her.

"What am I going to do with her, Mr Warren? I try to teach her her letters and she won't learn."

"Won't learn her letters?" Fred pulled a silly face that made Hanna smile in the tight-lipped manner of Bella.

"I don't like it. It is too hard to remember."

"I expect I started her too soon. After all, I was nearly thirteen when I learned."

"Perhaps Aunt Judeth is right, you will like it when you are older. It is a shame not to at least learn your letters."

"Why?"

The question exploded from Hanna as though it had been fermenting under a tight cork.

Fred and Jude looked at one another. Why?

"So that you can learn to read books," said Jude. "There's everything in the world in books. If you can't read, then it's worse than birds singing and not having any ears."

Hanna did not think bird song any particular loss. Jude had forgoten how hateful birds were to her when she was small. Then she had spent days wandering about fields clapping pieces of board to scare them off.

"I don't want to read books."

"Well, what do you want?" Jude asked.

"I want a house like Mrs Warren. And green chairs. And a white dress with red flowers and red ribbons and little pink shoes. And a big glass over the fire. And chairs with little thin legs." She went on to give an inventory of the front room at the Warren's and Molly Warren's dress.

"Well then, Miss," said Jude. "You will need to find yourself a husband like Mr Warren to buy them for you, because you won't get chairs like Mrs Warren's standing the market."

Summer 1788

> *I sometimes wonder what my life would be like if I had never learned to read and write. I cannot remember what it was like when I could not. As I see it, to teach all people to have this skill would not be difficult to arrange.*
>
> *Something Fred Warren said has been going round in my head.*
>
> *If little children were given no more than half an hour each day, the accumulation of learning in a year should be enough to let everyone have the elements of reading and writing by the time they were adult.*
>
> *There could be people like myself who could teach village children just the way Gilly was taught. Some schools have been set up, but what is needed is for it to be properly organized.*
>
> *I can see no objection to it. If every squire in every village gave the cost of the keep of one hunter, and the church let the vestry or some such be used, then in one generation every person could learn to read.*
>
> *The more I think of it, the more possible my scheme appears to be.*
>
> *There will be children like Hanna who dislike the work of learning something they think is useless. This means that perhaps it could only be done by imposing it on them. Yet that does not seem to be the way. It ought to be done as it was with me and Fred — joy of it on both sides.*
>
> *However, that is but a detail which can be overcome.*

Judeth Nugent

BEFORE FRED WARREN left Croud Cantle, he and Jude arranged to go to Park Manor together to look at Young Harry's library. So, on next Blackbrook market day, Fred walked back with them. He led his horse with Hanna in the saddle. She was sulky when Fred and Jude went up to the House without her, but could always be cheered up by a treat of food, and Bella said she thought she had seen ripe raspberries under the nets.

They went up the long front drive to the great house. The whole place looked entirely different from how it had appeared in the summer mists a week ago.

Now one could see how well chosen was the site of the original house in the lee of the downs. Standing four-square, its windows evenly spaced to balance the central, columned entrance, the imposing mansion faced the drive. It was surrounded only by grassland and a few Cedars of Lebanon, so that there was nothing to distract the eye from the lines of the building.

"I wonder what the House thinks of its new master," Jude said. "Looking at it from here I can't imagine young Squire Goodenstone there. It looks a few sizes too large – needs cutting down to fit."

Fred laughed. "Like a pony in a shire-horse stable?"

"That's it!"

It was not only the sun shining upon the house that gave it a different appearance, something else had changed. It had come alive. Windows were open, there were chairs and umbrellas outside, some small dogs were running in and out of the main entrance and white caps of serving maids could be seen moving about within the house. Quite different from the gloom of a week ago, when Jude had seen only Mrs Cutts and Mary Holly.

"Hello," said Fred Warren. "Looks like Young Harry has returned."

"Oh Lord!" said Jude. "You don't think we shall have to see him?"

They went to the side of the house and were let into the library by a man-servant. Fred had suggested that they might start by selecting for the Manor library all those books with the bright bindings that Master Harry had liked. Then make up a list of all rare and illuminated books, bound prints and maps.

They worked quietly for a couple of hours. Occasionally Fred would say something, explaining why a particular thing was special. He became quite animated about a book entitled, *The Historyes of Troye*, which he explained was a rare and early printed book. In fine mimicry of Young Harry's high voice he said, "Oh fudge, Warren! Don't want that old thing. Chuck it out!" causing Jude to burst into laughter that seemed inappropriate in the ornate room.

"I never thought Old Sir Henry had it in him," said Fred. "His choice of works is impressive. Everything from Atterbury's Sermons to illustrations of Cook's third Voyage."

The fact of it was that at the time when he had believed he was likely to become a knight of the realm, Old Sir Henry had spent a fortune bringing his house up to the scratch of high rank and had purchased the entire library from the estate of a parson who had more taste than his inheritors.

Fred was on the library steps and Jude writing at a desk when the door was flung open revealing Harry Goodenstone and a dainty woman. She was wearing a pink silk dress that touched the floor and a fashionable, huge, soft muslin mob-cap, frilled to match the dress. Before they noticed the two librarians, Harry raised his hand to his mouth like a trumpet. "Larhdies and Ginnlemen – tra-ra – Miss Car ... lotta."

"Oh Harry, you'm such a fool sometimes," she said, mimicking a Hampshire country dialect that did not match her elaborate dress.

Then they saw Fred and Jude.

"Ah," said Harry Goodenstone, quite unperturbed by the fact that his performance had been seen by them. "So you've made a start then, Warren. And Miss Judeth." He turned to the pink lady. "Lotte, this here's the one that slapped me in the face with her bonnet ... 'member I told you? Cheered me up no end. All that lot of mumbling old crows."

Jude laughed.

[107]

"I'm sorry, Mister Harry. I wasn't laughing about my bonnet, but
... " She stopped.

"Go on, what was it?"

"It sounds disrespectful to Old Sir Henry ... to Squire
Goodenstone. But it wasn't about him," and she told him what she
had said about crows at the funeral.

It was not extraordinarily amusing, but it did not take much to
make Young Harry laugh.

While this exchange had been taking place, the little pink lady held
on to Young Harry's arm, smiling at everybody and everything. They
were both a bit affected by a good sampling of Old Sir Henry's wines.

He patted her white arm. "This is my Lotte. I dare say the whole
village knows by now that Lotte has come to stay. Has it reached
Blackbrook market, Warren?

"Well, it don't matter who knows. I don't care a fig. The old devil
fancied a title for me. Threatened to cut me off. So now he's gone and
she's come." A little bantam cock crowing at a cornered hen.

"And now she can come, she says she won't. Put up every sort of
reason not to come. Says she couldn't live down here. She's fell in love
with the house though. Hey, Lotte?"

Lotte had moved away from him and was idly fingering some
books that were on a side table.

"What are you going to do with these, Harry?" she asked in her
low, soft Hampshire voice, not unlike Jude's.

"Chuck it out if you like."

"Well that'd be a shame," Lotte said. "There's a lot of work gone
into making these. You should always respect good work, Harry."

Apart from her elaborate cap and dress, Lotte behaved quite
naturally and, unlike Young Harry in his present state, had few
affectations. She was lithe and slim and talked and moved gracefully.
At first sight she looked about twenty; her face and arms were as
delicately pink and white as her dress and she had good, white teeth.
But when her features were not animated, you could see that she was
probably nearer Young Harry's age.

Jude watched and listened, quite fascinated by the unexpected
interruption.

Young Harry went and sat on the arm of Lotte's chair and spoke in
a normal, serious tone.

"Warren. I tell you this and you can tell the whole countryside if you care. Lotte and I have been together ten years. In London and Bath and places like that Lotte is treated like a princess, which is no more than she deserves. If I can rid her of this notion that she don't want to live in these parts, then she shall be the squire's lady." Then he returned to his cocksure manner. "Say, Lotte, let's give them a puzzle to guess you."

"Oh no, Harry."

"Oh do, Lott. I'll wager Warren's heard of you."

He spoke to Fred. "Lotte here is famous for her art. Here she is: 'Lotte'. You say you do not know her, but I will lay you a guinea that you have heard of her, even in Blackbrook. Come, Lotte – the nunnery."

"Oh, Harry. Sometimes you're such a babe with your games and puzzles. Very well." She smiled indulgently and got up.

"Wait!"

Young Harry pushed aside a table and drew two chairs together.

"Here." He beckoned at Jude. "Warren, here." He indicated that they should be seated, then adopted an exaggerated pose beside Lotte, pointing to the door.

"To a nunnery, go!"

"A minute, Harry."

Lotte took off her mob-cap and removed a bone skewer that was holding her hair up. The hair cascaded down to her wasit; fine, pale moonlight blonde and dead straight.

And from Jude's subconscious leaped the answer to Harry Goodenstone's puzzle.

She guessed the reason why Lotte did not want to come to live in Park Manor, in Cantle; why Mary Holly was here; why she had treated Jude so strangely.

Harry again took his pose. "I shall say Hamlet's line ... 'To a nunnery, go!' "

What subtle change came over Lotte as she spoke, Jude could never fathom, but there was a kind of enchantment in the room, her voice was clear and her Hampshire dialect curbed:

" 'O, what a noble mind is here o'erthrown!
The courtier's, soldier's, scholar's, eye, tongue, sword;
Th'expectancy and rose of the fair state,
The glass of fashion and the mould of form,

[109]

Th'observed of all observers – quite, quite down!
And I, of ladies most deject and wretched,
That suck'd the honey of his music vows,
Now see that noble and most sovereign reason,
Like sweet bells jangled, out of time and harsh;
That unmatch'd form and feature of blown youth
Blasted with ecstasy. O, woe is me
T'have seen what I have seen, see what I see!' "

THAT EVENING and the next day, Jude worked at anything that would keep her from spending any time alone with Bella. She believed that she was sorting out how best to tell her about Charlotte Holly without too much hurt, but what she was truly doing was avoiding an emotional contact so soon after the other.

When she had arrived home from the House, she had said she felt unwell and had gone upstairs. In the morning she got up early and started at once on the plot furthest from the house; hoeing, weeding, thinning-out. In the middle of the day she saw Bella stumping down the slope with a knotted cloth of food.

"Here."

Jude stopped work and took the bundle.

"She wasn't drowned with your father then. You wasn't bad, was you? You seen her."

Jude felt ashamed of her cowardly prevarication. "I didn't know how to tell you. Who did?"

"Dicken."

For the second time in less than a fortnight, Jude saw the scar-tissue that had grown over the twenty-year-old wound re-opened, as she told her what had happened up at The Big House.

"So she's famous then."

"Yes. The name she uses is Charlotte Trowell. Fred has read about her. He says she is very well-known."

Bella, her chin trembling, said with frustration in her voice: "Why then do she have to come back to Cantle? Why couldn't she a stopped up in London? Why couldn't she let sleeping dogs lie after all this time? What do she want – to rub our noses in it? Don't she think I had enough? Do she think he's here? If she wants her own back, she won't get it from the dead and drowned."

She paused. Jude did not know how to reply.

[111]

"Well," she continued after a while, "I suppose it's only natural now she's famous and got the Goodenstone money behind her. She don't have to care what people says."

"I don't think it is like that."

"Like what?"

"I don't think she wants to come back. I don't think Young Harry even knows she was ever in Cantle. He kept on about how he had persuaded her to come, about how once she got here she'd like the place. All this business about the library is because he wants to build her a little theatre there so she will like the house more. He thinks it is because she wants to stop in London. She's kept saying to him, 'Harry, you're such a fool. Harry, you're such a babe' and that's true. He is a fool. But he thinks the world of her."

Bella, who had been gazing at the ground about two feet in front of her, looked up at Jude.

"He must know. You reckon he lived with her ten years. Ten years, and he don't know she was here when she was a girl? It's beyond belief."

"Well, I don't think he knows. Why should he? She probably told him a cock and bull story. He don't strike me as being the brightest of men."

"He got a big shock coming to him, then. My eye, it'd knock a better man than him sideways, finding out something like that after all this time."

"After she had done that acting, Young Harry was pleased as punch. Fred and I said how beautiful it was, and it was. It was the most beautiful words I ever heard said.

"Young Harry said he'd bet I never knew what it was she was reciting and I said, 'Ophelia.' They were all surprised, because it's an old play. She seemed really pleased and she said to come and look at some more plays."

"Go on."

"We went into a little room off the library, just me and her. I didn't know what to do or say. I thought she was bound to ask something about me, just for talking sake. She said, was I Mr Warren's daughter? I said no, I was a farm girl.

" 'What farm's that, then?' she said. Perhaps she's a good stage actress, but she couldn't stop goose-pimples on her arms nor going pale when I said it was a farm the other side of the village. And she asked me straight out, 'What's your name then, Judeth?' and I told her and she said, 'A course' very quiet, to herself like. Then she said, 'I dare say red hair like yours runs in the family,' and I said yes, that it was like you and Jaen and Hanna. And we didn't have time to say anything else."

Bella was miles away, somewhere.

"Mary Holly was born old," she said, as though it was something that had been staring her in the face, but that she had not realised. "Not only that, she was born resentful, except to her – that one. They was as different as a corn-lily and a tater plant. Come from Rathley. I think it must a been one of the dairymen who brought Mary here. I seems to remember there was one called Holly when I first come here."

Jude sat quietly, waiting for her mother to go on. One word and Bella would be back again, saying, "Ah well, no use digging up old bones."

"I shan't never forget that morning Mary come round the back door. 'I believe our Charlotte have gone off', it's all she said. I knew who she'd a gone off with. She asked me if I knew where they might a been going and I asked her who she meant. 'The Master have been after our Charlotte.' And I knew she was right. I don't know how, but I knew." Bella gave a short snort of laughter. "I was sick right there and then. And I knew what it meant. There an't but one thing that makes you that sick in the early morning. It was you, Jude. I got to admit it, I could a done without you on the way just then."

Putting the puzzle of Bella together was difficult for Jude, but another piece fell into place.

"I never seen hide nor hair of neither of them since, and it's above twenty year ago."

[113]

FOR PEOPLE WHO work the land or keep animals, there is never a day in the year that is entirely free of work, but Sundays are easier than the rest of the week since only the essential work is carried out. Jude sometimes spent Sunday afternoons writing her journal or commonplace book, but more often she spent her leisure hours walking the downs.

Sometimes she took Hanna, but Hanna did not appear to feel the same thrill and love of the hills that Jaen and Jude had felt. Perhaps it was impossible when one grew up with no one of the same age to roam wild, invent games or make magic in a fairy-ring. Or maybe it was that Jude's affection for the chalk-hills was caused by a sensitivity to the air that had blown over them and the water that had filtered through them. Maybe Hanna was protected. She was content to stop with Bella and make ring mats whilst Jude climbed and roamed.

On the Sunday following her second visit to Park Manor, Jude's mind was on fire with all that she had learned over the last few days and with what might happen next. She had written for hours, hoping that might help her to sort her thoughts out a bit, but when she came to read it back, very little of it made sense.

Now, as she climbed Winchester Hill, she wished that she was as light and lithe as when she was six or seven, so that she could scramble to the top of Old Marl or Tradden and come racing down one of the gentle slopes, unable to stop. She remembered the freedom of near flight, when each step was a momentary touch of the grass, and the wonderful exhaustion at the bottom.

Winchester was the furthest hill from Croud Cantle. It's back was to the north and its shoulders were outlined with the fortifications. On Marl, Tradden and Beacon, the only visible signs of their use by people were the raikes, tracks and footpaths that criss-crossed over them. But Winchester was different.

Apart from the ruined fortifications, on the north side – where the blade-bones would be if they were human shoulders – there was an upright tree-trunk of a stone as big as a man. It was a mysterious object to strangers and a magic place to the witches and warlocks of the four parishes. South facing, just below the shoulder on the left breast was Bell Tump.

There was nothing there except a hump surrounded by a hollow and a ridge, as though some ancient god or giant had thrown down his hat and grass had grown over it. There was a tale that it was an ancient burial ground, but it looked nothing like any burial ground the villagers had seen. To be on the safe side, however, they tended to avoid the place.

So, down the ages, people had come and gone on Winchester Hill, but on that Sunday there was none left there but Jude.

It was high summer and from the crown of Bell Tump Jude looked down upon the geometric fields of the Cantle valley. Some were still bright green, some were straw-coloured and some, as at Croud Cantle, were mottled from the variety of the crops grown. Dunnock Brook and the village pond were symbols drawn on the valley floor.

Jude wanted nothing more from life at that moment than to sit and look. After a while, she lay back against the slope and gazed at the upturned blue bowl of the sky. Slowly she relaxed and was able to think separate thoughts, instead of the turbulent muddle of the last few days.

"Books by the yard don't get bought by riding to hounds, nor by entertaining and parties and the like. They get bought by taking land from people who have worked it all their lives." In the midst of going over some of the things her mother had said, Will Vickery's opinion jumped into her mind. Not only his opinion: Will Vickery the man approached her thoughts.

Sometimes, when Fred Warren talked to her about ideas that were written up in some of the pamphlets he brought her to read, Jude felt her blood course with excitement. Fred had visions and ideals. When he was speaking about a changed world or about ordinary people who had actually tried to change it by taking the law into their own hands, he excited Jude. He confused her, or she confused herself. Jude was aroused by talk of ways of taking hold of the world and shaking it up, so that people who had grabbed more than their share would fall on their heads.

On that same Sunday, also with a turbulent mind, Charlotte Holly, who had become Charlotte Trowell since she was last here, decided to walk out on the chalk-hills. The last few days had been a strain. She knew that she must either leave and get Harry to go too – and quickly – or go by herself. And she would have to tell him a lot more than she had ever done about the years after leaving Cantle; the years before she knew him. In any case, it was all bound to come out. And when it came out, she did not know how Harry would behave. He had always been jealous. He was pleased when men fell at her feet as Ophelia, but promised them a duel if they did the same when she was Lotte.

She had an affection for Harry. He had been generous, but for all his, "One day we shall commit matrimony, Lott," she realised that most of his passion centred around the other people she could become; the unreal ones, the fantasies she created for him as he watched her on the stage. One day he would not find in his bed the tragic princess he had seen die, or the little royal prince in doublet and hose that he had seen strutting in a make-believe world earlier that evening. He would find Charlotte Holly, the milkmaid who ran away to sea with her master.

She remembered Winchester Hill as a frightening place, not that she could recall ever having climbed it. There was never any reason to. Now that she was here, it appeared to be a good place to be. On the crest she came across the ruins, then climbed further down to a pile of stones. Once it had supported the wall of a dwelling of some sort on the left breast of Winchester, not far from the giant's hat of Bell Tump.

All that she could see of Park Manor from here were the cedar trees. She could pick out the pond and the church – she remembered them – and there, diagonally across, deep under the Tradden Raike, was the Nugent Farm. It looked very small.

From her seat on the stones, Lotte saw a movement a short distance down the slope. A woman, who had been sitting in a hollow behind a mount, sat up suddenly. Immediately Lotte recognized Tomas Nugent's daughter.

She realised that neither of them could move without the other seeing, so that there was bound to be another meeting. If it had not been for the strange relationship they had, Lotte would have taken to his daughter. She was one for first impressions, and she had liked the girl. Although she was superficially like Tomas's wife, as Lotte remembered her, Tomas's striking handsomeness had come through. Yet, judging from when she had seen her at Harry's house, Lotte felt sure that the girl wasn't aware of the impression her looks made on people. And she wasn't really still a girl. She must be twenty now, same age as Rosie.

The first part of that afternoon at Harry's Lotte had felt sure that the girl hadn't known that she was her father's ... Lotte wondered how the girl had thought of her all these years, what word the mother had used when talking about her – trollop? harlot? Those were the kind of words Cantle people would use. She was sure the girl had not known that Charlotte Trowell was her father's wench. At some point Jude had clearly come to realise it, yet had behaved as though she had learned her manners in Bath society.

Lotte carried in her mind a list of irrevocable hurts she had done to people. Prime among them was what she had done to the baby that Tomas's wife had been expecting. Not straightaway, when she had gone off with Tomas, but in later years when she thought about the little one growing up, shut away in Cantle, knowing that her father had gone off with a girl hired to milk the cows. She had tried to talk to Mary about it once, but Mary was always so bitter about Tomas's wife that it was impossible to get any sense out of her.

"What you worrying about them for? They'm living off the fat of the land that should have been ourn."

Mary would never have admitted it, but Lotte was sure that her sister had loved Tomas and was resentful when he married. It would not have mattered who Tomas Nugent had married, Mary would have hated his wife. What Lotte had done had just served Bella right.

Over the years, Lotte had withstood a good many knocks. She was tough. There wasn't anybody around; the girl could say what she liked. Lotte knew she deserved whatever she had coming from her.

Lotte rose, clearing her throat and rustling her dress to allow the girl to know that she was not alone. She walked the few yards that had been separating them.

"I never was up here before," she said.

"It's not my favourite bit, but I come here sometimes to get a different look at Cantle. On our side you are always looking across to here."

There was a brief silence.

[117]

"I was in Cantle before. You knew that?"

"Yes," Jude said.

There was a longer silence between them. Eventually Lotte said: "I'm sorry. I can't say no more than I'm sorry."

Lotte was standing and Jude had not risen. She looked up at the older woman.

"You got nothing to be sorry about to me," she said.

Lotte did not know how to react to the girl. She was years older, she had faced audiences in men's costume; spoken with lords and generals. Yet in this situation, with Tomas's daughter, she felt inadequate. It was the guilt. The baby Mary had suspected, the baby that she had thought of over the years was this quiet girl with the features and hair of her mother, but the good looks of her father.

"Why don't you sit down?" Jude said.

The two sat looking across the valley in silence for a timeless minute.

"It's all so bare."

What a strange thing to say, Jude thought. It was the opposite of bare. Except on the raikes and tracks where the chalk showed through, every inch of the down was prolific: from minute mosses to junipers, from ants to hares, from moths to sparrow-hawks.

Another short silence, until Jude said: "What made you say you was sorry?"

"Because I am. I've always been sorry. No that's not true. I got sorry after I realised what I had done, when I grew up a bit, when I began to think about you growing up. Village people have a nasty streak in them when it comes to that kind of thing."

"I never knew anything about my father, nor you, till a few days ago. I knew he went off and his ship got sunk and everybody was lost."

"It don't seem possible you could grow up down there and never hear something like that."

"People knew my father went off and was drowned, but they never knew you went with him. My mother says she told people that your sister and you had gone back to Rathley because of some trouble in your family. Just after there was smallpox there and nobody thought any more about it. She said nobody thought anything about two girls going off home and not coming back."

"Wasn't there anybody at your place who ..?" There was no

way of saying, was there nobody who knew your father had seduced me and taken me off to Bristol with him.

"No."

Jude picked a daisy from the mound, inspected it closely, not seeing it. Apart from Hanna, this was the first time that she had ever sat with anyone on the hills since Jaen. It was very strange that she should feel at ease.

"Do you mind if I ask you?"

"What about?"

"My father was drowned and you wasn't. My mother thought you must have gone with him. She knew where he was going off to."

"I should have gone with him."

"Why didn't you?"

Lotte frowned and looked across the valley in the direction of Croud Cantle, then turned to look directly at Jude.

"It's all a mess. It was so, right from the start." She shook her head at the memory of the mess. "Is it all right if I call you Judeth?"

"Mostly I'm called Jude."

"I think you'm more a Judeth."

Jude noticed that Mrs Trowell did not know how to take her. She spoke fairly correctly and with only a little of the Hampshire about her, but from time to time the old village style crept in. Jude had noticed that in herself. The kind of words she read crept into speaking, and her mother often made a joke about Jude having got on her Winchester-city voice. Not that Jude spoke in the society way that Mrs Trowell did.

"I don't want to upset you, nor anybody. If it had not been for Harry, I would never have stepped foot near the place again. But Harry has been good to me. You can say that – he's been good."

"It won't upset me if you tell me about my father. I never knew anything. Jaen said all she could remember was his blue velvet coat, and I grew up knowing he was drowned, most likely before I was even born."

Oh dear Lord! Lotte Trowell was suddenly aware that there were implications of her returning to Cantle that she had never even guessed at. She had thought all along it would be a mistake, but somehow, in the back of her mind, she had imagined that Tomas's farm must have disappeared along with Tomas. Because it had all happened twenty years ago, it seemed almost as though it had never happened at all. And now she had dragged the mess of the past twenty years back into the valley, just because she felt she owed something to Harry Goodenstone. All that she could do now was to tell the girl some of it, if only because she was entitled to know.

"I've been all over the place, and I haven't ever seen a more beautiful man than Tomas Nugent."

"That's a funny thing to say – beautiful. It is what my mother said when she told me about him. It's not a word you usually hear given to men."

"No. Yet there isn't anything else that says it. I always thought he was beautiful. But then I was very young."

Jude said nothing, hoping that Mrs Trowell would go on.

"When Mary took me over to Croud Cantle, your mother was working the place herself. She had the new baby."

"Jaen. She's married."

"Ah yes, little Jaen. It was quite a decent place, though Mrs Nugent worked us hard. That was what was wrong with Mary. It wasn't the being worked hard, it was being told by Mrs Nugent. Then one day Tomas – Mr Nugent as he was to us – turned up out of the blue. Everybody was talking about him, saying that things would look up. They reckoned he would be buying more stock and that kind of thing.

"Well, you don't want the details. He came down to the meads one morning when I was there, and he spoke to me about what cows was giving up best, and just said something about ... I'm sorry ... he said a thing about the sort of wife he had. Ah, Judeth, when I look back now and have heard that old story a hundred times since, I could sometimes cry to think what a silly child I was."

She turned a wry smile on Jude. "I dare say you know plenty of married men who have told you sad stories about their wives being so cold."

"I don't think they'd say it to me. They would think I am the one who is cold."

Jude had scarcely allowed herself to think about this, let alone say anything. Yet suddenly the belief formed itself in her mind and she had said it to her father's mistress.

Lotte made no comment. She knew what Jude was like, even if Jude had not realised it herself.

"There was one or two of the herd that would stand quiet on the meads and be milked. When I was there on my own he would come and talk to me. He told me about going to other countries, about things he had seen, and I thought it was all so exciting. Him being the master, and so – beautiful, coming down to talk to me while I worked. That's what makes me so surprised. You say nobody guessed that I had gone off with him. I'd have thought he must have been seen, and there'd have been gossip. He came several times."

From Bell Tump, Lotte could look across at the corner of the field by Howgaite Path where Tomas led her; where he had asked to be comforted by her; where her virgin body had been shaken by the unexpected explosion of ecstasy as she had looked up into that beautiful face.

In later years, she had always admitted to herself that it was not only because Tomas Nugent had said that he could not live without her, but because she wanted to repeat that experience with him.

"We went to Bristol. He said he was going back into his old business. I didn't know anything about that: only that it meant going in a ship and sailing to hot countries like he had told me of, and I'd have gone with him to the end of the earth."

… If he'd a said jump off Beacon Hill, I'd a done it …

"Yet you didn't."

"No. I stayed behind."

On Bell Tump: plucking at grass and daisies; sitting like sisters or friends under the blue bowl that the chalk-hill gods upturned over Cantle on hot July afternoons; Jude listened to the woman who had run off with her father and learned a bit more about him. He was a man who could cast a spell on women.

The sun that had been almost overhead when Jude started to climb Winchester Hill was now shining over her left shoulder, sliding towards late afternoon. Lotte thought that she had said enough.

"I told Harry I would be back to take tea with him. I couldn't abide being there. It all seemed on top of me. It was the coming back. The shock the other day – seeing you and realising that things and people I had thought about as though they was stories wasn't just that. They was true. I wanted to get away from Harry for an hour, so that I could try to sort it out."

"Have you?"

"There wasn't anything to sort out. I can see that, now I'm up here. I wonder why I ever thought it a frightening place."

[121]

"I'm surprised you think it bare."

Lotte Trowell rose and brushed grass from her pink, rose-budded skirt.

"You have very pretty clothes." Jude said.

"Harry buys them, so he chooses. He's going to have to realise soon – women my age don't go in for rosebuds."

"I think they suit you." Coming from Jude, no side, no flattery.

"That's a compliment that means something," said Lotte.

L OTTE TROWELL KNEW that she had made a mistake as soon as she gave in to Harry's pleas that she give the old house, "At least a bit of a try, dammit, Lott."

She knew that she should have told him years ago: the first time he had said his name and she had realised that he must be Old Sir Henry's son. But by then she had obliterated the Cantle episode: Tomas Nugent had gone; Charlotte Holly, the milkmaid, was gone for ever; and the actress, Charlotte Trowell, was well-known, with a bit of money, and never in want of a part. There were always plays being produced in which a naughty, pretty, country wife, coming into society for the first time, was pursued in and out of rooms and cupboards by sophisticated philanderers and a greybeard of a husband. Mrs Trowell's Ophelia was a delight, and gave her entrée into many famous salons in Bath and London. She could also give a good performance as a strutting young attendant or messenger in tabard and hose.

She should have told Harry years ago. When he said his name she should have smiled archly and said in her role of pretty farm wife: "Well then, Sir, you must know that I be the notorious Charlotte Holly, what ran away from Cantle with her Master." But she never supposed, at that time, that she would ever become beholden to Harry Goodenstone, or ever need to go near Cantle again. In any case, it was nobody's business but her own. She'd paid for it over and over.

Later on, the right moment never seemed to present itself, until eventually it was impossible to say anything at all. When he had pressed her to, "Give it a try, dammit", she persuaded herself that it was all so long ago, nobody would remember. So it might have been, had Mary not wanted to make Bella Nugent suffer, and had not Charlotte Trowell herself still looked so much like the milkmaid who had run off with the master of Croud Cantle. The man at Willow Farm had recognised her.

The whole of that part of Hampshire was such a backwater. The nearest towns of any size were Southampton and Winchester and she had never gone there. It was just chance that she had met Harry: one of the few people from the backwater who moved in the kind of circles in which Lotte moved. It was chance also that took him one night to a theatre where she had a small part. A part in which she rushed on stage with a message for the king, her legs encased in hose that reached right up to a short bouncing tabard.

The boy-woman had brought a flush of colour to Harry Goodenstone's cheeks, and from then on Young Harry had followed Lotte wherever she performed, with presents and propositions. Mary, who had always managed everything, had been Harry's ally. In the end, Lotte had to admit that Mary was right. She wasn't getting any younger, and men like him weren't three for a farthing, and so she said, "Yes, all right, Harry", when he offered her a kind of security as well as adoration. It was not only security for herself – there was Mary and Rosie to be provided for.

Considering what could have happened, it wasn't all that bad.

Right from the day she found Lotte in Bristol, Mary had protected her fiercely. Those had been grim and hard days. They were good milkmaids, a skill that was of no use in the part of Bristol where they were forced to live. Mary wanted for them to leave and get work on a farm, but Lotte still pined for her lover, and would not go far from where the Farmouth had sailed.

It had been months before she finally realised that he had never intended to take her with him. He said that on board the Farmouth wasn't any place for a girl; yet it was one of the pleasures that he had held out for her in the first place, them sailing off together. Then he said it wasn't any place for a girl in her condition, but her condition wasn't any different whether on board a sailing ship or on the dockside at Bristol with only a couple of guineas for company.

It was meeting Jude that had decided Lotte. It was meeting Jude and liking the girl so much. Sitting with her, then realising what a queer set-up there was. The girl was Rosie's half-sister. What did that make Lotte, but a kind of half-mother to her? Then there was Bella Nugent. Lotte didn't reckon that the situation Tomas Nugent had landed Bella in had turned out as good as her own, as far as comfort and that was concerned. It was just as hard working that place these days, and the hours were as long as they ever were. The girl, though: Bella Nugent was lucky there. The girl said it wouldn't upset her because it was all so long ago. Mary had said just the same thing, but they were wrong. It was all here and now.

And it was that realisation that made her determined to get out of Park Manor, out of Cantle and Hampshire altogether. Tomas Nugent had made people suffer when he was alive. If Lotte came to live at the House he would be doing it still, through her.

Mary had faults. If anybody knew, then Lotte did. But twenty years ago she had made her way across country to Bristol, then gone on and on searching until she found Lotte. Mary had picked her up, nursed her, and worked herself into the ground at any rotten work she could get. Those years had fastened Lotte to Mary with bonds of gratitude, but not affection. It was the one thing that Mary wanted above all, yet she stirred it in nobody. Mary had pushed and guided Lotte. If Lotte was a success, then so was Mary, for it was she who had seen that her pretty little sister had looks and grace that were saleable in better places than around the Bristol dockside. It was she that had protected her from any more Tomas Nugent's.

Loyalty, duty, gratitude, obligation – but no affection. Lotte had tried to love Mary as she used to when they were at Croud Cantle, but a bitter worm had bored into Mary and there was little left to love.

Right from the time Mary had gone to Bristol she had hardly said anything about Lotte's flight with Tomas Nugent. But living close for twenty years, Lotte had come to realise that her sister's bitterness was bound up with him. Mary had worshipped him from the time she was ten and went to work at Croud Cantle. He was fourteen. Lotte realised that it was not personal jealousy that Mary Holly felt towards Bella Estover. It was jealousy towards Tomas Nugent's wife. She would have felt the same about any woman he had married. But she'd had her nose rubbed in it with Bella Estover coming there like that, under the guise of nursing the old man. And then getting Tomas, who was still just a lovely boy, into a trap.

Mary had been forced to watch it happen, and Lotte knew that her sister had never really got over it.

Meeting Tomas's daughter like that had given Lotte a bit of the kind of backbone she had often wished for. It had occurred to her sometimes that she had never properly grown up as she ought. People

[125]

had pushed her about for years, and she had been willing to let them. It was much better, easier, not to cross people. Especially people who wanted their own way, thought they knew best – and often did, she had to admit that – people like Harry and Mary. But meeting Tomas Nugent's daughter had done something to help her stand up at last. She had sometimes wondered if she should have had more courage over Rosie. This time she would have to make her own decision. There was nobody else who could – for the sake of the girl.

When she arrived back at the Big House, Harry had gone off to look at his horses. There had obviously been trouble between Mary and Mrs Cutts. It was Harry's fault, of course. He ought to have sorted out with his Housekeeper where Mary fitted in the household. Mary had been ordering Harry about for years in the various smart little houses he had provided for Lotte, and in which Mary behaved as a kind of mother/housekeeper. She had no intention of taking second place to a paid servant at Park Manor.

Mary had always taken charge of everything, but on the Sunday when Lotte decided to leave, it was Lotte who called for all their boxes and bags to be brought up. She started packing before Mary could argue her out of it. She tried, but Lotte just went on piling her belongings into trunks.

"You mean you'll go? Now, just when you've got your hands on all this lot?"

"I don't want my hands on this lot. I never wanted it. We should never have come. What do you think it'd be like for the Nugent girl, and for ... " the name she had always avoided, "for Mrs Nugent."

"Ah, so that's it. You saw that girl and you've gone stupid and sentimental. What about Rosie? What about us?"

"We shall be all right."

"Do you want to go back to how it used to be? You're thirty-five, Charlotte. You're lucky to a got away with it this long. For sakes, look at me. Forty-two, and don't I look old enough for your mother?"

Lotte tried to divert Mary's pique from developing into rancour with lightness.

"Goodness, Mary, don't everybody look old enough for my mother."

"You'll have to tell him now. You can't just go off and expect him to put up with it. Any case ... " She didn't finish, but Lotte knew what she meant. If they didn't know already, people would remember a name like Mary Holly. Then add Charlotte and Lotte together and make a great deal of it.

"In any case, I've made my mind up. I shall tell Harry what I should have told him years ago. I never told him any lies. I never made out I was ever any more than I am, but I should have told him years ago."

Lotte had been thrusting skirts and gowns into trunks and Mary had been automatically folding and repacking. It was the first time that the older of the two sisters had felt herself at a disadvantage in any argument between them. It was as though Lotte had gone from the house a young girl and returned as a woman – the kind of woman Lotte sometimes became on stage. Lotte felt it too. She felt strong.

The door that connected her room and Harry's opened.

"What was it you should have told me years ago, Lott?"

Summer 1788

One of mother's sayings is, "things go in threes." It does not seem sense that they should, but it would be interesting to see if there is any pattern to the way events happen in people's lives. It does seem sometimes that when one thing happens other things do as well. When she says that things go in threes, she does sometimes have to bend events to make them fit.

Nevertheless, there do seem to be clusters of events that we remember. Jaen got married – I started market – I started lessons. For some while, nothing happened out of the ordinary. Then Hanna came to us – Jaen was ill – Daniel was born.

I began thinking of this because after a dull time, events are tumbling upon me.

Since I wrote a few weeks ago about reading the story of "The Vicar of Wakefield", I have had some ideas about writing. The first is that my style of writing this journal is not much different from the facts that I record in my Common Book, and often do not read any better than a receipt for apple jelly. If people in a hundred years are to read this then it should be as interesting for them as that book was to me.

The events I have learned of in the last few days are more dramatic by far than those Mr Goldsmith records, and I shall from here on attempt to write with less formality.

Yesterday, for the second time, I met my father's mistress.

She looks fragile, and her hair is fine and pale as the silk seed-head of a meadow thistle. Her name is Charlotte Trowell.

Although she's a woman, fourteen years or so older than me, and she is now famous for playing in Sheridan's plays and has appeared at theatres in London, we sat and talked as Jaen and I might.

[127]

We were on Bell Tump and she told me how Tomas Nugent loved her, and ran away with her. When she spoke of it she was looking down at the place where it happened, her look was sad and I wanted to put my arm about her, as once I did my mother. My mother was warm and soft and I felt the structure of her bones, like the soft body of a bird. I think that Mrs Trowell must be like a pink and white canary.

Hanna is the only human creature who ever puts a hand in mine or an arm about my neck, and who I can do the same to, yet there are times when it seems like holding back nature not to put arms round people, and let them do the same to me. I remember watching my mother wash Hanna's hair and longed for the feel of her hard fingers on my scalp. When Mrs Trowell was with me, I thought what pleasure there would be to touch the fine pale hair.

Hanna is my mother's only contact. Lately, when Hanna kisses goodnight to my mother, she will say, "Ah, you great baby", and I think she is weaning herself from Hanna's touch, as she did from Jaen and me.

She said that she would have jumped off Beacon Hill for him, my father, Tomas Nugent, yet he went to the milk-maid and loved her. Why? Why?

When I said to Mrs Trowell, that men would think me cold, she looked at me, then quickly away. Why? Does she see Tomas Nugent's blood in me? Was that what Jaen got from our father, his nature? The thoughts and dreams I have!

There have been women. In the bible. Salome. Delilah. The woman saved from stoning. Perhaps I am my father's daughter.

Why does my mother shrink from an embrace, even from a daughter? Why?

Jude Nugent

ALL THE WAY back to the holding, Jude thought about what she should say to Bella. When she arrived, she found that there was nothing to say. What Mrs Trowell had told Jude was impossible to retell. She could never convey what she felt about the woman. Bella would not understand how Jude could have any warm feelings: to her it would be disloyalty.

Summer was slowing down, the hills were changing colour. Knapweed, cornflowers and cat's-ear bloomed on and on and beside the tracks and raikes, pure, blue chicory flowered. Goat's-beard seed drifted everywhere, and although children were sent out daily with baskets to take fresh dandelion heads for wine-making, they could never keep up with the ever-blooming gold.

This year, the raspberries and other soft fruit had come in abundance, so Bella took on two girls to help with the making of preserves, jellies and cordials.

Fred Warren was getting busy again and had not come by their stall on the market morning following the Bell Tump episode. Jude was going round shopping for a few things before the market was over and called into Fred's small office in the grain merchant's yard to return his book.

"Did you know Ophelia has gone?"

Jude was taken aback.

"No!"

"I haven't been up to the House. It was the tenant at Mill Farm. He said that Young Harry had gone off again."

Whilst he was telling Jude, he was watching her closely.

"What else did he say, Fred?"

"Nothing very much."

"Oh Fred, I can see it in your face that he did."

"No. He started to say something, but I can never stand his gossip. I wouldn't stay to give him the satisfaction."

"Have you heard anything at the market today?"

"No."

"You will. It is nothing for us to be ashamed of, but they will all make something of it."

Suddenly, not knowing why, tears sprang to Jude's eyes.

"The one who should be hurt is dead and gone, but it is Mother and her they will tear at. Oh, the devil with tears!" She blotted her eyes with her cuffs. "My eyes always show so red."

"Judeth," he said gently. Then, in an attempt to hide his concern, put an arm lightly about her shoulders and said, "Do you want to tell me, Judeth?"

"My father ... Mrs Trowell ... She was his other wife."

His warmth and firm arm about her, the wholesome smell of grain in his clothes, and the concern in his voice, made her tears flow faster. He drew her closer and she cried on to his waistcoat breast. It was a marvellous relief.

Coupled with the relief, guilt. Confusion. At twenty, this was the first time a man had held her close and she liked the sensation. Oh, the many sermons on the sins of the flesh. The years living with her untouchable mother. Having no body, save Hanna's, close to her own since Jaen went from home. Fred Warren was like a relative. To be held by Fred and to enjoy the sensation was a gross sin of the flesh.

Anyone coming into the office at that moment and seeing the two, might have read into the scene something other than tutor-pupil relationship.

As did Will Vickery, glimpsing it for a few seconds before he hastily closed the door again.

The Park Manor story was a nine-day-wonder. Its details were altered and twisted out of recognition, and the fact that the Goodenstone name was involved added spice and malice to the gossip. Bella and Jude took Hanna to visit her parents. In Newton Clare, the story was that one of Harry Goodenstone's dairymaids had run off with a farmer, and he had got her back and set her up in the Big House.

Bella said that it was Jaen's right to know and, in a brusque manner, told her the bare bones of the history. At twenty-six, Jaen was a matron. Pregnancy, birth, still-birth, child-death, miscarriage. Her moods changed abruptly from tears to fury, and there were times when she found herself holding a dish and not knowing what on earth she intended doing with it.

When Bella finished, all that Jaen said was: "He had a velvet coat. I always remembered his coat."

Life at Park Manor and the management of its farms went on as it had always done during the owner's absence, ordered by housekeeper, agent, manager and solicitor. Only the solicitor knew where to contact Harry Goodenstone. On the Sunday evening, after Lotte returned from Winchester Hill, there had been a flurry of packing. In the morning, Mary Holly and Mrs Trowell had been driven away, soon followed by the master of Park Manor. There was a great deal of speculation, but it was not until the next day that anybody knew what was behind it.

Sublimated, contorted passion. Mary Holly would not leave without punishing the woman who tricked Tomas into marrying her. It was her fault that Lotte and Mary were not now in possession of Croud Cantle. There would have been none of that time in Bristol; no secret ready to jump out and spoil everything, if Bella Estover hadn't got herself pregnant and tricked her Master into marrying her. Well, now it didn't matter and Bella Estover would get everything she deserved.

It was Mrs Cutts who had the story from Mary. Mrs Cutts, with secrets and poverty of her own to hide. Mary could not have chosen a more suitable confidante, or one who was better at putting down her own kind: it distanced her from them.

IN THE WEEKS that followed, Jude worked herself into the ground. Long after Bella and Hanna had gone to bed, she was working. The hours she usually spent reading or writing, she spent on any physical work she could find – whitening walls, tarring beams or oiling woodwork. It was only when she was dead tired that she could fall into an oblivious sleep. If she did not get to that exhausted stage, she would stay in a half-conscious state, where her thoughts became distorted and terrifying, her stomach knotted with obscure fear. The only way she could cope was to try to censor her mind and quell her body on a treadmill of work.

Once or twice, she fell into a trance over the bread and cheese she took with her into the fields. The experience was frightening. She remained aware of her surroundings, and realised that she was not fully conscious, but could not pull herself out of the dreams. She would waken from the state, bathed in sweat. She had a recurring dream in which, with arms and legs bound and mouth gagged, she struggled and struggled to reach an ever-retreating summit of an Old Marl which was sandy and barren; or, gasping for breath, sank eternally into Howgaite meads, whose spongy marsh had become a swamp of sucking filth. Mary Holly often appeared in the dreams, ridiculing Jude's naked body as she stood on the steps of Blackbrook market cross, hawking blank sheets of paper. A draped angel with welcoming arms, from a picture that hung in Bella's room, appeared to her. It turned its back, its drapes and wings fell away. Though his face was away from her, she knew that he was beautiful, as he held out his arms to Lotte Trowell. When she awoke from the trances, the smell of grain-impregnated cloth was always in her nostrils.

Seeing Jude with dark rings round her eyes, Bella prescribed licorice powder.

"I'm all right," Jude insisted. "It's just the weather."

Earlier in the summer, there had been enough rainfall to swell root-crops and grain, but for weeks now the weather had been cloudless. No one could remember so many days of unbroken sun.

If the weather held, it would be a good harvest.

All over the county, rooks, clouds, gnats and midges were consulted daily for a forecast, and old people sniffed the air and reported on the state of their rheumatics. The weather held.

Every year, about this time, they took on extra hands at Croud Cantle for the digging and clamping of root-crops. This year, it seemed that there were more people than anybody could remember looking for work: not village people, but strangers from over the border of Sussex. Men who had left their families under the roof of some more fortunate neighbour, had come to look for a week's or even a day's work, if they could get it. People on their way to markets all over Hampshire noticed the increase in the number of men tramping the roads in search of work. But there was no more work about in Hampshire than in Sussex.

Harvest was always a time of tension. If there was going to be a poor yield, then it was vital that the weather held, for not a grain could be afforded to go to waste. If there looked like being an abundance, it was equally important.

To the landowners and tenant farmers, harvest meant profit. A thunderstorm could spoil crops and make for scarcities, which meant that the prices would have to be raised to maintain their income. To the agricultural labourer, a thunderstorm at harvest meant not only the depressing sight of seeing a season of work flattened, but also that employers would have an excuse to push wages even further down at a time when food prices would be high.

Many a crocodile tear dampened a landowner's cheek as he told Joby or Ned that they would all go broke over it. Wages were low and were likely to get lower. There was plenty of spare labour tramping the roads.

At Croud Cantle, the shelves were filling up with pots of sweet preserves and chutneys. Honeycombs were draining and the curds that had dripped from the gush of spring milk were turning into pale, acidic, Cantle cheese. Apples were laid out in the lofts and the new wine was clearing. Each evening Bella took Hanna to look at their stock, refreshing herself at the sight of their security for the coming year; Hanna smiling, pleased at the result of her part in the picking and pounding and stirring.

[133]

"Well now, lovey, there's a sight!"

Bella fluctuated in her opinion about Hanna's lack of interest in learning to read. Much of the time her reactions depended on whether Jude was trying to coax Hanna into learning or not. If she found Hanna chalking letters on a slate, she would comment that all anybody ever needed to know was how many beans made five. She was pleased that Hanna was turning out to be a good, practical worker. Bella understood Hanna.

On the Estate farms, harvesting was under way and the whole of the Cantle valley was greased with sweat and laden with heat. Men, women and children were out in the fields, where the rhythmic swish of sickles sounded like a breeze. But there was no breeze. Dust settled on sullen trees and bent backs.

The cutting of the first swathe was accompanied by the voices of the lines of men cutting; of women following on, binding and stooking; the chattering of children working at whatever they could manage. But day after day of unrelenting toil and heat gradually silenced them. Slowly, with the sun striking their backs, heat rising from the earth and dust and salt of sweat stinging their eyes, the corn was cut. The larger the area of stubble grew, the less was the talk. It was only when the sun had dropped behind Beacon Hill to restoke its fires, ready to rise again over Tradden in a few hours, that the villagers returned home. Men and women, almost all barefooted – the women with their skirts pinned between their legs – rocked home on wagons or dragged their feet along the tracks.

During the day, the only Cantle people left in the village were the aged men, whose spines were frozen sickles; the old women, who looked as though they were still yoked to pails, and the Reverend Mr Archbold Tripp, who was greatly occupied with an unprecedented crop of peaches, ripening against the rectory wall.

The weather held right through. Then, on the day before the cutting of the last stand of corn, the first cloud for weeks appeared far, far to the west, off the coast of Devon. Skies over Hampshire were still white-blue, but cattle and sheep began to become restless. Workers going back to the village, or to the out-houses of Park Manor, sniffed the air.

"Will it hold?"

"It's more'n a day off, I reckon."

"It'd better be!"

[134]

And so it had. Of all the days of toil and slog that had gone into getting the crops in, only the last was the one worth getting up for. And the rain had better not come and spoil the sport of clubbing, stoning, and setting-the-terriers-at: sport with wild-eyed hares and rabbits, rats and birds that had retreated into the central stand of corn, before the breeze of sickles.

It was not often that Bella chose, or had the time, to mix with Cantle people. The cottages, houses and church that comprised Cantle village was clustered west of the Dunnock. Croud Cantle was some way off, south-west. Most of the villagers either worked for the Estate or the tenant farmers, shared wells or drew water together at the ford, and so lived in close contact with one another. The only times that Croud Cantle had anything to do with their neighbours, except in passing on the way to market, was briefly after Sunday service – and at the cutting of the last corn.

It was one of Bella's few holidays and she never missed it. When Jaen and Jude had been little, like the rest of the village children, they had joined in chasing the bolting animals, clutching heavy sticks. Bella was quick and accurate, always taking home a good bag for their own dinners and some to take to market. It was the only time that the villagers could walk home openly with a game-bird slung over their shoulder.

Bella was up well before dawn, seeing to things before her day out.

Dicken, Johnny-twoey and the other hands came into the kitchen as always for breakfast. "Here." She put out large dishes of fermity. "Fill yourself up Jude, it a be a long day."

When he saw Jude's obvious lack of appetite, Dicken said, "I reckon Miss Jude ha' got worms, Master. She'm that pasty-faced these days."

Jude tried to eat the porridge at the same fast rate as usual, but it did nothing to fill out her hollow cheeks and eye-sockets.

Dicken was unusually full of chat this morning. "If it in't that, then it's some young feller breaking her heart. It an't worth it, is it, Master?"

"I can't see how you'd know Dicken. Your heart haven't felt nothing this many a year."

"Ha, only heartburn, and that's a fact."

All this unusual chit-chat gave an air of festivity at the breakfast-table and Jude made the effort to join in. She talked to

Hanna about the day ahead, and went off with her to pack some food to take.

The last corn left standing was in the fields that had once been part of Croud Cantle Farm, before Tomas had sold them to the Estate. From the house-place window, just as the sky was lightening, Hanna, who had been keeping watch, called that people were coming. So they left the kitchen to walk across the stubble of the cut fields.

By now the sun was up over Tradden. Most of the men were in clean smocks and the women in white aprons and large, old-fashioned, floppy linen bonnets. The children were in anything that didn't matter, which meant rags and tatters and short togas of sacking. Wagons crunched over the pebbles at the ford, carrying workers from other farms in the valley. Casks of special brews were put in cool ditches.

Nobody mentioned the smell of rain coming from the west.

It was bad luck.

Soon there was a ring of men, their thick smocks now abandoned, short stick in one hand, sickle in the other, swishing rhythmically into the brittle stems. Behind them, women and girls, barefooted, barelegged, bodice-strings hanging loose, petticoats pinned up between their legs, gathered armsful and bound the corn into sheaves. Bella and Jude joined in. Bella was in her element.

As soon as she set foot on the field, she made it quite plain that whatever scandal had been buried twenty years ago and had worked its way to the surface lately at the House, nobody had better mention it today. The few who liked something to chew on said that Bella Nugent was putting a good face on it. But the majority were in a genial frame of mind, glad to see her enjoying herself for once. They knew her great fault was her pride and her tongue, but for the most part people had to admit that she had gone like a bull at a gate to make something of that place after ... well, after what happened, and she hadn't made a bad job of it.

There was nothing like a whole day's work for the number of people gathered there: what with those who had come for the day out, the chance of a hare and the excitement. So the pace was slower and there was time for a bit of a bite and a sip or two. Just before noon, thunder rumbled from the direction of Tradden and every sickle hesitated for a split second: only the sound of the wagons coming back empty. By this time there was not much corn left standing, and a premature rabbit broke cover and surprised everybody by escaping across Raike Bottom track.

Jude had spent the morning in the circle with the girls and women, gathering and binding. The air was still and pressure began to build up in the valley. She felt as though she was strung up by her ears. Just after the bit of fun about the rabbit, the reapers and binders retreated to the comparative cool of the hedge-bottoms to rest. Lads took their chance to sit with girls they had hopes of, or had their eye on; most of the women gathered together to shriek at their own bawdiness and plait corn-stalks. Men swigged their fair share of cider and took forty winks.

Jude sat in the group with girls she had maypole-danced with; spent other Harvest days with. All but one or two were now suckling babies. She had not realised how much she had grown away over the last year. Last Harvest they had all been eighteen or nineteen. None had been married that long, yet only one or two had not given birth. This year, they seemed to have nothing to talk of except strong suck and salves for sore nipples.

"You better hurry up, Jude, or all the best one's a be gone."

"You mean babes or men, Kath?"

"What's the difference?"

And, with their new intimate knowledge of both, they were perked up with superiority. In their laughter was the bawdy shriek that would develop with each Harvest day, with every year.

Jude's mind needed some peace and rest. She would have loved to be able to take something from the placidity of the girls with wide-spread legs and sucking babes. There was not a single grizzling red-gummed Hanna among them, but then there wasn't a confused and tense Jaen, either. Subconsciously, Jude started to try to sort out what it was that separated her from them. Her ears became even more tightly strung.

She put on a good show of light-heartedness.

"Well, you know me. You always said I should have to get one made special."

"Man or a babe?"

"If she don't get a man, than she'll have to get the babe made special."

The breast-fed babes, indirectly fed strong cider, were put to sleep on straw in a wagon. It was the young mothers who first articulated the coming break in the weather.

"We shall have to watch out," nodding at the now massive bank of cloud coming from the west. It did not matter now, mentioning rain. The sport would be over by the time the cloud broke over the valley, and the Harvest supper could be held in one of the barns.

The corn left standing in the centre held a mass of small creatures, which had retreated before the swishing sickles.

This was the sport.

Ancient tribal ritual.

A shared lust to kill.

The other climax.

They arranged themselves in rings around the corn, each person placed so that if one missed, the one behind might not. Some men had fierce little terriers, quivering, scenting the fear in the corn. Some had ratting mongrels on short ropes, which they snapped across the dogs' snouts if they growled. Men, women and children held thick sticks and any bit of old metal that came to hand.

For them, at that moment, their field was the eye of the universe, the patch of corn the eye's pupil. Only that existed.

Individuals had melded into a whole. No leader, no led. All would know the moment of action. They waited, still and quiet, lulling the creatures in the corn into false security. Exhilaration fermenting, building towards climax.

Jude was on the outer ring, by the field gate which opened on to Raike Bottom Lane. The silent wait was probably no more than a minute, but to her it seemed endless. Her scalp seemed to shrink. Great nimbus clouds were spreading over the blue sky like dark, fast-growing lichens. Within their mass, lightning crackled. Tremors ran through her. She wanted to run into the corn. Run away. Run. Run. Any action that would release the upward pull on her ears and scalp.

First, the silence erupted.

Lightning hurled a clap of thunder into the echo-chamber of the valley. The dogs started: yelping and frenzied barking.

The stillness was broken.

The dogs were unleashed and bounded into the corn. Whoops and shouts rose from the hunters. They banged sticks against bits of metal. Everyone took an involuntary step towards the patch of corn.

Then the field erupted. First a pheasant ran out. Accurately aimed flints downed it. Before it had dropped, the dogs had flushed out the rest of the animals. More pheasant; rabbits racing in all directions at once. Hares bounding, turning, twisting. Rats, voles and dormice running. Every creature that ran met the hunters with their sticks head-on. Every creature that froze in terror had hunters after it, or was seized by the dogs. Every creature that had gone to cover in the tall corn gave up its moment of bloody excitement to the Cantle harvesters.

Jude had been involved in the excitement from the time she had been laid on straw in a wagon, alongside other babies. As a girl she had excitedly joined in the chase, running with the others amidst the thud of sticks and the blood and the lust that was still embedded in the canine teeth.

ONLY HANNA SAW Jude leave the field.

Her mind a jumble of images, Jude ran along Raike Bottom; around the marshy edges of Chard Lepe Pond, startling cows into jerky flight; over a cattle-gate at the bottom of the raike, and on up Tradden. She stumbled over every small undulation and mole-hill. With her breath coming in sharp gasps, she ran on, until the slope became too steep. Her path seemed impeded at every step. Sharp hooks of brambles and dog-roses clawed at her skirt, and fallen branches tripped her before she even noticed them.

She was scarcely aware of herself, or where she was going, except that she had to escape the scene in the field. The sudden image, as she stood holding her stout stick, of her neighbours – the girls she had played with; the lads who had been flirting; the bawdy women and laconic reapers – changing into a savage, bludgeoning tribe. The pent-up desire to kill something – not only hare and rabbit for food, but any creature that ran from the corn – anything. And it was not only the image of the villagers she ran from. She ran from her own image, child and woman. The image of a hand holding a bloody stick, cracking bones, pounding out life.

She ran to kindred spirits. Those who understood her, those she understood; those whom she could caress and who would caress her. She ran to the arms of the downs that surrounded the Cantle valley.

Eventually she sank on to the parched grass and lay panting.

By now the sky was heavy and dark. The sun was above the west downs, and as the cloud bank raced towards it, everything was briefly bathed in brassy yellow and threw dark purple shadows. Then the light went out, and the valley looked as though December had come suddenly.

Holding the stitch in her side, Jude saw the people she had just run from moving quickly about. Watching them, as though they were under her magnifying glass, she saw a knot of reapers finish off the last of the corn. Wagons moving; tiny dots of people going towards the field-gate; a stream of dots. Then, like disturbed ants, they went quickly in all directions, as a grey net curtain came between them and Jude.

The hissing grey came swiftly across the valley and the storm broke.

From the winter-dark clouds, lightning forked and sheeted around the hills. Sudden, brief, bright, white, shadowless glimpses of every bush and tree. Thunder like cannon-fire, crashing so loud that the ground seemed to vibrate. Then, along with lashing rain, hail-stones, large as beads, thudded and bounded off the dry, hard surface of the hills.

And Jude sat and watched the storm lash the Cantle valley and hills. Then she lay back and welcomed the stab of ice and the scourge of rain on her sun-reddened skin. As the hail and rain soaked through her clothes, through her skin, through her body and into the parched grass, it drained away her hysteria. She could have slept there without the terrible dreams she had had of late.

Presently she got up, chilled and stiff. The hail had stopped, but the storm still flailed the valley. The rain was falling so heavily and the surface of the hills was so hard with a dry crust of thatch and soil, that water ran off the surface and began to flow downhill in rivulets.

At the first heavy spots of rain, Bella and Hanna had cut back across the fields and arrived home just before the storm broke. Dicken, and the other hands who had gone down for the sport, trudged in and began their work, pleased with the furry bodies they carried and looking forward to the supper later that evening, which was laid on by the Estate for anybody who helped with the reaping.

Hanna set about seeing to the fire and seeing to the chickens, whilst Bella went to help with the animals.

"I reckon 'tis trapped, Master," Dicken said to Bella as they forked hay together.

Bella agreed with the local belief that a storm could not escape from the valley, but had to blow himself out. And it did appear so with this storm. The cloud had become a static slab of lead-grey.

"Where's Miss, then?"

"I don't know," said Bella. "I didn't see which way she went. When the rain started I cut off over the fields."

"She never did mind the wet."

Behind the farm, beside the Dunnock where it flowed south to the Solent, was a little-used track. Bella and Dicken heard the sound of horses come from that direction. They paused and frowned at one another. "Horses on The Track!"

"I'll see," said Bella, and went to the cow-shed door just as two riders came into the yard and up to the shed.

"Fred Warren, you'm soaked! See to your horses then go on in. Hanna's got things going in there."

Fred Warren and Will Vickery, on their way back from farms at Wickham, had been caught by the storm on the bare Corhampton Downs and had galloped the few miles to the nearest shelter: Croud Cantle.

They had weather-capes, but the rain had soaked into their neck-cloths and hats and boots. When Bella got back into the house, they were seated barefoot beside the fire, where their boots steamed. Hanna, the proper little farm-wife, had given them hot cider with cinnamon and ginger, and bread and cheese.

"Well, Fred Warren, you chooses some funny times to go gallivanting round the country," said Bella, as she removed the sack from round her shoulders and took off her muddy boots.

Fred and Will, bare-necked and barelegged, stood as she came in.

"And a pretty picture, too."

Bella perched on the edge of a stool in her usual, can't-hang-about-here-wasting-time attitude. She listened to the news from Wickham – the increasing land being given over to strawberries; a new mansion being built; the usual trouble there had been on Fair Day – to the sound of rain hissing straight down the chimney and pattering on the thatch.

Eventually Bella commented on Jude's absence.

"I can't think where Jude can have got to. She should have been back ages ago. Even coming up the lane don't take that much time."

"Perhaps she's sheltering in somebody's house," Will Vickery said.

"Jude ain't likely to do that."

"She went up the hills." Hanna's statement caused them all to look out at the sheeting rain and back at the girl.

"Up the hills?" Bella sounded as though Hanna must have meant something else, but at once guessed that Hanna was right. Jude had been acting strange this last week or two.

"I saw her go up Raike Bottom."

"But that only leads over Tradden, doesn't it?" asked Fred.

"How long ago?" asked Bella.

"Just before the rabbits came out. When it started to get dark. I saw her go off, then the sport started and I didn't see her no more." Hanna felt important at the interest being shown in her.

"That's hours ago."

Fred and Will watched the growing concern on Bella's face.

Fred rose. "We'll go and look for her. Come on, Will."

"You can't go out in this."

But already the two men were putting on their warm, steamy boots. They saddled up quickly and took the shortest route over the fields towards Tradden.

"Shouldn't we ask in the village first?" said Will.

"No. She'll be on the hill." He said this with such certainty that Will Vickery wondered what kind of a girl wouldn't shelter in the village but would go out on to a hillside when a storm was threatening.

There was no point in hurrying now that she was soaked to the skin. She unpinned her hair, heavy and darkened with rain. It whipped her face as she walked with the storm behind her.

Many of the plants that hold on precariously to the thin loam of the chalk-hills live close to the ground, like the chicory, plantains, and toadflaxes. Others, the harebells, the cornflowers and scabious, flower on pliable stems, nodding and bending before every gust. Jude walked down amidst them, masses of blue little whirling Dervishes, and she felt pleasure in them. She was tired: not the fevered tiredness she had worked for recently. The disorder that had been affecting her seemed to have gone.

Suddenly a gust of wind whipped her straw hat from her hand. It bowled across the hillside and caught against a stunted juniper bush. By now, the water running off the hills made every score and scar in the soil a miniature cascade. The track, where there was never a vestige of soil covering the chalk, was washed and glistening white. Its surface was so slick it might have been oiled.

As Jude ran for her hat she slipped on the chalk and slithered on, unable to save herself, until she crashed against the stunted tree.

When there is no grey curtain of rain on the downs, it is not

[143]

difficult to see a person from a distance. But today visibility was down to yards, so Fred and Will separated in their search of the wide expanse of downland. It was Will who found Jude. Unconscious and with her leg twisted into an unnatural position.

Practical, resourceful, no one in such a predicament could wish to be found by a better person than Will. It was not the first broken bone he had treated. Most of the others had been in his father's stables and he knew that the sooner it was straightened the better. If he could manage it before she regained consciousness, it would save her a lot of agony.

He carried nothing that would serve as a splint, and the hillside was bare of anything useful. Even the juniper had no branch longer than a foot. Will took off his neck-cloth and tore it into strips, but there was not enough. It was no time for delicacy and in any case, having several sisters, knew all about petticoats; so he removed Jude's and tore that also. Then he gently turned her onto her back, straightened the broken leg, and strapped it to the good one.

Either the storm had blown itself out struggling to escape the valley, or had moved on to Kent and Sussex, leaving an increasingly brightening sky from the west, so that Fred Warren could see Will from some way off. His horse found the slithery chalk treacherous, so Fred walked it down. By the time he reached Will and Jude, Will was just finishing the binding of Jude's legs.

Will looked up.

"She's not badly hurt, I think. Only the leg – it looks like it broke. It'll not be easy getting her down."

They each had weather-cloaks, which in double thickness proved strong enough to carry Jude in a kind of hammock in which her legs could be held stiff. With the horses following, they went down the steep slope of Tradden.

They made a dramatic tableau. Dicken saw them from the yard, always on the look-out for something to brighten his dull life. "Master, Master," he called. "They'm coming in with the body."

White-faced, with Hanna her little replica a step behind, Bella ran to meet them. Fred waved and smiled. In her relief, Bella searched for words to hurl at Dicken, but could find none at the moment.

Before they had reached the flat ground at Raike Bottom, Jude had begun to regain consciousness. Swimming in and out of the pain and the motion of the sling, she gradually became aware of the sky, the sound of horses walking slowly and the smell of cloth impregnated with the smell of grain. Bella's face came into focus, then the porch, the beams of the house-place, then, as they lowered her to the floor, blackness.

It was impossible to get her up the few, twisting stairs, so they brought Jude's little cot down. Jude's clothes and the strips that bound her legs, were soaked through. Before she could be put to bed, Bella had to undress and dry her. Fred and Will, in the scullery, rubbed their hair, but the journey down without their weather-capes had soaked their clothes.

All the time that Bella was drying Jude, dressing her in a woollen gown and wrapping her warmly, Jude gave little groans as she became conscious of the pain. Hanna hovered and helped, her face all concern and seriousness.

When Bella had finished, the men helped her to lift Jude on to the cot.

It was now well into evening. The sky was clear again and the whole countryside glistened and glittered as the sun sank down towards Beacon Hill. Will and Fred set off as soon as they could do no more to see to things at Croud Cantle.

Jude became fully conscious, and hearing Fred's voice in the yard said to Hanna, "Quick, before he goes, run and tell Mr Warren that Jude says thank you, and tell him I'm sorry I put him about."

EVEN THOUGH her leg was painful, Jude had some restful sleep that night, dosed by Bella with one of her opium simples. Bella put no faith in the Cantle wise-woman, so next day, Johnny-twoey was sent off to get the Cunning Man of Motte to call. He came later that day and pronounced a small fracture. He advised that the leg be kept rigid and bear no weight upon it. Bella paid him for a box of pills which remained on the mantelpiece along with her few other souvenirs.

"Well," said Bella, after he had gone, "that's what comes of roastin' off in a thunder storm."

This was the first time that yesterday had been mentioned and they were both aware that it was dangerous ground. One false step by either of them would land them in another quicksand of emotion such as they had recently experienced. Neither of them was ready to tackle it again so soon.

"I know, Mother. I'm sorry. It was so hot in the field, I wanted a breath of air. I thought it'd be cool on Tradden."

And so they settled for this explanation.

The few ailments that beset the tough Nugent household were put right by large doses of licorice powder for the innards. Bella's "Green Special" – her own receipt – pungent ointment for cuts and grazes, and a warm stocking, straight from the wearer, tied round the neck for throats and chests. Indispositions at Croud Cantle were rare and the remedies mundane, giving Hanna little scope for her desire to nurse and fuss over people.

Hanna was just eight years old. Firm and square like Bella, she had strong stocky legs and arms and good, capable hands. She had all the prominent Estover features: small nose and ears, pale skin that freckled in summer, and a soft, full mouth. The Estover eyes were small and close-lidded, and few people could have said what was their colour, but those who did get close enough to look saw that they were green-flecked blue – or was it blue-flecked green? And of course the hair – the fox-red, golden-red, flaming Estover hair.

Under Bella's tuition, Hanna had become a reliable little worker. Provided that jobs were scaled down to her stature, there was not much work on the holding that she couldn't do well. She was now much too valuable a worker to spend her time bird-scaring.

She and Johnny-twoey were, in many ways, much alike. Both were hardy; both found satisfaction in such common sights as seeing beans and seeds germinating; both got on with whatever had to be done without question or complaint; neither had done much childish prattling. Seeing them digging, dividing or taking cuttings in the herb plot that was the thirteen-year-old Johnny-twoey's thriving domain, it was impossible to tell whether they enjoyed one another's company. They were a serious and hard-working little pair.

Perhaps Hanna's memory of Jaen went deep, for she was never very easy in her mother's company. At Croud Cantle she was usually a staid, placid child who seemed to be quite pleased with life in a rather solemn way. But whenever they went to Newton Clare, she appeared to revert to an older version of the fratchety, red-gum baby of seven years ago.

Perhaps she was more intelligent than given credit for. Perhaps she had inherited Estover shrewdness.

There was a houseful of Hazelhursts already, so nobody was likely to want to take back one who was disagreeable and bad-tempered. At Croud Cantle Hanna was wanted. The memory of the two red-haired foster-mothers who had soothed her and rocked her into security certainly went deep.

One thing she was good at was tending any animal that was injured or ailing. Bella was inclined to say that she had a tender little heart. But in fact, the satisfaction that Hanna got from taking some half-dead creature and putting it on its feet again was akin to the satisfaction that Jude got from taking words and forming them into a satisfying paragraph, or that Bella got from taking raw berries and creating neat rows of preserves.

Having got over the fright Dicken gave them when he saw the body being carried down, Hanna felt excited at the thought of caring for the injured Jude. As soon as she saw the state Jude was in, she had put bricks to heat up to warm Jude's bed; had run for a shift and a thick wool cloak; had held them before the fire, so that when Bella had taken off the soaking clothes, Jude could be dressed and wrapped up warmly.

At the time, Jude was only half-aware of what was happening. She knew that Bella had wrapped her up, but it was only the next day that she recalled Hanna towelling her hair dry and the soothing feel of the warm wool on her chilled skin, and she guessed that the heated bricks and the warmth were Hanna's.

The morning after the accident there was a lot to arrange. Two of the weekly-hired women were kept on to do Jude's work and help on market day. Over the breakfast meal, Hanna went busily back and forth giving Jude her food and drink, fetching and carrying and helping her to hop about.

"I reckon it'd be best if Hanna stopped in the house for a day or two," Bella said.

"No. I shall be all right. I'm not dying."

"She can still see to the hens and that."

Unusually for her, Hanna spoke up, seeing the chance of nursing Jude slipping away.

"If she was to fall down again, Jude might be a cripple. You remember that little goat that fell twice?"

Remembering the little goat, Jude wanted to smile. But she didn't, and gave in to being attended by Hanna.

The great storm had caught some crops further west which were still uncut, and had been left as tangled masses to be reaped and dried as best they could. In the Cantle Valley there was no farm caught out and the Harvest Suppers were smug and festive. The air was humid again. Almost immediately, the brown sides of the downs began to show green, but although there was a return to blue sky there was more cloud about. Summer was running down and the days were shortening.

Jude was weaker than she had supposed she might be. For a couple of days she lay in her cot beside the window, lightly sleeping or watching the pigeons go in and out of the cote under the roof of the cow-shed. Her leg was bound between two cut-down rake handles. It ached constantly and stabbed hot pain when she moved.

Hanna's little face was for ever beside her.

"Do you want anything Jude?" "Is your leg hurting?" "Shall I prop you up, Jude?" "Shall I brush your hair?"

[148]

"I'll tell you what you can do. Fetch my big book down."

Although Hanna thought writing a dull occupation for anyone who might have lain there like a lady, she set everything up comfortably within Jude's reach.

"I'm going to write a story."

This did interest Hanna. Her only experience of what books held between their covers was from listening to Reverend Tripp. In his delivery of lifting up his eyes unto the hills from whence cometh his help, he caused the eyes of his congregation to glaze over. He could blunt even the Song of Solomon. Hanna could see no connection between "a" is for "apple", "b" is for "butter", and tales of witches and magic.

"Good Heavens!" said Lady Geraldine as she entered.

The chamber was high and hung all about with drapes and tapestries. She held a candle that flickered in the still air. The reason for her exclamation was the high bed all draped in some dark-coloured damask and a dark counterpane covering it. "Good Heavens! Does his Lordship expect that I shall sleep in such funereal surroundings?"

The writing of that first paragraph took Jude the best part of the morning, a lot longer than anything else she had done previously. That had come tumbling out of her daily observations and experience. This was very different.

As she lay resting in the afternoon, she thought about Lady Geraldine. Where had she come from? The more she thought about it the more it excited her. She realised that she had been influenced by her recent reading, but Lady Geraldine was Jude's own creation. If she went on and on thinking about her ..? It seemed possible that Jude could create a person with as much life as herself. If Jaen were dead ..? If Jaen were dead, then she would exist in Jude's mind as remembered images and impressions. Which was just what Lady Geraldine was, or could be. And her own father? To me, Jude thought, he is a character created from Bella's words and a few words in the Parish Register. And so he is for Bella ... and Lotte ... and Jaen ... For anyone who ever knew Tomas Nugent, he was images conveyed by words.

Jude felt that this was the most important thought that had ever come to her.

[149]

Later, Hanna came and sat beside Jude to hear what she had written, observing each word as Jude ran her finger beneath the line.

"And did he? Did his Lordship want her to sleep in that dark bed?"

"I don't know yet."

"Oh, Jude! You said it was a story."

To please Hanna, Jude wrote about Lady Geraldine for two days. She turned out to be Little Lady Geraldine, eight years old. Once lost to His Lordship as a baby and brought up by a poor woodsman and his wife, she was found again, became Lady Geraldine and the poor people were rewarded.

A is for apple had been boredom. But whenever Little Lady Geraldine appeared in writing, Hanna began to recognise words and letters. When the story was finished, Jude tied the pages together and gave the story to Hanna. From then on, Hanna's progress in reading speeded up, though she still found writing laborious and uninteresting.

The cloudless whitish-blue sky had gone with the storm. From her place by the window, Jude noticed the gradual change to a pinker sky with small cumulus clouds. The one branch of an apple tree that was visible showed some yellow leaves and reddening fruit.

On the third day, when Johnny-twoey came to fetch his midday food, he asked in his broad, halting way, "Miss Jude? Done you want to get out of the house?" When Jude said she would like to, but what with the cot and everything, he said, "Miss Jude? I could drag over the old trough what's waiting for mending."

Hanna frowned at his intrusion into her domain.

Placating her, he went on: "Hanny could fill it with hay, couldn't you Hanny? And make it soft."

The two children arranged the trough just outside the door. It was surprisingly comfortable. Hanna brought out Jude's writing things and it was there that Jude began her second tale of Lady Geraldine, which she did not read to Hanna or anyone.

There was a bit of Bella in Jude that caused her to feel that idleness was a dreadful sin. This she assuaged by doing such small chores as could be done without standing. There was also in her a bit of Tomas Nugent's Sybarite nature that hitherto had no means of surfacing. The two conflicting – Bella and Tomas – sides to Jude's nature were satisfied: by working extremely hard, but at the pleasure of writing her story.

The routine of the farm settled down around her. She soon learned to move short distances without help and she spent some time teaching Hanna. Coming a small way out of his shell, Johnny-twoey changed the hay daily, saying, "Miss Jude?" by way of greeting; reddening at the neck when Jude praised his good idea about the trough.

By early September, Jude had written and discovered a great deal about Lady Geraldine, who had become interested in a young man. He was unsubstantial and mysterious – to Jude as well as to Lady Geraldine. Then one day, Lady Geraldine fell from her horse. As she lay stunned, the young man found her and carried her back to his house.

Lady Geraldine's recollection of how she got to Trelford Court was hazy. The pain in her arm and the severe blow to her head caused her to become faint. The young man was gentle, realising what permanent damage might be done to the arm should it be found to be broken, or should the motion of the horse make the condition worse. Her head lolled on his shoulder and she smelled a strange odour of ..? Lady Geraldine, in her fainting state, could not bring to mind what this might be until she heard the sound of sails as they passed the mill. Of course, it was the wholesome smell of freshly ground corn.

I T WAS A YEAR when there was an abundance of crab-apples, blackberries and sloes. Although Jude was able to get about the house and yard with the aid of a stick, she could not go out this year into the fields and lanes to pick the wild fruits for making their preserves and wine. So it was left to Bella, Hanna and Johnny-twoey to go out every afternoon, leaving Jude to prepare windfall apples and break up the sugar-loaf.

As sometimes happens just before autumn, there was a short spell of summery weather. Bella had taken the young ones to pick in Church Farm Lane and Dicken and the hired labour were digging up root-crops and putting them in clamps for winter use. Jude had finished preparing fruit and was sitting on a kitchen chair outside.

Although she had started the Lady Geraldine story to keep herself occupied, it had recently become marvellously absorbing to her. Lady Geraldine's adventures were trivial, but Jude had discovered that there were many and various ways of producing an effect with words and punctuation. The discovery excited her. Lady Geraldine's obsession with finding the identity of the man who had rescued her had been written in several different ways. Jude was fascinated at how she might change the story by the way she wrote it; like changing her tone of voice when speaking. She re-read some of her many broadsides and her few books with a new awareness, comparing the way that they were written with that she had done.

She was sorting out her latest episode of Lady Geraldine when she heard a horse being ridden quite fast from the direction of Corhampton. And just as she had hauled herself to her feet to see who it was, Harry Goodenstone rode into the yard.

He was beautifully, fashionably dressed: all red cloth, shiny buttons, ribbons and roll-top boots, and another of the large hats with a buckle in front, blue to match – clothes not at all suited to galloping

a horse over Corhampton Down. He reined in his sweating mount and
sat for a moment looking about him, as though he had come to a
crossroads and did not know which direction to take. Then he saw
Jude and dismounted. Jude greeted him. He did not respond, but stood
holding the reins of his horse, looking at the house, the yard and
outbuildings.

"The trough's there," she said. He appeared not to hear. "Or that's
the stable."

He still said nothing, but led his horse to drink. Then he let it go to
graze the grass close by.

"You look hot, Mister Harry. Can I get you some cider?"

"Yes," he said, in the high, tortured-vowel voice that was as
fashionable and awkward as his clothes. "All right. Cider would
be ..." He trailed off and sat down on the chair Jude had been using.
Leaning on her stick, she hobbled into the house and came back
unsteadily, carrying a mug of cider. Harry took it from her and drank
it off. Jude stood before him, leaning on her stick.

"D'you want to come into the house, Mister Harry?"

"No. No." He spoke slowly, preoccupied. "Is this all?"

"All?"

"I thought it might have been larger."

"It used to be. The land ... there used to be more, at one time. But
all that part down by Howgaite was sold to Old Sir Henry – Mr
Goodenstone. All those bottom fields belong to The Estate now."

"Yes. Hmm."

She began to feel apprehensive. The years of unquestioning
security had long gone. The more she read about land and small farms
throughout the whole country being absorbed into the large estates,
the greater was her realisation that any holding as small as theirs was
insecure; particularly since she had been told about the casual way her
father had sold off the land and then left. It was quite possible that
Croud Cantle was not even legally her mother's.

Jude was not able to stand for longer than a few minutes at a time.
Soon her leg ached badly, but she could not politely ask him to get up
from her chair.

"I'm sorry, Mister Harry, but I shall have to go inside. You're
welcome to sit there, long as you like." She left him sitting outside still
looking around at the outbuildings and barns.

Since the Sunday when she had last spoken to Mrs Trowell, Jude

[153]

had heard nothing of anybody at Park Manor. The only person likely to have brought news out to Croud Cantle was Fred Warren, and he was busy riding all over the county buying up crops of cereals. It was a queer situation. Jude did not know what to do next. It did not seem probable that he had come to Croud Cantle accidentally. No one coming from Corhampton to Cantle would use that track, unless they intended coming to the holding. She could not go and ask him what he wanted. Perhaps he didn't want anything. Perhaps the fancy just took him to ride into the yard. Men like the Goodenstones were seldom held back by want of time, money or arrogance from doing what they wished on the spur of the moment. Perhaps he was riding by and just thought, I'll go and have a look ... Perhaps it was something more serious. It was queer and she was uneasy.

She could see him from where she sat. He struck her as a pathetic-looking creature. For some reason his clothes always appeared to be a bit large for him. Possibly he thought it disguised his narrow shoulders and thin neck, whereas they emphasised those features. And why, as his beard was so pale and meagre, didn't he go clean-shaven? From where Jude observed him, he had the appearance of a silly youth. But he wasn't. He was a rich and powerful land-owner in his mid-thirties, and Jude was uneasy, not knowing why he had come.

After about five minutes he rose, came towards the house, walked straight in and, apparently apropos of nothing, said, "Tell Warren to take the books. I shall arrange it."

"Yes. Thank you. When I next see him, I'll tell him."

As suddenly as he had come into the house, he went, saying as though finishing a conversation he had been having, " ... but of course it was all before your time."

Jude followed him out, but before she got to the door she heard him riding off, not towards Park Manor, but back in the direction from which he had come, to Corhampton. No sooner had he gone than she heard another rider coming towards Croud Cantle from the opposite direction along Howgaite. It was Fred Warren.

Compared to her last visitor, Fred looked solid and normal. He greeted her with a good handshake and smiles; cheerfully running on a bit to hide some self-consciousness that he occasionally felt in Jude's company these days.

"Judeth! I have neglected you. I hope you didn't take it amiss, me not visiting the sick. There was nothing I could do about it, though.

[154]

Needs must when the Devil calls, etcetera. We have been so busy, I can't tell you! There's a business going for sale up near Salisbury. Mr White is thinking of buying it up: though why he wants to spread as far as Wiltshire with all his rheumatics and gout, I don't know. He sent me to look it over, and what with that as well as everything else, it's a blessing I've got Will, and that's a fact. And here am I going on ... So how is the invalid?" He seated himself on the ground close to Jude's chair.

"As you see. Almost well. Fratcheting because I'm so tied down here."

Jude offered him a drink of cider, but he refused, saying he would rather talk. The talk, however, was no more than polite comment about Bella and Hanna and prospects of good harvests. There was an awkwardness, a kind of formality between them.

Fred felt ill at ease because he knew that something was wrong. On the day of her accident he had noticed that her dress was pinned up for field work and that her legs and feet were scratched and cut, as though she had been running from something or somebody: she had not mentioned the incident and he did not like to ask her about it. Also, since the day when he had glimpsed her figure through her thin dress, he found himself sometimes remembering it, uneasily.

Jude's contribution to the awkwardness sprang from the show she had made of herself in his office. She did not want Fred asking her how she came to be on the downs that day in that state. There was also the fact that she had become aware that Lady Geraldine's mysterious rescuer was recognisably a more youthful version of Fred Warren.

"Young Harry was just here. He says you are to take the books."

There was the awkwardness; politeness, as though they were newly met.

"Ah yes, we must get down to it."

"Yes, soon as I can get about again."

And so they circled around one another and the unspoken things.

He asked her how she had been spending her time. Jovially: "I see you've got the old book out."

Jude felt uncomfortable at what was beneath Fred's hand as he patted the binding that concealed grown-up Lady Geraldine. She told him that she had written a story for Hanna. When he asked to see it, she said, "Oh, it isn't any good." But he pressed her into reading it to him. She had just begun when she was interrupted by one of the hired women wanting to know where to store some beets. Jude put down the book and went with the woman. A breeze riffled the pages, showing Fred a great more close writing than Little Lady Geraldine. When Jude returned he asked her about it. She protested, saying that it wasn't anything.

"If it wasn't anything, Judeth, you wouldn't have written it. You were never embarrassed before to show me what you have done."

"That was only my histories and notes. This is different. When you make things up they come from inside your head. They're part of you, your own thoughts, and if other people read them, it's like ... well, you are really letting them see right inside you. You haven't got any protection; you're letting people know what you are like."

Jude sat with the open book clasped to her protectively.

"Why go to the bother of writing them down? Why not leave them inside your head then?"

"Because I wanted to make up a story."

"What good is a story if you won't let anyone read it?"

"It is just to please myself."

"Then you needn't have gone to the bother of writing it down, need you? You already had it in your head."

Slowly they were getting back somewhere on their old footing. He was the Fred of five years ago – Mr Warren the tutor – arguing with her, making her see things for herself, not telling her, making her work it out.

The short silences between them became more relaxed. Eventually, giving no explanation as to how she got to this point in her argument, Jude said, " ... and that is something I never thought about before ... you don't think about Shakespeare being a real man ... I shouldn't want to let anybody know I was thinking things like that."

"Why?"

"Because of what people might think."

"About what?"

"About me, I suppose."

"I see. It runs like this then: if Judeth Nugent wrote a story called *Macbeth*, then people would be sure to go about thinking that she must have secret thoughts of murder. Or if she wrote *Hamlet*, then there must be a bit of a mad Ophelia in her, or a bit of an incestuous queen."

Jude flushed at his directness. "Well yes, I suppose that is it."

"Do you think any the worse of William Shakespeare that he had a

[156]

bit of mad Ophelia and bad Gertrude in him?"

"People never think so badly of a man as they do a woman in that kind of thing. They would think a woman shouldn't write about such feelings."

Fred broke a short silence by saying, "You'll be wasted, Judeth, if you never do anything but give orders about clamping beetroot."

Jude felt elated at this confirmation of her own secret estimation of her ability. But her mother's denigration of people who were too clever for their own good or who got above theirselves always coloured her opinion of herself. Bella's conscience was always perched on Jude's shoulder, so she put herself down, laughing.

"You think I should write plays about mad girls and bad women?"

"Be serious, Judeth." He spoke as he used to when she had occasional fits of waywardness as a young girl. "Back in the summer I tried to get you to talk about it. 'Don't push me Fred' was what you said. Remember? 'Don't push me'."

Still clutching her book, Jude studied her fingernails.

"Can you write stories?" Fred asked.

"I don't know. Honestly. I don't know how to judge what I've done so far."

"Do you want it judged?"

"I suppose I do."

"Well?" He stared her down and she handed him the book with a pretence of negligence.

"All right, Fred Warren. Now you will know what I am like."

She went indoors, not bearing to watch as the mad and bad in her was revealed to Fred; worse, wondering whether he would recognise himself in the young man. As she waited she began to realise how important it was that he should have a good opinion of what she had tried to do. Slowly, apprehensively, her unconscious ambition became conscious.

I want to write proper books, real books.

Elation and hope, deflation and dashed hope. Libraries and books with "J. Nugent" embossed in gold. Endless milking, churning and frozen earth. Images in quick succession. Books were not written by country girls who milked cows and stood on Blackbrook market.

There was about half-an-hour's reading in grown-up Lady Geraldine. After about that amount of time and with as much nonchalance as she could affect with her stiff leg, Jude took out to Fred a dish of small cakes.

He sat deep in thought, staring at the cover of the closed book.

"Go on then," Jude said. "You can say what you like."

"That's easy to say. But what you said earlier ... Won't you take criticism personally? What if I don't like Lady Geraldine?"

"You aren't supposed to like her."

"Ah!" Fred looked pleased.

Fred was the best sort of critic. He took her seriously and knew what she was capable of. He wanted her to succeed and did not find it necessary to make polite compliments or useless comments. Between them they took Lady Geraldine apart: talked about her, criticised her and speculated on her future.

"What are you going to do about it then, Judeth? And don't you dare tell me not to push you."

"Do you think I can write? I mean really write, so that people will want to read it."

"You don't need me to tell you, do you?"

"I believe I could do it, but would people want to read a serious book by a woman? Let alone somebody like me who haven't ever done anything except grow things and stand on Blackbrook market."

"Well, well, so it's to be all Lady Geraldine, and Princess Lavinia or Bishop Somebody and Admiral Whatnot? Judeth! People who stand on Blackbrook market are the ones worth writing of. You have said so yourself. The others aren't one in a thousand; their loves and lives are trivial in comparison."

"All right. Supposing I did manage to write something about ordinary people, would somebody print it?"

"Women are writing."

"Farm girls?"

Fred recited a few lines of "Drink to me only with thine eyes". "A bricklayer wrote that – Johnson – you know."

"I know. But he was a man. Ben!"

"There's nothing stopping you calling yourself Ben."

"But not Judeth!"

"Would it matter what you were called? The important thing is for somebody to write a book where the characters are people thrown off their land; people tramping the roads looking for work; hungry children. And about girls and boys in villages like yours who have been falling in and out of love like the Lady Geraldines."

"And half of people are women!" Ideas that had been collected and stored burst out like wheat from a ripped sack.

But Fred was in full flight with his own ideas.

"In France at this very moment there are farriers and bakers and stonemasons – the kind of people we see every day in Blackbrook – who are rising up together, trying to make their lives better. That's exciting; worth writing about."

"The women are part of it. They are affected by it all."

"Right, that's what I am saying. This life is by far more important and more interesting than Squires and Duchesses. You could write about them."

"But not as Judeth or Jane or Dorothy!"

"It is what is between the covers of a book that is important, not the name on the spine."

"You can say that because you won't ever have to pretend that you are Judeth or Dorothy to get taken seriously."

"What you must do is to write. Forget the details about your name. Writing should be all about how people deal with the problems they are faced with. Dammit, Judeth – the greatest problem your Lady Geraldine ever has to deal with is to discover the identity of Will Vickery!"

The fire of argument that had started furiously in Jude's mind was suddenly quenched.

Will Vickery?

Will Vickery! Jude fairly blushed. Not Fred Warren at all. Will Vickery.

She had allowed somebody to step into her mind and ferret about finding out secrets about Judeth Nugent. Not just that: to discover what she had not realised was there. Fred was right. Will Vickery was Lady Geraldine's rescuer, the man with the smell of grain in his clothes, the man who aroused the lady's passion. The man Jude liked very much to write about.

It was what she had been afraid of, what she had tried to explain to Fred before she had allowed him to see the book. Revealing herself. Exposing herself to criticism. Allowing others to make assumptions about her from what she wrote, with them not knowing everything. Writing was like rumour and gossip: people could never know the whole truth; only enough to chew over and make something of. Jude had been a bit prepared for Fred seeing himself in the hero's character.

[159]

She could have made a joke of it, saying: "I don't know any men except you and Dicken." But she was not prepared for the discovery that Will Vickery was roaming about in her unconscious.

"I hardly know enough of Mr Vickery to put him in a book."

Fred did not answer immediately, but idly turned over the pages of the old accounts book, then said suddenly, "I write verse."

"Fred, I never knew that."

"Nor does anybody – till now. Oh, it isn't any good. The reason I'm telling you is that I feel somewhat guilty, and it seems fair I should tell you. I got you to let me read what you had written, and put to you all those arguments about what's the good of writing if nobody's going to read it ... "

"And you haven't never let anybody read your poetry."

"Verse, Judeth, and not good. Anyway, the merits of them don't make any difference. It's just that I'm saying I know you're right about letting people see right inside you; letting them know your most secret thoughts that you sometimes don't even let yourself know. Like Will Vickery."

Jude blushed again and could not meet his eyes.

"It's the test, Jude. If you are going to write about flesh and blood people, love, passion and so on must be there. It's already there. Lady Geraldine is not really about aristocrats: it's about Cantle people."

Life on this farm was little different from others. In Judeth's childhood she had worked as hard as any: had her feet and hands frozen and aching with chilblains; been wind-blown, sweat-soaked, and rain-drenched. Yet somehow she had survived with her mind intact. There were others like her: delivering unorthodox sermons in tin chapels; printing and handing out political broadsides; addressing any small gathering of people who would listen to their belief in a radically new kind of society.

Fred Warren occasionally saw something like it elsewhere in nature – a few ears of corn that were taller, more productive, or could better withstand the extremes of weather than the rest of those in the field. It was from such sports that cornseed continued to improve.

"Aren't I right, Judeth?"

Before she replied that of course the story had nothing to do with Cantle people, Jude reflected – as Fred had taught her to do when she was a girl.

"Then you don't think that Lady Geraldine is really a lady?"

"Is she?"

"I don't know any ladies," she smiled, remembering his old tactics. "Oh, Fred, I think my brain would have gone rusted ages ago if you didn't come and make the wheels turn sometimes."

"So?" He adopted his old schoolmasterly tone. "What do we conclude, Judeth?"

"That Lady Geraldine is nothing like a true blue-blooded lady, and I ought to have put her into a farmhouse and called her Polly Nettleship."

They were laughing together at Lady Geraldine's great surprise at suddenly finding herself transformed into Polly Nettleship. They had slipped into their old, relaxed, familiar way, their earlier discomfort apparently abated, when Bella's voice cut in.

"Well, it's nice for some people, Fred Warren. Sitting about whilst you gets others to do your work for you."

They looked up. Jude avoided everybody's eyes when she saw Will Vickery coming through the gate with Bella, Hanna and Johnny-twoey. The mob of emotions, suppressed a short while ago, threatened to riot again.

"I met Mister Vickery coming out of Eastfield's farm and he been getting down crab-apples for us like nobody's business, all along the lane there."

It was as much as Jude could do to keep any tell-tale expression from her face when the full meaning suddenly came to her. Fred was not the man she hazily recollected bending over her on Tradden; it was not his coat that had exuded the evocative, comforting smell as she swam in and out of consciousness; it was not Fred who had removed her petticoat and torn it into bandages.

As he took Hanna down from his horse and helped Bella with the baskets of fruit he had been carrying, Will Vickery was also forced to put on an expression consciously hiding his thoughts.

When Will first met Jude, he had been very taken with discovering such a girl in that God-forsaken little farm. She had a look about her which conveyed intelligence, eagerness and curiosity. After that first meeting, he believed that he had come upon as near a perfect woman as he had ever thought to exist. Unsophisticated – a girl who scarcely ever left this place; yet, apparently, a serious reader. Simple – doing the hard-labour of growing and rearing; yet, according to Fred Warren, a good businesswoman and an amateur local historian and recorder. The idea of the work-hardened hand of a young woman being employed in researching and writing excited Will Vickery's imagination. To add to all that, she had the most striking looks and colouring.

Then he had opened the door of the office and seen her enclosed in Fred Warren's arms and he felt that he had been let down. Will Vickery was a man to reason intelligently with himself and had come to the conclusion that to feel like that was very foolish. It was not his business what she did and it was hypocrisy on his part, for he professed an open way of thinking about all kinds of freedoms. He concluded that it was not up to him to give an opinion on the girl's behaviour.

Yet, of course, as soon as he saw them with their heads close, laughing together, he did.

When Mrs Nugent spoke, Will saw the expression on the face of the woman he had once thought to be near-perfect. He noticed her avoidance of their eyes.

Jude, likewise, saw his expression.

Bella had recently done a deal with a packman carrying coffee beans. It was never Bella's policy to take much notice of the claims of packmen, but this one had held some of the crushed beans for Bella to savour. "Tis like a tonic to get you going twice as fast" was a recommendation to Bella. So she exchanged some of last season's sweet-jar for some of the beans. She had to admit that she was rather partial to the taste as a treat, and it was worth the trouble pounding and crushing the beans. She insisted that Fred and Will try out this new drink.

For the rest of the short visit they talked of nothing except what a treat the coffee was; whether it was better with some cream; what a great season for sloes it was; did that mean a good or a bad winter? Will remarked that most likely it meant there had been no frosts when the sloes had been in bloom, which drew from Jude a spontaneous exclamation at the sense of his observation: then she quickly avoided his eyes again.

It was coming up to Plough Fair Week at Blackbrook. As the men were preparing to leave, Fred said that if they were going to ride over for a day or two's holiday, then they should use his house as a base from which to visit the fair on any day they chose. Bella said she didn't know, what with Jude's leg this year and that kind of thing. He suggested Jude might stop with Molly and him for a few days. When

Hanna insisted on being included, he said, "The more the merrier."

"I couldn't, not with all the fruit and that to be done," said Jude, aware of her weeks of idleness when she hadn't even earned her bread. Yet really she was longing to go. Bella had taken them to Plough Fair Monday ever since she and Jaen were able to walk the distance. It was one of their few holidays.

Jude loved to be part of the crowd: to hear the raucous music, the shouts of horse-dealers, and see the sights and side-shows.

"I don't see why not," said Bella. "After all, in a week or ten days it'll all be done with. Anyway she an't a lot of good about the place like that."

That was just like her mother. She would grump and make you feel uncomfortable if you didn't pull your weight, then suddenly do something like this. Jude had learned to take Bella's good moods while they were going.

In Bella's opinion, Plough Monday ought to be enough for anybody; but if Mrs Warren was agreeable – and you'd better be sure she is, Fred Warren – then Jude and Hanna might go over and stop a day or two.

H ARRY GOODENSTONE'S strange visit to Croud Cantle originated from the meeting of Jude and Lotte on Bell Tump and Lotte's removal from Park Manor, but the actual dash from Lotte's lodgings in Old Portsmouth took place that morning.

A change had come over Lotte since the Sunday encounter with Jude on Bell Tump: not dramatic or noticeable to anyone who knew her less well than Harry or Mary; but something subtle was changed in her whole demeanour. It was as though she had been a shiny chess piece this last twenty years: moved by others, easily, on a slithery board. Now she had become magnetised on a metallic board, a resisting pawn. Her old chess-masters were nonplussed.

Lotte appeared to be growing a shell of protection against their playing upon her feelings of guilt, responsibility and duty. Ever since Tomas Nugent had sailed off and Mary had found her – then later when Harry Goodenstone had offered his protection – Lotte was never free of the awareness that she must be grateful, always grateful to those who had saved her from herself.

It was true that, in the Bristol days, anything might have happened to Lotte without Mary there. Mary had given up a good job and tramped scores of miles to find her. Mary had been a mother to her, and twenty years of reiteration of this truth gave Mary a strong claim to gratitude. It was true also that with Harry Goodenstone around, jealously guarding his expensive fantasy, she was to some extent – at least whilst not in the theatre – protected from other men with other fantasies. So Lotte had a duty of gratitude to him as well.

Lotte was not entirely dependent upon Goodenstone money. But the style of living that he had set for them had put Lotte to a great deal of expenditure from her own income on the kind of gowns and flowers that went with the smart carriages and good addresses he provided. Had she led a simpler life, she would have had a nice nest of savings against the day when there would be no more offers for her to play the country wife or young messenger. As it was, she had a little put by to provide for Mary, Rosie and herself in a simple way.

Although Mary was plain and drab and took no interest in her appearance, she wanted to live no other kind of life – unless it be in greater style. It did not matter to Mary when visitors took her for Lotte's companion; or handed her hats without a glance, as though she were a maidservant; or even that people were openly incredulous that she was the sister of the beautiful and graceful Charlotte Trowell. Mary had everything she wanted. She was living in greater luxury than she had even known to exist when she was a milk-maid. So when Lotte had shown reluctance to accept Harry Goodenstone's offer of a grand life at Park Manor, Mary had played on every one of her sister's weaknesses – particularly "poor little Rosie".

"Don't you care about nobody except yourself?" was always Mary's stab to Lotte's conscience whenever there was a difference of opinion.

But this time, for almost the first time, the stab was deflected.

"Yes, I care about everybody except myself." A hint of character overlaid Lotte's bland features of enduring youthfulness.

Mary did not know how to handle her sister's rebellion.

Mary had managed to contain the first outbreak. This was at Park Manor, when Harry Goodenstone had walked in on their packing and asked what Lotte should have told him years ago. Mary had jumped in before Lotte could speak and confessed to him that it was in Cantle village that they had spent their early years: a touching performance of a true story without its essential central theme and lacking some of its important characters.

Harry Goodenstone had said dammit, he didn't care a faddle where Lotte came from, if he wasn't master of his own village to do as he pleased, then where was he master, and as for the rest of the county bores, they could cut him dead if they chose to, he did not need them. He and Lotte had enough of their own sophisticated and entertaining friends not to need the kind his father had.

He had put down Lotte's determination to leave, to her being away from the theatre and needing to act up a bit, so he indicated to Mary that they should humour her and allowed the packing and the exodus to go ahead. He followed them.

Lotte's order to the coachman to drive to Portsea had no thought behind it. It was the first place that she could think of near enough to drive to at that time of day – and where she was a stranger. They found lodgings that night and the next day took rooms in Crown Street.

It was outside Lotte's rooms in Crown Street, some weeks later, that Harry Goodenstone had flung himself upon his horse and rode back the fifteen miles to Cantle.

He had only got as far as the top of the Ports Down when he realised how unsuitably dressed he was for racing off like that. He had got himself up in his new, fashionable, rust-red coat, intending to have it out with Lott and insist that she go back to Park Manor. After all, he'd waited long enough to gain his inheritance. He was convinced that the old man would not have hung on to life so tenaciously had it not been for the fact that he knew his son was waiting to step into his place. Since their arrival in Portsmouth, Harry had taken rooms at a hotel that was full of naval officers. He had not much liked it, but had no option. It was the only place with rooms of any size. Lotte's lodgings were out of the question. She was still acting up.

From the hill, he could plainly see the tracks over the downs on the Isle of Wight, the Langstone mudflats, and the shining harbour full of small craft and naval vessels. Uncultured place, swarming with seamen, rough and full of themselves in their gold braid and buttons. He longed for Bath. Of all the places Lotte chose to act up in! Of all places to discover that one had been betrayed, lied to, deceived. Of all places to find oneself in and be told that the little messenger who ran on to the stage in tabard and hose was a woman near his own age; that the naughty, innocent, country-wife with baby-like hair who ran round the stage dressed in rose-bud gowns and hiding in cupboards had hidden her whole history ... All these years there had been a child hidden away somewhere. A child! Twenty years old!

Lotte had spoken like a peasant. Not just acting up. Streaming out her dirty history. She had had enough! The sister could do nothing but stand and watch. She had had enough. She kept saying that. Acting, acting, acting: twenty years pretending to be somebody else. If you want a girl to live with, then clear off and find one – or a boy!

He could have coped if she had been a sweet, mad Ophelia, singing naughty songs ... but this! The thirty-four-year-old peasant had taken from him his little messenger.

The Goodenstone in him came out. The trait that caused them to get whatever they decided they wanted, be it boy/woman or the farms and commonlands of Cantle. The trait that caused extra wings to be built on to the Park Manor House; that caused cottagers to be put out so that game-birds might be brought in. That trait which made it impossible for two male Goodenstones to live under the same roof rose up within the rust-red breast and he hit out. Earlier that day he had demurred for half an hour over whether to buy a riding-crop with a tail of animal hair or a short silver-inlaid stick. He had chosen the crop.

With it he struck out at Charlotte Holly, the woman who had taken from him beautiful Charlotte Trowell, messenger and naughty country wife.

For the first few miles' mad gallop out of Portsmouth, Harry Goodenstone had gone without direction. It was only upon finding himself on Ports Down, overlooking the naval town, that he took stock of where he was. He had no conscious desire or plan to go in the direction of Cantle, but it was towards there that he started his horse into a gallop again.

Within the cloud of jealousy and spiteful, thwarted possessiveness that enveloped him, an ice-crystal of reality formed. The reality of the names and places he had forced Lotte to tell him – degrading her, hurting her, salting his own wounds, working up the Goodenstone in himself. The first crystal to form was about the name, Nugent. Not about the man who had been the violator of his fantasy, but about the girl who had attended his father's funeral; the same one he had seen in the vestry and then in the library. The daughter was another woman who belonged to the violator, and for a short while he had turbulent thoughts of avenging the old harm with some new.

As he rode inwards from the coast – up over the windy hills, down into the moist, moss-ridden, Meon valley then up, up again on the south-west face of Tradden Raike – his dementia slowly withdrew. He was left fatigued; left only with a voyeuristic desire to look at the previously insignificant, independent little state within the Goodenstone kingdom: Croud Cantle farm, where the violation had taken place.

On the high point of Tradden, where the enormous beeches forever rustled leaves and clicked twigs; where red-brushed squirrels bounced about or watched what was going on as they chewed beech mast; where fur hunted fur and feather swooped on feather, Harry Goodenstone reined in his horse and saw none of this.

[167]

His full attention was upon the valley. His valley. The Goodenstone valley.

He sat astride his horse and viewed the main source of his wealth and power. He suddenly saw it as he had never seen it before; as his father and the grandfather who had made the first move to enclose and claim the valley, had seen it. Not as Jude saw it, as a thing with a life of its own; ancient, independent of god or man. Jude saw it as a creature; a spirit to be venerated and loved, yet untouched and untouchable, owned only by itself. Fashionably-clad and perspiring, the owner of plans showing fields and commons, the legal possessor of rolled documents with seals and ribbons viewed the valley. He was suddenly seeing, vaguely, that this valley had something to do with what made him Harry Goodenstone; with what made him Squire Goodenstone, Master of Park Manor and its surrounds.

Throughout his Young Harry years, his father and other landowners had appeared ridiculously obsessive about the possibility of losing a few acres of land, or the rights to something or other, or even game-birds and the odd sheep. They talked as though the hordes were at the gate: death, bankruptcy, litigation, natural disaster and men who wanted a share. The most frequent subject of their conversation was how to maintain their hold – strong laws and strong fences. The ownership of good land was their birthright and theirs only. How to keep out the hordes was an ever-present problem. One of their best strategies was to unite, consolidate and entail, and the most effective means of bringing this about was through marriage.

As soon as Old Sir Henry knew that his first child – and, in the event, his only child – was a son, he felt that the Estate was properly secure, and that eventually it might be united with one of the adjoining estates. He had not bargained for a silly and wayward son who thought that the wealth and power he had been born to was indestructible. Had he perhaps taken Young Harry to the top of Tradden in his most impressionable years, said all this is ours and on the other side of Winchester Hill is the Berol estate, explained the compound interest of joined estates, instilled in him a fear of cracks in defences and a horror of letting in the hordes – then he might have saved himself years of anxiety about his foolish son.

Instead of the practical demonstration, Old Sir Henry had imposed restrictions, made rules and attempted serious argument with a boy who was interested only in pleasing himself. Young Harry could not see that his relationship with Charlotte Trowell had anything to do with his father, or the future of the Estate. Old Sir Henry saw her as a pleasure-seeker, like his son, who would assist the Estate down the slope to bankruptcy. She destroyed, as well, his hope of joining the estates of Cantle and Motte through marriage. Fortunately he died in ignorance of the origins and biography of his heir's mistress – and in ignorance of the possibility that his lands might get back into the hands of the peasantry.

Harry Goodenstone was beginning to realise.

The valley was his and the valley was himself. Without it he was nothing but a small man on a large horse. Without the fields of corn, barley and wheat; the flocks of sheep, the herds of beef; men, women, dairy cattle, pigs, and the land on the valley floor, plus whatever could be dug from beneath its surface – without these possessions, the Goodenstones existed only on the level of ordinary humanity.

These thoughts did not come clearly, logically or in any order, but simply as an awareness of what ownership, power and the right to rule meant.

The possession of Charlotte Trowell suddenly appeared trifling in comparison.

BLACKBROOK FAIR was a fair by ancient charter, held on the third Monday of September. For more than six hundred years people had been saying that Fair Monday weren't the same as when they were young. Even so, for more than six hundred years people from all over Hampshire and West Sussex had continued to flock into Blackbrook on the Monday; and on the rest of the days of Fair Week, when fair and market combined.

Good or bad harvest, wet weather or fine, it was a pause in the lives of the rural community and a diversion for urban dwellers. Everybody who could make the journey went to Blackbrook sometime during Fair Week, and the streets thronged with people: velvet jackets rubbed stiff linen smocks, silken flounces jostled home-spun woollen skirts, and traders took pence as willingly from brown and calloused fingers as from finely manicured ones.

During the four or five days preceding Fair Week, children in the area rushed out whenever they heard unfamiliar-sounding carts and wagons, calling to others to look, look, quick, look. These wagons, thrown over with bright covers, were often highly decorated in gilt paint and gaudy colours; with symbols and pictures illustrating – without restraint – the extraordinary powers, entertainment, wonder, magic and horror to be expected when the proprietor had set up his stall.

Gipsies, who had been trekking the country in small family bands since early in the year, now began to make their way into Hampshire, bringing their beautiful, sprightly ponies and horses to trade with each other – and beautiful-looking and apparently-sprightly animals to sell to undiscerning Hampshire Gorgios. Local people were suspicious of gipsies, and everyone had some apocryphal tale – vanished children, missing sheep or pigs. Nobody knew the truth of why gipsies should want to take children when they seemed to have more than enough of their own, but it was likely that gipsy women envied local mothers their white-skinned offspring, or something like that. For all their prejudice against them, the sight of the first gipsies going to Blackbrook started the anticipation of pleasure in the hearts of the local people. By Sunday, every available field in the area had been rented out to the travelling people.

Jude and Hanna approached Blackbrook. They were each riding a donkey and carrying extra clothes in a bundle. Hanna was unusually animated and excited, as much because they were going to stay in the house that Hanna idealised, as the novelty of staying for the whole of Blackbrook Fair.

She saw a bear being led along the road on a chain; then in a field a cage on wheels with a canvas cover down so that no one could get a free look before the fair started; even a laden and covered farm cart looked as though it might be something. Look Jude! Look! It was difficult to believe that it was Sunday.

Being able to walk without pain and no longer having to lean on a stick, Jude felt free and light-hearted. Occasionally she thought of the dark hole in which she seemed to have lived during those days before she ran from the field, but once she was back to her old self she found it difficult to recall how she had felt then. It had been a very strange illness – if you could call it that. The invitation from Mrs Warren to stay in Blackbrook for a week, and Hanna's bubbly chatter, infected Jude with almost childish excitement.

The Warren's house in Blackbrook was very much different from the one in Motte where Jude had spent her Sunday afternoons learning to read and write. Fred's one hundred pound partnership, his aunt's advice, but mainly his hard work and likeable personality had finally provided Fred with work he enjoyed, and Mrs Warren with a house in the town. It was situated away from the main square; yet even here the fair was spilling over, with strings of little flags, notices, and graphic pictures of dancing bears and others animals which snarled and clawed out at passers-by. Look Jude! Look!

Mrs Warren greeted them warmly.

People who had known her as Molly Tarrant, the grocer's pretty daughter, said she had worn very well. And she had. From her pink, plump shoulders to the top of her curled and beribbon-capped head, she had worn very well indeed. Her eyes were the same bright colour, her nose as pert, her lips as full and her eyebrows as nicely arched. But four live children and others that might have been – if not for the hand of God, who plucked one fevered baby from its cradle, or a thick bitter concoction that plucked others from Molly before they were hardly the size of a bean – were commemorated by legs roped with veins, a belly with an ever-pregnant appearance, breasts that had begun to sag, and glands that did not always function reliably.

Considering the fifteen years of marriage and child-bearing, it was true that Molly Warren, at the age of thirty-two, did seem to have worn very well below her frilled-lace neckline and strings of beads.

Overawed in the presence of wonderful Mrs Warren's fine house and rustling dress, Hanna became her usual more serious self for a while and showed nothing of the excitement and delight that were frothing in her eight-year-old soul. She missed nothing.

"There my dears. Make yourself at home. I let Peg and the others have a little walk down to the Market Place – you wouldn't think she was fourteen, getting all excited about a drummyderry animal. Mr Warren went out to unlock the store. There been that much call for feeding stuff, unexpected, he had to go out Sunday – day-of-rest or no."

She had an easy way of speaking to everybody, learned early in childhood in the grocer's shop. She had never lost her urban Hampshire way of talking, which was tight and a bit whining: but to Hanna it was "town" and sounded much better than their slow country talk. She took it all in.

"There's room in the cupboard and there's some room in the chest of drawers. When you've put your things away, come down and we shall have some tea."

As soon as Mrs Warren had gone back downstairs, Hanna rushed to Jude and hugged her about the waist. With an explosion of withheld anticipation of pleasure, she said, "Oh Jude!"

Jude was stirred by the unusual sparkle in Hanna's eyes. The day to day routine at Croud Cantle never caused Jude or Bella to think too deeply about Hanna, except to be sure that there was nothing wrong with her. They took her to market and occasionally to Newton Clare, and she appeared to be contented, but looking down at her now, Jude remembered her own unspoken desires at the same age, when she had wanted very much to be always going to Blackbrook like Jaen. Jude was sorry that she had not thought about giving the child a few more pleasures.

[172]

Jude swung Hanna round. "We shall have the loveliest time we ever had in our lives."

"Can we see the drummyderry?"

"All right. We shall see everything. Be quick and put your things away so we don't waste any time."

Even though she was bubbling over, she was still neat and methodical in putting away her few clothes. As they were going downstairs she whispered to Jude, "What is a drummyderry?"

Mrs Warren and the young girl who lived in as general help had laid tea. Hanna's eyes widened at the sight of the pretty cups and cut-cake laid on an embroidered cloth. At Croud Cantle they "laid-up" on high-days and holy-days, but nothing that her grandmother owned was so covered with flowers and birds as the pieces on the Warren table.

There was a sudden eruption of noisy voices and Fred came in with his four children.

"Ah, they've arrived!" said Fred.

The youngest boy slapped the back of a chair with his cap.

"We was too late for the dromedary. They'd took him back to Johnson's field and Peg wouldn't let us go."

"Manners!" Fred took the cap and slapped the boy on the head with it in a friendly way. "Sam won't ever be invited to meet the king." He hit his son playfully again. "Say good afternoon to Judeth and Hanna."

Peg, Freddie and Jack each said good afternoon and Jude remarked on how grown up they all were since she had last seen them. Mrs Warren poured tea and they all ate cake as though it wasn't a treat, except Hanna, who did everything a bit behind the others. She watched them to learn how to manage cups in saucers with spoons sliding around.

They discussed whether or not there would be a chance of seeing the dromedary if they went out again. Mrs Warren said she wasn't having anybody late in for supper, so Fred said that he would go with them and have them back on time. As soon as they had finished eating, he took the five young people off, leaving Jude, whose leg was aching a bit from the ride, to give a hand to Mrs Warren and the girl.

In the kitchen, Mrs Warren exchanged her fancy cap for a plain one and covered her flouncy dress with a white coverall, and plunged straight into an explanation about why she preferred to do her own

[173]

cooking. You had to know her for a while to be able to follow her silent train of thought, which sometimes led her to answer questions that had not been put.

"It's not that I wouldn't, it's just that I've always been used to doing it my own way. (Millie, pickles.) And your mother is coming over tomorrow then? (A bigger piece than that Millie.) The children's been all very excited having you come to stay. You was always a favourite, specially with Jack. (Cut that into slices, Judeth. Saves a mess in there.) He's quiet. Don't say much."

Jude moved about under Mrs Warren's directions and very soon the tea things had been removed and a good supper laid in its place.

The rest of the evening passed quickly. In the Warren household, everybody appeared to want to say something important at the same time. The four Warren children were obviously encouraged to join in discussion, causing Fred obvious satisfaction when they expressed opinions. He drew Hanna out, prompting her to tell about the various preparations for the fair that they had seen on their walk. Life at Croud Cantle seemed gloomy when thought of in such lively surroundings.

When at last Fred said they'd all had enough treats for one day, the three boys all protested.

"There will be another day of treats tomorrow. Mrs Nugent will have her dinner with us and Will's coming for supper."

Jude went to bed with mixed feelings about the next day and stayed awake a long time, enjoying sharing a bed with the warm softness of Hanna's relaxed little body. She remembered Jaen, thinking momentarily how uncomplicated life had been then.

Mrs Warren refused any offers of help from Jude, telling her to make the most of it, there'd be plenty of work waiting when she got back to the farm and, in any case, she had help coming in. Fair week meant a lot of extra work at White's, and Fred would be busy. So Jude went out with Hanna and the Warren children, with an injunction from Mrs Warren to go into Fred's if her leg gave her the least trouble.

Jude took the children out early. The Market Square and side streets were transformed. Little booths and stalls formed a sort of parallel but ramshackle, colourful, town-within-a-town. Already people were streaming in from outlying villages, wanting to get a good day in before they had to leave in order to get back in daylight.

Already there was a constant chink of coins being handed over in exchange for knick-knacks and trinkets of design only found at fairs; for humbugs, hot-clove sweets, Emsworth oysters and cockles; for goes at three thimbles and a pea, looks at freaks and peep-shows; for futures seen by gipsies and for Fair beer – which was not much different from everyday beer, except that it was served in smaller measures at the usual prices and was drunk whilst walking about the streets – and for a potent hot drink made from rum, sugar and cream which was drunk in a hot little booth.

Bella had provided a bit of money for Hanna, but there was much to do and see without spending anything at all. She was quite content with the free entertainment and the look at the disappointing dromedary, which Jude paid for. They agreed that the dromedary depicted on the painted notices, galloping across a desert with a mysterious, robed rider, was not much like the smelly creature they had crowded into a canvas booth to see. That made Hanna open up, and as they wandered about Blackbrook she gradually lost her reserve until she was chattering and skipping about. She was particularly animated with Sam and Jack, who were nearer her age and whom she had seen once before, on the occasion of the short call at the Warren's house that had made such a lasting impression upon her.

In the middle of the morning, Jude heard Bella's voice calling. Bella was wearing her high-days and holy-days skirt – the one she had got for Jaen's wedding – and an old-fashioned but pretty jacket that Jude had not seen before. The first words Bella said were, "I had it for years and it still fits me," smoothing the waistline self-consciously, not saying that it had been packed away since the last time it was worn – at her own wedding. Hanna talked non-stop for five minutes, and they all went round everything again so that Bella could see it too, until it was time to go back to the house.

As they passed The White Horse, a large and prestigious coach-house, a well-dressed man emerged from the public rooms. He was approaching the age of fifty, wearing a coat of fine cloth which he filled well, and a hat with a buckle which suited him finely. He looked prosperous and important.

"Bella. A rare day when you takes a holiday."

"Ben Hannable. Ah well, 'tis only one day."

He had raised his hat like a gentleman and given a little nod in Jude's direction, to which she replied with a polite smile.

[175]

"You looks pretty well, Bella, and the rest of the Estovers." He patted Hanna's head.

"You looks well yourself, Ben Hannable. There must be more money in oil than vi'tles."

"Fingers in pies, Bella, fingers in many pies." His expression was smug and confident. He rearranged it to a ponderous solemnity.

"You heard about my tragedy?"

Bella said that she had not.

"Mrs Hannable. Died all of a sudden. Four months gone of a child. Only twenty. I'm surprised you hadn't a heard. It was a terrible thing to me, but I got over it."

"I'm sorry to hear it. I hadn't a heard you was even married, Ben."

"Ah, a couple a year ago. Rose Cash as was. You wouldn't a known her, come from Andover."

Jude walked on with the children and after a minute Bella caught her up.

"You wadden very polite."

"If I'd have stayed there another minute, I don't know what I should've done. His tragedy! Terrible for *him*!"

"Ah well, I dare say he was hoping for a son."

The way Bella said it. It had never entered Jude's head before. They walked in silence for a few minutes, being jostled and forced to step aside in the crowded streets.

"Should you have liked a son?"

Bella's answer came too slowly to be reassuring.

"No. Always clod-hopp'n about the place, scerfing food out of house and home. But there, they don't give you other worries, I suppose."

A street-seller with a cage of bright green birds gave a good excuse not to continue the conversation. They were back to enjoying Fair Monday.

Back at the Warren's there was a laden table to which Croud Cantle had contributed generously. Fred joined them briefly, then went off to Blackbrook again in company with the children and with Peg in charge. Mrs Warren insisted that Jude rest her leg and Bella insisted that she help in the scullery, from where Jude could hear the confidential murmur of their conversation. There was less difference in age between Jude and Mrs Warren than between Mrs Warren and Bella. There was, however, a great difference in Jude's status. She had

[176]

no personal knowledge of men and childbirth, or the changes wrought upon women's minds and bodies by both. Consequently they kept their voices confidential as, inevitably, they talked of little problems and remedies.

Mid-afternoon the three of them walked out again. At about four o'clock, Bella said that she'd had enough of Plough Fair till next year, and in any case she'd better get back to see what mess they'd made of things without her there. Before she went she gave Jude some money to buy herself something decent – "don't thank me, thank the bees and them that'll pay fourpence ha'penny a pound for combs this year." Apart from small coins, Jude had never had any money of her own. Everything they needed, except for haberdashery kind of things, Bella bartered for or did deals over.

Jude found unexpected pleasure in having the money.

Mrs Warren, Jude and Peg prepared the various dishes for supper, whilst Hanna and the servant girl fetched and carried things. Freddie, Jack and Sam went out to meet their father.

"Judeth, you must let Peg do it. She is a very genie," was the end of a thought about Jude's hair, spoken aloud.

With Bella gone, and nipped only slightly by conscience that she was pleased because of it, Jude felt that she could now begin to enjoy herself. The cheerful, easy-going atmosphere of the Warrens and the knowledge that she was taking part in Blackbrook Fair – living in its midst – gave her a strange feeling of recklessness, and she cheerfully fell in with the suggestion. Under Mrs Warren's guidance, with Hanna following every movement, Peg rolled and pinned and bound the red mass into a fashionable shape.

As with the money, Jude felt pleased at the novelty of this time-wasting. She liked the look of herself, in spite of a feeling that the pins would never hold.

"You should get yourself a dress, Judeth," Peg said.

"Yes," agreed her mother. "With the new, narrow skirt."

"That stripe we saw; the silky sapphire."

"Oh yes, she would suit that. Narrow skirt and stripes – it'd make you look a six inches taller, Judeth."

Jude laughed with pleasure at the frivolity of the conversation. "What would I want with a sapphire dress on the farm?" Bella's training. Automatic reaction to small follies and gallivanting.

"You could put it away till you get married, Jude," said Hanna.

[177]

Jude laughed, carefully because of the upward pull of her new hair. "Well then, I shall have a striped dress, though it's likely to be out of fashion by then."

"I thought you could marry Mr Vickery, Jude," said Hanna. "He's the right size for you."

Although she felt that her colour had risen, she saw from her reflection that it had not. Peg's face, however, was quite flushed, but she tried to behave naturally and unconcèrned in the face of talk about Will. Will Vickery. Her Will.

Jude with fashionable, high-dressed hair, felt poised enough to have supper with the king himself.

"A pulpit's what he ought to marry," said Mrs Warren, now receiving Peg's attentions.

"Is he a preacher?" asked Jude.

"Not in that sense, not in church. But he do go on about things. Mr Warren's quite bad enough, but when the two of they's together! I told him, it's a special treat and it's got to be a jolly supper. Singing! That kind of thing."

EXCEPT FOR the years following the Black Death, when people were scarce and physical work better valued, English employers of farm labour have always believed a good employer is one who makes the occasional enquiry about the Old Bronchitis, Nice little Ratting-terrier or Fine Litter of Pigs. No matter that it is arthritis or a whippet, it is the thought that counts. They are firm in their belief that a word from Master compensates for poor wages and bad conditions.

The employed have never thought much of that idea. But at least if His Lordship rides by and says to a gardener, "How d'e do Briggs", or, "Plucky Little Dog That, Briggs", or his gracious daughter sews a flannel shirt for the gardener's child, then the gardener is left with the impression that he is some sort of a person because His Lordship called him Briggs – even if his name was Norris.

On the other hand, should His Lordship uproot Briggs from the place and people he knows, set him down in a strange and unwelcoming place, visit the estate only on rare occasions when the fancy takes him, and cannot remember either Briggs or Norris ... then Briggs, or Norris, or Vickery for that matter, is likely to emerge from the fog of "How d'e do Briggs", and little flannel shirts and begin to realise that he has never been other than a possession to his Lordship. The fact that His Lordship does not actually own Briggs is neither here nor there. His Lordship owns ... My gardener, My fishing-rod, My harpsichord, My Head stableman.

When the Duke of Berol acquired an estate in Ireland, he removed some of his servants there and then lost interest. He was instrumental in the making of Will Vickery. Vickery senior, the Duke's head stableman, took the Duke at his word and expected a new and better life there. Instead, Vickery found that he was resented by local workers, the family were cut off from relatives and friends, and the

Duke seldom came to see the results of his employees' labour or to say How d'e do? Gradually the Vickerys were forced to see the Duke's low estimation of their worth: in proud people like the Vickerys, it rankled.

The forced exile and a festering discontent compounded by the absent and careless Duke of Berol, instilled into the five young Vickerys an awareness of what's what and a radical way of thinking. "That's never right", and, "If the law was up to me ..." were phrases greatly used by them. And for all its faults, the five children grew up knowing that England was a desirable place to live in. When Barnabas White decided that Warren needed an assistant, Mrs White – who had been a Vickery – remembered her cousin's son, who was working right up North.

Will Vickery had no striking good looks, was not much above average height or breadth and did not concern himself much with having shiny buttons and frogging on his coats. Women of all ages found him attractive. He looked them directly in the eye and paid attention to their point of view. He had been brought up in a household where five women had views about everything and would be taken seriously.

He was always a welcome visitor to the Warrens' house. Although Will was, at twenty-six, only eight years younger than Fred and six years younger than Molly, the fact that he had no partnership in business, no house, wife and family of four to provide for, made the age differences appear to be greater. Fred liked him as a fellow-radical. Molly had fallen for him in a maternal way and fed him extra slices of red meat as she did to her boys: they needed building up. Peg, at the same age as Juliet when she loved Romeo, had equally strong passions. It was pain and pleasure when she met Will; it was torture and delight to sit at table with him. It was misery to have heard his name connected, even jokingly, with Judeth's.

It was with mixed feelings that Will walked from his lodgings. He had imagined the evening over and over again. She intrigued him. He had only to catch sight of a head of red hair these days. He had not realised that there were so many. After the episode when he had seen her in Fred Warren's arms, he had argued with himself that he was reading something into it, and had begun to convince himself that the tutor stood in for the father. When he had found her on the downs, the sight of her half-dead had overwhelmed him. Then, on that day when he came upon them laughing together at the farm, all his painful doubt returned. He wanted to see her. He didn't want to see her. He wanted to see her again in Fred Warren's company, but not if his doubts were confirmed.

The Warrens were still unused to their new affluence, and tended to be lavish and extravagant, so that to be entertained to a meal by them was to sit at a laden table and be plied with delicacies by Molly and wine by Fred. Fred had never shaken off the influence of the boarding school, and Molly was still a grocer's daughter: they had dinner at dinner-time and supper at supper-time and they mixed with people who were like them. Dinner was in the middle of the day, supper was in the evening.

No matter in what kind of a bad mood one might be before sitting at supper with them, it was sure to be driven off soon by their very affability and generosity.

Apart from Will, there was Mrs Gardine (an old friend of Mrs Warren) and her husband, and Mr and Mrs Carter, who lived in the next house to the Warrens, with their son James: a total of fourteen to supper.

As the evening went by, impressions crowded upon Jude. There were a few late roses, a bowl of polished apples and a branch of candles. Everything seemed red and warm. The wine, the apples, the roses, the heavy curtains; even the white walls flickered pinkly. The three married women wore dresses of pretty colours, embroidered and flounced, with either ribbons or feathers in their complicated hair. They made good wine at Croud Cantle, but it never achieved the headiness of that at Fred's table, neither was it served in glasses with stems. The lightness of spirit she felt earlier increased. She found it easy to talk.

Mrs Gardine and Mrs Carter knew her, of course, as the market-girl who came to stand on the market outside the Star. They couldn't get over how she joined in the conversation. If it wasn't for her hands and her brown face, you couldn't a told she was a farm girl.

Will was seated opposite Jude. Each tried to catch a look at the other unawares, so inevitably they were constantly catching one another's eye and not quite knowing what to do when it happened. He did not know what to make of her. She appeared to be all contradictions. Her hands holding the delicate glass had rough skin and nails. She moved them constantly, as though speaking a second language. In contrast to the other women she was poorly dressed. She

[181]

had talked with enthusiasm about the possibility of buying a new dress, yet never felt obliged to apologise for her present work-a-day clothes. And she had her hair more strikingly arranged than any of the other women. His work took him to farms every day; he saw farm-girls every day, many prettier than she was, but he had never seen one so ... He only realised that he had been staring at her when she spoke to him. "This will be your first Plough Fair then, Mr Vickery?"

"It is. I've always worked in the North since I came from Ireland."

"Do they have big fairs like this, that goes on for a week?"

"There's Goss Fair in Nottingham."

She asked him about it; he told her about it being a goose fair; then she asked him what went on and he told her – both of them being drawn into a short conversation quite separately from the rest of the table.

When Will arrived at the Warrens' house his affable manner hid an unconscious anger, at Judeth, Fred and at himself. Every time he stole a look at her he found that she was looking at him, and he could not decide whether she was artless or wanton. Then, over the short conversation about fairs, he discovered that he did not care. If she was on over-familiar terms with his superior, then she was! If she was not the near-perfect woman he had idealised, then she wasn't! All he did care about was that he wanted to know her better.

As they talked, Judeth lost the embarrassment she had felt about him ever since Fred had shown her the true identity of Lady Geraldine's ideal lover. Why should she feel embarrassed to have written Will Vickery into her story? Most likely he would be an ideal lover. She was not even surprised at herself having such a thought.

"Well, I've been to Fair Monday, but never been for the whole of Fair Week. Perhaps we should see some of it together."

She said it as naïvely as Hanna would have. Surely, Will's subconscious concluded, it's impossible that she's the kind of woman I've been thinking? She would have used more guile; would have worked the conversation round so that I would make the suggestion. I've been wrong.

After the meal, they all sat around like a country family at ease. Fred sang, Mrs Gardine told a long tragic poem and Sam played a tin whistle he had bought at the fair. Nobody minded that it was tuneless tooting, there was an infectious merriment in the room. Nobody wanted to make a move to break up the party, but Hanna and Sam kept falling asleep, so when Fred suggested that they all go together next evening and walk about the fair after dark, everybody was pleased to go home with the prospect of the same good company the next evening.

Hanna, full of pleasures and food, was asleep as soon as she got into bed. It was Peg's room that Judeth and Hanna were using, whilst Peg slept in a tiny attic above. The attic was virtually part of the bedroom and had no door, and for a long time Judeth heard no steady breathing to show that the young girl was asleep. There is always a readiness to say about a youthful passion, "You will get over it", but until it is got over it is quite as painful as a mature emotion. There was nothing Judeth could do: she was the last person Peg would want to confide in.

The habit of writing for at least an hour every night made it difficult for Judeth to go to sleep otherwise. She lay with Hanna breathing deeply beside her. The night was full of strange sound. There were always noises at home: the tree branch that rubbed the roof; mice; the wild animals and the domestic ones; squeaking, lowing, grunting; Bella's snore coming through the thin partition. There were animal noises here: horses and other strange ones – the dromedary perhaps; mice here, too; Fred's rumbling voice and the edge of Mrs Warren's Blackbrook whine; strangest of all to Judeth was to hear voices coming from outside the house. It had never occurred to her that people were ever out in the streets this late at night.

Judeth put her arm around Hanna and felt a fierce burst of love and compassion for her. She had watched her off and on all day, as the gaudy booths and flags and gew-gaws and useless trinkets and the calls, drums and tin whistles had worked trumpery magic on the children. Vitality. Excitation. As Judeth herself had experienced with the cheerful Warrens and their cheerful friends. She felt a pang at the thought of taking her back to the milking, churning, fetching and carrying; to the uneventful evenings and days where her only youthful companion was the reticent Johnny-twoey.

Apart from that, she lay awake feeling pleased with life. She wanted other people to be pleased also, but reality intruded. Whilst she had a week of pleasure, somebody else was doing her work. Judeth's very existence had been brought about by a past distress for Bella. The source of Judeth's pleasure was the cause of Peg's unhappiness, and the reason that Judeth and Bella could have Hanna

[183]

was because Jaen could not. Pleasure was never unadulterated. Not for somebody like Judeth, whose conscience was primed by Bella at an early age: It's all right for some!

Jaen.

It had been on another such few days of visiting, in Rathley, that Jaen had met Dan Hazelhurst.

Jaen at Rathley.

Judeth closed her mind. There were things there; long-buried, unhealed. It would not stay closed. Jaen had gone to Rathley. The flicker of an image ... the little bantam that Judeth was always saving from the great, aggressive cock with his jerky head and bright, fleshy wattles as he followed the little brown bird about: she taking little runs, fluttering, scrambling from his attentions.

Younger than Jude was now – Jaen. She had escaped briefly the uneventful evenings at Croud Cantle, where she was not even able to lose herself on Crusoe's island or Gulliver's problems.

Jaen, relieved for a few days from the milking and churning, the field-mud and the barn-mire; from the damp chill of the dairy, from their mother's queer ideas about dust motes; and scrubbing red tiles, and obsessiveness about taking water from the deep well. There hadn't seemed anything odd about that, living on top of it, but away from it ... Their mother was strange. She did not mix with Cantle people, or they did not mix with her.

Jaen. Perhaps it had been flowers and polished apples. People. People laughing. People who sometimes let themselves go. A room that was red and warm, with more flickering flames than were necessary to light it. Perhaps Dan Hazelhurst had sat across the table and Jaen had felt a pang at having to return to the isolated life at Croud Cantle.

But history would not repeat itself. She had a vague recollection of being with her mother, talking about Jaen. It must have been soon after Jaen got married; they had hardly ever talked very deep about her since. Jude thinking, I won't never do anything like that and make Mother unhappy. Yet, wasn't it Mother's fault? If she hadn't always been so sharp. If she had only sometimes given them a bit of a hug or something, or let you put your arms round her. She never did. Jude had a picture – perhaps just a feeling deep in her mind: she was very little, trying to climb on to the wide expanse of her mother's apron ... Bella's firm grip on Jude's elbows as she was firmly planted back on the floor ... damp, cold, red tiles.

Slowly Jude drifted up to a point where she looked down. Occasionally when she was on Tradden or Old Marl she had experienced a kind of remoteness, as though what went on below was not to do with her. At this distance from the farm and her mother, with the draw-string loosened, she felt very remote.

What would it have been like if their father ..? But Croud Cantle without her mother in charge was unimaginable. The Tomas Nugent she saw in her mind's eye was young, beautiful, in a blue coat. He did not fit the real world of the mire of the yard. She could not picture him prising vegetables from frozen clamps, or bending his back in the field with scythe or sickle, working, rivulets of sweat running clean through his dirt. Would there have been more warmth with him there? Had he run away from the cold of the farm? Had he been the cause of it? Had it descended upon their mother, or had she brought it with her? On the rare occasions when she let herself go – at the reaping, this very morning when they had gone round Blackbrook, Bella in the pretty, old-fashioned jacket – it was as though the strings that held her upright when she was on the farm, stumping about, straight-backed and square-shouldered ... it was as though the tension on her strings slackened and she became rounded, soft and bending.

Judeth heard the abbey clock strike three o'clock. Peg was asleep now with deep, regular breathing; Hanna jumped from time to time. As Judeth drifted into sleep she was not actively thinking of the prospect of the next day or of meeting Will Vickery again. He was there, though, complicating her thoughts. Her thoughts had led her to the point of seeing clearly the effect that Tomas Nugent's nature had had upon their lives. Mother, Jaen, herself, Mrs Trowell, Hanna – and the blacks he had traded in. He had only been about Will Vickery's age.

Although Molly Warren took life very much as it came, she had not much enjoyed the years when they had lived in Motte. Now that she was back in the place where she had grown up, she was content.

On the Tuesday morning, Mrs Warren took her visitor about the town.

"Peg will take the children and we shall go about like sisters. You will call me Molly."

Jude felt frivolous and self-indulgent and needed little persuading to dip into the money Bella had given her. Molly Warren seemed to know everybody in Blackbrook. Although Jude knew people from the years of standing on the market, Molly belonged. She had been born and bred there, the grocer's daughter, part of the class of small trade – I'll scratch your back, you scratch mine was their philosophy. Molly had no difficulty in buying the sapphire stripe cheaply, or in getting a promise of having it made up quickly.

It was during Fair Week that thrifty housewives bought their cotton, pins, needles and buttons in quantity for the next year. Jude was caught up in the pleasure of handing over coins and receiving little packages. She laughed each time she said, "I don't know what I'm going to do with it," but still went on buying bits and pieces of frippery and ornament and went back to Molly's house feeling quite intoxicated with her rashness.

Later, many of the party of the previous evening met to take their walk round the Fair together. Hanna and the boys, having spent hours wandering about, knew every interesting and exciting stall and constantly insisted that they look at this or come and see that. Peg walked sedately apart from them, until James – who had hitherto suffered in her eyes from being too young and living next door, but was now aided by a fashionable coat and hat with gold braid – began to be a bearable companion. Will walked with Molly and Jude, and Fred with his neighbours.

The voices inside Will were unquiet, conflicting. An angel in one ear insisted that he walk beside Mrs Warren and Jude and be pleasant to his employer's wife, making casual conversation; a devil in the other bawled at him. His hands wanted to listen to the devil; to feel the texture of wild, red hair and the shape of waist, breasts and shoulders.

His experience of girls had been frivolous and playful on his part, and his experience of women had been erratic and flirtatious. He had never been serious for much longer than it took to persuade them to respond. The loud voice in him said that Jude was very different.

Her enigma was the combination of reserve and quiet exuberance, naïvety and knowledge. For Will Vickery there was also the excitement of the farm-girl whose fingers could equally well manage the teats of a goat or the shaft of a pen – milk and ink; the girl who could read the signs of potato blight and read Dean Swift. He had the strange notion that she was a blank page on which the most profound knowledge had been written. He was sure now that his first impression

had not failed him – she was a near-perfect woman. He was beginning
to love her. Sacred-profane. Spiritual-carnal.

Jude's emotions were not like his. She was excited by his presence
and would have been glad to have been walking about only with him.
There was something open about him; almost as though his past,
present and future were written in his look. He was no enigma. Her
feelings for him were those of Lady Geraldine, who had wanted
a wholesome man – compassionate, to be sure; intelligent and
non-conformist; a man out of the usual – but above all wholesome,
smelling of grain.

The week seemed both endless and fleeting. The Thursday was the
day when the Blackbrook market-day and the Fair combined.

They had arranged that Bella would come as usual, would sleep at
the Warren's and go home the next day with Jude and Hanna. It
needed a great amount of organisation and orders for the farm to be
left in the care of Dicken, Johnny-twoey and the hired labour. Dicken
didn't know what had come over the Master, traipsing off up
Blackbrook twice in one single week, and wondered if there wasn't
summat up, what with Miss Jude gone and all that. There'd been a lot
of traipsing off like that before Mrs Hazelhurst had got herself wed.

The dress was ready on Wednesday evening. The dressmaker
brought it in a large wicker basket. Jude, with Hanna taking in every
inch of the sapphire stripe, had to stand on a stool in the little sitting
room whilst the dressmaker made adjustments upon the advice of Mrs
Warren. Peg, now that she had discovered that they had all
unconsciously been living next door to an exceptional young man
who found her charming, was happy to watch. Apart from the
removal of a bow which they all said wasn't Jude, the dress fitted well.
Peg did up the red hair in a simple bandeau style. Jude was
experiencing sensuous fabric against her skin for the first time.

As she viewed herself in Mrs Warren's mirror she said several
times, "I never dare be seen in it," but not meaning it, and, "I don't
dare think what Mother's going to say," but not caring. She knew that
she was outwardly transformed and that when she walked she would
be inwardly transformed also. "I could nearly pass for a lady if it
wasn't for my hands." She was sure that Fred still thought of her as the
child who wanted to learn to read, and thought that he would be
astounded at the woman in the latest fashion. But most of all she
wanted to astound Will Vickery. As she sat before the mirror she

gazed inwardly at Will Vickery standing behind her, his hands tracing the line of the stripes over her waist and hips.

"Look at her, she's miles away." They laughed good-naturedly at her momentary confusion.

"I was just wondering when I shall ever be able to wear it after today."

Next day was the usual market day. It was raining; the first of the cold rains that brought down whatever remained of the scarlet and gold autumn to trample it into winter mire. Jude set out early for their usual place outside the Star to wait for Bella, but it was the best part of an hour before she arrived, leading the laden mules.

"Trust everything to go wrong at the same time," was her greeting.

As they unpacked and set out their produce under a little awning to keep the rain off, Bella went on and on about the things that had gone wrong: the unreliability of the casual women, the hens, and this rain, and winter was setting in and that was the end of using the short-cut because the Dunnock was up, and all that drag over Winchester Hill. She was sullen and terse. In no time at all she had pulled Jude down from the high plain of enjoyment she had been on.

On Monday her mother had been a different woman as she had walked about in her pretty jacket with Mrs Warren, relaxed and almost smiling. Jude had expected to see her like that today. Instead she was in the trough of one of her moods and made Jude feel guilty about her few days of idleness and pleasure.

It was unfair. It was Mother who had persuaded her to go. Jude had said right at the beginning about all the work. Mother had said she would keep the casual workers on. It wasn't her fault that they weren't reliable. It wasn't her fault that the Dunnock was rising, as it did every October. The women were probably all right anyway. It was just Mother – never satisfied with people's best. She probably went poking around as she always did, instead of leaving people to get on with things.

Why had she said they should come to Fair Week if it was going to be like this? Why had she given Jude money to spend if it had to be paid for by being made to feel guilty?

Jude had looked forward to telling her mother about the trumpery things, the bits and pieces of little use and value she had bought this week. She wanted to introduce Will Vickery's name into their conversation. And the dress. She had looked forward to putting it on to surprise Bella, but she knew how it would be received by her in this mood. The sideways glance from head to toe would say, "It's all right for you, my girl. Some of us had to work hard while you was traipsing around." She could not bear the thought. Neither could she mention Will Vickery's name and allow her the opportunity of taking the light out of it.

Bella dreaded these moods descending upon her out of the blue. When they came, she hated herself. She knew what she was doing and could not stop it. One day she would go to bed feeling normal, then wake up the next day looking out through a black curtain, with a great lump of anger, bitterness and misery in her.

Nobody understood. People went on leading their easy lives: no responsibilities, taking her for granted, laughing and joking. She ached to tell somebody, yet it was the last thing she could bring herself to do. It was weak. People would show pity. That was about the worst thing that could happen to Bella, being pitied.

She wished that she had been able to say to Jude, "Don't take no notice of me, I feel that rotten today." When Jude would have said, "That's all right. Why don't you go on round to Mrs Warren's and have a talk to her? It'll cheer you up?" And Molly Warren might have said something jolly and the black curtain might have lifted. If only ... But the darker her mood, the heavier and more bitter the lump, the less able she was to say anything except what hurt other people.

Bella knew that Jude was expecting her to ask what she had been doing, how her leg had been, and had Hanna been enjoying herself, but she could not bring herself to do it.

In the middle of the morning Molly Warren and the children came to see them. Hanna chattered away, tumbling out everything she had seen and done. Bella arranged her mouth into a tight smile for the child.

"Well, you have got a lot to say for yourself," was as enthusiastic a response as she could manage.

"Shall you come to the house?" Molly Warren asked.

"Thank you, no. The river was coming up, so I dare say I shall have to trail back over Winchester Hill."

"Perhaps I had better come home today," Jude said.

"Oh not today, Jude!" said Hanna. "Mrs Warren is going to have a party. We never had a party."

Bella fed her resentment. "No, you stay. I shall be all right. You stay

[189]

and have your party ... " the unspoken end of the sentence implicit. "You go on and enjoy yourselves while I'm dragging back to the farm."

Jude flushed with anger. They were being punished for enjoying themselves. Why was she like that! Why did she get like this with people? Why couldn't she be a bit more bending like Mrs Warren was? This time Jude was not going to be intimidated. Usually Jude was placating, allowing her mother to take her mood out on her. And it did no good. She wasn't going to start on Hanna too. So she said in a falsely pleasant voice, "Well, that's nice. We shall have the party and go home Saturday then, like we said."

They had not really settled when they would go home, but Jude settled it then and there.

Molly Warren sensed the tension between Judeth and her mother and did not stop long. She asked if Bella was sure she wouldn't come in for a bit of something, but Bella refused.

For the rest of the morning Bella and Jude spoke only when necessary. Bella was nonplussed by Jude; Jude was determined not to climb down. They packed the panniers.

"There," said Jude, "I've packed it so you can ride home."

Bella's immediate response was to reject any easement. She needed to foster her resentment, but Jude was out-flanking her. It would have suited her to let Jude watch her having to walk, but she had no excuse.

"You a be back on Saturday then?" Bella said tersely.

The first-time stand that she was making against her mother's intimidation gave Jude a feeling of elation. She felt powerful standing up to the black mood. She would not give in.

"I expect so, Mother. It's a shame you won't come back to Mrs Warren's, but there, if you want to get on back home ... " Jude planted the suggestion that Bella preferred to go back home without visiting, that Bella was doing what she wanted to do.

The rain that had started that morning set in. People still came in from the rural areas. Many travelled on foot, trudging clayey tracks and slithery raikes to have a look at the old fair. It was often the only time they left their hamlets and villages. They wondered why they couldn't hold Plough Fair in May, like Wickham, or July, like Portsmouth. The weather was always treacherous at this time of year. For some, the rain decided them. They were too old for that sort a jaunt any more, and anyway it wasn't like when they was young, you never saw a good cock-fight these days, and the dogs seem half-afraid to have a go at the bull, and bears wasn't half the fun they used to be years ago.

Young people didn't seem to mind. After all, you had to work in the rain so you might as well enjoy yourself in it, and Plough Fair only comes once a year, and who knows what next year might bring? For a good many the answer came in less than a year – the weeks just before harvest always brought its crop of Plough Fair Babies.

When Jude got back to the Warren's, Mrs Warren had everybody getting on with a good bake-up. Used to the Croud Cantle evenings of pie-making for market, Hanna got cheek-burning praise from Mrs Warren and the two women who had been hired for the day.

"Just look at that. Neat and pretty as you please. You a have to teach Peg to crimp pastry neat as that."

"Look, Jude," Hanna said, all excited. "It's for the party."

Molly insisted that Jude have a bit of a rest of her leg, seeing as she'd been on it since early. Jude sat in the hot, busy kitchen, where the boys were put to take turns at the spit and keep the fire in, and the women and girls prepared the very substantial courses that any grocer's daughter considered necessary for a party. None of the fidgety little bits of more elegant society, but heavily encased game pies, huge roasts, meats – cold-cut, jellied and pressed – and a whole poached salmon.

The kitchen, scullery and pantry were filled with people, talk and movement. Lamps had been lit and it was warm, in contrast to the wintery October weather that had pushed its way into a late September afternoon. An image of Bella and the pack-horses going over Winchester Hill came briefly into Jude's mind, but she had made up her mind. She had been thinking about her mother and had come to the conclusion that there was something in her that drove her to choose the hardest path. It was as though she was punishing herself for something. Jude had intuition enough to suspect that if she was not careful she would become like her.

She put the image of Bella firmly from her mind and threw herself into the pleasure of preparing for a party. She began by saying that she would start on the making of a special punch that she had heard of and recorded in her journal for posterity. Freddie said they should call it Posterity Punch, then they all joined in, topping one another with witticisms, childish and hilarious.

[191]

Fred came home. With the help of the boys, he moved furniture from place to place, until they had made a space for games and dancing, room to lay up the supper and somewhere for people to have a game of cribbage or hand of cards.

He had been really pleased to see Judeth open up this week, and little Hanna jumping about as an eight-year-old ought to. There had been times during the week when he found his eyes fixed upon the curve of Judeth's cheek or the rise and fall of her breast, but as soon as he caught himself he pulled his mind away, aware that it could only spoil the fineness of their relationship as well as the intimacy that had grown up between Molly and the girl. Fred was glad of that. There had been a time in their flirtatious youth when Fred had called her Jolly Molly – it summed her up, even in her matronly thirties. She was what a solitary, intelligent girl like Judeth needed to bring her out of herself.

He was glad, too, that she and Will appeared to be interested in one another. Somebody like Will was exactly what Judeth needed to allow her to develop, to encourage her to reach out. Perhaps she would be able to make something of the writing. More and more women's names were appearing on book spines. It was true that none of them, as far as he knew, was a farm-girl whose only education was gained from the junior in a grain-merchant partnership, and from whatever books came into her hands, but that did not mean that they had any more ability than a girl like Judeth.

All of Fred's idealism – the liberty, equality, fraternity call that was in him – was, in a way, invested in Jude. Quite apart from the fact that she was a woman, she had everything else set against her chances of succeeding: her station in life, her isolation, her lack of contact with like minds and the hard labour she was committed to. In a way she was his hope for the future.

Once or twice in recent years it had occurred to him to wonder what would happen to the little farm in a few years' time. Mrs Nugent was not the woman she had been when he first arrived in Blackbrook, and she and the elder girl had stood on the market. It was difficult to tell with a woman who drove herself as she did, but she must be quite elderly now – well past forty. He had a picture of her: the hair that was always escaping from her cap had a lot of white in it; her cheeks were sunken from loss of many teeth; her uprightness was more stiff than held erect. Probably her expectations were that Judeth would marry an estate worker or some farming son, as the elder daughter had done. Then she would hand over the place to them whilst still holding the reins. What would happen if Will came into the picture? Fred did not see him in any kind of role such as farmer or horticulturist and market trader.

When they had done as much as possible on the Thursday, they all settled in the kitchen, ate a made-do supper, talked about favourite jigs and dances the fiddler must play, and wrote lists of what they must remember to do the next day. It was to be a big entertainment with at least twenty invited friends and neighbours. From Jude's seemingly endless money she had bought something for the party for each of them. Only trumpery from the fair stalls, it is true, but delightful to each recipient as they opened the packages containing black neck ribbons and waist-fobs for Fred and the boys, painted handkerchiefs with the words "Plough Fair" amidst the flowers and birds for Mrs Warren and Peg, and a beribboned and embroidered apron and a pair of red silky slippers for Hanna.

Jude enjoyed every moment of the new experience of pleasure in choosing, buying and giving. "If only" ... the two words that so often prefaced thoughts of her mother. If only Mother could have allowed herself that experience instead of awkwardly thrusting the coins upon Jude, saying, "Don't thank me, thank them that'll pay fourpence ha'penny a pound for combs this year."

Their money was hard earned, no one would deny that. It was thumped with chilblained hands from churns; boiled from pans of scalding syrup; expressed from cows in ankle-deep mire; dug from frozen ground; gathered a few ha'pence at a time on Blackbrook Market. It was a representation of their collective labour and a means of keeping body and soul together, but it was also a means of rising above that. People needed to be frivolous sometimes. Keeping body and soul together meant more than sustenance.

Until now, Jude had not thought about money. But with the new experiences, and getting away from Croud Cantle, she realised its potential for freedom.

THE PREPARATIONS went on all Friday morning. When everything was ready the women went round the house with satisfaction.

By Croud Cantle standards the house was large and luxurious. There were separate rooms for sitting, receiving visitors and for eating, as well as the kitchen and scullery in the basement. The furnishing of it reflected the happy childhood of Molly Tarrant, who had been brought up in the back of the grocery shop where every bit of floor-space, every wall and every shelf was filled. Some of the younger members of her stratum of Blackbrook society had started going in for alcoves displaying nothing except a single vase in the new Wedgwood; left elegant space between elegant chairs in order to show off neat chequered carpets, and talked of "style".

"Why, it looks as though they had the bum-bailiffs in. They might as well live on Salisbury Plain if they don't want no more comfort than that!" was her comment upon them. Jude would have agreed with those sentiments. She enjoyed being surrounded by floral patterns, braid trimmings, velvety textures and little ornaments and knick-knacks on mantelpieces and every other flat surface. Apart from the space that Fred had cleared for anybody who wanted to jig to the fiddler, the whole of the ground floor was crammed. The room that was known as Mrs Warren's little room held the arrangements for cribbage players. On the other side of the passage the supper was laid up.

"It seems a shame to eat it," said Jude. "I should like to take it home, just as it is, so that I could look at it – like a picture."

She said it lightly, but it was an expression of what she felt about going back home. She wanted to take with her something of the essence of the Warren household: chatter, frippery, the clutter of Molly's furnishings and Fred's books and papers.

[194]

The female members of the household went upstairs to wash and change. Mrs Warren had engaged a hairdresser to call early so that she could put on her new turban head-dress long before necessary.

"If you leave things like that till there's people all around you and you have to be concentrating on them, you forget you're wearing something new and you don't get the full pleasure."

,She offered the hairdresser to Jude, who declined, saying that if Peg did not mind then she would prefer her to do it. So Peg was allowed to have Jude's share of the hairdresser's attentions, and finished up heavy with pleasure and pinned-on curls, frizz and ribbon. Mrs Warren then called Fred to be attended to.

"He's always had this notion about a wig bringing him out in a rash," Mrs Warren confided. "Well, I have to admit he do get this on his neck when he wears one, but this man has got Fred made a nice toupee of real hair which can't surely bring him out in spots? He is very careless of how he looks about the head. I don't hold out no hope of him if he hears how men of fashion in London and places is going back to wearing their own hair."

The hairdresser agreed. If it became the fashion for people to wear their own hair, how would anyone tell a gentleman from a cowman? Why, the next thing you knew linen smocks would be in fashion, and skills such as his own would be lost in a generation and they would all be starving in the streets. So Fred was shaved, bewigged and powdered in the latest Blackbrook fashion.

They were waiting, dressed, powdered and perfumed, for the first guests to arrive.

"Do you know what occurs to me?" said Fred. "We are waiting to go on stage, like players."

"You say some queer things sometimes, Fred," said Mrs Warren.

"I can see what he means," said Jude. "There's going to be a play here tonight. We are actors waiting to go on and the other players are just putting on their costumes."

"That's a nice idea, now you put it like that," said Mrs Warren.

"I hope it won't be a dreary play," said Freddie, suspicious of any gathering in which he was expected to attend to neighbours and other boring old people.

"How can it be dreary with all this?" Hanna indicated generally the splendour of their surroundings.

"What shall the play be called then?" said Mrs Warren.

"The Jolly Rabbits," said Jack, whose schoolboy humour was understood only by Sam until he explained the "warren" connection.

"I would call it, 'Lady Geraldine's Grand Party'," suggested Hanna.

The play started with the arrival of the Gardines, Carters and James, the guests of the Monday supper. Mrs Gardine and Mrs Carter – in confidence with one another quite amazed at what you could do with a market girl if you put her in silk and saw to her hair – complimented Jude on how pretty she looked.

"See, Mr Carter," said his wife, "this is the sapphire stripe I told you was coming in – and this straight style."

Mr Carter said it looked very well, but he was more a man for old-fashioned things, which was evident from his untied physical wig of a style that had been in fashion when he was a young man.

Jude sat beside him in the little card room, talking as though she had known him longer than the four hours of Monday. Hanna was listening, watching, not wanting to miss anything, wanting to be everywhere at once. He was a genial little man of sixty or so, who said he liked nothing better than a game of cribbage and a good old-fashioned supper of the sort provided by Mrs Warren. "None of your little glasses of ice-mush that's put out at supper these days, but an honest pudding. It's a great pity fermity has gone out. We was brought up on fermity." He gnashed his teeth at Jude. "Fermity grows you good teeth!" If his own unusually full jaw was anything to judge by then, if it did not grow teeth, it kept them in the gums.

"Fermity hasn't gone out with us," said Jude. "We never have nothing else in the mornings, do we Hanna?"

"Show us your teeth, Missie."

Hanna did as she was bid.

Holding Hanna's jaw, Mr Carter leaned over in his wife's direction.

"Look at this. Good fermity teeth!"

Mr Carter was one of those people who, in company, do not converse very much – unless they find a companion who starts them off on a subject dear to their heart. They will then talk constantly, and of nothing else. Having met a young woman who was the living, breathing confirmation of his belief in fermity, he did nothing but extol her virtues and her teeth.

Whilst Jude was entertaining Mr Carter, she saw Will in the

passageway. She marvelled that she had been so unobservant as to scarcely notice his looks the first time he came to Croud Cantle. Nobody would, have said he was handsome, and if each feature were to be described individually without seeing the face – a tilted nose; full, bowed lips; wide eyes – one might have been forgiven for believing these were the features of someone as effete as Harry Goodenstone. But he was indeed a man, head and foot, and with no doubt about any part between.

Will came to where Jude was sitting and immediately Mr Carter talked to him about teeth and fermity.

"It would be in the interests of Barnabas White, if you was to try and bring back good fermity breakfasts to people in towns. He's a grain dealer. It'd increase his sale of wheat no end and he'd not even have to take it to mill." He offered Jude's teeth to Will as proof of his point, and Will took the opportunity to hold Jude's chin between thumb and finger and look with merriment, not into her mouth but into her eyes. And Jude did not lower them.

The house was soon filled with many of the trading people of Blackbrook. For the most part they were still close enough to their origins not to have too many airs and graces, yet had sufficient income to have no worry about where the next meal was coming from, with something over to buy their wives and daughters fur for muffs and tippets.

Not knowing how to play at cards – and not understanding why anyone should like to when there were people to talk to – Jude moved about the other rooms and passages. Earlier, Molly had said: "It will be such a treat to have you and Peg to help at seeing they'm all comfortable. There's mostly Blackbrook people as know you already that's coming. I can't wait to see some of their faces." Molly had felt it a great achievement to get Jude into the sapphire stripe and take up her hair. It went as much against Molly's grain to have an undecorated person as to have an undecorated wall or side-table, and now that Jude was less plainly got up Molly claimed her, displaying her and looking for compliments.

"What do you think of our dress then, Kathleen?"

"Why, Molly, you've done wonders. I shouldn't ha' known you ... "

Here the compliment tended to trail off – how should they address Jude? Most Blackbrook people knew who she was, had known her since she was a little thing standing with Bella Nugent outside the Star. She was the pie-girl, the butter-girl, the cheese seller, but not a shop-keeper, not one of them. Yet here she was visiting with the Warrens, and on first-name terms. And the Warrens, you couldn't deny, were higher even than Alfred Herbert the draper, who had put up his name in gold letters above his shop and who never soiled his hands these days with dimity or bombazine. Could you call her Miss Nugent, when you knew who she really was – even though Bella Nugent was reckoned to have a long stocking with gold coin in the toe from her deals with the honey merchant. Or should you use her first name? But first names were strictly for close acquaintances and servants.

Jude was quite unaware of the terrible quandary that the shop-keepers (who planned for their children to take a step up the ladder) were in. Like everyone else, she was born with the knowledge that one's betters must have curtseys bobbed to them, have forelocks tugged, be allowed free passage, and that kind of thing. What Jude did not know was how many betters there were these days or the trouble they had with protocol. Throughout history it had been simple: you followed the example of the Church. There were those to whom God had given the right to communicate directly from the privacy of their own private chapel or pew – and everyone else. Now, however, society was beginning to create for itself a complicated classification system in which any grocer who changed his shirt on Sundays might pay for the privilege of having himself partitioned off from his inferiors when praying.

Blackbrook traders and their wives were constantly having to weigh respectability against money; acceptable trades against the dresses and houses they provided. It was difficult having to decide whether an apothecary was higher or lower than a surgeon; whether the grain fortune of Barnabas White was to be preferred to the elliman money of Ben Hannable; or where a pie-girl – who you might not tell from one of themselves if it wasn't for her hands – fitted in.

Solving their problem, she said, "Call me Judeth, if you like."

"Well, she seems a nice enough girl," was the general opinion.

Mrs Hart, though, born a bailiff's daughter and married to a well-off lawyer, considered herself to be of some quality in Blackbrook society, and thought it a mighty dangerous thing to raise country people up, and girls especially. She knew 'em!

Mrs Carter agreed. "She can read and write you know."

This information made Mrs Hart even more concerned. "I never found a need for it, and you won't find a better run home than mine. You'll agree that, Mary?"

Mrs Carter agreed, extolled the running of her own home and added that any woman that did her job properly shouldn't have time for anything of that sort.

"I should a thought there was enough to do on a farm without a man, as it is, and it don't hardly seem like what I know of that mother of hers to agree to such a useless thing in a girl."

But as Molly Warren had given the information not only that the pie-girl could read and write, but that it was her husband, Barnabas White's junior partner, who had taught the girl, they had to agree that you never knew what people would do and that Bella Nugent could find herself having trouble with that girl.

Jude was quite ignorant of any interest in her as Molly drew her into the circle.

Jude had danced on many a Mayday and at harvest supper but to have a fiddler in the house was a great novelty. She would have loved to dance, but her leg was still not fully recovered, so she had to watch when all the young people danced their elders off their feet, enjoying themselves a great deal more than they would when they achieved the higher social position they expected. Will danced himself breathless with Hanna as partner, who giggled and laughed with pleasure. Peg, whose heart appeared fully mended, linked arms and twirled with young James Carter.

Jude and Will were constantly caught in one another's eye, and often found themselves standing or sitting close. Time had the quality of being both slow and rapid. Each would make a dozen new discoveries about the other only to find that a mere ten minutes had passed: then suddenly the party was finished. Will's warm, dry hand held Jude's quite long in taking his leave.

"I have to be in Cantle before quite soon," he said.

"Well, then, I hope you won't miss calling on us."

Between these two lines of farewell and the eye-holding they made other promises to each other.

Only the thought that Will Vickery would come there made the return home bearable. She had done the journey between Blackbrook market and Cantle scores of times, feeling content that she was

[199]

returning to the security of the farm and her protectors, the chalk-hills. Yet this seemed to be a going-away rather than a return journey.

They started for Cantle early and were waved off with promises of other visits very soon. Fred had a call to make in Motte, so rode with them: he upon his heavy horse, Jude and Hanna upon the donkeys. The day was dry and the cloud-layer was a grey slab. They agreed that after the rain the lower track was likely to be impassable, so after leaving Blackbrook they took the southern road which eventually branched. One part became the track over the crest of Winchester Hill. Saturday was the last day of Fair Week and people were streaming into Blackbrook. Boots, hoofs and wheels churned up the rain-moist surfaces. It reminded travellers of the winter quagmire that lay ahead, especially along the stretches of road where landowners did not fulfil their obligation to put down stone or hoggin, making life for carters, coachmen and people who earned their living like Bella Nugent doubly hard.

Jude had expected that Hanna would have been as reluctant to leave as she was herself, but she appeared to be quite happy.

"It wasn't too bad after all, was it?" said Fred.

Jude pulled her brows together, realising that he was joking her, but not quite sure about what.

"Giving yourself time off."

"It has spoilt me for a quiet life. I shall want a party every week and visitors every day."

"I think you will have one caller quite frequently." He raised his eyebrows at her.

"You mean Mr Vickery?" said Hanna. "He said he was coming."

"I do mean Mr Vickery. He's got a good many calls to make on the Berol estates, so he will be going close by Cantle."

"I hope he does then," said Hanna. "He is nice. He is nice, isn't he Jude?"

Jude had to agree that Mr Vickery was nice.

THEY LEFT FRED in Motte, went on up Winchester Hill and down past Bell Tump. It was only a matter of weeks since Jude had sat there with Mrs Trowell, yet it seemed almost as though most of her life had been lived since then – everything crammed into that short space of time. All the experiences: the terrible harvest day; the weeks of convalescence; the attempt at writing; Harry Goodenstone's strange visit.

Then the whole crush of experience in a week. Living surrounded by comfort and pleasure, being in rooms full of people and holding conversations with more than one person at a time.

There were, too, the conflicting emotions stirred by her mother's grim leave-taking; the new physical awareness of herself. The same old desire to touch and be touched, to hold and be held, to have contact with another human being – as with the warm, dry handshake of Will Vickery. As she half-listened to Hanna her mind was on fire. She felt as though she had glimpsed another life through a crack and that she had only to push at the door and step through into it.

From across the valley, as they went down Bellpitt Lane, they could see Croud Cantle: the pinkish brick and grey flint of the cottage and dairy and the adjoining barns with their sagging roofs – like a small, natural outcrop on the green slope of Tradden Raike. Jude's experienced eye saw where crops had been cleared and where the rough turning of the soil to catch the frost was under way. She noticed the small changes that had taken place, where the trees in the orchard were almost bare and most of the hives had been dismantled down to their stone walls, leaving only one or two wearing their conical, straw hackles.

Hanna called excitedly, "I can see home," and urged the donkey forward.

"Take care!" Jude told her.

[201]

"I want to see Grandmother and I got all my presents to give."

Jude felt a familiar pang of guilt and a wince of anguish at the mention of Bella. It would all be spoiled. She knew how warm experiences of frivolous pleasure, stored away, could become instantly mildewed if Bella dampened them – it's all right for some! She felt guilty at not being as pleased as Hanna at going home. It's the place you ought to want to go to more than anywhere.

"When we get home, Jude, I got a present for you as well."

"Goodness! A present!"

"It's from the money you gave me. You got to promise to use it every time. Will you Jude?"

"What is it?"

"Promise."

"I can't promise to use it if I don't know what it is. It might be knitting pins, and you know what a tangle that'd be."

"Oh, Jude! It isn't anything like that. I got one for you, one for Grandmother and one for me and we shall all use them every day. I shall make Grandmother promise; then when I go to the fair next year I shall get some ... " Hanna began giggling. "I nearly told you. Then you would guess what the present is. Promise Jude. It a make us like Mrs Warren."

"All right, I promise."

They were almost home, going along Howgaite Path, when Hanna said, "The best present is for Johnny."

"You brought something for Johnny-twoey?"

"A course I did. I wanted him to come to the fair, but he said he couldn't leave the farm. I think Grandmother could have let him. So I brought him a thing."

"Is that a secret too?"

"If I show you, you won't tell?"

"I won't tell."

Hanna reached inside the bodice of her jacket and brought out a fist of soft paper in which Jude assumed there would be a lump of clove or peppermint fair-sweet, but when the paper had been carefully unrolled, a small, blue china bird was displayed.

"Look," she said, cupping it in her hands like a live creature.

"It is beautiful," said Jude. "What is it for?"

Hanna gave Jude a look such as children do when they are amazed at grown-up stupidity at something blatantly obvious.

[202]

"It is for looking at and holding," she said. "I shall tell him to make a little shelf to put it on – like Mrs Warren."

Hanna had brought with her mementoes of the fair that were unlikely to be mildewed by Bella.

As they approached the house, Jude felt apprehensive because of the tension there had been between them on Thursday.

IN PORTSMOUTH on this same Saturday afternoon, Charlotte Trowell was sitting beside Mary's bed waiting for a doctor to call.

There was nothing she could do except replace the vinegar and water press on the delirious Mary's forehead, and anoint the terrible boils with unguent. She suspected that there was nothing that the doctor could do either.

At about the time that Lotte and Mary had arrived in Portsmouth, a ship had docked on which – it was later learned – smallpox had broken out. A great number of those on board had died and been put over the side, as had some before they reached death, such was the panic at its outbreak in a confined space with nowhere to run to.

The ones who were left when the ship docked were mostly those who had received the Turkish treatment. No one knew how the treatment worked – except that a mild form of a similar disease appeared to give protection from the more deadly variety. There were some, though, who had received the Turkish treatment but had not survived; and some who had neither the Turkish treatment nor the disease. It was they who carried the smallpox into the seaport.

They first heard that there was smallpox in the town at the time of the rift between Lotte and Harry Goodenstone. It was a bad time. The weal that Harry had left across Lotte's face had become infected, and Molly was frightened that Lotte had picked up the smallpox. They consulted a specialist in pustular disease, who said it looked like the malignant pustule which was thought to come from animals. He wondered whether it had been an animal that had caused the injury, but Lotte said no, it had not been an animal.

A burning lash. The coarse tassel of animal hair on the riding-crop. The seared and broken skin of her cheek and brow.

As it turned out, Lotte was fortunate. The boils were not malignant

and slowly responded to fomentations, so that eventually her lovely
face returned to the condition in which Harry Goodenstone had last
seen it – except for a puckered and purpled furrow that ran from the
bridge of her nose to the lobe of her left ear.

This consultant was a specialist in the treatment of smallpox by the
Turkish method. There was no doubt that when it worked, it worked
well. One received a mild illness and was for ever protected from the
worse form. They had both received such a fright about the infected
wound that he had no difficulty in persuading them to be treated.
They each had a few days of feeling unwell, then Lotte recovered; but
the disease raged through Mary until the specialist had to admit that,
"There are people who take badly to the treatment," and yes, there
were unfortunates who "did not respond to the point of recovery."

"Do you mean she might die of the treatment?"

"I fear the possibility."

And at about the time that Jude and Hanna were going up
Howgaite, the doctor's fears were confirmed and Mary Holly died too
delirious to realise that she never got her own back on Bella Estover
for turning up that day and marrying her beautiful young master.

WOOD-SMOKE HAZE was quivering over the broad chimney-stack of Croud Cantle farmhouse. The house-place door stood ajar. The red tiles were still bright in patches where the damp from Bella's morning cleaning of them was not yet dry. Everywhere seemed quiet. Jude had half-expected to be greeted by the sight of her mother stumping across the yard with her pails, instead of which she appeared at the door in a clean cap and apron as though it was Sunday morning. For a moment Jude was taken aback, her mother appeared quite changed. She had not realised how much white there was in her mother's hair, how sunken her mouth was from losing teeth, and how much like other women who had spent their lives yoked to heavy pails she had become in shape. For the first time, Jude realised that her mother was getting old.

"Well, there you are then," she said. "I didn't know what time you might a been coming."

Hanna jumped from the donkey and ran to her Grandmother. Bella was obviously pleased, but only with long experience of her expressions would one know that. In response to Hanna holding her hand she said, "Well, what a lot of fuss. Anybody'd think you been gone a twelve-month. Before you gets too excited there's your animals to see too." Still, she did not release the child's hand, but held it and went to where Jude was holding the two donkeys.

Bella took one of the straps, and looking just over Jude's shoulder said, "Well, you're back then. Didn't you have no trouble, or did you come over Winchester?"

It was only being away and being able to think, without things being all on top of her, that had enabled Jude to see that Bella's uncompromising attitude, her frigidity and moods had become worse of late. She had made up her mind that she would try to start off on the right foot, whatever her mother's mood. Jude would make her peace, but would never again be intimidated by her. And here was Mother, suddenly looking an old woman, going as far as she knew how in trying to be nice.

They led the donkeys away to be unloaded.

"We came over Winchester. It seemed sense after what you said about the Dunnock track on Thursday."

The mention of Thursday caused them both to hesitate momentarily. The moment passed when either or both of them might have resumed the unspoken animosity of that day: they were acknowledging something. Neither of them could have put into words exactly what: it was emotion of their subconscious. On Bella's part it was, perhaps, that her powers were subsiding and Jude was in the ascendency; on Jude's that a trap was being prepared and that if she did not run from it now it was inevitable that she should fall into it. Whilst Bella's subconscious thoughts were tinged with melancholy, Jude's had panic and anger involved. She automatically pressed them down.

She smiled, "We said, if there's anybody knows when the Dunnock track's passable, then it's you."

Bella looked properly at Jude. "That's true."

Back in her own room that night, Jude thought how it was that you live day after day after day, with changes happening imperceptibly. Like her mother's white hairs appearing singly and like her teeth being lost one at a time. The way her own body had changed over the last six or seven years, from the first small swellings beneath her bodice to her present fullness of womanhood. It wasn't only the small physical changes that went unnoticed either.

Hanna had been not much more than a year old when they brought her to Croud Cantle, but had been developing sides to her nature that were unsuspected – like her buying that blue china bird for a lad who did the rough work. Obviously none of the changes took place in secret, they were simply unobserved. When she thought back she could see that the lad had changed too: from the small boy who had become attached to Croud Cantle in the same way as the cats, pigeons and dogs, to a lad of thirteen or fourteen who had thought to turn the old trough into a day-bed for Jude. It was possible that he would like to have a blue china bird without Jude knowing it: for all that he had been as much part of Croud Cantle as any of them, she had seldom given him much thought. It took something out of the

[207]

ordinary to happen for one to take a fresh view. It had begun with her fall and continued with being away for a week.

They went into the house, where Bella had prepared a nice meal for them, with a brew of tea instead of the everyday milk or cider.

"Wait, Grandmother," said Hanna, when Bella told them to come on it was all ready.

"There!" she said, and placed three small packages on the table. "Jude promised to use hers all the time. Will you, too?"

"You can't promise things blind."

"It won't hurt. It's not like, hold your hand out and you gets a rabbit-turd for a joke."

"I shouldn't hope so."

"Will you? It a be a bit like Mrs Warren's."

Bella's expression changed momentarily, and Jude noticed. "Well, let's open our parcels, and we shall know what it's all about."

When the wrappings were removed, three cups were revealed. Very like Mrs Warren's, except in quality. Brightly coloured and fanciful roses flourished, and here and there an unintentional blob of paint or a speckle in the glazing told the secret that these were not the pieces that the pottery would want its name attached to, so had sent them to be smashed. Thus sprang a sub-trade between the pot-smashers and knick-knack stall traders.

"An't they beautiful?" said Hanna. "If I has any money next time then we shall have saucers; then we shall have plates."

Jude was afraid that Bella would not be able to stop herself from saying something hurtful. The cups were obviously an unintentional comment by the child upon the way they lived, and Jude could understand it. Croud Cantle contained nothing decorated, glossed or swathed. With the exception of Jude's own shelves and a few geraniums in the windows, nothing but useful objects were displayed.

"Let's use them straight away," said Jude. "But they're so beautiful, I reckon it would be a shame to use them all the time in case they got broke. I reckon they should be holiday cups."

Hanna had not thought of the danger to the beautiful cups through use, and she had been a regular breaker of their plain ones.

Bella's subconscious was dealing with the infiltration of frivolity and the possibility of treachery by another woman who would woo away this last love of her life. The first had gone to Lotte Holly, the second to Dan Hazelhurst. Jude had inevitably been lost when she had entered into the world of books and ideas which made her different. Now Bella was in danger of losing the most precious of all: the child who had come to her as an unexpected gift with no hurt attached. Bella had indulged the child with the week of nonsense at Plough Fair and Hanna had come back with the kind of fancies that would make her dissatisfied.

Consciously or unconsciously, Bella put her best face on it and poured tea into the cups. "I must get Dicken to get out some good long nails to hang 'em on."

The lives of the inhabitants of the Croud Cantle holding were of varying degrees of interest to several Blackbrook people.

Mr Carter started a revolution in his own household by insisting that everyone should have a bowl of good fermity to start the day. The cook, who considered herself mistress of unleathery kidneys and non-glutinous kedgeree, was affronted at being asked to deal with such countryfied ingredients as plain wheat and milk, but Mr Carter held the money bags.

In the Warren household, Peg was no longer attracted to older men and now saw James Carter for the wonderful creature that he was. Sam and Jack had been surprised to find that they missed the little girl who had not been afraid of any of the monsters in bottles they had paid a farthing to see at the fair and who, moreover, had not told that they had been there when they had been forbidden to go. Mrs Warren felt quite at a loss, and wished that Peg would be a bit older soon so that she might be got up in a bit of style and they might go about a bit in a sisterly way, as she and Judeth had done.

"I don't understand how that girl can bear it stuck all out there," she said to Fred on his return. "Why, it was bad enough when we was living in Motte, and that fair gives me the shudders to think of. From what I've heard, Cantle is nothing but a hamlet, and you reckon they lives a mile or two outside?"

"Not a mile or two."

"But cut off."

"It's out of the village. But not everybody is like you, Molly. Because you like living in a town, it doesn't mean everybody does."

"She liked it here, you could tell."

"Judeth always did like visiting us when I was teaching her, but she always went home happily enough."

"Well, she didn't this time. I think if she could she'd a stopped here."

Fred had to admit to himself that he had seen a different side to Judeth this week. He had seen the possibility of her losing that which made her so dear to his heart: the contrasts in her, the conflicting emotions she roused because she was a naïve and innocent country girl from the back of beyond who read poetry and political broadsheets; a girl who worked barefoot in the fields or stood on the market by day and compiled information about common people almost in secret. A unique girl in Fred's eyes. He thought he saw what he had always been unconsciously afraid of happening – that she would not remain his creation hidden away in the hamlet at the foot of the downs.

But it was he who had suggested the visit, so there was no one to blame, and if eventually she was going to come into touch with people in a social way then it was better that his hand was still guiding her. Also, it had been a pleasure to see her so flushed with enjoyment, surprising herself and everyone else with her unexpected ease of manner.

Will had the greatest interest in the inhabitants of Croud Cantle. Whereas Fred had taken the raw clay of the young Jude and wedged, shaped, fired and now glazed it into the woman, Will saw the finished object.

He had sown wild oats with several pretty girls whose bodies were strong from hard labour, and he had been enchanted by one or two daughters of vicars who could read and enter into a theological discussion; but the idea of the two within the one woman compounded her attraction for him.

Although most of his doubts about the scene in his superior's office had been put from his mind, now that he had observed the two of them together during Fair week he still needed to know of any complication. He hoped that his first opinion of her would be confirmed: that she was emotionally untouched, yet, because of what she must know from reading Shakespearian passion, emotionally sophisticated at the same time.

His relationship with Fred Warren was not straightforward. Had they been equals, Will might have asked a direct question. But although Fred had befriended Will – had offered first name terms, invited him into their home as an equal and discussed more of business than was normal between employer and employee – the fact remained that Fred was a partner in White's and Will was very much a junior both in position and in years.

ON THE MONDAY after Jude had returned home, Fred and Will were riding together in the direction of Salisbury.

"I have to go to see the Manager at Berol about the malting grain, if you remember. I thought I'd call in on the Croud Cantle place ... " He hesitated, searching for what reason he should give for calling, feeling slightly ridiculous – there was no need to explain. "I said I would be going through Cantle."

Fred's expression was bland. "You're honoured. They don't have many visitors at the farm."

"Have they always lived like that? Just the mother, living outside the village? They seem to be shut away."

"Not entirely shut away. They come to Blackbrook when the roads are passable. That's a good many weeks."

"That leaves a good many when they don't, though. And I didn't mean shut away in that sense – I reckon we were more cut off than that in Ireland – it is rather that I get the impression their isolation is from choice."

"Mrs Nugent is an excellent woman. From what I know of things, she was left alone to run the farm – well, it is really only a smallholding. It provides them with a living, though. They work very hard for it."

"I believe Judeth cannot go on living like that. She ought to meet people with ideas. She is an intelligent young woman."

Fred did not immediately reply, but rode on, gazing at the perked, chestnut ears of his horse.

"Intelligent, yes." He withdrew again.

He did not know when it had first begun, but for some while Fred had been thinking about Judeth in the years ahead. He was never able to imagine her in a satisfactory situation. His mind rejected the thought of her running their farm, as it rejected the idea of her with a husband and family. The only image that he could accept was of her sitting at a desk in a book-lined room. He could not even fathom what she would be doing there.

For a while he had thought that she might follow her interest in recording a history of rural life, but she was doing that as a simple hobby. Recently, when he had discovered that she had been writing, he had temporarily felt satisfied that he had perhaps created a woman novelist. But he had come to realise that to progress with that art she needed a great deal more experience and learning than she already had or he would be able to give her.

He had watched her with Molly, enjoying the dressing-up and that kind of thing. It was a part of Molly that he had always found attractive to him. She bathed everyone with her good spirits when she was engaged in satisfying her appetite for pleasure, colour and comfort, and in seeing that others were likewise fed. But Molly's qualities were not at all like Judeth's. The thought of her living the life of a wife and mother as Molly did, was incongruous.

When he first encountered her enormous enthusiasm, he had responded, feeding her with some of his ideals and feeding his ideals upon her. Peg and Freddie were now of the age Judeth had been then, and for all his parental pride, he could see that they did not approach her in keenness of mind and ability to think. He had been carried away. Instead of leaving it at reading and writing, he had primed her enquiring mind. He had not realised how concerned he would feel, or what a responsibility he was beginning to feel. If she could not find a way to use her intelligence in a way satisfactory to her, Fred would be guilty of offering a starving person a morsel then removing the dish.

He felt a sudden need to talk about it, and Will's remarks gave him an opportunity.

Will had begun to think that Fred would say no more.

"Intelligent. But what is that going to do for her? As she is now she's neither fish nor fowl."

Will's spontaneous response surprised himself. "I want to marry her."

That response surprised Fred also. He had seen them together at the supper last Monday, where they had conversed in a friendly way. Fred had been pleased: he had thought at first that Will had seemed off-hand with her, then at the party they had appeared to be getting on well. But he had not realised that Will had any serious intentions

[213]

towards Jude. "Does she know that?" he asked.

"No, I hardly knew it myself until now. But I am sure of it. She is the most remarkable woman I have ever met. I look at her hands – it is her hands I think that ... I can hardly explain what I mean ... it is her hands ... "

Fred inwardly finished the sentence. Enigmatic? Two women in one? But before he had time to reply, the subject was taken from them by the weather.

They had cut off across country, and were now on the old Roman Road which was high up and, in parts, a bleak no-man's-land. On either side was open downland with no sign of habitation as far as the eye could see. The grey cloud that had earlier been a slab overhead, had become lower and turbulent. A strong wind got up.

"Did you feel rain?" Fred asked.

"Yes, big drops."

They fastened weather-capes about them as they rode. They urged their horses, galloping into the wind, cloaks ballooning beneath the flapping capes. The sky quickly darkened. Large hailstones came like flung handfuls. The horses, with nothing to protect their eyes, flinched and jerked as the ice stung. The men hunched into the head-on storm.

"I didn't expect this." Fred shouted. "I thought we should easily make King's Sombourne."

"Can you see any shelter?"

"Isn't there an inn somewhere here?"

"Yes, near the Garlick signpost." Will's words were almost carried away. "It's about a mile off to the left."

There had once been a hamlet on the old Roman road, but that had fallen victim to enclosure long ago, so that what had once been the ramshackle homes of cottagers were now heaps of rotting wood, clay and flint, grown over by bramble, dock and old-man's-beard. Whether one called it the determined independence or the pig-headed stubbornness of one family, the fact remained that several generations after the destruction of the hamlet, the inn still remained.

Isolated, kept going by means of a minute piece of growing land, by poaching, brewing a good ale and sheltering travellers like Fred and Will who had underestimated the distance they had to travel and the freakish weather on this moorlike terrain, an innkeeping family had staggered on from generation to generation, picking a living from their tight-fisted circumstances. Now it had deteriorated into scarcely better than a hovel.

Before Fred and Will reached shelter, a whipping wind with hail and rain for its cat-o'-nine-tails scourged and drenched them. A man was holding open the door of a decaying stable.

"Get you in, masters. The boy'll see to the horses."

The two drenched men handed over their horses to the care of the man and ducked through the low doorway of the inn.

It was a low, beamed-ceilinged, oblong room with a hearth, window and two doors each as a central feature of the four walls. Fred was immediately reminded of the house-place at Croud Cantle, except that here there was the more usual cottagers' stamped floor, giving the place a characteristically earthy smell. At one end was a rough dresser holding a variety of ale-mugs; beside it was one tapped and one untapped cask. There was a small fire on the hearth, which a woman was blowing with squeaky bellows. When they entered, rubbing their faces with their fore-arms and shaking their cloaks, the woman gave them a rotten-toothed grin, then returned to breathing the fire into life.

Will and Fred removed their outer clothes.

"There," said the woman, pointing to a settle and indicating that was where they should put their clothes. "Come, come." She rose from her knees and pulled stools close to the fire.

They sat before it, grateful for the smoky blaze.

The woman went out and clattered about in the adjoining scullery. Then the man came in.

"Jonah Smith, sirs. For my sins, keeper of this place. You were lucky to be near to us, sirs, or you would a had a good soak. Where were you heading?"

Surprisingly, his speech, although having broad-vowel Hampshire about it, was not like a countryman's.

"Salisbury, but we thought to reach King's Sombourne dry."

His silvery untrimmed beard and hair receding each side of a widow's-peak gave him the superficial look of a man older than the forty or so years his physique and brow suggested. Although he had some kind of damage to foot or ankle which caused him to limp, he was an erect, handsome-looking man, except for a dent in his skull – not a scar, but an indentation that started at his eyebrow and ended somewhere under his abundant hair.

[215]

He drew ale into three large pots, shook and sprinkled powders from various small tins, then mulled the brew with hot irons from the centre of the fire. The ale hissed and steamed a fragrant cloud.

"There sirs!" He handed Fred and Will the steaming drinks and joined them as though one of the company. "Bess won't be long with your food. You might as well settle, this won't blow itself out this side of midnight."

"Very well. We shall put up here for the night and start away early."

The woman hung a pot over the fire and in half an hour the three men were enjoying a good rabbit stew.

When they had finished eating a boy came silently in, cleared the table and went silently out. From his height, he appeared to be about eight or nine years old, and although he was unwashed and unkempt, with coarse nails and hair as long as a girl's, his fine features and large eyes showed that he was likely to grow into manhood with striking good looks.

"That's a fine looking lad," said Fred. "I have a boy about the same age. Your son?"

Smith made a laughing sound. "Is there any man knows the answer to that old question. Yes, he's as near my son as any man's." He stood two mugs of ale on the table. "Take your ease, sirs. I shall see that Bess has got out blankets. It'll be two cots in the front room, if that will serve?"

Fred agreed that all they wanted was a night's shelter and rest, and that anything clean would do. "I never like to pay to feed another man's fleas," he said.

Smith limped off, leaving Fred and Will to share the red glow in the darkening room.

They talked a bit about the adjustments they would have to make in regard to their King's Sombourne and Salisbury visits, then sat each gazing into the fire, Fred smoking one of the long pipes that Smith had made ready and placed on the hearth.

The boy came in with an armful of thick logs. Fred tried to draw him into some kind of exchange, by asking him whether he was good with a sling, did he have a good dog of his own, the kind of question a boy would respond to. But this boy answered only in yes-sirs and no-sirs. He made up the fire and retreated.

On the logs that the boy had placed carefully on the fire-bed, bark and bits of dry ivy flared and cracked, moisture oozed, sap frizzled, then little whistles of steam escaped from the cut ends giving off the aroma of apple-wood. Fred and Will gazed at this display so intently that you might think that log burning was a new phenomenon.

At length, Will said, "What I said earlier – about Judeth. What do you think?"

"It's what *she* thinks that is relevant. You say she doesn't know … you haven't implied … anything about marriage?"

"No, nothing." There was a short silence. "Well, what do you think?"

"I think it would complicate her life."

"Complicate?"

"Yes. But if she were to marry any man, then it should be a free-thinking man with radical views."

"You know that I am that. What do you mean about complicating?"

"Up to now her life has been simple enough to allow her to be the two women. I said, didn't I, that she was neither fish nor fowl; what I suppose I meant is that she is fish *and* fowl. She is only at the beginning of what she could become. Did you know she is trying to write a book?"

Will shook his head.

"What she has done is nothing better than imitating, but that doesn't matter – she is experimenting. She needs … she needs to go on living without complications. If she were to marry now, then it should be to a man who could cook and scrub and sew – and see to it that she had no responsibilities such as children."

Will looked thoughtfully into the cats'-tongues of flame licking the apple logs.

"What did you mean about her hands?" Fred asked.

To have revealed himself to such an extent whilst riding beside Fred, speaking the words into the open, anonymous downland, high up on the old road, had been like speaking aloud to himself; intoxicated by articulating what had, till then, been vague thoughts. But face to face in the gloaming room, illuminated by the bright fire, Will felt restrained, embarrassed almost. What he had wanted to say about Judeth's hands seemed suddenly too suggestive, too revealing of his own carnality.

"I hardly know," he said.

[217]

"I do." Fred paused a moment. "I think of it as her Mary Magdalene quality."

From Will's expression he seemed about to protest.

Fred smiled and put up a hand. "No, no, don't misunderstand. Any woman with two unexpectedly different sides to her nature is doubly attractive. Mary Magdalene must have been so after she had anointed Jesus's feet. That is all I mean. A parson's wife serving in a gin-shop, a duchess performing high-way robbery, a farm-girl who reads *Othello* for pleasure. Hands that deliver lambs and write journals."

"Do I take it from that, that you find her attractive?"

For a moment, Fred's instinct was to rebuff his junior, put him in his place for taking liberties from their situation, but he quickly realised that in this they were equals. They each had equal call upon the other over questions of Judeth.

"I have known her for seven years, from a child. She has been under my roof scores of times, alongside my own children. I have as much concern for her future as though she was Peg."

For a while there was silence, except for the twin sounds of rain pattering on mud and crackling from the fire. Where the inhabitants of the inn had gone they had no idea, but there was no sound from them. It was entirely dark outside now. The room had become a confessional.

Eventually Fred said, "Mrs Warren was the jolliest girl in Blackbrook. I was the most solitary man ... lonely almost. She brought me to life. I have been alive ever since. Molly and the children are all in all to me." He gazed inwardly.

"Our desires are terrible traitors, aren't they? Well, in marriage they are. I tell you, they desert you – leap upon you when you're least expecting. Disloyal, faithless things, desires. You will perhaps think it a dishonourable thing to say of a woman, but there is no sensible reason why they are not attacked in the same way as ourselves. I occasionally look at Molly when she's in company, playing up like a girl, and wonder what prankish thoughts she is secretly plagued with."

It was as though the two men found themselves outside normal society, otherwise Fred Warren would never have spoken such private thoughts. The isolated inn, the monosyllabic woman, the silent boy and the dubious feelings they had about the man; a feeling of remoteness, their two faces each illuminated for the other in the dimness of the room – it was as though they were, for the now, not

[218]

bound by the accepted codes. It was only this feeling that gave them temporary liberation, lulled them into exchanging of confidences without even thinking whether they would ever regret such openness. It was an intimacy that men suspect women of sharing with one another, and long for themselves: the indulgence of admitting to anxieties and emotions, talking of them to someone of one's own sex.

"The bonds of marriage are conscious, civilized – mature, I suppose you could say. Wayward desires are not really any match. Even the best of marriages is not easy."

Silence again.

Then, "I would be less than honest if I said that I have not thought of Judeth once or twice ... for a brief moment ... " he trailed off. With a trace of aggression, "If you expect to be any different, however faithful you are ... The thoughts leap at you, leap. The only defence is to forearm; keep minding of what misery is caused by a moment of indulgence, of weakness. A marriage is always under attack, you know."

Fred appeared to have come to the end of his train of thought, and for several minutes only the rain and the hissing and creaking from the burning logs disturbed the quiet.

Then Will said, "It was in the town office that I came upon you. Quite accidental."

Fred looked puzzled.

"You and Judeth. I opened the office door. Ah sure, but you didn't see me. You ... she ... you were holding her." For a moment the image flashed at him, and he received a spurt of curdling jealousy.

"Ah." Fred nodded. "Yes, I know the time. She had learned something about her father that few of us could take without breaking down. I shan't tell you about it. That is for Judeth, if she wants you to know. It was nothing of the sort that you have been thinking. It goes to show how little we know one another. Not only you and me – all of us."

The explanation came to Will like a draught of heart's-ease.

"No, I think I've always got you for a better man than that." He smiled. "It was all the fault of me jealous thoughts that came leaping on me that day."

A door banged in another part of the house.

Time and place reassembled around the room.

Intimacy retreated.

[219]

Fred took up another pipe and lighted it, Will rose, stretched and went to look out of the window.

. The two men mended the small cracks they had made in their own emotional defences.

They could hear Smith's voice, the rattle of fire irons and pots, then Smith came into the room.

"Without lights, masters? I told Bess to see to it before we went out."

He offered no explanation about where they had been, but his shoulders were damp, leggings and boots were wet, and his face was flushed from being outside.

Fred protested that they were happy enough in the fire light.

Smith lit some old-fashioned rush lights, and a tallow candle or two.

"There, sirs, that's more civil. Andrew has seen to the horses and we shall have a brace of pheasant – fresh I'm afraid, but Bess is good with a pheasant, I can say that in her favour, if nothing else."

He drew off more ale and once more joined them as though of their company, this time discussing the merits of his ale and the details of his brewing methods, pressing them to try mead and other of his country wines. There was no doubt that the man was skilled at producing all manner of alcoholic beverages.

From the scullery came the cranking sound of a spit turning and an occasional word from the woman, and soon the smell of roasting. In a while the boy came in with knives, a loaf, cheese, butter and apples. Then the woman brought in a dish with three crisp-skinned birds, and a bowl of potatoes that had just come from the ashes.

"Ready," she said, and retreated.

Again Smith acted as though they were his invited guests.

"Please, sirs, join me."

The two men did so readily. The food looked and smelled appetising. Smith carved the birds and handed round the floury potatoes. It suddenly occurred to Fred that perhaps they had been mistaken: perhaps the place was no longer an inn and they had intruded upon a private dwelling. But then he recalled that Smith had mentioned other travellers, though he behaved like no inn-keeper Fred had ever come across.

"What about Mrs Smith and the boy?" Fred asked.

"Bess? She'd never eat in the presence of such gentlemen as

yourselves, sirs. No more would Andrew. They've rarely been in the presence of strangers for longer than five minutes."

Smith apparently had no such objections and ate and offered with the social grace more likely to be found in Fred's own circle than in this decaying inn on the old Roman road.

Later the boy came and cleared away. Fred and Will said it was an excellent supper, but Smith apologised for the freshness of the pheasant.

It occurred to Will that the earlier disappearance of Smith and his subsequent reappearance with wet clothes and three fresh – very fresh – snared game-birds were connected. It was by no means the first poached pheasant that Will had enjoyed. The knowledge that someone had put one over on a landowner gave flavour to game-birds that no amount of hanging could impart.

Smith filled half a dozen churchwarden pipes and drew some fine brandy from a small keg.

"Your healths, sirs. It is a pleasure to have someone to sit with after a meal. I like to hear what is going on elsewhere, being we're so remote up here."

The inn-keeper seemed to have rapacious need of companionship and related every story in a grandiose manner. He clutched at Fred and Will's attention, wanting to know all about the unrest in France; and when Blackbrook was mentioned he questioned them upon every detail of the place. He related at tedious length how the blow to his head had "caused him to drink Lethean waters", how he had come to the inn, how he had "perfected a brew that was, as you can judge Masters, bettered by none", and how his limp was from being recently gored by a bull. They talked until the rush-lights guttered out and the fire became a red glow on the white ash-bed.

Will would have preferred to retire early and go over in his mind what Fred had said about Judeth and have some thoughts about the future, but Fred liked nothing better than to sit before a red glow and talk.

When they retired for the night, Smith thanked them warmly for "putting a light to wicks of memory that had been snuffed out."

"It's an ill wind," said Fred. "We have done a day's good deed. I could not bear such isolation."

"It is the woman and the boy I should think needs a good deed done to them," said Will.

"That's true," said Fred, then after a minute, with a wry smile, "'Tis a pity that you aren't a man to cook and scrub and sew, for you would fit my requirements in a husband for Judeth in respect of a free-thinking man with radical views."

Smith had been right, the storm did not abate until Fred and Will were soundly asleep. They set off early. The boy brought out the horses, their flanks shining and manes brushed like thoroughbreds. Will gave him a gratuity. "Andrew, you're very good with horses, my own father would be pleased to have a lad like you about the place. I never came up to his standards of grooming."

For the first time in the eighteen or so hours they had been there the boy showed some response. He smiled broadly. Will had a warm moment of recalling Mr Carter and Jude at the party. He longed to see her again; the day spent at the strange inn meant a day longer that he must wait to see her. The boy's smile brought back to Fred and Will a sense of normality. They mounted their horses. "Fermity teeth," said Will, and after a second or two Fred remembered and they rode away laughing with greater gusto than the comment would normally have warranted.

Smith, Bess and Andrew watched the riders until they were specks on the straight, old road.

"I'VE COME at last," was Will's greeting, his mind and body alive at the sight of her.

"So I see. I am pleased."

There had been a fox in one of the chicken-coops overnight and Jude, wearing a thick head-shawl and with her skirt pinned up, with bloodied hands and a pail of heads and carcases, had an air of serenity. She might have been gathering spring flowers.

"I've been all over the place this last month."

"Yes, I saw Fred. He said you were away."

"Do you want a hand? Did he take many?"

"Only the four in this coop."

The formality in their conversation was not in their expressions. They looked and looked away constantly as though it was not safe to allow their eyes rest upon one another. Jude could easily have made a move towards him, held out her hands to him as her instincts insisted. She looked down at them and said without affectation. "Well, that's not nice. I've finished here."

They went up to the house, stopping to feed the remains of the chickens to the pig and to draw a pail of water. In the scullery, Jude picked at the knot of her head-shawl with her fingertips to keep the blood and filth from it.

"Let me," Will said, stepping close to her.

"I can manage."

Almost imperceptibly, Will recoiled, like someone thinking that a glass window is space until the last second. In his reaction, Jude saw a flash of recognition of the situation – I can manage was Bella's rebuff – and a revelation of understanding. The danger of being hurt, rejected, disillusioned that is attached to responding to another human being.

She smiled. "Even so, you do it," and she held her chin up.

[223]

Holding the knot, he pulled her head towards him and they kissed; gently, briefly, a touch of lips – sensuality more intense than a longer, harder, more voluptuous contact.

With that brief, gentle contact the damsel-fly emerged. Jude, the damsel-fly, whose casing had been cracking for a long time, but to which she had held on because she did not know how to live without it; but who now discovered that her hunger for contact with someone could not be satisfied through the prohibiting shell; who realised that in order to spread fragile wings and fly free it was necessary to expose the vulnerable self, to exchange the safety of the opaque, inhibiting armour for the dangerous freedom of contact. The emergence of the modest damsel-fly often goes unnoticed when there are large dragonflies about. It is necessary to be on the look-out for it.

Bella saw the change, but Will did not.

As she scrubbed her hands he stood watching her, silently. He followed her into the house-place. Bella and Hanna were working in the dairy.

"It is getting on for dinner-time. Will you stay?"

He stayed for an hour and ate bacon and bread with them. Dicken talkative, Johnny-twoey watchful, Hanna chattering about things that happened at the party that no one else had noticed or remembered, Bella amiable and Jude open, her senses picking up every particle of his presence that she was able to. Will, enlivening their dinner with news from other parts of Hampshire, unobtrusively held on to Jude's gaze from time to time, from which she did not try to escape.

After that first visit, Will came to the farm whenever he was in the vicinity. He also tried to arrange to be in Blackbrook on market days, although as it got on into December the journeys from Cantle to Blackbrook were unreliable. The days were getting so short that they needed good weather to be able to get there, sell their products and get home again before dark.

Bella accepted his visits without comment. Ever since their first meeting when he had surprised them all with his outburst about Jude's right to the Goodenstone library, Bella had always been pleased to see him. It was obvious that Jude was most to do with his more frequent visits, but Bella always welcomed him as a visitor to them all.

"Well, look, Hanna, here's Mr Vickery come to see us. That's nice to see you, Mr Vickery. You'll stop and have a bite?"

He often came on Sunday afternoons, stopping only for an hour

[224]

because of the short days and treacherous roads. On the Sunday before Christmas, Bella said that she did not feel up to going over to see Jaen and Dan this year, which they usually did if the weather was good enough. She said that if Will wanted to ride over and eat with them she would kill the big goose and cook it early in the day, so that they could eat at dinner-time and not in the evening as they usually did.

Jude anticipated the visit with contentment. Whenever Will was there she felt calm and at ease. His voice, still with a hint of accent and an occasional turn of phrase from his childhood in Ireland, pleased her; his easy manner with Hanna and Bella pleased her; the good-natured intensity when he spoke of his beliefs and convictions pleased her.

December 1788

Last Sunday, Will Vickery was with us for two hours.

He is very knowledgeable on government and such. I am very ignorant about it, but I do want to know more.

He is very earnest on the subject of co-operation of ordinary people. His belief is that if people were somehow organized, then because of their great numbers, government would be in everybody's hands and such things as poverty and ignorance would go. This is such a simple plan that it seems that there must be a flaw in it — but I cannot see one. I asked him how he would get Young Harry to share out his estates, and he said that they were not his estates and that people would take back their stolen lands by law.

For fun I asked him how he would go on with our place, but he took it serious and said that as it could not be worked without Dicken and Johnny-twoey, they should have equal share with ourselves. And I had to admit to myself that there was some justice in what he said, for although Dicken is now very old, he was working here before mother came, and as for Johnny-twoey he now works like a man, and the herbs and plants we sell come entirely from the plantation he has made himself.

There are many reasons why I am delighted to see Will ride into the yard. Some are written only in the journal of my memory and not in this record of day-to-day life. One reason why my heart leaps when I hear a horse coming along Howgaite, is that I know my brain will be stimulated with new ideas if it is Will Vickery who is riding.

How do some women manage to live all their lives with the kind of man, even if they have good looks and are jolly companions, whose ideas are stiff and uninteresting. The only desirable man, to my mind, would be one who's outward appearance is conventional. He should dress simply and have a gentle manner. This outward appearance would hide such advanced and rebellious ideals that would uproot order.

WILL CAME early on Christmas morning. Jude had killed the goose a few days earlier and it had been hanging in a shed safe from the fox until Bella was ready to pluck it.

The day before Christmas Eve she sat with her knees spread, holding the bird with her wrists and pulling at the down and feathers. Something half-remembered from her childhood floated to the surface. Keeping a rhythm with her hand movements, she sang over and over, "Wha-at care I for my goose-feather bed, with the sheet turned down so bravely-O? What care I for my newly wedded lord? I'm off with la-la da-da-da hum hum-O".

They had rarely seen her like this. You could probably count on the fingers of one hand when she seemed to be enjoying life. There was one time, a really good honey year when she had sold above twenty heavy hives; Hanna's coming, there had been a period then when she smiled; going out to join in the harvest-day sport; and Jude remembered her mother's supressed amusement on the day of Old Sir Henry's funeral, but it was short-lived. If only ... if only.

Hanna knew Bella's moods well enough not to be seen watching, so laughing into her cupped hand, whispered to Jude to listen and come and see Grandmother playing the goose. Jude, standing behind Hanna, holding her giggling shoulders, looking in at her mother's square back moving as though in some seated dance felt a catch of sadness. If only ... if their mother had been able to sing a line or two of a song, let her hand rest upon Jaen and herself when they were younger ... If only she could have let herself be easy like this more often.

Jude had only recently begun to realise how silent and cold their home was. What their life would have been without Hanna she just could not imagine. When she tried to, she saw two featureless statues, standing separately in the house or the dairy or far apart in the fields.

[226]

She could never visualise Bella and herself as two moving women. She was beginning also to realise what effect Bella had on herself and Jaen and she was determined to watch herself and not go about with life hanging like a millstone about her neck.

It was something Hanna said that made Jude realise why perhaps Bella was making such an effort with the Christmas dinner.

"There won't be so many people, Jude, but do you think Grandma's party will be such fun as Mrs Warren's?"

"It isn't how many people come that makes the fun, it's ... "

"Being partyfied?"

Jude laughed.

"Like that," Hanna said. "Laughing is being partyfied. Mr Vickery is always laughing, isn't he? But still, four people is not many."

"Then we shall have to laugh twice as much and sound like eight."

Bella brought in the goose. They all worked together in the warm and steamy kitchen which smelt of fruit and spices, preparing little tarts and cakes. Hanna said, "Grandmother, I want us to ask John to our party."

"Who in the wide world is John?" asked Bella.

"Well, if you don't know who John is! He only lives here."

"Cheek, Miss!" chided Bella. "You mean Johnny-twoey? Come for Christmas dinner?"

"Yes," said Hanna. "He never goes anywhere."

"You can't ask farm-hands to something like this."

"Why not? He always eats his dinner here other days. And harvest supper."

"This is a ... It is a family do. There's places and times for workers, but this is a family do."

"What about Mr Vickery, then?"

Ah, well. Bella didn't quite know what to say about Mr Vickery; it wouldn't do to say anything too serious.

"He's a friend. More a equal than Johnny-twoey."

"John is my friend and he is just as equal here as I am. And he don't like being called Johnny-twoey, and I wouldn't if you was to call me Hanna-Hazelhurstey."

It was so seldom that there was occasion to even think of Hanna's second name, let alone say it that – quite apart from her statement about the boy – Jude and Bella paused in their work. Hanna was a Hazelhurst and not theirs. She could be gone from them on a whim of

[227]

her father at any time. The bright little redhead gone, leaving two isolated statues: a thought too chilling.

"Well, lovey, it's all right you saying you wants him to come, but he's a funny lad who always has kept hisself to hisself."

"He would come. He would if you asked him, Jude."

Jude remembered the blue china bird and Hanna being absolutely sure that the boy would like it.

"All right then," Jude said, "if you think he would like it."

Bella did not contradict, but looked momentarily at Jude and then went on rubbing salt into the goose.

"Oh, he would like it. I told him everything about the party at Mrs Warren's and he said when he's got his own place he will have a party every Saturday night."

"Well, now, so he's to have a place of his own, too." For a moment Jude detected a whiff of sarcasm, but it went. Bella quickly remembered that she was talking to the little redhead that could at any moment be taken away to Newton Clare.

"How do you know so much about him? He never says two words when I'm about," Bella said.

"Well, I talk to him and he talks to me. We tell each other everything. When he has saved enough money, he is going to get a plot and grow pot-herbs and plants and trees and then sell them."

"And where's he going to get all this here money then?"

"I expect from you, isn't he? He says he reckons you are putting it by for him – the wages. He says you would have to take some out for his keep, and he probably didn't earn much when he was little, but he says," she had to stop to draw breath, "he says he works as hard as Dicken even if he is not quite a man, but he does his job proper."

Jude kept quiet, waiting to hear what her mother had to say. She herself was taken aback by the unexpected shrewdness of the boy. All of that had been going on in his head as he came and went. "Yes, Miss Jude. All right, Miss Jude. Where do the Master want the hurdles put?" Blushing and apparently inarticulate. True, they had never paid him. He had gone from a seven-year-old throw-out from the Toose family to a youth taller than Jude and Bella without really being anybody. Dicken also worked for them, he also took orders; but he argued, talked, garrulously sometimes; approved or not as the mood took him of anything and everything to do with Croud Cantle. He also came and went about the place, but Dicken came from home and went back there each day. John Toose had a room in an outhouse.

"Hmm." Bella beetled her brows and sucked her bottom lip. "Hmm. I dare say he is owed a bit o' back pay."

"He won't want it yet," said Hanna very seriously. "He says it will be four or five year till he can set up a place on his own."

"Has he thought where he would live? He would have to get a place with a cottage," said Jude.

Hanna carefully placed pieces of chopped fig and blobs of honey on to the squares of paste she had carefully cut out. John had never talked about where his venture as a plantsman might be placed.

"If he had some land close by," the answer to the problem came clear, "he could live here just the same. I know! He could have that ... you know by the spring, the little strip along Raike Bottom, near the pond."

ON CHRISTMAS MORNING Bella, Jude and Hanna went to a special, early service. There was heavy frost and boots crunched, whether on frozen mire or grass. Although it was still dark and they had to take a lantern to light their way down Howgaite, the church was full.

The box pews of the more prosperous amongst the Cantle God-fearing – the miller and a tenant-farmer or two – were occupied. There was even somebody in the Goodenstone pew. But gentry – when not addressing the Almighty in their own chapels – prayed enclosed on four sides by high, carved panelling, and came late and left early; privately, secretly almost. None of the common villagers, on full view in the open aisle at their devotions, were given any opportunity to know whether or not it was Young Harry.

Perhaps the reason that the church was so full at this early hour was because the early Christmas service was the only one when the Reverend Archbold Tripp did not spend fifty or sixty minutes passing on a lecture that God was unable to give the Cantle flock, except by means of being interpreted by Mr Tripp himself. Well it an't no good keeping a dog and barking yourself, would likely have been the villager's view, had the question arisen. The question never had. Hampshire in general was not keen on questions about established order, and Cantle was insulated by its beautiful, high mounds of chalk from infiltration or from even the mildest of dissenting thought.

To the surprise of Bella and Jude, Hanna said that Johnny-twoey would come to the party. When Will arrived, the boy was seated in the place he usually occupied when he came to eat in the kitchen. Hanna was bending over his shoulder entertaining him with the pages

[230]

of Little Lady Geraldine, reading slowly and underlining the words with a forefinger.

Molly Warren would not have recognised the Christmas dinner as a party, but in terms of Croud Cantle it was a great celebration. When Will said that he hadn't had a goose like that since he last tasted his mother's cooking, and for sure he reckoned that the fig-puddin' was better than her's because Mrs Vickery was no hand at all at making suet puddings light enough and never pretended that she was, Bella looked enormously pleased. She explained how it was with suet; you had to chop to just the right fineness and it was something she had learned in her childhood and it was something you never forgot.

Although, nowadays, Johnny-twoey often took his dinner in the kitchen along with the rest of them, the fact of being told by Hanna that it was a party overwhelmed him. Most of the time he concentrated on his plate and spoke only when offered more food. Bella and Jude looked at him with a new curiosity since Hanna's revelations about his ambitions, but still found it difficult to believe that he was ever involved in such a complicated conversation as Hanna had suggested.

Jude could not remember a time – except at harvest suppers in the days of Rob and Bob and occasionally Gilly, when she and Jaen were little – when the table had been so laden with food. To drink there was some of Bella's Love-apple wine; clear pink and dry, made five years previously from a good summer crop and just potent enough to loosen the tongues of the three adults and dispel formality.

The meal was over soon after midday. Will paid his compliments all over again after patting his belly and saying he would have to go for a run before he could eat another morsel.

"It's decent enough out. You could go and pick a branch or two of holly. It'd be nice to see some in the house again," Bella said.

Jude began clearing the table. "Hanna and the boy a give a hand to do that. Put on your boots and show Mr Vickery ... "

"Ah-ha," said Will, "you said you'd call me by me name."

"Go and show – Will – where that good holly bush is, down by the Manor gates." She nudged a smile at Will. "'Tis Estate holly by rights, but we'll have a bit of our own back."

"Why, Mrs Nugent, you'll have me up before the Magistrate enticing me to do such things as stealing Estate holly."

Observing her mother flushed from the wine and smiling, being indulgent, joking even, Jude thought: She'd have been a lot happier if Jaen and me were sons.

The sky was blue as June and the air sharp enough to spike the hollow behind the bridge of the nose if one drew breath too deeply. A hoar-frost of frozen dew clothed bare trees and hedges in imitation foliage and worked lace edges on the deodars and cypresses in the estate park. At this time of year the sun was too low to melt frost on the lower slopes of the enclosing downs, but gave green tops to them for an hour or two. The air was so clear that the bells of Winchester cathedral could have been heard by anyone on the top of Old Marl, which was unlikely on a day when gentry and labourers alike walked no further than to bow heads before the nearest altar.

Will and Jude walked briskly cross-country, down through the Croud Cantle plots and meadow and across the corner of the estate field from which Jude had run three or four months ago. They talked quietly, agreeing on the fineness of the day, the good that this heavy frost was doing to the land, the large number of rabbits there seemed to be about, and the marvel of how tiny birds like snipe which don't weigh hardly nothing at all manage to keep fat in winter when other birds sometimes fall starved from their roosts.

The holly bush was lush with berries and Will took a branch that was bristling out into the track at Raike Bottom.

"Are you all right now to be walking uphill?" Will asked.

"I've been part the way up Tradden."

They started up the gentle slope.

"We'll turn back as soon as you find it too much."

"This is Judeth Nugent – not Bella."

He turned a smile on Jude. "Isn't she the one, your mother? That day," he hesitated for a fragment of a second, remembering another image of that day, "when I was hold'n down the branches and she was pick'n off the crab-apples. She was telling me everything from how to make cheeses to how to charm away warts." Will laughed, "I couldn't get a thin word in sideways if I'd a tried."

His view of Bella was so at odds with the real Bella that Jude felt confused. She did not even know that Bella could charm warts, let alone talk so that a person couldn't get a thin word in sideways. Jealousy, possessiveness, reproach. If she told him what her mother was really like, how would she appear in his eyes? Yet she wanted him to know about the coldness and the rejection. She wanted him on her side, to herself. There were niggling, mean thoughts rushing through her.

"It's a pity she wasn't like that at home."

"Is she not, then?"

"No."

"I can hardly believe that. I was just thinking when she was cutting up the goose that she was like me own mother – it was never father who took the carving-knife in our family. Mother stands there like queen o' the tribe. I'd not felt so much at home for a long time."

"What is your mother like?"

They were walking uphill, Will carrying the holly-bough over his shoulder. He laughed. "Well, I tell you, there's times when she's as prickly as this and I should a had sense enough to pick this on the way back." He put the bough down. "I'll get it later."

Free of the holly, he unceremoniously took Jude's hand in his. "Mother? Dark, darkish, middling in size, I suppose you'd say. And she would always call me Billy. I'm reckoned to take after her in looks, so you can tell she's a handsome woman."

"Be serious. What is she like? What kind of woman is she?"

"Seriously, she's never got over being cut off from her home and family. There's never a day passes without she's talking about home. Home! Seriously I think that, deep inside her, she's bitter – no, no, not bitter, resentful. No, you'd get the wrong impression of her. She's angry. Ah, that's what. Father's a bit like that, too, but I think he's like it because he feels useless. You know, always seeing to horses that nobody rides. The waste, extravagance, that kind of thing. But her anger is because we were moved over there on a whim, you might say, just to be there in case anybody of the Berol family fancied a week or two there for a change, and she had no choice but to go with me father."

As he had been telling her this, his hand had been clasping Jude's, hard. "She's probably been living in Ireland now longer than she did in Hampshire. Yet she still talks about being sent off, like sheep to market, to a land where they can't talk King's English. It's as though they only landed yesterday."

They had reached that part of Tradden where the gentle slope ceases and the climb becomes more steep. Where nothing ever grows taller than eighteen inches or so except for clumps of willow-herb in summer and the humps of brambles, now winter-bare revealing the structure of their shape. In them brown clots, where, in the early part of the year, pairs of neat wrens had made bulky homes, and garden warblers had woven clever structures. Will and Jude stopped spontaneously and looked down over Cantle.

"We've come further than I thought. Is your leg all right?"

Jude nodded absent-mindedly.

He suddenly realised that he held her hand in a tight grip. He relaxed his hold, then said in his more usual soft tone, "Oh, look at your white fingers, I must have stopped the blood." He felt her knuckles with his lips. "You're frozen."

Jude drew towards him and shared the warmth of his cloak, which he held out, wrapping it about them both.

The few touches and kisses that they had exchanged had been like the first when Jude had been cleaning up after the fox: gentle, spontaneous, playful almost; the sort of kisses Will had exchanged plenty of times.

But not Jude.

The experience of being this close to somebody desirable was nothing dewey-new to Will. He had wrapped his cloak about girls before. The only difference now had to do with this tense, strange, enigmatic girl. A certain heightened sensuousness; a perplexing importance. They stood side by side, their eyes directed upon Cantle, but not seeing.

Whilst she had been disabled and, more recently, since returning from Blackbrook, Jude had often been engrossed in thoughts about herself. She was trying to tease out a tangled and knotted mass. Her emotions were like sinews or fibres that were constantly dampened, softened, then dried out and hardened. Brittle. Unreliable.

Early in the summer there had been all the softening hope of assuaging her thirst for knowledge through Young Harry's books, and the unadmitted fear of what would happen if she started down that path. Don't push me, she had said to Fred Warren. Yet had she been honest with herself she wanted to be pushed, not to have to decide for herself, to be faced with a fait accompli.

The softening and hardening stresses: firstly of meeting Mary Holly; then the physical and mental breaking through Bella's barrier, putting an arm round her mother, listening to her history with Tomas Nugent. Then meeting Lotte Trowell on Bell Tump, quickly followed by the complexity of feelings when Fred had comforted her.

It seemed as though all through the long, burning days of last summer and the weeks of hard labour without a break in the weather, her emotional fibres had been so stretched that they had snapped on the day when she had wildly run on to Tradden.

Again, now, on the same loved and lovely swelling of the chalk downs she felt panic. The damsel-fly was out of her familiar, shielding, distancing shell. At the same time that she was feeling apprehension and the urge to escape from the brace and buttress of Will's firm warmth, she instinctively kept close to him, tempting and testing herself. Tense. Wanting. Needing. Her old hunger – to touch and be touched. Not knowing how to deal with intense feelings. Afraid, yet fearless.

Will's thoughts were uncomplicated, his action straightforward. Beginning with a kiss that was not gentle or playful.

ON NEW YEAR DAY, Will Vickery made a brief visit, but
it was a visit in passing. It was a round-about way of
passing, for he could have taken the coach from outside the Star at
Blackbrook, close to his lodgings, but preferred to pick it up on the
Corhampton Road and leave his horse to be stabled at the inn there.

Barnabas White wanted to know more about the possibilities of
using steam-power in the handling of bulk cereals, and as the north of
England seemed to be the place to find out he was sending Will as his
eyes and ears.

Will stopped for only half an hour at Croud Cantle, and with
Hanna chattering and Bella wrapping delicacies to sustain him on his
journey, the lovers could exchange only conventional words and
colliding glances. All three came out of the cottage to watch as he
attached Bella's package of little gifts to the horse's saddle. The mud of
the yard was frozen hard and breath spurted white.

"Let's hope the ground have thawed a bit be the time you gets
back," said Bella.

"Ah, to be sure," agreed Will, standing with his back to Bella and
looking directly at Jude. "Springtime and the grass soft, it's a time to
look forward to." He limited his smile to his eyes as he looked at Jude.
She reddened at the meaning of his look and pulled her shawl close
over her cheeks.

"But I haven't any intention of bein' away till then."

The New Year brought a surprise to Molly and Fred Warren. The
combined facts of something being not quite right ever since her last
confinement, and the regular use of a brew of pennyroyal and bitter,
herbal concoctions (sold under many different labels such as Special
Restorative for Women), had led Molly into the certainty that Sam

[236]

would for ever be her youngest. After ten years she felt that she could relax into matronhood.

Fred's first thought was that it would be rather good to have a baby about the house again. Molly's first thought was that she hoped she might not be so long in labour this time and that it might be a girl who would pay for dressing pretty.

The baby would be born in July and would be known, like many another, to be the result of its parents having been Fair Mondaying the previous October.

On Christmas Day, when Jude had lain upon the bones of Tradden, cushioned by frosty grass and beneath the warm, flesh-covered bones of Will Vickery, the possible consequences of the liberating joy of their loving had not occurred to her. She had thought many times about what had happened to Jaen, but if that lesson tried to get through now, Jude ignored it, and in the contentment and ease that followed she felt nothing but well-being and confidence.

Fate? Chance? Good fortune? Something ordered the fallow, last of Jude's December moon-cycle days to coincide with that Christmas Day. Jude never had even one day's disquiet. No waiting for the days to pass, no bitter remorse, no promises of the deaf god of women, none of the anxiety and disquiet that had followed Jaen's day with Dan Hazelhurst. Not that Jaen had emerged from her casing as fully-mature as Jude: Jaen had not been ready and her fragile wings had been damaged, never allowing her to fly again.

It was not until Jude heard, soon after Will had gone North, of the unexpected Warren baby, that the full realisation of how easily and with what recklessness, abandonment and impetuosity she had endangered her own ambition to be, do ... something – she did not yet know what. Except she did know that it was not to live her life like Jaen, Mrs Warren, or the Cantle girls she had watched in their cow-like apathy last harvest day.

The fact that Jude did not say much when Bella told her what she had heard about Molly Warren's condition from market gossip, had little to do with that news, but more to do with a sudden flood of understanding. Understanding of Jaen, of Bella, of Lotte Trowell and even of her father and of herself.

Judeth Nugent, who believed herself to be unlike others, now saw her true likeness to them. She saw how easily anyone may be carried

[237]

away by passion, by desire, by the old need – to touch and be touched. She saw, too, the knife-edge on which she had been poised on Christmas Day. She had not realised it until now.

How Bella must have been carried away by Tomas Nugent! Even after he had abandoned her for five years, she had seen him and again submitted to her need for him, and perhaps would have taken him back yet again if he had returned. There must have been a moment when Tomas looked at Bella as Will Vickery had looked at Jude, arousing such a heady force that the real world – of December frosts and anguish – became, briefly, inconsequential.

She saw that Jaen's need was probably much like her own; remembering how they had always huddled close in their bed, not knowing that their vague unsatisfaction was to do with their absent father and a mother who could not bring herself to take the risk of showing love again, even to her children.

Jude understood about the ecstatic moment when young Charlotte Holly had been unaware of anything except her passion for her master.

How near she had been to finding herself stepping blindly into the quicksands of a life like Jaen's or Bella's. She had taken one step into the sucking marsh and her foot had been guided to a small patch of firm ground. If the hand of a god had saved her, she had no faith that it had been that of the father-God who spoke to the Reverend Archbold Tripp. It must have been some more ancient deity, whose bones she had often felt beneath her and whose four breasts were Tradden, Beacon, Old Marl and Winchester.

January this year began with daytime skies that were as blue and high as summer and which, at night, were overwhelming to anyone out after dark. Infinite black plush and glitter. Clear, brumal air, carrying the terrifying shrieks of vixens on heat far across the Hampshire countryside.

It was the time when humans gave way to nature in the management of the soil. After harvest it had been roughly turned and left in clods for frost to break down. This January the sunny, clear, bitter-cold days went on and on. Frost penetrated the land, deeper and deeper.

It was the short break in the crop-growing season when repairs to implements and fences were done. Usually Bella was here, there and everywhere, ferreting about in every corner for rotting wood or sagging fences. This year, though, she spent a lot of her time indoors: she did her usual work in the dairy and storehouse, but left Jude to see to the rest. Guilty and sharp-tongued at Jude's tentative enquiry, was Bella all right?

"I can have a few twinges, can't I, without everybody making such a ta do of it? I an't as young as I was – none of us is," she snapped. What Dicken had said about the Master having her stuffing knocked out was becoming more noticeable.

"What's up with the Master, Miss Jude? She look like an old 'umpety hen 'smorning."

"You better not let her hear you say that."

Dicken pulled a knowing face. "My eye, I knows better'n that and that's a fac'."

They were working on saving a huge old cherry tree that had provided fruit and preserves for years, but had been battered and broken in a storm. Jude and Johnny-twoey were holding up a heavy branch whilst Dicken sawed at it. They were shapeless with garments against the cold.

"Miss Jude?"

Dressed in an assortment of old jackets and anything else that came his way, his chilblained and chapped hands wrapped in rags, Johnny-twoey spouted white breath as he took more than his share of the weight. Although still by no means talkative, encouraged by Hanna he had recently been slowly coming out of his shell, but he never spoke without the preliminary, asking permission: Mizz Nugent? Miss Jude? Hanny?

"Yes, John?"

A moment of pause as the three of them got over the hurdle of his new naming.

"Miss Jude?" The little shock of suddenly being John caused him to forget the arrangement of words he had formed before venturing to say them, and blurted out instead, "When the Master's too old and Dicken's gone, what's going to happen?"

What's going to happen?

"Dicken's not going, are you Dicken, not yet?"

"Can't last for ever, Miss Jude, and that's a fac'. I'm older'n the Master by a bit."

What's going to happen?

[239]

"Three score year and ten, at's what the Book says we'm due for ... "

What's going to happen?

" ... but there an't many as I knows gets their proper share. I sometimes asks my old 'ooman who gets them years which an't used?" – Dicken's own wit always had caused him a good many laughs – "and she says they'm give to passons and jukes and the like of they ... "

What will happen!

" ... and I reckon she got something there, for I never knew a passon in these parts that didn't have five or six year above his own share. Well, I says to her, it must be the good Lord as looks after his own, and she says, or Old Harry," he indicated horns with his forefingers, "and I says, perhaps it's having a good swig of communion wine every day. When you comes to think on it, there might be some't in that. Jukes and that lot, you don't catch they drinking no ale nor cider, oh no me boys, t's all red wine, and tell me if it don't stand to reason at red wine helps your blood, and your health'n'strength's in your blood."

And so, as often happened when Dicken got going, the original topic or question got covered in the moss of his garrulity and was forgotten.

As soon as she had an excuse, Jude left them to get on with the clearing up and wound-painting of the old tree.

It was Saturday. Except in the seasons of planting, thinning, harvesting, Saturday afternoon had become accepted at Croud Cantle as an afternoon to be taken at a more leisurely pace, when some of the less arduous tasks were undertaken. In winter Bella attended to hives and skeps; in summer to collecting any swarms and later on to the killing of them, then to taking the honey. In spring they collected elderflowers and may-blossom to make the quick wine, the fizz and sparkle of which was always echoed in Jude's feelings, as the chalk-hills and the Cantle valley seethed with regeneration.

At this early part of year she had often used her precious bit of leisure for reading or writing up her journal. Often she would try to persuade Hanna that it wasn't unfair to have a reading lesson on a Saturday. If only she saw what fun reading and writing was she wouldn't find it hard to learn, but Hanna – firm, square, Estover Hanna – would rather tidy shelves or help with the bees.

On this Saturday, still dressed in her layers of clothes and her thick boots and shawl, Jude cut a thick slice of bread and left Hanna to tell Bella that she was gone out.

"I'm glad you an't growing up strange, Lovey. She been like that since she was littler'n you – and Jaen too. They'd a slept up Tradden if I'd a let them. An't anybody else walks up hills unless they has to." As she often did when saying aloud some of her puzzled thoughts about Jude, Bella went on and on.

"I remember asking her once what she saw in walking up a great, barren, steep lump like Tradden. Barren? she said. Why there's something new every time. New? I said, I suppose this year's grass an't the same as last year's. That's right, she said. I said to her that people would say she wasn't all there, but she only laughed. She said, perhaps I an't, and I said that's tempting Old Harry." She pointed a hank of raffia at Hanna in emphasis. "You remember that, Lovey. It's like crossing your eyes and the wind changing. Everybody knows it's tempting Old Harry, yet you can tell by all the cross-eyed people about that they will still do it. It don't never do to go against things. She's gone off up there in the dep of winter. Anybody can see her from the village and you can't blame them if anybody starts saying she an't all there. Twenty years old! I'm glad you'm growing up with some sense."

As Bella was rambling her puzzlement at Hanna, Jude was through the scrubby trees at the back of the farm and climbing the steep slope of Beacon Hill.

THE CANTLE FACE of Beacon was north: its steep slope rose up like the sides of a bowl from the flat valley floor. The other three hills, more gently sloping, were criss-crossed with tracks, raikes and footpaths and were travelled over by people on foot, on horses or upon donkeys. Wagons and carriages mainly used the long track up Bellpitt Lane and over Winchester. This gentle slope was the easiest way in and out of the valley, and may have been a reason why the Romans had built fortifications on the high vantage point close by. The upkeep of this track was the duty of Cantle landowners. As the majority of it was Estate or Church land, and as only the Goodenstones and Reverend Tripp owned anything on wheels, it was the Estate and the Church who made sure that it was always useable. By rights Croud Cantle should have contributed some labour to this work, but no one had ever approached Bella Nugent about her duty.

Usually when Jude went out on to the downs, she went instinctively to the part that suited her mood at that particular time. Instinctively, because she had never thought why she went in this or in that direction. Each hill had a character and an atmosphere quite different from the others. As the four hills were almost a circle, except for where the river made its way through, outsiders would find it difficult to know where one hill began and another ended. There were no noticeable indications, not even the river, for part of Beacon was cut off by it from the main hill and was joined to Tradden. But the people of the valley knew which part was which.

Furthest from Croud Cantle was Winchester Hill. Slouching, sprawling, facing south, facing the dark side of Beacon. Mysterious, with the ruined fortifications, the barrow, and the upright slab of alien stone over the crest.

Its partner, Old Marl, also faced south, on the left of the Dunnock. For some reason more trees grew on that hill than on the others. Old

Marl sat upright behind the big House, behind the Estate and the Goodenstones, as unaware of them as of others who had scrabbled there before: small tribes, thin, wary, who grazed on seeds; others who gnawed red flesh and fish, aggressive, suspicious. For the most recent tribe, the Cantle people, Old Marl was the least accessible of the four, because the Goodenstones owned the land at its base and any tracks that once existed were now grown over. On Marl, keepers and poachers fought a constant battle with wits and cunning.

Tradden, probably because Croud Cantle was at its foot, was the most familiar to Jude. Her first steps outside the farm were taken there. Tradden purified their well-water, filled their pond and washed down essential particles into their soil. It darkened before the rest, but the morning sun shone upon it. Tradden had spread its knees and made a lap where Jude had cried for Jaen; screamed inside her head on the killing day; taken peace and satisfaction from Will Vickery.

Beacon Hill. In bitter January, Jude had chosen to walk there. Great lumps of its chalky skeleton protruded in places, bare of any vegetation. It offered no welcome. Even in summer it never had the open warmth of the rest of the downs. It had never mellowed. The other downlands often wooed Jude into stopping longer than she had intended, offering, it seemed, a greater amount to interest, more varieties of creatures. Although Beacon was well flocked with sheep and some goats, it was scarcely ever walked upon by any humans, except for shepherds and a few agile berry pickers in late summer, and men who came on rare and special occasions to light a beacon.

Jude climbed Beacon Hill, following the faint track to the Point where she sat and ate her bread.

What will happen when … ?

Why do things always have to be pushed under my nose before I realise about them?

Beacon Hill might be lonely and barren, but in the crystal-clear air, from the highest point in the county it was easy to see for miles. Jude looked down on the tiny patch that was Croud Cantle and then out over the swelling downs: Blackbrook abbey to the north, Corhampton and Wickham to the west and south and further south to the far horizon where the waters of the Solent sparkled.

When she turned back to look at the valley again that bright line was still in her mind. Cantle was cramped, confined, isolated and the farm was not even part of what little community there was. Below her level of consciousness, something rankled. Discontent. She could see the field she had run from in panic on Harvest Day. The buried memory of it rose again, turning over her stomach and drying her mouth. She could see Park Manor. The discontent curdled into resentment. There was something wrong when a fool of a man like Harry Goodenstone owned all the farms, all the land, everything and everybody in that valley.

Take the books! I've got more brains in my little finger than he's got in his whole body and he don't see that books have got any more value than a bunch of dead daisies. He been taught from the time he was little – been to a university even – and all he'd ever done with it was to have himself dressed up in fancy clothes.

Slowly the resentment drained away. She faced the sparkling southern horizon. It didn't do any good getting het up. She had come out to try and think about what Johnny-twoey had said. How long could they keep going as they were now? Dicken was already too old to do some of the heavier jobs. Johnny-twoey would be a man in a couple of years. Mother, like Dicken, was worn out by years of long hours and hard labour. Jude looked at her own hands. How long would it be before her fingers stiffened too and her knuckles became round balls that were fiery hot? The sensible thing to do would be to take on somebody younger than Dicken. But we could keep on Dicken and he could share Mother's work ... and we could get a dairy-maid and ... and ...

And I could ... ? What? What? She wanted – something, to do – something. She was like an athlete; full of power and energy, ready to burst into a run, but finding that the race was the other side of a high wall.

She had started writing a book about the Nugent women, but it was slow, solitary. Since her stay with the Warrens, except when on her chalk-hills, Jude liked to be with people. The people in her book were no substitute for flesh and blood; the information in the Journal was intended for descendants who were generations ahead. She would have liked to tell them face to face and get their response.

A BOY WITH a handcart waited outside Lotte Trowell's lodgings in Portsmouth whilst she collected together the last bits and pieces from the backs of drawers and cupboards, as Mary would have done. Mary had always seen to that kind of thing. Lotte had never bothered much about half-used bottles and pots and would have left them.

"You'm a fool, our Lotte. You worked for that."

"Oh Mary, it's only lavender water."

"It had to be worked for, didn't it? If you leaves it behind you only have to work for it all over again. One day you might be glad of it."

Most of her things had been put into store until she had decided what to do. It had taken her a long time to sort everything out. She had no real plan for her future; the only thing she knew was that everything had changed. For the first time in her life there was no one to decide for her. From the day Mary had fetched her from home to work on the farm at Cantle right up to now, there had always been somebody telling her what was best for her. Now she had to make some decisions of her own. So far she felt pleased with her achievement. She put everything into store, except her warm and practical clothes.

The only journey she had ever taken without Mary was the one from Cantle to Bristol with Tomas Nugent. The secrecy of the plan and the clandestine way in which they travelled had obliterated every thought except the romantic and exciting future. Sometimes Lotte thought that at coming fourteen she should a' known better; at others she was run through with bitterness, especially when she went to see Rosie. Tomas Nugent couldn't help being lost at sea, but he was a grown man and he certainly should a' known better than to leave a young girl there in Bristol.

She scarcely noticed the streets as she followed the boy pushing her

travelling boxes, and was surprised at her lack of emotion at leaving.
She had tucked easily accessible handkerchiefs about her dress,
expecting that sadness would descend upon her at having to leave
Mary in a grave in Portsmouth, where it seemed to Lotte that the only
permanent residents were the dead.

The bustle of preparation in The Sallyport yard was soon got over,
and Lotte was on the first leg of her journey into an unknown future.
For the first time in years she felt that something was happening.

Pilley Heath was not more than fifty miles to the west as the crow
flies, but because the south coast is split both at Portsmouth and
Southampton Water, Lotte's journey was long and meandering. The
other travellers had little to say to one another once the effects of The
Sallyport spiced rum had worn off. Lotte, with her hair and hood
arranged to cover her bad eye, sat like a sober and quiet governess
looking out through the grimy, clammy window. The coach paused at
the top of Ports Down, to recover those passengers who had had to get
off to lighten the uphill load. It was where Harry Goodenstone had
stopped for breath. Like him, Lotte looked down upon the harbour,
the mudflats and the sandbanks. She hoped never to have to see the
place again, but Mary was there and you had a duty.

It had been an unlucky place. But that was daft, wasn't it? When
you thought about it you could say that about anywhere, right back to
Tomas's farm. Bristol, where she had sunk about as low as anybody
could, but then Mary had come. You couldn't say that was bad luck;
what would she a' done without Mary then? Perhaps that was the time
they should have gone back home. It was easy to say that now, and
thinking about it Mary was probably right: they had enough to get on
with there without adding to it. Lotte did not often remember that she
had other sisters, and brothers too. Was Ma and Pa gone? Years ago
most likely ... they'd be well over sixty.

Some places had been lucky – like London, where she had got her
first real chance. That afternoon when both young Mr Hamlyn and
young Mr Locke had been taken with the fever and hadn't been able
to go on. Up until that time her only parts had been walking on and
standing about. It was funny how she hadn't realised that other people
couldn't remember a part almost word for word after hearing it once,
like she could herself.

She smiled to herself as she looked out on the bright, frozen
countryside of south Hampshire. That was a good moment.

Everybody being all at sixes and sevens trying to find somebody to learn the Horatio lines before the evening performance; Mr La Rousse discovering that she knew Horatio's part as well as almost everybody else's and telling everybody that Mrs Trowell was destined for a great career. Well, it hadn't been a great career. She had always been too young-looking and high-voiced for the really good parts. Always been in demand, though, and even though I say it myself, I was good at the naughty wives' parts – and the boys in doublet and hose. She had only got to have somebody read over a part a few times and she got it. That was lucky; there wasn't many who could do it.

London had been unlucky as well, though. Mary had said they couldn't go on letting Rosie travel about with them. She wasn't a baby any more. It was getting harder to keep her hidden away. Lotte hadn't seen anything wrong in letting anybody know about Rosie, but Mary had said that Lotte was too young to understand what it would mean to her future. Mary's arguments had been persuasive, realistic.

"She an't ever going to be able to keep herself. She won't be capable."

"I don't care. I'll look after her, I'll keep her."

"What with? Is any company going to keep you on if you got to go about with a great girl who perhaps won't be able to talk nor perhaps even know what's going on about her? The audience'd laugh you off of the stage, doing 'phelia. The only thing you got that they wants is that you always looks like a twelve-year-old. And any case, what man's going to look twice at you with a child that isn't all there?"

Lotte hated Mary saying things like that about Rosie. Mary never could understand that it didn't matter if some people were like that, they didn't do anybody no harm; and anyway, who said Rosie wasn't all there? Not Lotte. Wasn't she the happiest creature alive?

"I shan't ever marry anybody!"

And nor I shan't, thought Lotte. That was one thing she was still sure of, even though Harry Goodenstone and Mary were gone.

In the end, Lotte had agreed that she would let Rosie go so long as they could find somebody who would look after her and bring her up being kind and gentle. Rosie didn't have to be brought up ladylike or anything like that, just so as she wouldn't realise that she was different. It had taken them months to find somebody suitable, then at last they had come across Constance Sylver, who was in pretty much the same boat as Lotte; but she was trying to keep body and soul together by dressing and painting up the actors and powdering wigs backstage.

One day, Constance had been forced to bring her child to the theatre with her. It was a drooling, moon-faced, slant-eyed child, who smiled and smiled. The way that Constance had been thrown out by the great actor-manager had proved to Lotte that Mary was right. That had been lucky really – Mary being kept at home with the runs that day – she hadn't been able to interfere when Lotte had gone to see Constance Sylver. It was funny, looking back. Things had quite often come out all right somehow, the few times Lotte decided something for herself.

Lotte had made a bargain with Constance Sylver. If Constance would take Rosie and bring her up as near to ordinary as she could, then Lotte would provide for them all: Rosie, Constance and Constance's little Eileen. Lotte had to admit that she couldn't have done what Constance had. People had treated her rotten, especially at first, when she had gone back and tried to live in her own village. It was better now that they had gone to Pilley Heath. It was hardly even a hamlet, more a settlement of charcoal-burners on the edge of Savernake. Constance could stand it if strangers were nasty to her, but she said they hardly took any notice. Constance reckoned that it was because the charcoal-burners were looked down on by ordinary villagers ... so she was really quite content there.

You'd think your own kind would treat you better than that, though, but then you can understand in a way – times being hard enough without having any more burdens. It was hard enough for people with their health and strength looking after their old people, their lame, their idiots. Not that Constance and the children were ever burdens to anybody. Lotte kept her end of the bargain, even though it meant all those years of Harry Goodenstone.

It had broke Lotte's heart at first, but Mary was probably right. It would a' been bad enough if Rosie had been like anybody else, but you had to watch her all the time. Lotte wouldn't have minded; she loved teaching Rosie to do things other children could do naturally. It had taken ages for her to learn to hold out her arms to have her shift put on, but after she did get the hang of it they were both so pleased. Rosie was so loveable and pretty. Rosie. Why ever had she christened her Rosalinda? Rosie was exactly right – like the wild roses; pink and open and ...

Remembering, Lotte's eyes brimmed and she had to be careful not to blink in case they should run over in tears.

She didn't know what they would do now. She had gone over it a dozen times in these last weeks since Mary died, trying to work things out.

When Mary was ill, Lotte nursed her night and day, not really taking much notice of the bruise and grazes Harry Goodenstone had made. When the place started to become hot and sore Lotte did wonder for a bit if she had got smallpox, but the apothecary who had looked at it said it was just festering; probably from face-powder or one of the other concoctions women put on their faces. He had seen the same sort of thing enough times. Lotte had scarcely listened to all that, just as long as she hadn't taken the smallpox and could nurse her poor, tortured Mary.

She forgot the irritating wound until the day after Mary had been buried. Then at last she had a good look at herself. The stiff-hair trimming of his riding-crop had made a kind of burn on the skin. It had blistered and let the infection in and the wound had healed like a burn, leaving a pale mulberry-coloured scar that was shiny and tight. She was too busy to think much about it then, but Lotte had felt a kind of relief when she had realised what a mess that part of her face was.

The woman sitting next to Lotte in the coach was wearing a high and complicated wig under a wide and complicated hat which, for a start, was a nuisance to those on either side of her; but Lotte had noticed when standing behind her as they climbed on board that the woman had far more than the usual number of wig-lice: so many, apparently, that there were some on the ribbons of her hat. You expected to pick up more than usual on any coach, but when the woman took her seat Lotte was conscious of all the time she would have to waste when she got to the other end, getting rid of the fleas that would certainly overflow on to other people. So Lotte tried to make as much space between them as possible, but each time Lotte edged away half-an-inch, the woman spread into it until, at last, Lotte had only part of her allotted space.

Finally Lotte turned to the woman and sweetly, as she always spoke, asked her if she would mind moving along. The woman was about to say something, but then drew her cloak close over her breast and quickly made good space between them.

Lotte, grieving over Mary and preoccupied of late, looked out at

[249]

the world. When she stepped back into it again, she saw that it was much as it had always been and was not surprised at it. The world, looking back at Lotte, reacted as it would on finding an unsuspected slug on the underside of an open lily.

The world had reacted to Lotte's face in this way several times in recent days, but it was only now, with a bit of respite from everything that had been going on since Mary had been stricken, that this reaction of the world registered in her conscious. She did not feel hurt or angry, but intrigued.

Well, well! What was it? Not the scar itself ... half the population has got some mark where things has festered, teeth rotted and gum-boils has eaten into their jaws. And ringworm marks. Why, on the farm everybody had the ringworm patches on them. It wasn't just the scar being ugly either. Good Lord, there was enough of that about, too, especially in places like Bath, where you saw men who looked like they were bloated bodies dragged from the river they were so full of fat meat and red wine – and others, women too, with poxt faces. No, the woman hadn't drawn away from her because of that. Why, the nest of fleas the woman wore was a worse thing to sit next to than a scar. True, it was a nasty scar, especially when you compared it to the other side. That was probably it. People don't like to have things like that jumped on them. Lotte had arranged her hair and the hood of her cloak to hide it as best she could. That wasn't right, it caught people unawares. She had to admit she would be the same herself. If Mary had got over the smallpox, she would have had to go about with her face full of holes and pits and people wouldn't have taken much notice. What always shocked you a bit was suddenly seeing something through a veil: an empty eye-socket where you expected to see an eye.

Then and there she decided that she could do without that kind of thing. She was going to have quite enough problems as it was, without people suddenly going quiet when she turned her face. She pushed back her hood as naturally as she could and went on looking out of the coach window, giving her fellow-travellers a good chance to see that she wasn't really a pretty woman. For a minute or two she felt a bit self-conscious, but was soon lost again in thinking about the changes she was making and how they were going to cope.

There was the jewellery. Mary had always said they should put every penny into good stones. She had reckoned that they were better than gold coin if you had them in really good settings. And Lotte had been surprised when she had come to look in the false bottom of the chest: there was above three hundred. Surely three hundred ought to keep them for years; and that was in addition to what Mary had kept tied about her, beneath her clothes. Then there was the place Harry had bought in London which was supposed to be Lotte's, but Mary had seen to everything like that. Surely Mary would have said something if Harry hadn't made it secure? There was one thing about Mary: she had always looked after them all right in that way; her head was screwed on all right. When it came to things like that, Lotte didn't know where to start. Mary had always managed to get the last penny out of any manager. Never mind, they'd manage somehow.

Lost in confusion of thoughts, Lotte noticed the cold and discomfort of the journey only superficially, and was putting up at the Dolphin in Southampton almost before she realised it.

ARRY GOODENSTONE was not a man for much deep thought, but he had recently been thinking about things – things to do with himself, the Estate, the farms; what he was going to do now.

He had simmered down a bit, but there were times ... especially when handling a riding-crop. He would slash it against his knee-boots or leggings, giving himself quite a thrill at the remembrance of letting go at her.

He decided to spend some time at Park Manor and see what was what. He rather liked the idea of becoming a landowner of the new style. Young Harry Goodenstone. A fellow to bring in new ways of doing things. Never be afraid of trying something new. Harry liked that idea.

"Say! Have y'seen Young Goodenstone's new scheme? Smart young fella. Show us old'ns a thing or two."

"Heard about Harry Goodenstone's latest idea for sheep? Trust him to be first with anything new."

Recognition. Esteem.

He thought that it could be like leading the very latest fashion of dress. Recognition as a leader in ... well, growing new crops perhaps; a new style. He wondered whether he could have all the cottages on the estate painted. Green? he wondered, or blue? Or a lovely lapis lazuli colour he had commented upon at a little spa. It would make quite a lot of difference when riding out to see squadges of colour tucked here and there. His father had spent a fortune on the house itself, yet when one moved away one was confronted by the cottagers' squalid, mud-coloured hovels, and Harry thought he might brighten them up.

He had recently been finding out more about their estates abroad, and was surprised that so much of the Goodenstone income came from places he had never even suspected till now. He could not always remember whether it was India or Indies, but he thought perhaps he could take trips to those estates. He liked the idea of going somewhere where it was warm. He saw himself taking a sea voyage and having a look at where his money came from. See tea and coffee growing. He wondered what a tea field would look like. Then he saw himself going in for government.

Parliament. Harry Goodenstone knew that he would only have to let it be known that he was willing and he would soon be offered a seat. He thought up some ideas that would go to present the kind of forward-thinking man he knew he was. He had heard men talk about the new spirit with admiration.

He wondered if he might start a school? He had heard only last year that some noble duke or lord had started a scheme for teaching peasant children. Or a library open to the public? One had been started in Southampton, and Harry had heard very great praise heaped upon the person whose idea it had been.

If he was going into Parliament, Harry thought, people would have great regard for a fellow who was advanced in his thinking, travelled to foreign places, and was philanthropic to boot!

So when the new year came, and Harry Goodenstone had some thoughts about his future, he began to see that life might be quite as jolly thinking up schemes like these as choosing coat-cloth or going after a new horse, and he could still keep up with fashion, of course; the latest plays, London, Bath, that kind of thing.

The thought that had begun to germinate on the day he had looked down upon Cantle after riding hell-for-leather out of Portsmouth now took root. That one had to defend what one owned; side with one's own kind against the rest. Harry decided that perhaps, after all, his father had had something there, and that it was a good thing that he had not gone rushing back to Portsmouth.

BELLA HAD ALWAYS been a one for special days. She never said anything to anybody, because when you came to look at it it was a bit soft: there wasn't really anything special about the day you were born. Not to say you should make anything of it when it came round every year, and Easter wasn't the same two years running. But remembrances would go through her mind whenever it was a holy day. She would recall others – that Whit Sunday, twenty years ago, was the day when ... One St Crispin's, must a been when I was about eight ... Every spring she remembered previous springs and tended to mull things over every Christmas, and times like that. She often felt a bit down when she realised that another year had gone by. For some reason a new year was worst of all. If you looked back over the one just gone there never seemed much to crow about, and if you looked forward there didn't seem no reason to think things would get much better.

She didn't even know what she wanted to happen. These days she just wanted to let it all go. What was she – forty-five, forty-six? Yes, nearly forty-seven – plenty of women had passed on by that age. She didn't particularly want to die – there had always been a suspicion at the back of her mind that Heaven and all that was a bit of a carrot the Church held out to keep everybody going – not die, but just sort of let it all go.

Twenty-odd years she had been keeping the place going. The times she had wanted to run away from it all! Once, when Jaen had been just a girl and Jude not much more than a baby, she had gone to see a lawyer about selling up the farm. She had no claim, according to him; no proof that Tomas Nugent was dead. In time the farm might pass to a son. No son. Come back in ten years, and if your husband has not returned ...

[254]

The ten years was long up. Sometimes she thought she would do something about it, but it never seemed to be the right time. Anyway, what was the use? There wasn't nobody to hand it on to. Jude would settle down in time: if she didn't marry young Will there'd be somebody, and if he wanted the farm then he'd have to see about all the legal side of it.

If only she'd a had sons. She'd been sure Jude was a boy. The way she was carrying, high; the slow way she moved in the womb – not like Jaen, always jumping and turning months before she was birthed. Perhaps it was God's judgement on her for praying she wouldn't have another girl. Perhaps it was His way of showing her that it don't do. He had not only give her a girl, but one who wasn't ordinary, nor easy to get on with. No, she didn't really believe that it was a judgement: that's what They liked you to believe. Even so, the fact remained. Jude wasn't never easy; always made you feel she was getting the better of you somehow. Always "at" something or other. There was something striving about Jude, and women never ought to be like that.

If only Jude had been a son. Now, if a boy had a learnt to read and write, he could a made summat of it, instead of all that stuff Jude had wasted so much time on: people dead and gone, who wasn't anybody even when they was alive. Giving in to Jude like that had been a mistake. She'd only intended it to be something to take her mind off things after Jaen went. That's what comes of being soft! Every time you gave in and did something soft there was trouble. If she hadn't a give in to Jaen that time. It had went to Jaen's head – and look what happened. She'd a been soft with Jude. The money that had gone into that week with the Warrens! Money put by for years in case she had to pay lawyers to get the farm sorted out. True, there was money left, but she'd been too hasty. Mind you, Jude hadn't made no fuss about being laid up all that time, nor still don't, Bella had to admit that. Even though she still walks a bit dot-and-carry-one with her leg. But life's hard, and it don't do to be soft against it.

All Bella wanted was for it all to go away so that she could sit back for a year or two and let somebody else take over worrying. This place needs a man. Why didn't Jude have the rumgumption to see Will Vickery couldn't take his eyes off her? He'd got more than his share of Adam in him, that's for certain. But you couldn't never talk to her. She'd look at you in that clever way, and you'd feel her looking down at you if you mentioned something like that. You never knew what she was thinking. Deep? She was deep all right.

It was funny, though, she'd never wished Hanna had a been a boy. A boy wouldn't never put his arms round your neck, and boys wouldn't never let you dress their warm little body, nor be content to do the baking and seeing to the hens like that little Lovey did. Hanna wasn't deep, she was a proper little woman. There wasn't no doubt, Hanna would make somebody a good little wife. She'd be all right.

IT WAS HANNA'S FUTURE that occupied Jude's thoughts following her climb up Beacon.

She knew that she was coming to a kind of crossroads and had been approaching it for quite a time: that much was now clear to her. She could continue on the old, familiar road of land, animals, home, farm and market. There were plenty of people who would give their eye-teeth for that kind of security. Security and going on having the kind of independence they had. They didn't have much, but it was worth having.

She could take the second road – marriage to Will Vickery. He hadn't asked her, but he would. It was temptation itself the thought of him. Will, the man; the warm, hard body. Will; non-conformist ideas, secrets, hidden behind the conforming face he presented to the world. The stimulation – two men in one. Will the lover, who had been the means of her discovering that there was a kind of flying ecstasy she had not suspected. Will Vickery, who believed that there was nothing to be ashamed of in their enjoyment of one another.

But what happens when that fades?

What would Will be like when they got to the stage when he got used to her? Home and children were just a small part of a man's life.

It was the same in the few marriages she knew anything about. Even with people like Dicken and his wife. For all the long, hard labour of their lives, Dicken still came off best of the two. He was master in his own home. He got paid for his work and could say how it was spent: if he wanted to drink it away in the Dragon and Fount, then nobody could say him nay; and the same if he wanted to buy his wife an extravagant shawl, or bread for his family. He had the say.

The third road, you went down blind. Once you took it, you probably had to keep going. Plenty of men took it. Her father had. He had said, in effect: I've only got one life and I shall live it the way I want to. Any young man of twenty – it didn't matter whether he was the highest or the lowest in the land – if he felt as she did, unsettled, searching for something, could just go off and see if he could find what it was.

That's what I should like. That's what I want ... what I need.

There was no knowing where the third road led, but it seemed to Jude that if she did not break free of the farm and at least try to do the vague something that goaded her, then there would be more episodes like that when she ran out of the harvest field. Going that way meant pleasing nobody but yourself, and you had to be strong and not be turned back because people needed you or you needed them.

This train of thought, started on Beacon, went round in Jude's mind for days. By the end of January she was still as unsettled as ever. She had some idea that perhaps she ought to go and live in Blackbrook to see what she was capable of doing, but she still kept coming back to the problem of what to do about Hanna. She felt responsible for her now. Bella could rub along all right with some help, but she could not bring herself to think of leaving Hanna, isolated except for the company of the ageing Bella and Johnny-twoey.

Will returned from the North in early February and rode over to Croud Cantle at the first opportunity. The place came alive with him. Bella fussed and Hanna giggled. As soon as Jude saw him dismounting in the yard, wearing the cloak in which he had enveloped her on Tradden, she could hardly meet his eye. She had thought of the moment of meeting again a hundred times. In imagination she could greet him dispassionately, resetting their relationship, putting it back to where it was before they had made love on frozen Tradden.

She would be light about it, almost as though it had never happened. It was just an unguarded moment, the wine had gone to her head.

But she had not taken into account the lovely way he spoke, the trace of Irish, the last few words of his sentences rising then falling, and the amusement there always seemed to be in his voice. She had forgotten the arousing, masculine smell of his clothes, and had forgotten, too, the way his eyes could suggest something that the rest of his features, his manner, his conversation did not. So when he doffed his hat and said politely that it had seemed a long time since he was last here, his eyes, flickering up and down her figure as he said "here", passed her a more intimate message.

Jude knew that, if she was not going to allow herself to be lured down into domesticity as they had lured one another down on to the frosty surface of Tradden, she would have to be forearmed against his charm and her own desire to love him again. She would need to be stronger than ever Bella had been with Tomas.

She had a lesson from Bella and Jaen. They had been blind to the consequences of giving in to your nature, as she had to admit she had been blind herself on Christmas afternoon. She had been lucky that once.

That first visit after returning from the North was only a short one, as he was out on business for White's. He was puzzled by Jude.

"Is everything all right?"

"Of course. Did you have a good journey?"

She was polite and nice. He had expected anything except politeness, friendliness.

Jude was relieved that he could stop only a short while and that Bella and Hanna were there. It gave her the chance to deal with the sensations that had leaped at her unexpectedly, such as when she saw his breath spurt, swirl and eddy, white into the frosty air, breath that had been inside him, part of him; and again when she noticed how the long muscle at the back of his leg flexed and hardened beneath the cloth of his pale-coloured riding-breeches as he put his foot into the stirrup. Indeed, there seemed to be no part of him safe to look at; no part that she did not want to touch, hold, caress. It was not going to be easy to keep him at arm's length.

"I shall be this way again quite soon."

"You make sure you are then," said Bella.

And when he came that way again, Jude saw to it that she was fully occupied with necessary work. Supervising and helping Dicken and Johnny-twoey in the opening up of some clamps of vegetables for market.

"Jude, you might a left off doing that for a minute today and come in and talked to Will," said Bella.

For a few seconds Bella looked at Jude, who would not look back. "I said to him, why not come to Morning Service on Sunday, and I'd make him a rare good pie. In his lodgings he don't never get no good cooking. I thought you might do one of your rabbit-pies with a lot of herbs and the apple wine. You know, like you do."

[259]

Oh Mother! I can read you easier than a book.

"I had definitely made up my mind to take Hanna over to Jaen's and I've told Hanna now. We haven't been since before Christmas," Jude said.

"Well then, another week won't hurt."

"We can't really leave it any longer, especially now the weather's set fine for a bit. Get into March and it'll as likely change and we shall be into planting-time, and you know I always hate that road when the trees drip."

"Trees drip everywhere."

"Not like they do on that mile or two going into Newton."

"The days a be that much longer if you leave it a week."

They wrangled on for a few more exchanges until Jude said, "Oh mother, just because you asked Will Vickery to stop and eat on a Sunday, it don't mean I have to be here as well. You enjoy each other's company. You'll be able to make a to-do over dinner. You'll both like that."

Bella did not know what to say. Jude kept stirring the frizzling bacon and potatoes; trying to pass Will's visit off, as though it was nothing to do with her.

"He don't come to see me," Bella said at last.

Jude did not answer.

There was strain between them the rest of the week and early on Sunday Jude got the two donkeys ready and set off with Hanna. Bella knew that Jude had the upper hand. Nothing had ever been said about Jude and Will Vickery. To all intents and purposes, Will was no more than Fred Warren's assistant who paid friendly visits to Croud Cantle when he was in the area, and who Bella had invited to share their Christmas dinner. Nothing more. If Bella had chosen to invite him again then that was all right.

She came to the door as Jude was tucking shawls about Hanna.

"What shall I tell him?"

"Who?" asked Jude, intending to appear preoccupied.

"Jude! You know blimmen well."

"Will? Tell him Hanna hasn't seen Jaen for ages and now the ground has started to warm up we shan't have much time. There'll be plenty of other times when he can come."

"LOOK HANNA!" I called, as we rode down Howgaite on the promised visit to Newton Clare, "the fairy-soldiers' plumes are out." This was the name Jaen had given to the tiny, brilliant scarlet tufts of the female hazel catkin.

There were times when it seemed that Hanna and I should change our roles; when she, with her seriousness and responsible outlook, should be the aunt and I the niece. She was always kind to me in my fanciful enthusiasms, but gently disapproving. "Oh Jude, you are not much of a lady, are you?"

It was soon after dawn when we left. The weather had become milder and blustering winds were beginning to get up, which did not please me because such weather always makes me uneasy. There had been deep frosts all winter, and much of the underwood of holly, birch and ash was stripped of its lower bark by rabbits, who will take anything for sustenance in a hard winter. Hares, too, had been at many of the hazels. The young shoots being cut off clean as if by a sharp knife. Here and there I saw the first signs of regeneration: the slight swelling and shine of new buds in leaf axils of the traveller's joy; its clots of beard, which had been white and fluffy in the autumn, now brittle and tattered. I cannot remember when I first noticed this death and regeneration going on together, but it seems that I have seen it a hundred times. It never fails to fill me with an emotion that I cannot give a name to, but it is a mingling of joy and regret.

My sister and her husband lived then at Ham Ford Farm. Dan Hazelhurst, no longer farming the small acreage he had started with, had gained more land and had now turned almost all of it to wheat-growing, so that their fortunes depended entirely on this one crop.

It was several months since I had brought Hanna to visit her parents. I saw at once that Jaen was yet again pregnant. I say "yet again", because it was less than nine years ago that she was a bride. Hanna was eight, and had five younger brothers, and I know that Jaen had been through at least one "misfortune".

I did not know whether to congratulate or commiserate, so I hugged her and patted her mound, and said smilingly, "What is this one to be then?"

"A Hazelhurst, no doubt," she said, without any suggestion of a smile.

I wished that I could have picked her up and run back with her to Cantle. Back in time; to when her hair was abundant and the same colour as the wreaths of rest-harrow flowers she let me bind into it; back to when the worst of our problems was to remember not to walk upon our mother's bright floor with muddy feet; to when she took me by the hand and led me out on to the great green breast of Tradden Raike.

She petted Hanna, holding her face and smoothing her hair but, as always, they behaved to one another in a polite and restrained way. I have often wondered what Hanna thought of the arrangement; living with her grandmother and aunt whilst her mother cared for an ever-increasing family of little boys. She never wanted to stay there very long.

"Goodness, child, you gets more like Jude every time I sees you," Jaen said.

Hanna looked at me as though she did not know what to make of that.

The house was empty except for Jaen and one or two girls who worked in the house and the dairy. Jaen said that Dan had taken the boys to morning service and to visit other Hazelhursts, but her legs were too swelled up to do that these days.

"I'm glad you come, Ju," Jaen said. "The packman had some coffee beans, which he says is the fashion, and I thought I would give us a treat."

For the time that it took her to grind the beans and brew the drink, she was quite animated and jolly.

Hanna, already bored – which she seldom was at Croud Cantle – went out with one of the maids. The girl did not appear to be much older than Hanna, but already had the hollow-eyed look that many little servant-girls get just before they drag themselves into womanhood.

"Oh Ju, I wish you wasn't so far away. It's so lonely."

Jaen said this same thing every time I visited, and I never knew what to reply. I did know, however, that it was not so much that she was isolated, for the house seemed always to be bursting with people and children. It was that she felt cut off from people who knew her, knew Jaen Nugent, knew a person who belonged to herself – not Young Dannal's mother; not Baxter's or Francis's mother; not Dan Hazelhurst's wife.

"I wish I could come over more often," I said.

This was not true. It was no pleasure for me to see the deterioration of my pretty, lively, intelligent sister, whose imagination had been more vivid than that of Dean Swift – ah, what sparkling adventures Gulliver would have had under Jaen's guidance.

We sat with our feet in the hearth, sipping the bitter, aromatic drink and saying how delicious it was; talking in a desultory way about mother, the farm, what was going on in the market these days when, almost mid-sentence, she said, "You got a young man, Ju."

I was quite taken aback, firstly because we have always been a reticent family and secondly because she did not frame a question. It was a statement, an observation.

"You been listening to gossip, Jaen?"

"Never a word."

"You know what they say about Jude Nugent – she wants a man made to order."

"Oh Ju, I care that much about you." She took my hand and stroked it as one strokes the head of a cat. "Don't keep it all inside." She just looked at me, her head on one side, and said, "Ju, I can see. It's writ all over you."

I could never hide anything from Jaen. When I was very little she would say, "It's writ all over your face," and I would be puzzled as to what was there, never having seen my face. Again, now, I knew what was writ on me.

"How serious is it?"

I could not meet her eye.

"Oh Ju! You haven't gone and ... " My cheeks burned, because I knew that she would find me out as she always has done. She sounded quite anguished, her voice rose. "Look at me, Ju. Go on, look." She stood before me, her swollen belly at my eye-level. She tore off her cap and she clutched at her front hair. It was sparse and straggly, with little left to suggest that she had once had hair as red and bouncing as a squirrel's tail.

"This is what comes of that half a minute of enjoyment."

I tried to calm her down, telling her to hush or the girls would hear. She lowered her voice and sat down again, but she was in such earnest that I wished I could laugh at the very suggestion that I had been loved by Will Vickery.

"Jaen, it wasn't anything. It was ... "

She came and sat beside me in the chimney seat. It was the first time that she had put her arms about me since the day she left home and was married, when I had been so bitterly grieved because she had abandoned me for Dan Hazelhurst. Now I was so overcome by her action that I told her about Will Vickery; of how I liked him and how much I was affected by him.

"If you can dout that sort of fire, Ju, then dout it. It an't worth it. Lord help us, if I haven't learned much in life, I certainly learned that. I wish somebody'd a told me when I was young."

Jaen spoke as though she was a generation older than myself instead of only six years, but she must have come to realise that I was now a woman and no longer her toddling sister, for she talked to me about the time when she had gone away for a few days and had met Dan Hazelhurst and conceived Hanna.

"It was only a moment of foolishness, Ju, and it can alter your whole life. I was young, but I don't think that makes much difference. It was just ... Well, you know how big and handsome Dan is. I was overcome by all his attentions. A course, I hadn't never known nothing like it before, him telling me how pretty and that I was. I never knew it was possible to get into that state where nothing don't matter except pleasing yourself and him." She made a thin, tight line of her lips. "It an't worth it, Ju." She lowered her voice, speaking almost to herself. "There's times when I wishes him to Kingdom Come. To him, it's just his rights as a husband, and his pleasure. To me it's all this." She laid a hand on her belly and raised her skirts to reveal huge, white legs, looking like rolls of lard and knotted with purple veins. I drew in my breath at the sight of them.

"It's all right, Ju, it an't nothing but water. Most of it will go when the baby comes." For a moment she closed her lids over her eyes, as though to blot out any thought of that event.

"And you don't intend to marry him?" she asked in her ordinary voice.

"No," I replied. "Since I learned to read and write, I know just enough to show me that there's better things than growing salads and selling pies, but being tied down to a husband and children isn't one of them, even if the husband were Will Vickery."

"What shall you do, Ju?"

"I don't know. I would like to get away from the farm. I don't even know what I can do. I don't see how I can know till I know what goes on. Do that makes sense?"

"There might be summit goes on in other places that don't go on in Cantle that you don't know about?"

"I heard the other day that there's public libraries starting up in some places. Well somebody has to work in them, and it'd be just the kind of thing I'd love to do. But you wouldn't never know they even exists in a place like Cantle. Jaen, I want to do something, something, something! I shall go off my head if I can't use it."

"I thought you was writing a story."

"I am, but that's just my pleasure. I want to do something that's going to make a bit of difference."

"If you'd a been a man you could a gone to sea." She withdrew into her mind, as I had seen her do throughout my childhood when she let her imagination wander, and gazed at the flames licking at the base of the black cooking pot.

"You could a been a privateer, putting to sea and going to countries where there's all different kinds of birds and fruit and that, and you could go to places like Gilly Gilson used to tell us of, where water shoots out of the ground already boiled. Just imagine that. And you, being that much cleverer than the rest, you'd a soon been the chief one, and when you'd a captured a ship, you could a ... " She suddenly seemed to see the steaming cooking pot, then covering her nose and mouth in her cupped hand, just like an embarrassed child, said, "Oh Ju, an't I a fool!"

It was good to see Jaen laugh, properly. There have been times when she has seemed very strange, getting het up over little things and getting shrill with the children and the maids, and never laughing, except in a forced way.

"Well, I can't go to sea, so what am I going to do?" I said.

[265]

"You always been pretty thick with that Mr Warren what taught you to read. I should a thought he might be the one to ask."

I had already thought that I might talk to Fred Warren. The only trouble with that was in Will being close to Fred and Molly, and I believed that they would have been pleased to see Will marry me. But as beggars can't be choosers, I said to Jaen that I would do as she suggested.

We had about one hour to talk, in which we returned to something like the intimacy of our girlhood, strengthened by Jaen's acceptance of me as an adult. Then the spell was broken by Hanna coming back.

"What you been doing, Child?"

I don't think I ever heard Jaen call Hanna by her given name after she came to live with Mother and me. Hanna, picking it up from us, always referred to her mother as Jaen.

"I did the butter, and got the eggs from the banties."

"You don't have to do that, we got girls to do that, and anyway it's Sunday-day-of-rest."

"I like doing it, Jaen, and there isn't anything else to do."

Soon my brother-in-law returned with the little boys, and the house seemed suddenly overflowing. The children were red-cheeked and wind-blown, and brought in with them a healthy smell of children who have been running in the fresh air.

It was easy to see how the young Jaen had been captivated by Dan. He was a very tall, manly man, of such a breadth of chest that his jacket-fastening – like the strings of the leggings which encased his tree-trunk legs – gave the impression of creaking under the strain of encasing such an amount of muscle. There had been a time when I thought that he was so knowledgeable about government and reform and that kind of thing, but his ideas were immature and uninformed in comparison with those of Fred Warren and Will and, unlike them, he never considered women capable of joining in such discussion – or that it was their place to do so.

He greeted me in his usual way.

"Still not married then, Judeth?"

It was an implied criticism, because of that time when Edwin Hazelhurst had kept calling on me. Dan, thinking what an honour it was for me to be courted by a Hazelhurst, had not forgiven me for spurning his brother. Because I was still not married at the age of twenty-one, he probably thought that I now rued that day.

"That's right, Dan, so I've still only myself to please."

"Well, Girl?" he said to Hanna. "You've come on a bit since we last saw you."

"Have I, father?"

"She's been doing the butter, look, all done nice in the mould."

"You'm good at that kind of thing, then?"

Why did I go on and on so about how good Hanna was at everything? I suppose I must have wanted him to praise her, instead of which he said, "Well, I reckon then, Girl, that you'd be a real help here to your mother."

At first I did not comprehend the full meaning of what he had said, so I gushed on.

"I can't tell you how much Mother has taught her," I said, and I laughed, "I wish she'd be half as good at learning to read and write. I've been trying to teach her." I poked Hanna jokingly in the ribs. She did not respond, and it was then that I saw how wide-eyed and apprehensive she was as she stared at her father.

What ever did she feel? That neat, square, stocky little girl, looking up at her huge father. Her father, yet almost a stranger. She knew Fred Warren and Will far better than she knew Dan Hazelhurst.

THE ANGUISH of that day is bound to stay raw and tender, as is any memory involving the heartless treatment of a vulnerable child.

During the whole battle for Hanna – for that is what it became – she stood white as a sheet, never saying one word. Then, when she at last realised that I had used up every argument I could lay tongue to; when it was apparent that there was nothing left; no reason, no threat, no right that would allow her to return to Cantle with me, she ran from the house with her own water running down her legs and vomited yellow bile in the yard.

I ran after her and drew her into an outbuilding. She was acutely embarrassed. Humiliated at the physical manifestations of the shock and her fear. Tears and mucus ran down her face. She kept repeating, "I couldn't help it, Jude. I couldn't help it," and I kept answering, "It's all right. It doesn't matter." Wet stockings were the least of our troubles, but the removing of them at least gave us something to occupy our hands as I knelt to help with the unknotting of laces. Suddenly she flung herself at me, sending me off balance and we finished up sitting on the straw of the barn floor, with me rocking her and murmuring meaningless sounds that were intended to be comforting. I could scarcely believe that the tense, cold, clammy, clinging small body, was warm, soft Hanna.

We had come full circle.

Full circle from that Christmas Day when I had rocked and comforted her once before, a wretched, teething baby who had come to live with us at Cantle; full circle to this day, over seven years later, when with that terrible, chilling unexpectedness her father insisted that she return.

A great, hard ball of emotions were gathering like a carbuncle in the pit of my stomach. Pain, anguish, misery, despair – yet I could not allow it to burst whilst I held the tormented little girl. Had Dan Hazelhurst appeared at the barn door at that moment, I believe my passion would have been uncontrollable. I should have run him through; pierced his dominating, high and mighty chest with the hay-fork. I was so furious at the way he could just step into our lives and order them, that the plates of muscle would have been as unresisting as rendered lard.

My teeth clenched at my hatred of that man.

When I took Hanna back into the house, Jaen was apprehensive, clutching her locked fingers under her bosom and rocking slightly back and forth. She kept saying the same things, over and over in a strained, wheedling, whining voice. "Why not let her go back, Dan? It's all too strange for her. Let her go back. I can manage. She's only eight: what bit of work she can do here won't make much difference." And to me she said, "I didn't know, Ju. I swear I never knew."

"She stays and there's an end to it. We don't want none of your Nugent nerves and fancifulness again today, Missis. Nor none of your tears or sulks, Girl." Hanna flinched but now stood solidly, a little Bella Nugent, facing whatever she had to face.

And he stood there, God, warming the backside of His breeches at the fire.

On that little patch of earth, that was what he was: insensitive, arrogant god. He held the lives of Jaen, Hanna, and the little boys. He ruled, too, the servant-girls and milk-maids whose parents, in their poverty, had virtually given them to him on the basis of an exchange of work for bread. None of them were anything without him and what he owned. They had no say in the gambles he took in the management of the farm; in how many pigs they should keep; in how much butter should be on the table. When it came down to it, not one of them had any real say in their own lives; what they ate, drank or were dressed in.

As the wind sometimes blows through the valley clogged by mists, so it blew through my mind. When it was cleared of the obscuring wants, desires, ifs, and buts of everyday living, I could see one fact clearly, standing isolated like the eccentric, mysterious stone on Winchester Hill.

People like me, ordinary men and women, are bound about by unjust laws, written and unwritten: rules; oppressive customs. Poverty, fear, lack of education and plain exhaustion from work keep

[269]

us from breaking free from their hold upon us. But as I was now, unmarried, unattached, I was free of one set of laws – those which subjugate women in marriage. I was not held by the rules, nor enmeshed in customs.

I did not have to marry. I did not need to marry.

This was the one freedom that I had.

To remain a spinster.

No judge, minister, lord or bishop could take that freedom from me.

The smoke did not clear as I stood there; these thoughts did not occur to me in sequence or even in words at all. But seeing Jaen, clutching and unclutching her white-knuckled fingers and Hanna, bewildered and distraught, there was an amalgamated thought that summed up the rest: Never!

I went away from Ham Ford Farm and out of Newton Clare in a stupor of anguish.

I had no idea how long I had been there. The sun, which was only visible through occasional cracks in the scudding cloud, had swung round and had already begun to drop down. The wind that had been gusty earlier in the day was gathering strength, was loud and turbulent.

The distance between Newton Clare and Cantle is not great, but the state of parts of the road have always been renowned as the worst in the four parishes. Having Hanna's donkey as well as my own meant my progress was slow. And, of course, I was preoccupied. However was I going to break it to my mother?

Had the Goodenstones not effectively stopped all reasonable exit from Old Marl by enclosing the land at its base, then I might have travelled as the crow flies and been at least in the village before the light failed, even if not actually home. As it was, there was no quicker way home than to go a slightly longer route along the Tradden Raike.

When I reached the steep slope, I dismounted and led the two beasts, one of which was always difficult if it had no panniers or rider. It stopped and started so many times that it was dark by the time I reached the summit. Being Tradden, I knew every hummock, hole and track, and because the chalk was so close to the surface, footpaths and raikes showed up as if drawn upon the grass.

I had just started the descent when the animal stopped and refused to move. I tried sitting upon its back, but it would not budge. I wondered whether, by some sense that animals have, there was some danger, or whether it could hear a sound over the uproar of the March winds; but I could see or hear nothing. A tiny glimmer of light far down, from our farm window. The anxiety I was feeling over my mother increased. I could feel the strain of the day building up. I wanted to rush on towards facing my mother with the terrible event. I wanted to get the imagined distraught face of her out of my mind and into reality where I could cope with it. I wanted the distracting wind to calm itself and allow the air to become peaceful.

At last, when I could bear the stubborn animal no longer, I whipped it across its back with the leading rope. It gave a loud bray and raced off across the downs. I let it go, making no attempt to get it back. The good beast followed me. After a few minutes, I saw a light moving along the narrow track that leads up from the farm, then a call: "Ju-deth. Ju-u-deth." I recognised Will's voice and called back to him.

By calling out from time to time, we soon met. As soon as I saw his outline and heard his deep, gentle voice, a kind of dry sob broke spontaneously from me. I felt as though I had been submerged in a deep pond and had forgotten to come up for breath until he reminded me. He took the leading rope from me and held the lantern out at arm's length, looking along the track.

"Where's Hanna? What has happened?"

"They've taken her back." I think my voice was trembling, certainly my hands and legs were.

He pulled me gently into his shoulder and patted my back, as one would a child who has fallen down. There was great comfort in his action, but I pulled away at once.

"I must get down to tell Mother."

"Ah, just take it easy a minute." He raised the lantern high and waved it slowly back and forth a few times. "Your mother is waiting by the yard gate. She'll go in now I've given her the signal. You're trembling like a leaf. Just sit and rest. Here," he unstoppered a small pocket flask and handed it to me. "Go on, it's good French brandy."

I swallowed a mouthful and felt the searing passage of the liquid as it branded my throat then spread out into my body, relaxing it. Oh, Will, how gentle, how firm as a rock, how reliable. Will Vickery, calm, un-godlike. As he went with me down Tradden it did seem the most desirable thing to have someone who loved me enough to share the weight of the awful misery of Hanna's loss to us. I was quite sure that he did love me. Marriage tempting. The road that was signposted and known, going that way with someone who loved you.

"Jude! Jude!" My mother's voice rose up from the valley. Breaking into my thoughts, she broke the spell. I called a reply.

"Your mother thought you might a had an accident or something. She was expecting you long ago. I stopped on to keep her company. When it began to get dark, I said I would take the lantern out."

He kept the one-sided conversation going as we went slowly down. I could think only of how I was going to break the news to Mother. I cannot bear seeing people suffering, miserable. I cannot cope. I do not know what to do. No doubt I shall appear indifferent to her desolation. Words are useless, weak things, when it comes to expressing the deep emotion of compassion.

In the event, it was not necessary to choose words. When we reached the bottom of Tradden, Mother was in the yard holding a lantern, but the moon was now flooding light so that she could clearly see that there was only one donkey, and that Hanna was not with us.

I wanted to get it over. "Mother, Hanna ... "

She interrupted me. "He took her back."

Not a question – a statement. Inevitability.

"Yes," I said.

"I always thought he would, one fine day, once she got useful enough."

Once, long ago, I had found her crying over Jaen. It was a shocking thing to me. Women did cry – but not my mother. I had thought her to be granite-solid, and was so disconcerted at finding that she had a hair-line crack, a flaw that she was ashamed of, that I had put my arms about her. And this is what I did.

She did not flinch or move away. I do not believe that she even realised that I had made this move towards her. She stood, running her hand over the dip in the donkey's back, as though she was blind and was looking to find something there. After about a minute, which seemed long-stretched – Will and I, useless statues, waiting – she said, "I had thought I should a had her another four or five years. I never thought he'd a took her so soon."

"There's another baby on the way," I said.

This seemed to bring her back from wherever she had been.

"He should a been born a bull, then he could at least a put it to some use."

If I had expected anything, it was not her dull acceptance of the blow. Perhaps she had been waiting for it ever since Hanna came to us. Perhaps she felt a strange kind of relief that the blow had fallen. While I was still quite young, I realised that my mother's philosophy was to expect the worst and be thankful if you got anything less.

"You go in," Will said quietly. "I'll see to the animal."

"You still here, Will?" she said, apparently surprised at hearing his voice.

He took the lanterns and the donkey away and I went into the kitchen with Mother.

"I told Dan that I would go and live in, till Jaen was on her feet again, if he let Hanna come back here."

She started preparing some food, her actions automatic.

"He wouldn't have that, I'll be bound."

"No. He said it wouldn't be long before she would get too big for her boots. I think he means like me."

"He never liked you learning her to read."

She handed me a thick crust of bread and lard and laid another plate out for Will.

"Will should ought to stop here tonight. He was that good when it got dark and you hadn't come home. He's a good lad, that. There an't many like him about."

"It's a pity it wasn't him that Jaen met," I said.

It was my message to her not to expect anything to come of me and Will.

"You'm a fool, Jude!"

It was not the fact that Will broke in on that exchange that we said nothing more on the subject – there was nothing more to say.

After a bit of discussion as to whether I should sleep in with my mother and Will use my bed, he insisted that he was perfectly used to rolling up in any odd corner. Will moved about the kitchen as though he was entirely at home. Mother called him "Lad" or "Will Lad", leaving no doubt in my mind that they had been getting on like a house afire. The more I thought about it, the more I saw what different lives we should all have lived if Jaen had brought somebody like Will to Croud Cantle.

We sat for a short while, eating and talking about nothing very much except whether the donkey would return on its own, or whether I would have to go searching for him.

"I'm going on up, then." Ever since we had come into the house, although I had not realised it, I had watched every move my mother made, so that a series of detailed pictures and observations was imprinted on my mind. As she passed behind Will's seat, I saw that she briefly touched his shoulder, then quickly returned the wayward hand to her pocket. Why do you find it so difficult to touch anyone, Mother? I do not need a reply. I know why. It is commitment. The first step towards rejection and hurt.

When my mother had gone to bed, I told Will that I was sorry I had gone off like that and not stopped and had dinner with him. If I wanted to keep him at arm's length, that was not the way. It was childish and hurtful.

"Ah, that's nothin' now," he said, "not compared to what happened. If you hadn't a gone, I don't suppose it'd made a deal a difference. I suppose your brother-in-law would a taken young Hanna back in the long run."

"She was the centre of Mother's life."

"You could tell that. It's a terrible, terrible thing for her." He was so concerned for my mother's feelings.

You'm a fool, Jude! I looked at him seated on the ingle-bench, gazing at the smouldering log, bending forward, elbows on knees. His unremarkable face, framed by unremarkable hair, intelligent eyes, sensitive, sensuous mouth. Desire for him flowed through me. I stopped my thoughts from going in that direction and began to clear away the remains of supper.

"Things are bound to change now, aren't they Judeth? It's not a small thing that's happened y'know."

"I know," I said.

"Your mother was telling me just today that she's only keeping the holding going for Hanna."

"I know she is." I tried to make a joke of it, "She doesn't put much faith in me as a farmer."

"That's not true, she's got nothin' but praise for you."

"She keeps it a dark secret then."

"It's not her way to be able to say the things she wants to."

"She says them to you."

"That's because I don't put up any barriers." He spread his arms, and mockingly said, "No taboos – never a one. Wide open as a barn door."

You'm a fool, Jude.

I would be safe with this open man. When Will Vickery stood with his back to the fire, he warmed the breeches of a humble man. I do not mean a servile man, for he had a very proper pride: I mean that Will was a man without arrogance. Best of all about Will was his good humour.

I was carrying things into the scullery, when he placed himself directly in my way and put his hands on my shoulders.

"Marry me, Judeth."

I brushed his fingers briefly with my own, and shook my head. "No, Will."

We were standing close, looking directly at one another.

"I thought that'd likely be your answer, but I hoped it wouldn't."

"I wish it was different."

He took away the things I was carrying, put them back on the table and led me to sit opposite him before the fire.

"It's not because of what happened?"

For a moment I thought that he was referring to Hanna.

"Up there, when we didn't bring back the holly."

We both smiled, remembering our abandonment of the holly-bough.

"No, no. That's one reason why I said I wish my answer was different."

"I wondered, maybe, if you thought I was treating you lightly."

"No. I never thought of it as you treating me. It was us – both. You just made it seem not a shameful thing to do."

"Why then? You seem to like me well enough."

"More than well enough."

What could I say that did not sound perverse? To like someone more than well enough was not a bad basis for a marriage.

"I don't think I can go on ... " I found it almost impossible to give a simple explanation. Whatever I said was bound to come out sounding pettish: "I don't want to go on doing the work that I am doing", because the answer to that is, "Few of us do!" Would he understand if I told him that my brain is on fire?

"Can I make you understand, Will? All round these parts, there's families who haven't got enough food, no home, only rags to stand up

[275]

in, and they're being moved on all the time to the next parish and the next and the next. Mostly they are good, decent workers, who grow the food and build houses, but they finish up not having either. Yet there's people like the Goodenstones, who never do a hand's turn, with more of everything than they ever need. That's wrong!"

I was stumbling along, but Will was nodding, encouraging me to go on.

"If I was rich, if I was educated, if I was a man, it seems to me that I could do something."

"What d'you think it'd be, then?"

"That's it – I don't know. With just enough money to keep him going, a man would be able to ride from place to place; perhaps holding meetings, putting out broadsheets – things like that – just saying to people that there are terrible things happening that should be put right. I don't even know whether it would do any good, but at least it would be trying."

Will said nothing. He appeared intent on filling his pipe with tobacco, carefully pulling the shreds apart and arranging them, as though it was a most important and delicate operation; but he was gazing into the fire.

"Go on," he said at last.

"I can't," I said. "I don't know what comes next. Every day my mind seems to get hotter and hotter with this idea that I should do something more than growing things and selling them on the market, and just thinking about how terrible it is to see so many people walking the roads looking for work."

It was the actual speaking my thoughts that made them real. Confiding ideas to a journal are a poor substitute for expressing them to a responsive human being. I met his eyes and smiled wryly. "Do you think I shall end up like Holy Joe, going round the markets telling people, 'Repent Ye!'?"

"There's a way to do that – not Holy Joeing, but doing something to change the old ways that cause all that – and still marry me," he said.

"The two of us up on your horse, travelling the markets to say, 'Repent ye'?"

He was silent for a minute, as though gathering his thoughts.

"When I asked if you'd marry me, that was only the opening question about ... ah, I'm about the same as yourself, things go on at

[276]

the back of your mind, vague sorts of ideas. You say to yourself, 'If I had my way, I'd do such and such.' What I wanted to ask you about was, if you married me, would you be willing to go right away from here? Could you live up in the North, or the Midlands?"

I was taken aback. I had never had the least idea that he had any intention of leaving Hampshire.

"Judeth, there are such things happening there. Things that's going to turn this country upside down. By the end of this century, spinning and weaving and making cloth, all that kind of thing, is not going to be done by one family in one house. Judeth, they are building places big as churches, where hundreds of people will work together."

I could not imagine what he was describing.

"It sounds as though it would be a great muddle. Hundreds of people, all working in one building: why, the noise alone would send anyone mad."

"It wouldn't be a muddle. Everything will be separated out. In one place there'd be rows and rows of spinners, say; in the next there'd be all the weavers; and so on and so on. Any sort of an article will be made in that way. From toasting forks to shoes."

"Do you mean that the grain merchants will work like this? I can't see how. And why would you have to go so far from where it's all grown."

"No, no. I'd not be staying in the grain trade. What's been offered to me is the chance to do something so exciting as to make your hair stand up."

His eyes sparkled and he seemed exhilarated with the vision.

"If you believed in Fate, you'd say that's what it was that sent me to lodgings where there was staying ... Ah, that doesn't matter, the how it came about."

He gathered his thoughts again.

"When this new way gets going, of putting hundreds of weavers under one roof, there's a terrible danger: the power of one man over the many he employs."

"I can't see that it will be any different from what it's always been here. The same as Harry Goodenstone; they've always been able to do as they want."

"Ah, sure, but can you imagine what it will be like when every man in a town works for the same master? It could be even worse than that. Whole counties could be given over to one kind of skill. Say every pair of boots was made in one place – you think I'm an eejit, but that's what it will be like. Can you imagine the power that one master would have? It wouldn't be a matter of a few families from several villages tramping the countryside looking for work: it'd be whole towns, whole counties."

"All right, supposing a whole town is given over to making the boots. How ever would the boots get from there to here?"

"Roads, roads and more roads. A great network of turnpikes between the towns. All those men who are tramping about looking for work will soon find it, making all the new roads."

"I can't say that is a very rosy future for them."

"It isn't, but if these new labouring guilds get going, then men will be able to stand up for one another. Imagine, Judeth, imagine Goodenstone's estate manager says he's going to finish with sheep and go in for grain, and he throws the shepherds off the estate and out of their cottages. Now, what if every farm worker in this valley refused to work at any job? What if every farm worker in Hampshire refused to work ... every farm worker in the country ... until the Goodenstones worked out some decent arrangement with the shepherds?"

"It would need a lot of organising."

"It will, but you have to start somewhere. It's already started. It's what I want to do, Judeth. I want to be in on making this new sort of guild possible. It'd be the means of changing everything, turning it all upside down. Men'd be their own masters. There's no end to what men could do if they was organized together. Like an army, except that it'd be fighting for a better sort of life, a fairer share out. It's the same thing you want. If we got married, we could go for a while to the north, learn, then come back here and start organizing cowmen, builders, carpenters into great guilds of workers."

My mother's presence overhead forced him to speak quietly, and this restraint caused his enthusiasm to sparkle in his eyes and tense one hand into a fist, which he kept thudding into the other in emphasis. He caught my hand and pressed my fingers tight. "Judeth, it'd be the most satisfying life imaginable, wouldn't it?"

I did not know what to answer. He was so fired with enthusiasm that I felt myself being singed by those same flames. I withdrew my fingers from his hold and put a log on the real fire.

The wind was still gusting round the chimney, plunging down into it and sending white wood-ash and smoke into the room, then sucking back again, sparkling and crackling dry bits of bark. The dairy door, which had needed oiling weeks ago, creaked and squeaked its hinges. The apple tree close to the house clicked and clattered the long shoots of last season's growth. The chain that held the yard gate rattled as the wind forced against it. All this restlessness and noise had been going on for hours, but it was only when I tried to take in what Will had said that I found it disturbing. I have never liked blustering winds.

"It would be satisfying, Will. Even if it doesn't succeed, it would be satisfying."

He looked directly at me as he had earlier and said again, "Marry me, Judeth."

"No, Will," I answered again.

He thrust his lips and eyebrows into an expression of disappointed resignation, but I believe that he was well able to accept it in his enthusiasm for his new work.

"Why won't you, Judeth? We'd make such a pair."

"You'd be celibate then?"

He was half-smiling and puzzled.

"Will, we'd never be a pair in the way you're suggesting. We should likely have a child every year, and what sort of a guild missionary should I make then? No, Will, until there's some way for women to have families or not have them, as they choose, then there isn't a chance for us to do anything or be anything."

"You would be a great help and support to me, Judeth. To have a wife on your side, a wife who believed in the radical changes we'd be working for ... why, I can't tell you how much help it'd be."

"If I said, 'All right, Will, we'll get married, but I've got such a burning ambition to ... to, say, teach all the poor children in Cantle and Motte to read and write because once you can read and write the world becomes different, and you begin to understand why We does the work and They get the rewards?' If I said to you, 'I believe it would turn the world upside down, and you'd be such a help to me if you would stop at home and cook and clean and raise our children – would you marry me, Will?'"

As I spoke, I discovered that what had been a rag-bag of thoughts seemed to stitch themselves together into a patchwork whole. What came out made sense. I had never spoken at such length to him. Our exchanges had previously been a tacking-on of my ideas to his, for the most part because we did have a basic agreement: that the unjust society in which we lived must be changed. I believe that he was quite surprised to hear that I could suggest an ideal equal to his own.

It was not until I had finished my outburst that I realised that tears were running down my cheeks. I was rejecting a chance of a life with this compassionate, ardent, intelligent man. If my mind was on fire with the desire to be filled with learning, then my body was equally on fire for desire to be filled with Will Vickery.

But it was not many hours since Jaen had torn her cap from her ruined hair and lifted her skirts to show her distorted legs, and said, "Look at me, Ju. Go on, look!"

When we parted early next morning, Will kissed me gently, more like a brother than a lover. "Your way is more likely to turn the world upside down than mine."

On that morning, the wind had dropped and it was beginning to feel more like spring. I was filled with a strange mixture of feelings: sadness, relief, calm; as well as feelings of excitement, anticipation. I was expecting to have to spend time searching for the donkey that had run off, but it was calmly cropping the grass close to the gate.

My mother came into the yard to bring Will cold meat from yesterday and some bread wrapped in a cloth. She had dark rings of sleeplessness around her eyes. As soon as he was gone we each started our daily tasks. As she went off into the dairy, Mother said, "It's none of Dicken's business, but he a go ferreting on till he makes summat of it. You tell him what you like, but I don't want not a single word about it spoke to me," and she went off to uncloth some cheeses for Thursday's market.

I found Dicken mending and sharpening some tools and told him that Hanna was gone to stay at Newton Clare.

"Master won't like that, then, I'll be bound. Be her acomin' back, then? I always said she wouldn't never stop here long, not once she was big enough to give Miss Jaen a hand. Miss Jaen all right?" Dicken was like the bees: if you did not tell him what was going on, there was trouble. I have no doubt that every happening at Croud Cantle was related at the Dragon and Fount, probably with embellishments; for Dicken was one for gossip.

I then went to find Johnny-twoey. Yesterday, as I was leaving Ham

Ford, Hanna had fastened her arms in a dead-lock about my neck. As I unwrapped myself, she said with great earnestness, "Tell John that I haven't left him, Jude. You've got to tell him. Please, Jude, please don't forget. He won't have anybody now. He will stop talking again."

"It's all right," I told her. "He'll have me."

"But you won't always stay there. I was going to stay there." She sturdily swallowed her misery.

I promised her that at least for now I would see that he did not stop talking again, and that I would bring her messages from him the next time I came to see her.

As always when I spoke to John Toose, he flushed shiny red.

"John."

"Yes, Miss Jude."

"John, Hanna is stopping over at Newton Clare."

"Yes, Miss Jude?"

I felt quite sorry for the lad. He would miss Hanna's companionship. Amost a foundling, he had been living and working on Croud Cantle since the very day we brought Hanna to stay. As he stood there, as he had throughout his young life, waiting for someone else to order his day, I realised that he deserved more than a brief half-truth of a message. John Toose owned a small china blue-bird, a present from Hanna. Only she had known that John Toose was a boy who would rather have a china bird than a twist of fair-mint sweet as a gift.

"No, John, that's not the real truth. Hanna has gone to live with her mother and father."

An even deeper flush and a tightening of the muscles round his mouth were the only signs of his feelings that I could see, plus the fact that he did not say, "Yes, Miss Jude".

"She has a mother and father, and brothers, so it is probably best for her to live with them."

"So have I got, too. I got a mother and father. We said – Hanny said, and so did I – about that. We was better here than there. I said, and so did Hanny, that it was better being just one on your own, not having to be with them. They must a made her go there. She wouldn't a gone unless they made her." Adding a "Miss Jude" a few seconds after his quiet-spoken, halting outburst.

"She gave me a message to tell you. She said be sure to say that she hasn't left you."

A small glow of pleasure lit his face.

[281]

"That's all right then, Miss Jude."

He stood, patiently awaiting anything else I had to say. " ... because once you can read and write, the world becomes different, and you begin to understand why We does the work and They get the rewards ... " My own theoretical ideals turned upon me and attacked. To young John Toose, at the very bottom of the heap, I was "They".

Twisting my promise to Hanna that I would not let John slip back into not talking, I said, "I promised Hanna ... would you like me to teach you to read?"

"Miss Jude? I can read."

I knew that he could not, for he had never been a day off the farm in years.

"Miss Jude? 'Little Lady Geraldine' – every time I was good, Hanny read it to me."

I smiled inwardly as I imagined the scene. Square little Hanna, who found it such an imposition to have her lessons, rewarding the tall lad with a "reading" of the story I had written for her and which she knew by heart.

"Well, then, that's a good start," I said.

I said that he could come into the kitchen for one hour every evening, and I would show him how to go on with his reading, and perhaps later to learn his letters, and he said, Yes, Miss Jude, at every juncture. I was just walking away when he came after me. "Miss Jude? Would you ... ? would they ... ? If I could just go and see Hanny sometimes. So I could see she was all right. I wouldn't get lost, I shouldn't think. I could ask Dicken how to get there. I would do my work just the same."

"I'll do a barter with you. If you work hard at the lessons I shall give you, I'll start taking you to market so you'll learn that, and the next time I go over to Newton Clare, you shall come too."

I had said to Will that once you read and write the world becomes a different place, and in teaching John Toose that is what happened. However, it did not come about in the way I had been speaking of, because it was for me that the world became a different place. I remember Fred Warren once telling my mother that it was a pleasure to teach me, for I absorbed what he taught me like parched earth, or something like that. If that is so, then I understand what he meant by it. After the trudging, cajoling and pushing to try to get Hanna to learn something, teaching John Toose was as different to teaching Hanna as the flight of a sparrow-hawk is to that of a broody hen. If you showed him a speck of knowledge, he swooped down upon it, devoured it, and hovered waiting for more.

I was sure that my mother would not like the idea of him going to stand on the market, and was prepared to have to stand up to her to get my way, but she said that it wasn't a bad idea because her legs had been playing her up going all that way to Blackbrook, most of the old ones were gone on, and the market wasn't the same now the young ones was taking over. And so, without any great to-do, Mother, who had held Nugent's stand outside The Star for twenty-odd years, stopped going to market.

As soon as Will had gone on that Monday morning, I told Mother that Will had asked me to marry him and that I had said no.

"It's your life, I suppose, but you mark me, you're going to live to regret it."

THROUGHOUT THE following year very little changed in the routine of our work. We missed Hanna deeply. At first, the pain and loneliness without her was unremitting, then slowly I was able to fill the space in our lives that had been hers so that in time I could go for an entire morning without thinking about her; but she was never really far from my thoughts. It was at that time of day when she would have been washing her hands and getting into her night-shift that was worse, when she would play mother and me off against each other for the favour of seeing her into bed. But I filled the space that been hers with other things, believing it best not to dwell on that which cannot be altered.

John Toose entered into our lives rather more than previously. At first, when he came for his lesson, Mother – also I suppose filling Hanna's space – would sit apparently absorbed in one of her evening occupations, rubbing herbs, spinning, or cutting little covers for preserve jars or for patchwork. Gradually she began to take notice of what was going on.

"What was that bit again, Boy?" or, "That an't never right." Sometimes she gave him the big Bible and asked him to read the Begats, or the In The Beginning. One evening after I had read The Song of Solomon, she said, "Now, if you could write summat like that, Jude, it'd been worth it." I did not ask what the "it" was.

Johnny-twoey (I made every effort to remember to call him John when speaking of him, or to him, but the name that he brought with him as a child was difficult to drop) came in for his reading lesson every evening, except on those days at the height of planting and harvesting when we all had to work till we dropped. However, Hanna's repetitive recitation of Little Lady Geraldine had given him a good start, as he could already recognise a fair number of words from their pattern and shape. It was a good method for teaching a boy who found it easy to distinguish five or six different varieties of mint which, to most people, looked very similar. He had no difficulty in telling apart such words as "Lordship" and "Ladyship", so I continued teaching him by showing him a word and telling him what it was.

I thought often about his kind of ability, and began to wonder whether John Toose's ability was not exceptional, whether I was not the oddity that I seemed to be. Perhaps all the rest of the Toose children, Cantle children, crow-scaring children everywhere, were equally capable: all that any child needed was the interest and the opportunity to learn.

He was not the best of market traders, being too shy to approach people, except when explaining to a housewife about some herb or flavouring he had succeeded in developing in the plot at Croud Cantle.

I saw Fred Warren quite frequently on market days, and Mrs Warren made it her business to come and talk for a few minutes until, round about May and June time, she became too breathless from carrying her expected child to walk very far. And now that Mother had given up going to market, I could never leave the stand for more than a few minutes. However, on one occasion, I did go and talk with Fred in the front room of The Star, where I could keep an eye on John Toose.

"I'm sorry that you refused Will," he said. "I'd have thought that he would have been right for you, Judeth. He's hit hard by you not accepting him. I should have thought you could have put your brains to work with him. He's going as soon as I can find somebody to replace him, you know? I only wish I had the chance to be involved in it all. Mankind is on the verge of a great leap forward."

I said that yes, I knew, and that likely my mother was right and I should live to regret it.

"Would you have married him if he'd have stayed here, working for White's? If he'd have been more steady?"

I would not have been kind to tell him that, had that happened, Will and I should probably have become a replica of himself and Mrs Warren; that I shrivelled at the thought of living the conventional, smothering life of a Blackbrook trader's wife, a second-hand life, filtered through the husband's experience.

Perhaps I do Fred Warren an injustice, for over the years he had encouraged me to look beyond the end of my nose and to read

[285]

pamphlets by visionary thinkers, but I believe that his own reformist views – as with those of Will – did not go as far as reforming his own scullery and kitchen. Womankind was not about to take a great leap forward. But I had such a warm regard for my old tutor that I never liked to say anything that appeared in any way to reflect badly on his views. So in answering him, I jokingly said, "That's too many 'ifs' for me to sort out," and went on to talk to him about Johnny-twoey.

"Oh, Fred, it's all so vague in my mind," I said, "but what I should really like to do is to start giving lessons to all the Cantle children, like you did to me. Sunday afternoon and an hour or so at other times. It'd have to fit in with their work, like it did with me."

Fred's expression was lit with interest and enthusiasm for my idea.

"You'd have a hard job to get them, Judeth. There's few poor families that can afford to have their children idle. Times are too hard."

I have noticed many times, when Fred is enthused with thoughts of an ideal world, how his eyes sharpen, he makes extravagant expressions with his hands and becomes a speaking pamphlet. It is then that he is at his most endearing.

"But if we could do it ... Judeth, if you end ignorance, you end poverty; if you end poverty, you end all the afflictions of mankind!"

I soon had to leave him and go back to Johnny-twoey, but by that time Fred was already talking of "we", and said that he would put his mind to it and we would meet again to see what we might do.

"The scheme needs a benefactor, Judeth. It needs a little money."

"Why?"

"It will fail if you don't have some time and a few materials. You'd need another hand to take on some of your work, a room somewhere, slates. Judeth, if we are going to try, then we have to do it in the very best way we can. It's not going to be like me teaching you and you teaching that boy. Everyone is not as enlightened as your mother."

I left him, pondering that thought. My mother was enlightened? Yet something must have prompted her to make the arrangement with Fred, to have bought me a book in which to write. Now she was beginning to take a bit of interest in Johnny-twoey; preparing something for him to eat when he came in for his lesson; commenting, "That an't bad, Boy", or, "You'm coming on".

In July, Mrs Warren gave birth to a girl; a pale little creature with a misshapen head and bruised from its struggle into the world. It happened the day before Market Day, so I went to see her after we had finished our selling. She was bright-eyed and flushed. The long and agonizing labour than she had been anticipating with fear for six months had proved to be longer and more agonizing than she had ever imagined; but that was all over now. She had what she wanted, another girl – because you could always dress up a girl so pretty. I was pleased for her, knowing how much pleasure she had got from getting me into a silk dress and showing me off at the party as her handiwork.

The baby, being very small and weak anyway, had not the strength to stand up to its own birth, and died after three days. Mrs Warren's pink, bright-eyed appearance turned out not to be that of health, but the onset of child-bed fever, from which she died only days after the baby.

I went to pay respects before the funeral. Looking down upon her, with her curls showing upon her forehead, and with the child in her arms, she looked more like a pretty girl holding a doll than a matron of thirty-five. Fred appeared bewildered at the funeral, staring into space and having to be prompted by young Peg, who was already trying to take the place of her mother by comforting Freddie, Jack and Sam.

Mrs Warren did not lack company of women in the churchyard that year. There were so many deaths from the child-bed that charms and spells that had not been needed for generations were made by grand-mothers. The Canon of Blackbrook Abbey, on hearing it rumoured that the dark arts of women were again rife, spoke loud warnings of damnation and denounced the women who put faith in the practices of heathens and witches. But many women, in dreadful fear when their time approached, and knowing from experience that grandmothers were wise as Canons, received whispered advice from old women. As there were more women who survived the scourge than died from it, the reputation of the grandmothers rose high, and for a year, charlock all but disappeared from the fields and waste places.

On the Sunday following the death of Mrs Warren, I could not bring myself to attend church. I had nothing to say to a God who could throw misery about the world like handfuls of gravel, scattering it without knowing or caring where it fell. Nor would I attend the service for the sake of appearances. A God of Love? A Heavenly Father?

I thought it a great pity that our Creator was not a Heavenly Mother, who might be a little on the side of the women; of Jaen and Mrs Warren. And perhaps to understand women like myself, who have additional

[287]

needs to those of motherhood to fulfil, and would not think it unnatural to seek to find fulfilment. God gave men a free gift of parenthood, yet had made women pay a high price for it.

As Jaen had said, if I'd have been a man I could have gone to sea. If I'd been a father, too, I could have gone to sea. That was the entire difference between my mother and my father, between Will and me, between Fred and Mrs Warren. Becoming a father had never distended a man's legs with water. A man's part in the begetting of his child was in pleasure. If the woman had pleasure it was paid for: by shame, sometimes, and worry, always by pain, and very often by death. I could talk to no one of my blasphemous thoughts.

My mother made little comment when I said that I should not go. Since Hanna had been taken away we had had few arguments. She was uninterested, spiritless and let me go my own way, saying only, "Ah, you'm too deep for me these days." After I had missed Morning Service for several weeks, Reverend Tripp waylaid my mother at the church door: "I told him, it wa'nt no good asking me what you was up to these days."

ON EASTER SUNDAY, when I had said that I would go over to Newton Clare my mother had said that her back was playing her up too much from all the planting. I believe that she could not stand seeing not only Jaen attached to the Hazelhurst clan, but now Hanna also. It did not matter how often Mother said that Hanna was an Estover to her fingertips, there was no getting over the fact that she was Hanna Hazelhurst, and my mother could not bear it.

So I let this be the promised outing for Johnny-twoey. He had not had much time to prove that he would keep his side of our bargain, but I was very sure now that he would.

In the eight or so years that he had lived at Croud Cantle, he had rarely been further than the church, except on a few occasions when he had gone down to the ramshackle cottage in which the rest of the many members of the Toose family lived. Certainly, until he began going to market, he had never been out of Cantle parish. The more aware I became that it was not an inarticulate, almost invisible hand who had been working for us for all those years, but a person – a John Toose – the more I felt that we owed him, not simply the unpaid wages that Hanna and he had talked of, but some experience.

To go over Tradden on a morning like that Easter Sunday was of such pleasure to me that I wanted nothing better than to be there for eternity. The bramblings that had been about in unusual numbers during the long, hard frosts, had flown and had been replaced by swallows and cuckoos. Corn buntings were jingling and I looked for a nest. I wanted to see what the lad had to say about bunting eggs, which look as though they have handwriting upon them. He looked puzzled, and said so seriously that I was not sure whether he meant it or no, "Miss Jude? They'm very small kind of words." Meadow pipits climbed singing into the sky, only to be outsung and outdone, as always, by their rivals, the larks. Bees pushed their way into early

[289]

purple orchids and dead-nettles. Although it was early for butterflies, a few brimstones, peacocks and, my favourites, the blues, flittered about on routes that were as complicated as scribble, in search of flowers ripe with the honey-dew into which they uncurled their tongues. There were even one or two slow-worms, elegant creatures, curled and still, sunning themselves and looking like brooches and clasps wrought from gold or bronze and dropped by some passer-by.

The visit at Ham Ford was not a success. It wrenched at my heart to see Hanna. At Croud Cantle she had been a hard, willing little worker, taking her share in everything she could manage; but in her parent's home she appeared to be working equally with the paid girls. I know it was Sunday and it was quite likely the other children had their chores during the week, but it did seem to me that in the very short time she had been living there, all of them seemed to take it for granted that Hanna would fetch and carry.

She asked if she could take John to see the farm. "Ah, all of you clear off out for half an hour," Dan told them. Hanna's face dropped; I saw that she wanted John to herself. I said that I would go with them, thinking that I could take my small nephews away from Hanna and John.

"Oh no, Ju, stop and talk with me. We shan't have long," Jaen said. But Dan's great length stretched out as he dozed acted as a barrier to free talk. Jaen could not walk outside with me. Her legs and feet were now so distended that if she pressed them the indentation stayed like a finger imprinted in bread dough.

I asked Jaen how Hanna was settling in. "She's all right, Ju, you don't have to worry about her. She says it's noisy here." Jaen smiled wryly. "Sometimes I think noisy an't the word for it. When they'm falling out with each other, it sounds like feeding time in the piggery. She a get used to it. She's a nice little thing."

A nice little thing! If Dan had not been there I should have been more frank about what I thought about them treating Hanna more like a village girl than a daughter. But the Hazelhurst men were all touchy, and if I wanted to make sure that I would always be welcome to visit my sister and my niece, I had to watch my tongue – as mother and I had always done – to keep him sweet.

Most of the information I got about Hanna was from Johnny-twoey. When we left, Hanna had been polite and straight-faced with me.

"Hanny says she can probably come back after the baby's birthed. Can she, Miss Jude?"

"I should be surprised. It's her home there."

Jaen's sixth son was, as she had predicted, a Hazelhurst, large and loud. There was less than seven years' difference in age between Little Dan'l and baby George, and all six were as alike as peas in a pod. After Daniel, Baxter, Francis, Richard and Gregory, they had run out of family names, so this baby was given George, after the king. Like Hanna, he was inconveniently born in August, when every hand was needed in the fields, so it fell to Hanna to help Jaen through the three weeks in her bed.

It was, I believe, George's birth that helped sustain Hanna during the great change that took place in her life. She became fiercely attached to the baby; willing to share him only with my mother and, of necessity, Jaen. She dressed and rocked and carried him about, for all the world like a wren or a meadow pipit caring for a cuckoo. On two Sundays, Johnny-twoey had gone to Newton Clare on his own.

Since he had been doing the market, I saw to it that he was paid wages properly.

Mother was reluctant. "He chose himself to come here. He've been kept all these years, and I've always give Amos Toose something for his lad."

How could you say that the small boy had "chosen" to come? He had been sent by his father. In my opinion, now that the lad was over fourteen, some proper arrangement had to be made. I ticked off on my fingers the amount of work he had done, even when he was a small boy. She had to agree that it wasn't all one way, and from the time that he was ten or eleven, he had been more than earning his keep. She was adamant, though, when I suggested that we owed back wages. "Mos Toose have had one less mouth to feed all these years," was her final word. So what I did was to allow the boy to keep a few pence from the sale of the herbs and salads that he grew so well and that had become an important part of our sales.

One Sunday Johnny-twoey went to Newton Clare alone. On market day of that week, he had spent much time and asked my advice several times about buying a thing for Hanny. What he finally decided upon was a discoloured brass bell, not much larger than a thimble, that he found on a dealer's tray of penny and ha'penny bargains.

[291]

"Miss Jude? He a be all right when I cleaned him." And so it was. After he had removed the grime with vinegar and salt, he burnished the brass until it was smooth and gleaming. I guessed why he had chosen the bell. When he had finished cleaning it, he brought it to me to see, flushed with pleasure at the first purchase that he had ever made.

"Miss Jude? I a tell you why I got the bell. It's a joke on Hanny, because she tole me that the birth-mark that Little Lady Geraldine had on her was a bull and it wa'nt, was it? I shan't tell her that's why, though, on account of she won't like it if she finds out I read it for myself that it was bell and not bull. Perhaps one day she a find out, when she comes back and starts learning again. Then I sh'll tease her on it."

That was probably the longest speech the lad had ever made to anyone other than Hanna. I felt pleased that he was gaining confidence.

"Miz Hazelhurst gid me a dinner, but I didn't tell any a they about Hanny's present. She don't want they to know."

From time to time over the next months, Will called at Croud Cantle whenever he was near. I watched for him when I was at the market, and was disappointed if he was away and did not come to see me. It was foolish. It was I who had made up my mind not to marry. No one had forbidden me: those closest to me – Mother, Jaen, Hanna, Fred Warren – would have been delighted. Yet not foolish, for I had no control over the kind of emotions that attacked me. The more I tried to put him out of my mind, the more vivid was my sense of him. When he was out of my presence, I could not bring his whole face to mind, I could bring only one feature at a time into focus; yet I was aware of every hair, every pore and cell of him, and found it strange to think that there was a place where he existed and people who could see him when I could not.

His visits at home were pleasure and pain. If he stopped for a meal I had sometimes to force my eyes away from him, from his mouth; the pointed formation of his front teeth as he bit hard into an apple, his lips glistening with juice; from his eyes which, catching me out in looking at him, half-closed their long-lashed lids and raised them to me, passing a message that Rev. Tripp would consider sinful between unmarried people.

I took to not looking directly at him, but soon found that a lock of hair curling into his ear, or the contrast between the smooth skin on his upper face and the textured lower part, were almost as disturbing to me as a direct look. The moons on his finger-nails, the curling hair on the backs of his warm, dry hands, and their sinews as he held riding crop or dinner-knife; his blunt finger ends tapping the table-top as he emphasised a point. If he laid a hand on the table, I was the table; if he rasped his chin with his hand when considering a question, the sensation was repeated in my own hand. Had there been some law wherein it was laid down that Judeth Nugent must become the wife of Will Vickery, I should gladly have obeyed. As it was, the decision was mine. That was the pain.

When he left, it was suddenly. Two days before Christmas, almost exactly a year since we had loved one another; a year since I had felt the frost of Tradden beneath me and the warmth of Will above; a year since I first had to contend with not only my brain being on fire, but my body also. I wanted Will, I wanted children, I wanted ... Ah, what was that third thing that I wanted ... wanted so much that I turned away from the other two?

He came to the farm in the morning. Dull December. A morning of gloom against the coming, official joy of the celebration of Bethlehem. Its sombreness seemed more appropriate in view of the experience of some of the mothers, more humble than the Virgin, who were known to me: Jaen, with her ruined legs and poor pod of a body, Mrs Warren, and other child-bed women who had, by proxy, fed their babies whilst still in the womb on Croud Cantle butter, honey and salads and who were now in a neat, new row together in Blackbrook churchyard.

Clouds were thick and low, saturated with the moisture that they would not release so that they could drift up and on towards Sussex. The Cantle valley was dark and oppressed, and had been for days. The hills were gloomy and heavy, as though their bones were not chalk but granite; the folds and crevices in Tradden and Old Marl were black, and distant Winchester was almost obscure for want of light. The river Dunnock lay across the valley like a hawser made of lead.

"Judeth. My chance has come. There's something going on in the North. The fellow I met last winter has asked me to join him." He did not say what he was going north to do: I did not ask, nor did I wish to know. It would be better not to have any image of what his life there might be.

I did not trust my voice, so I nodded and secured my bottom lip from within, nipping it with my front teeth.

"Won't you even think of coming next year, perhaps? I would not press you to get married, only to join me – join us – as a member of the group who are working to change events."

I shook my head. He knew that I was unlikely to change my mind. He looked crestfallen, but not so distracted that his new venture would be seriously inconvenienced. I believe I hoped that he might find someone more suited than I to fulfilling what he needed in a wife, but whether that is true or a myth that I have made for myself I cannot truly say. It is most likely that it is myth, for as I rejected him, I wanted him more than ever. I hesitate to say "loved him", for had I truly loved him, then I believe that I could not have let him go without me.

In many ways we were two of a kind. Passionate, sensuous, selfish and single-minded. Had my single-mindedness led me to domesticity, then we might have been as happy as two people living together could be. As we said our farewells, I trusted myself once more to hold his face briefly between my hands. I held his ears and ran my fingers down his jaw, feeling its shape, feeling the texture. And smelling again the earthy, tantalising, warm scent of grain that drifted from his cloak.

Mother wept as I had seen her do only once before, on the day that Jaen was married. Now, though, she was an old woman weeping. Like an aged mother seeing off a son who goes to war, her tears brimmed, ran and dripped in a constant stream. She wept silently. As Will rode off down Howgaite I put an arm about her shoulders – and she let me.

In unspoken agreement we did not admit Christmas Day to enter the house. Last year had been so vastly different.

Mother went down to the church, but only briefly. She came back with the news that banns had been called for Henry Goodenstone and Amelia Eames-Coates.

"And he an't doing himself a bad turn there," she said. Which was true; for the Coates Estate, which was close to Havant in south Hampshire, was large and they owned rich properties in eastern countries.

We sent Johnny-twoey to spend the day with his family, and told Dicken that if he saw to the beasts in the morning, we would do the rest of the watering, feeding and milking. We said little to one another and Mother went to bed as soon as we had eaten supper.

That night I had the first of the recurring dreams that fever my sleep. It was not one of the more unbearably terrifying of dreams. The entire night was a pink-coloured canvas in a gilt frame, blank except in one corner where, never moving, were two minute figures: a woman in the silk dress Mrs Warren had got made for me linked arms with a stiff doll-like figure of a man. Hovering like a kestrel was a silver fish with a head at either end of its finless shape. It quivered but,

[295]

like the figures, never moved. It was a still, silent dream, so that I do not know why I should have awoken on Boxing Morning trembling and relieved that the night was over, for there were none of the sucking whirlpools or shifting sands or falling into bottomless wells that came later and were understandably frightening.

WHEN, ON A STEEP SLOPE, a person misses their footing, stumbles and begins to run headlong, it is the
direction of the first step that implies the entire flight.

In the January of 1790, I received a message which was to be my
first step in running headlong.

The message must have caused great speculation and comment in
Cantle, and at the Dragon and Fount in particular, for it was Dicken
who saw it arrive and came hurrying for me on his rickety legs that
were by now as bent as though he were permanently ducking under a
low roof.

"Master Jude. Come quick. Ol Blackwell have rode over from the
Big House with a message. He've still got on his gold buttons under
his cloak."

Oliver Blackwell was a young Cantle man, who had been taken on
in the Goodenstone kitchens as a small boy and was now famous for
his rapid rise to an unspecified position where he wore gold buttons,
ribbons and braid, and often travelled with Young Harry, or Squire
Goodenstone as he was lately called – in his hearing at any rate.

Grand, handsome when his teeth were hidden, his wig well-kept
and plentifully powdered, Ol Blackwell was without doubt Cantle's
most esteemed son. He was about my own age but, because of our
virtual isolation, knew me only distantly, as did all Cantle children.
He therefore addressed me with the name which was written on the
letter he carried.

"Miss Nugent, my master sends his compliments and requests a
reply at your earliest."

He stood, allowing Dicken the full treat of inspecting the spectacle
of ribbons and gold buttons, whilst I read the note.

"Miss Nugent, As you may have heard, I have lately become
engaged to a lady of a sweet nature, whose philanthropic views I

[297]

believe you would find of interest. Please attend at Park Manor at eleven on the morning of Thursday." This was followed by a flourish of curlicues which I took to read Henry Goodenstone, JP.

This was the first missive of any kind that I had received and I was forced to reply on a page torn from my journal.

"Dear Mr Goodenstone, If Thursday was not Blackbrook market then I would be pleased to call upon you. I could come on Friday at the same time if this should suit you. You need not send another message unless Friday is not suitable."

I did not sign it, nor did I possess wax for sealing, but my message – as if it mattered at all – was safe in Ol Blackwell's illiterate hands.

Having received no further message, I started out for Park Manor on Friday morning just after the church bell had struck the half-hour, cutting across the fields by Chard Lepe and over Raike Bottom so as not to have to go via the ford and the eyes of Cantle village.

I had been forced to read Young Harry's note over and over again to Mother. She questioned me about philanthropic views, wondered how I could be interested and speculated on what it could mean.

"I hope she don't think we got money. If she thinks we got money you tell her we an't hardly got enough to keep body and soul together. Don't go pleading poverty, but don't let her get you saying we can put up even a brass farden for church candlesticks or hassocks. We been kneeling on bran bags long enough without no trouble, and we can go on kneeling for a good whiles yet."

It did not take much for her to become fidgety about the security of our ownership of Croud Cantle.

"Don't let on about nothing. If any of They thinks that there's as much as a shilling going into anybody's pocket except theirn, then they a go after him like a ferret after a rabbit."

I tried to assure her that it was unlikely that the holding had anything to do with my being summoned up to the Big House. "Philanthropy is giving something away. We never did settle anything about the books," I said. "It's something like that, I'll be bound."

"They never gives nothing away for nothing. It's how everything comes to be theirn in the end."

Just as I was going she came close and said quietly in my ear, even though we were the only two in the yard, "Don't get mixed up in nothing, Jude. There been too much mixing up and that, one way and another, with that place and this."

"What do you mean? Mrs Trowell?"

She did not reply, but frowned at me as though I was hiding the answer to something she was puzzling about.

"You all right, Mother?" I asked.

Her face suddenly cleared and she looked about her as though she had not been aware where she was.

"A course I'm all right. Why shouldn't I be?"

That moment of puzzlement was something that I had seen a few times lately. Sometimes I thought that she could hear something that was inaudible to me; other times she would look at me as though I had suddenly lapsed into a strange tongue. Once, just after Will had gone, I noticed her sitting beside the pile of logs on the hearth and picking off small pieces of moss as though she was attempting to steal something from under my very eyes. She would watch me until she thought that I wasn't looking, then lower her hand, pinch off a wisp of moss, secrete it in the palm of her hand, then unobtrusively transfer it to a fold in her shawl. I wondered if, perhaps, she was remembering a childhood game and replaying the moves, but did not convince myself.

I thought of Will as I walked quickly over the frozen furrows of Howgaite fields. I watched coots on the little Chard Lepe pond, and thought of Will. I made mental notes, for my journal, that some hazel catkins were so forward that they had already stretched to their fullest extent, and saw two nettle-creepers fussing about low in the hedgerow as though ready to nest. I tried not to think of Will and hoped that as the time and distance between us grew I should not think of him so often.

This time I went directly up the great drive to Park Manor and round to the side entrance. A little servant took me to Mrs Cutts' room. Mrs Cutts looked at me as she had done on a previous occasion – as though I had done her harm – and called me 'Miss' with contempt. I have never known anyone to walk with such whisk and jingle as Mrs Cutts. She led me to the hexagonal library where I had first encountered Mrs Trowell and where she had so delightfully recited from the play, *Hamlet*.

The last time that I had seen Squire Goodenstone – how impossible to suddenly think of him as squire – was over eighteen months previously, when he had arrived out of the blue at Croud Cantle. The change in his appearance was very surprising. He wore the plain, short jacket and dark waistcoat of a country gentleman; his boots sported no ribbons; his neck-cloth was soft and amiable. Most surprising of all was his hair. It was covered by neither wig nor hat: in fact, he had little to cover, except for a fringe over each ear across the nape of his neck. He had given up being a ridiculous dummy for fashionable clothes and had acquired some dignity.

He addressed me formally with a "Good morning, Miss", in his high, unmanly voice and thanked me for coming. He began awkwardly, saying that now that the banns had been called, he and the Hon. Amelia Eames-Coates were soon to be married. He went on to say that this lady was of the most charitable and virtuous kind.

"In fact, she is of such a noble mind that there is nothing that she does not do to try to understand and forgive others."

I said that I was very pleased that he was so fortunate. He peered at me somewhat, as though to fathom something more under my polite comments.

"So the past is the past. There's nothing anybody can ever bring forth in the future that will ever disturb the lady who is to be my wife."

I wondered if he had called me here because he suspected that I was capable of "bringing something forth". I was annoyed at the suggestion.

"I can't believe there's anybody I know of like that, Mister Harry," with an emphasis on the "I". "And as far as I am concerned, your past, your present and your future is not of much interest to me so long as you keep your hands off my mother's land."

He looked astonished.

"What interest should I have in that little corner?"

"The same interest your family have had in every other little corner of this valley."

I was being over-bold and knew he would think me insolent, but I could not stop myself. "There was a time when every field in Cantle belonged to the people here, and now you've got them."

He was not at all roused by my fieriness, replying mildly, "It was not unlawful, not plundered, you know."

I was pleased with myself for holding back the retort that if it were not plunder then it was pillage and, in any case, the outcome was the same: the people had lost their land and now he held it.

It was a strange meeting. But then I had never had an encounter with him that was otherwise: Old Sir Henry's funeral; the vestry and Howgaite Path; this same library, when he had brought Mrs Trowell to Park Manor, and lastly, his unaccountable call at Croud Cantle. For a girl who, by his standards, was a peasant, my relationship with Harry Goodenstone was a strange one. Aside from that of servant, the only other relationship that may take place between a village girl and masters and masters' sons is a squeezing, fondling, ravishing one. Masters believe it is their right. My father, master of Croud Cantle, had taken the milk-maid. The only part of the story that was unusual was that he eloped with her. Harry Goodenstone had only looked at me once in that way, and I do not believe that he was overly serious.

Although there must have been a score or more of servants grooming the great mansion of Park Manor and preparing food for its occupants, no sound filtered through to the room in which we sat. The book-lined walls deadened all sound except the crackle of burning logs, the gentle clock, clock, clock of a swinging pendulum and the sound of our voices, which seemed to travel no further than the foot or two that separated us.

I was aware of the eccentricity of our situation and wondered if it occurred to him. That a powerful and wealthy landowner should write a polite invitation asking a village girl to call; that she should sit in his library and talk as though to an equal; that a housekeeper of the calibre of Mrs Cutts should bring in cups of chocolate and small biscuits.

Before today, I had seen nothing in Harry Goodenstone except a silly man who behaved like a youth that wanted his own way. But, I supposed, since he had been able to stand up to Old Sir Henry and had gone his own way living with Mrs Trowell, flouting convention by bringing her to Park Manor, he might not be altogether the silly fop-doodle that he appeared to be. I discovered that I had a small spark of regard for him, the kind of spark that is as disturbing in people we despise as blemishes and faults are in those we like or love.

He waved me to sit in a chair closer to where he was.

"There was a time, a year or so back, when I might have wanted to take your land. Take it and try to obliterate it. But that is not possible, is it? If I could dig a pit a thousand feet deep to try to gouge out the past, I should not succeed. I assure you that I have no desire to own your small-holding, even if it were possible to do so. In any case, I believe that my," he gave an odd smile, "hated plot was sold to the Estate years ago."

In the dead-sound, unreal atmosphere, I felt no restraint on what I might say.

"Mister Harry. It isn't any secret to me what my father did. He infected my mother's life, Mrs Trowell's life and Mary Holly's; and I think yours, too. He made money out of buying human beings, transporting them from their homes like beasts and selling them."

He made no response, but sat watching my face with a puzzled expression.

"I feel that he ought to have infected my life as well, but it's queer, I haven't any real feeling about him one way or the other – it's almost as though it is something I read of. If you've got any fears that my mother or me's going to be any bother to you about that connection, then you can put them out of your mind. My mother's like you; she'd dig a deep hole if it'd make it go away. She don't want anything except to forget it. She hadn't ever talked about it, not till Mrs Trowell came. I liked Mrs Trowell. Isn't that strange? I liked her very much."

He still did not respond. He stopped looking at me and turned his gaze into the flames licking the burning log. I absently read book titles. I had nothing more to say. Our conversation had taken such a turn that the original reason for my coming seemed to have been forgotten. When I looked back at him I saw that his eyes were brimming tears that he made no attempt to hide.

"Jealousy. I have always been ..." He trailed off, gazing back into the fire. Suddenly he roused himself, rubbed his hand down his face, pinched his nostrils and rubbed his chin, as though awakening from a doze. "If we could get rid of the worst things by gouging out the places where they happened, the earth would be a honeycomb."

I nodded. Had the more serious Harry Goodenstone always been there under the ribbons and buttons and over-sized hats, as his hairless scalp had been there under his wigs, or had he changed? I still did not like him greatly, but I did see a human being that I had not seen before. But perhaps the change was in me.

"Well, now. To the purpose of my note." He seemed to be searching for a way to start. "You read and write." I nodded. "Warren taught you. It was just Warren teaching you. He gave you lessons. Tell me how you did it."

"It was a bit haphazard. It had to be fitted in when it could."

"It did not interfere with your proper work?"

"When he lived in Motte I used to go on Sundays and he would give me things to do, work, things to copy. Sometimes when I saw him in Blackbrook I gave him what I'd done, then he would tell me about it next time I saw him. I don't sleep much, so I had all that time, practising my letters by candle."

"Could you not have done it otherwise – I mean than working at night?"

"It would have taken a lot longer. I learnt quite quick. In a year, about."

"When ..? Is ..?" He scratched his chin, and again I noticed a sensitivity when choosing his words, a maturity perhaps, that I had never noticed in the past.

"What I mean is, are you spoken for? In marriage. When shall you marry? You seem to have managed to escape so far. I am surprised. You are ... you must have attracted many of the young men in the four parishes. You have good looks. I should say you're tough and strong: make a good wife for any farmer, a girl like you."

I bridled inwardly. Master and village girl. He would not dream of making such a personal comment to the Hon. Amelias of his world. I should say you got noble blood in your veins milady. Good record for sons in your family: make a good wife for any lord!

"I'm no longer a girl and I have a bent leg."

I had no idea why I should have said such an extraordinary thing to him. A bent leg. It is true that the injury I received on Tradden had never properly mended, but I had never thought about it a great deal. But suddenly it seemed that the badly-knit bone was very significant. For the life of me I could not have said why.

"That has never been an obstacle to marriage."

"I shall never marry."

He started to say something, but changed his mind. He began again. "Could you run a school?"

Without hesitation I said, "Yes, I could. I could do it very well."

My mind and my stomach were churning at the possible outcome of this conversation. An answer to a prayer that I had never prayed. Fulfilment of a dream that I had never dreamed.

This was what I wanted.

The unspecified need that I had tried to explain to Jaen crystallised.

[303]

I needed to be given a school in which to teach. Had he mentioned some other project, that might have been my unspecified desired object. But he said, Could you run a school? and at once that became my ambition.

"What if you were offered the chance to do so?"

"I should jump at it." I looked at him directly, daring him not to be playing jokes on me. "I should seize it, take the chance in both hands and nobody should make me let it go."

He smiled at my enthusiasm. I knew then that he was serious.

Later, after an hour of discussion, I was once more walking down the long drive. I found myself the first and only teacher in the first and only school in Cantle.

The details were not set then, but the unusual wedding gift of a "small school for the poor children of your village, Henry", that had been requested by the Hon. Amelia Coates (a kind and philanthropic lady), was going to be provided.

My mind was in uproar. A muddle of thoughts. A swarm buzzing. Ideas and fears, confidence and doubt. But, running through the chaos was a straight, calm line. It was like a beam of light shining through a hole into the dark: it was direction and fulfilment, it was self-respect and dignity. All those other things that were going on in my mind were mere moths and midges flitting around the steady beam.

I made no bones about it to my mother.

She was sitting on the little bench in the porch, watching her red tiles dry off.

"Well?"

"I'm going to be a teacher."

"A what?"

I think it would have made as much sense to her had I said, I'm going to be an organ-grinder with a monkey.

"Well, we can't sit around here all day. You wasted enough time as it is."

Fridays at Croud Cantle have always been given over to the clearing up after going to market. Baskets, boxes, jars and all kinds of containers have to be scrubbed with soda, scoured with salt, bleached, dried, and made ready for re-use. I put on my old skirt and sacking apron and started on this least pleasing of all the tedious jobs about the farm.

As we worked, I told her of the scheme and quickly put her mind at rest about taking on extra hands to do that work on the farm which I would have to give up.

"He wants me to teach. Well, not him, his wife that's going to be. Teach the village children, like I'm teaching Johnny-twoey."

"Oh, that'll do'm a world of good."

My mother's reaction was probably typical of others that I would encounter. People who worked the land, lived from hand to mouth on next to nothing. As soon as a child could walk it was set on the road of labour that it would follow all its life, so how many fathers would send their sons into a classroom when they might be earning their bread following the plough. There would be some who would be able to see beyond the downs, and I would have to start there and hope that others would follow.

"It will do them a lot of good in the long run. Things won't change overnight."

I could have wished that our benefactress had been different, but beggars can't be choosers.

My own view of the "lady of a sweet nature and of philanthropic views" was uncoloured by her immense fortune and whatever else it was Harry Goodenstone saw in her: my description might have been "sentimental and self-indulgent". She was a widow, four years younger and four inches taller than Young Harry and had a love of hats on which perched many tiny, stuffed birds. The ten years of her previous marriage had made her a dignified matron at thirty-one, different in every respect to the dainty pink and white Mrs Trowell. Perhaps that is why Harry Goodenstone settled upon this lady, or perhaps he wished for a more motherly woman in his life.

On my first interview with her she told me at length how she had once heard a sermon spoken by a wayside preacher, "of a most stirring and poetic turn of phrase", and upon discovering that he was once a ploughboy and had been taught to read, she had ever since thought what an infinitely better place any village would be if the poor could be taught to read in the manner of that preacher.

As she was telling me this, my hopes sank. I remembered what Fred Warren had told me about a charity school he had once attended where poor children received very elementary instruction in their letters and a great amount of teaching about the touching of forelocks, curtseying and other graces that would make them less hobbledehoyish when they went as servants. I was determined that I would have nothing of that and questioned her politely about what I might do.

"I leave it entirely up to you. Mr Goodenstone has recommended you as a labouring child who learned to read. Indeed, he told me how he discovered you first – studying in the church, was it not?"

I said, yes, I had done a great deal of work there. I did not mislead her, neither did I tell her much about what I hoped to do. I knew that I was treading on shifting sands. I passionately wanted her school – no, not her school, my school.

The next time I went to Blackbrook I talked to Fred about the plan. He was very excited and said that he would ride over to Cantle on the following Sunday. It had been my intention to find a room and let it be known in Cantle that here was a school for any child who wished to come.

"Why should they want to come, Judeth?"

The answer ought to have been simple, but I did not know it. I never really understood what it was that prompted me to want to bend my mind to learning, puzzling, remembering facts. But I did know how the reluctant Hanna could be persuaded and what it was that drew Johnny-twoey. It was the "and then? and then?"

"Curiosity, Fred. I shall begin by reading to whatever child I can persuade to come, and each time I shall stop at a point where they want to know, 'and then what happened?' But they shan't know until they have learned one letter, a word, a fact; anything."

"A carrot hung before the donkey to make him move?"

"Not quite. Usually the donkey doesn't get the carrot until the end of the journey, but my children will get a bite of it every time they take one step forward: not enough to satisfy them, but enough to get the taste for more."

That seemed to be perfectly sound reasoning and Fred said that he would like to help me. "It's what I need, Judeth."

He was right. Since the death of Mrs Warren, he seemed to have lost all his enthusiasm.

"Losing Molly and Will together like that," he added.

I was surprised to hear him speak of Will like that.

"Do you miss Will? I thought your new man was doing very well."

"I never liked any man so much as Will. It's not to do with the business. There was never any man I could be so open with. I doubt if we ever get two chances of finding such friendship." He tapped the back of my hand with one finger, as he used to do when I was his pupil and had made a stupid error, "You should have married him, Judeth. He might not have gone, if you had said you would have him."

"And he'd have been straining at one leash to be with his precious group and I should have been straining at another to be making a school, and in the middle would be some poor marriage being strangled to death."

"You wouldn't have needed the school. You would have had children of your own. You could have rowed them up at the kitchen table and made that a schoolroom."

He was making something of a joke of it, but he was half serious. I imagined Jaen, rowing up her flock of little starlings and hobbling round on her ruined legs with a slate in one hand and a ladle in the other, trying to capture rowdy Hazelhurst attention.

"You're the one that started me off, Fred. You used to ask me where it was all leading, what was I going to do? I thought you wanted me to do something. You didn't ever say what you thought I could do, just, 'What are you going to do, Judeth?' Even when Young Harry started off that business with the books I thought you had some idea that it would lead somewhere. But it didn't. It was you opened the top of my head and stuffed it full of pamphlets and broadsheets and poems. And now it's all overflowing. It's like a bee-wine: when it's ready you have to keep on giving part of it to somebody else, else it dies."

"Judeth, you are an extraordinary woman. I shall never know how you came about."

I had been bent over the table, making notes of what we had been planning, but his changed tone made me look up. His mouth was slightly open and he momentarily closed his eyes, as though controlling a slight pain, but it clearly was not that. I looked down and quickly started writing again. Dear God, how our desires leap out at us when we least expect them! He recovered himself as quickly as I did, but we each knew that he had been watching the rise and fall of my breast, and each knew that his aroused look had, for a moment, roused me. It was a natural, simple desire. He had not had Molly's warm, jolly form next to him for many months, and Will, who had shown me that my body could soar like a lark, was several days' ride away.

[307]

March 1790

I am my father's daughter. I begin to have some understanding. I believe that I understand how, when he saw and desired Charlotte the milk-maid, he took her and did not much heed the consequences. The moment of passion was all. It is what Jaen warned me of in our nature. "You can dout the fires, Jude," she said. Jaen knows that there are fires. She knows that, at that moment with Dan Hazelhurst, she could not dout hers.

If I had been a son, then I think I must have been another such seducer as my father. I do not believe that I love Will Vickery, yet I have been quite obsessed with thinking of him. It overflows. It is as though I suffer from a malady, a returning fever, a longing for a man. Not any man. I have looked at young men working in the fields, men who are strong and young, and have not found them desirable. At least not so desirable that I would lose control of my feelings and be led into the act as I was with Will.

My desire for Will Vickery is bound up with his being a visionary, a radical. I believe that the moment of fever over Fred today was my awareness of his idealism; the fact that he is a man who is not afraid of revolutionary ideas; a man perhaps willing to flout conventions, to question and to try to change the old, bad order.

If I suffer my "malady" only for radical thinking men, then perhaps I am saved, for I have not found the world is overly full of them.

J.N.

Afterthought.
But then, I do not know the world very well. That was an uninformed statement — the kind of thinking that Fred Warren chides me for.

I F DESIRE could pounce upon two friends such as we were, then it was necessary to be cautious and aware. I was determined not to let my body rule my brain. Keep myself aware of the consequences. A shrouded Mrs Warren with her arm encircling her shrouded dead baby; weary Cantle girls of my age, whose only desire was to see their children behind a plough or with a husband; the misery that never left Jaen's eyes, any more than the pain left her legs; my mother, who had lived with bitterness in her for twenty years or more. The moment of pleasure for women is paid for by a lifetime of pain: the consequence of giving into desire is subjugation.

I knew that I should have to be careful of stray and wandering thoughts of Will Vickery; then immediately put myself in danger by walking out on to Tradden. I had to live in sight of the place where he had found me unconscious, where we had walked and loved and where he had come to find me on the night of Hanna. Perhaps I went there to test myself, to see if there were ghosts to be laid. There were, and they were vivid, lively shades. Some nights they would visit me and draw sustenance from me in my dreams, leaving me like a moth sucked dry by a spider.

The last time that I had such fevered nights was just before I had run away from the harvest killing. Then I had worked myself into the ground; kept myself awake until I fell into an exhausted sleep because I was afraid of my dreams. Now I allowed the dreams to come, even when they were full of violence and menace I let them come, for I sensed that this was the lesser of two evils.

Squire Goodenstone and the Hon. Amelia Coates were married in June. The whole village was given an unexpected holiday and provided with more food and drink than they had seen in a lifetime.

The feasting and dancing went on long after the couple had been

[309]

hauled up the drive of Park Manor, in a flower-bedecked carriage, by estate workers. Seeing this I felt sullen and angry that those men did not see the indignity of their action. They were already used as little better than animals by their masters, certainly worse housed and fed, yet would still voluntarily subject themselves to the indignity of actually replacing the horses with themselves. It was just such acts that Will and I had had many conversations about and I wished that he was there to talk to me.

If I did nothing else in my little classroom, then I would try to instil into Cantle children some respect for themselves; open their eyes to the fact that it ought to be the Harry Goodenstones who should perform acts of humility; it was the Harry Goodenstones who owed a debt to the villagers, not the reverse. But I should have to be subtle and it would not take place overnight. What I hoped to do in my little school was something practical to bring about some changes, as Will was doing. It would be a raindrop in a pond, what I could do, but at least I would be doing something. And to achieve anything I would have to smile falsely at the Mrs Goodenstones and Young Harrys of the world. It would be a means to an end – I would never prostrate myself before them in the way that the estate workers did.

When Harry Goodenstone had first spoken to me of the school, it had seemed a very simple thing to do. All that was necessary was to employ someone to replace me on the farm and go to market with John Toose; to find a classroom and make a plan of teaching. By the end of the year only the last two had been accomplished.

It was difficult to find someone to replace me because I had grown up with the work and into the routine. I was everything from manager to labourer. I mended fences, baked Croud Cantle pies and sold them on the market; I kept accounts and records, planted, tended, harvested, killed chickens, took the house-cow to the bull and sat with farrowing sows.

Every suggestion I made seemed not to suit my mother. I would suggest someone who would be good for fieldwork and she would say, "If you thinks one o' they Gritts is getting their feet under my table, you got another think coming." Or if I thought of some good dairywomen who might be able to cope with the marketing, she'd be too old, too fly-be-night, have sticky fingers, "and we shouldn't never have a brass farden to our names if we let she loose up here."

I realised eventually that if the school was ever to get started then I should have to be firm, but I did understand that there would be an enormous upheaval in the way Croud Cantle had been run for years. I also wanted her to be fairly satisfied with the arrangement, or there would for ever be friction. In the end, it was a series of unconnected events that helped solve the problem.

Rob Netherfield, who used to work for us until a few years ago when he married and went to live in Andover, came back to the village. His wife had died giving birth to their second child, and Rob had brought his babies back to where they would have aunts and grandmothers to bring them up whilst he went out to work as a fencer, hedge-layer and general repair man. Rob had always been a favourite with Mother, so when I suggested that we might have an arrangement for him to come in a few hours regularly, she said, "You leave Rob Netherfield to me."

They were very difficult months for her. I don't believe that she really thought that my head had been turned by Mrs Goodenstone, but her acid tongue whipped out at me occasionally, "I suppose you won't want to dirty your hands with that kind of thing now you'm in with the gentry?" Or she would feign ignorance: "Ah, I don't know nothing about that. I have to leave that to people who've been properly learned."

By one of those coincidences that we tell one another are extraordinary but are, in fact, quite commonplace when we begin to examine the facts, Bob Pointer – who had left us to work for his brother at about the same time as Rob – also returned to Cantle. Bob's brother had put everything he had into a small herd of dairy cows and had lost everything he owned in an outbreak of cattle fever. He turned up at Croud Cantle looking for work at exactly the right moment. He knew the place like the back of his hand and set to work at once. Almost overnight, then, Croud Cantle was working much as it had done some years before.

The third event that helped to free me was that Ted Carterage, who worked for the Estate, was gored by the Mill Farm bull, leaving Maisie Carterage, to whom he had been married only a few months, a widow. She was also left without a roof over her head when she was turned out of the Estate cottage by the Goodenstone Agent. Maisie, who had worked in the kitchens at Park Manor, was relieved to be given the chance to come and work at Croud Cantle.

We made some hasty renovations to the house. Rob put in a better floor under the roof and mended the walls, so making the attic into reasonable sleeping quarters, one of which Maisie moved into with her few possessions. I continued going to Blackbrook with Johnny on market days.

By Christmas I was able to go to Mrs Goodenstone and ask her approval of the arrangements I had made. She had agreed to pay me a monthly sum from the time that I took over the back room of a small trading store that had been run by the Bassett family for generations. I believe that it had once been quite a thriving little business, something like a static packman, but now that Annie Bassett was old and befuddled, the shelves held little more than some rusted pins, a few lengths of faded tape and some disintegrating thread.

Christmas brought a letter from Will and as on earlier occasions, when his other letters had disturbed the thick curtain of work with which I surrounded myself, it brought more and vivid dreams. Dreams of thundering horses, tumultuous clouds and fearsome chaos, wherein a small crack appears in the earth and spreads until the entire world needs only a tap for it to shatter into fragments.

Dear Judeth,

I hope that you will read this letter to Mrs Nugent so that she will hear that I wish her health and happiness in the coming year.

It seems both a long and a short time since we had that excellent Christmas dinner and you and I went to look for a holly branch. Do you remember that we did not find the holly and Hanna said that it was a good thing as little goblins with hot needles lived in the red berries? Is Hanna happy now that she has been living with her mother and father for almost two years?

When I read that about the holly to myself, I again thought what a fool Judeth Nugent must be to give up the chance of living with a man such as Will for years of struggle with dull-eyed Cantle children. No, they should not be dull-eyed. I would tell them everything that I knew; brighten their eyes, as Fred Warren had brightened my own when he had taken trouble to teach me.

I did not read that part about Hanna, for we said very little about her. I rode over to Newton Clare as often as I could without appearing too intrusive, but Mother never came at all. They were not visits in the true sense of the word, for Hanna still appeared distant and Jaen seemed often dispirited and apathetic and not inclined to talk much.

I do not know what to tell you of the work that I do here. Sometimes it seems that a year's work has achieved nothing except a few lists of names. But I think we must not expect too much too soon. Men who are having to cope with an entirely new way of life; of working shut up, of working cheek-by-jowl in a crowd, of living in rows of cottages strung together, are not too concerned with any long-term betterment of their lot. Many are satisfied with the few pence more than they got labouring on the land. So we must work slowly and diligently. Eventually it will be seen that every working man needs to join with every other and that is all that they have to bargain with against the Power and the Gold.

His letter went on much in that vein and I could hear his voice in every word and sentence. I lost much sleep over it.

[313]

FRED CAME OFTEN to help me. He rolled up his sleeves and
together we scrubbed the room behind Annie Bassett's.

When I was little and Rob Netherfield worked at Croud Cantle,
he seemed like quite an old man, with his bushy black beard and
balding head. He was actually not much more than a dozen years older
than myself and now that I was adult and, in everything but name,
mistress of Croud Cantle, there was a kind of equality between us.

"Here, young Jude. Be that right you'm starting a Sunday school?"

"Not a Sunday school."

"At's what Dicken reckons. He've told everybody in the Fount.
The whole place knows Young Harry's paying you to get a Sunday
school going."

I could well believe that the whole place knew if Dicken was
telling. I had already heard from Maisie that Dicken had put about and
later had to deny that, "The'm all sixes and seb'ns up there, 'cause
Master Jude's getting wed."

"The whole place is going to have a surprise then," I said.

Because I knew that he was more loyal than Dicken, and did not
have cronies in the Dragon and Fount who would be told before the
Goodenstones made their intentions known, I told Rob the true reason
for the changes taking place at Croud Cantle.

"It's a ill wind, Jude."

I did not understand his wry smile.

"Young Harry – he'm going to stand for Parliament in the Four
Marks seat, what old Sir Nobby as got drowned have held this thirty
year."

"I hadn't heard that."

"I should ha' thought it was all over Blackbrook."

It was true, I had heard nothing about it. But I did see what Rob
meant by it's an ill wind. Opening a school for the children of his

estate workers would show Harry Goodenstone as forward-thinking and modern. It was becoming the very thing for men to be thought enlightened. Perhaps the original idea had been the Hon. Amelia's, but Rob was probably right in suggesting that Harry Goodenstone had seen that it was not a bad scheme to become involved in. But I did not much care how my school came about, so long as it did.

Rob became very enthusiastic and a great help.

"I shouldn't a minded learning to read, Young Jude."

"There won't be an age limit. You can have a front seat."

"I'm a bit old in the tooth, but I shall see my two little'ns gets you to learn them. Can you do numbers, too?"

"Not that well, but good enough."

"It's numbers at be as important as reading and writing. You have to know how many beans makes five so you don't let no Sir Nobbys or Young Harrys put nothing over on you if you can help it, or if they do, at least you knows how they'm doing it."

I got to know a side of Rob Netherfield which I never suspected existed. I do not know how we got round to it, but one evening he told me of events that he had been involved in north of Hampshire; of one or two small gatherings of farm and estate workers which had been held in the heart of woods on common land at dark of night. Men and women talked of banding together so they might approach landowners and magistrates to get wages raised to something above the starvation level they were at present. They talked of banding together, united, so that no one person would have to face the wrath of their masters alone, or be penalized individually.

"But we was all so afraid, Jude. Even there in the pitch of night, with our faces all muffled up, we were afraid that there was arse-lickers, if you a pardon the expression, or folks with little'ns so hungry that they'd sell us out to the magistrates, who'd have us as riotous assemblers or summit."

I told him what Will was doing in the North.

"Ah, Young Jude. If he'd a wanted to get people together to make use of the power of our numbers and our labour and our skill and that, then he ought a stopped round here. It a be a bloody sight easier getting people united when they all lives and works close. It's when they'm scattered in penny numbers like we are in these here villages round here that it gets hard."

He mended windows and boarded up holes and helped me

[315]

lime-wash the walls. Gradually, by flickering light, slowly, with our breath streaming white in the cold of the January evenings as we worked together, we talked, got to know one another, gained a respect for one another. Rob Netherfield was unread and could not always find the best words to explain his ideas, but he was as radical in his views as Will and Fred, and fiercer than either, for Rob had always lived much closer to hunger and poverty than either of the other two.

It was the first day of March when I walked up to Park Manor to tell my benefactors that the schoolroom was ready. Although I was eager to be there, I walked slowly. It was more like late April, calm and warm. Where Chard Lepe flows out in winter on to parkland, marsh marigolds were out.

Jaen. Marsh marigolds and Jaen and watching tadpoles; tucking our skirts between our legs like women gleaning, so that Mother would not know that we had been down near the Chard pond; the greeny smell of the clear water; watching caddis-fly larvae lumbering along the bottom; my skirt always, at the last moment, dropping its hem into the water; running in the wind to dry it before going home.

If I were God, I should not reward goodness with an eternity sitting on my right hand, I should give the reliving of times of complete happiness and peace. With the smell of bruised lush grass, and the sight and feel of the marsh marigolds, those hours with Jaen would be heaven enough.

One thing that I had not even thought about till that morning was how much time I would have from now on to go off wandering over Tradden and Winchester. Harry Goodenstone said that he expected the schoolroom to be open whenever children could have an hour away from their work. It was an unsatisfactory arrangement, for few parents would say that there was ever an hour when there was not something to be done. Although I could not have described it as such when I was younger, I have always felt as though my brain was being fed when I wandered over the downs with no purpose other than to wander.

At the Big House, Mrs Cutts disapprovingly led me into the presence of the Goodenstones. Dicken's gossip had foundation: there was to be a next generation of Goodenstones, and Young Harry reminded me of nothing so much as a bantam cock fussing about a large red hen. I sensed at once that Mrs Goodenstone's enthusiasm for village children who became wayside preachers had waned in her absorption with herself and her own child.

Rob had seen what might happen. "What a you do, Jude, if it's all a five minute wonder?"

It was not possible. It was a wedding gift, a token of affection between the two. The lady wanted her schoolroom so much that she had asked for it as that token.

"Ah well, just so long as you don't expect too much," Rob had said, "then there's no harm done."

"Ah, Henry, of course, it is the reading girl come. I had forgot," said Mrs Goodenstone.

I felt a flush of humiliation rush to my face. I accepted that I was Bella Nugent's girl, the market girl, pie girl, or even that queer Nugent girl up the lane, but the way she said "the reading girl" made me feel like a two-headed calf in a booth at Blackbrook fair.

You thinks too much of yourself, my mother would have said.

I think that Harry Goodenstone saw my discomfort and said, all jolly, "She's Miss Nugent. They have the little farm on the other side." Adding for my benefit, "Which I assure her I have no interest in acquiring."

Mrs Goodenstone smiled, intent on threading and knotting coral beads for the baby.

"We will leave Mrs Goodenstone to rest, and talk in the library."

I bobbed as much of a curtsey to her as I could manage and followed him out.

"Mrs Goodenstone has been required by her physician not to tax her strength in any way and to keep her legs raised."

Even legs encased in silk and resting on fine embroidery may not escape the disintegration brought about by carrying a child, and for a moment I loathed Harry Goodenstone for having brought that upon her. It was ridiculous, for quite obviously the lady was entirely taken up by the wonderful creation she was involved in.

"Of course, Mr Harry," I said.

The little bantam seemed to preen himself. " 'Sir' Henry before very long. Before the child is born. And quite likely, Sir Henry Goodenstone JP, MP."

I said that I was very pleased to hear, all the while aware that they were going to abandon me and the schoolroom. I could not bear to hear him go through all the preamble that would lead to the inevitable excuses and explanations.

[317]

"Then I expect you will find it difficult to take much interest in the little schoolroom?"

At least Harry Goodenstone thought that he should make an excuse. His wife, I believe, would have simply forgotten that she was ever interested in such a scheme.

"It is not so much that I shall not take interest and I, we, certainly should like to see you getting the children starting to read. But we shall be spending a great amount of time in London, and we also intend to visit and interest ourselves in our plantations and estates on the other side of the world."

"What do you want me to do then, Mister Harry?"

"Well, you have no doubt gone to some trouble and we," he giggled as he used to do with Mrs Trowell, "The Lady Amelia and myself, will arrange for a sum of money to be held by my Agent to keep you going for a year."

A year! It would take that amount of time to get half a dozen children even to make a start. It would take years; slow, hard years, to make anything like a school in a place like Cantle. Apathy, poverty, suspicion; all had to be worked upon.

"I had hoped for longer than that," I said. "We have made some big changes at home, extended some rooms, taken on some more labour."

"That is a very good thing to do, improve your property. Never wasted money, and labour is cheaper by the day: get twice the work out of any one man these days. Nothing like low wages to get the corn growing. Your mother will know that, she'll be glad of the extra labour."

Only a few short months ago I had thought what a change for the better there had been. I had found a spark of regard for him. A disturbing spark, because he then no longer fitted easily into my opinion of him as a silly, immature man. Now, however, he had returned himself to a place where I could regard him without any warmth at all. He had become everything that Old Sir Henry had been, and I knew exactly where I stood with him now. I knew, too, that I needed the money he had promised, so I swallowed my pride.

"Well, Sir Henry." He made a deprecative gesture, but enjoyed my flattery in the premature use of the title. "I was relying upon you to get children into the classroom. I think it will be difficult if you don't let it be known that you expect your estate workers to allow their children to come there. I think that once it becomes accepted we shall not find it so difficult, but at first it will be your ..."

"I see, I see. Very well. I shall tell Kyte that the schoolroom has my blessing."

I thanked him and went home, but did not tell Mother what had happened.

A few days later I went to Blackbrook, taking Maisie as well as Johnny-twoey so that I would be able to get away from the stall to see Fred Warren.

He was in his little office over the grain store. As I entered, sadness swept over me. Spaces left by Mrs Warren and Will had settled gloomy and grey in corners, along with the dust from corn husks and wheat ears. I told him how we had been let down and once more in that room my taut nerves snapped, my voice broke and tears welled up. It was over in a minute.

"It must be something about this room, Fred. I hardly ever cry anywhere else."

"You will try to be strong all the time, Judeth. You should let yourself cry sometimes."

"Weakness, Fred."

"You are your mother all over again."

"Fred! I am nothing like her."

He only raised his eyebrows and pursed his lips. I thought I remembered someone else using that phrase, but perhaps it was in the dreams. Did people think I was like her? I sometimes caught myself stumping about in a purposeful way very like Bella's. But it was my leg, still not straight, that made me walk like this. Fred was wrong. Not like my mother. No.

By the time I left him I felt hopeful again. He said that he knew people who might be willing to put up some money to keep us going.

"There are two approaches, Judeth. Those men who will help because I shall tell them Young Harry has money in it and they'll want to be associated; and others who will do so because I shall tell them that he's backing out, letting us down, and they will want to show him up. I should have thought he would have kept you going until he's actually got old Sir Noddy's seat. But then, Amelia Coates is one of the Noddy clan, so there's not much chance that Young Harry will not get it."

[319]

IN JUNE, almost a year to the day from their marriage, a son and heir was born to Sir Henry and Lady Goodenstone. The birth coincided with hay-making, so another moonlit supper was given for the villagers. There Sir Henry made his first appearance as Member of Parliament for Four Marks and gave a speech, at the end of which he announced that the schoolroom was not being used as his lady had hoped and urged the people of Cantle to recognise the value of their children being able to read.

After that, the number of children who came on a very irregular basis rose from eight to eleven. Most of them were quite small children who, I suspected, were being sent to "Annie Bassett's Reading", as it had become known, because they were the least able to contribute to the family. But I did not mind. Little children learn surprisingly quickly and quite soon a few of them could recognise some words and make a good attempt at their name.

Fred would often ride over and sit holding and guiding a child's hand, making letters, as he had done mine. His own boys were all at school and Peg had settled into her mother's place. He contributed to the expenses which were very few, apart from what was paid to me. I had suggested that I ought not to take anything, but Fred insisted that it was unprofessional to think of such a thing, and I was amused at first when he said, "People who work without a salary lower the standing of the whole profession." I hardly thought that one woman, in a small back room, teaching half a dozen ragged, cottagers' children would undermine the universities, but I agreed to the principle. As always when I needed to sort out ideas, I wrote to Will.

Dear Will,

These weeks have been agreeable and pleasant. Although I still have only a few children to teach, I feel that I am doing something useful; something I am good at and have been searching to do.

It is a usefulness quite different from working on the farm. The wage I receive is very small and I should find it difficult to eke out a living if I did not live at home. But my wage is very important to me. It is a symbol that I can live – a woman can live – using her brains and talent. Independence. It is quite different from being a governess, for a governess is treated like a servant by the family and kept at arm's length by the servants. I should dislike that very much and, with my tongue, I don't believe that I should last long.

I continue to work many hours at Croud Cantle. I still help with the baking and go to market. But I think of myself as a teacher. I am proud of being such. Independent.

You see how you have been saved. What a very bad wife I should have made.

I feel a great urgency about my work. The poverty in this area is distressing. Many people are on the edge of starvation. They live in abundant and fertile Hampshire and Sussex where corn is grown, cattle fattened, milk and cream and eggs produced abundantly: it is almost impossible to believe that they starve amid such plenty, but they do. Many of my children are little bags of bones. They have bow legs and streaming noses, such things that you will never see on the Goodenstone child, nor any other that has enough food to grow on.

I need to make a spell so that these children of mine will suddenly be able to read fluently and I shall be able to stuff their heads full of ideas, so that they will ask, "Is this fair or right?" and when the answer comes, "No!", they will go on to ask what they might do about it.

Is it any wonder that people says, "She's a queer one, that Jude Nugent!"

By the end of the summer, Sir Henry and Lady Goodenstone had closed their Cantle house, leaving only a small staff, and had taken a house in London for the coming season.

Just as the "Amelia Goodenstone Fund" was running out, Fred came up to the farm with the news that Mr Benjamin Hannable was willing to put enough money into the fund to keep the little school going. It would be an entirely new account – "The Benjamin Hannable Foundation". The title was, like its instigator, typically overdressed, but I did not mind, just so long as I could keep my children going. Recently I had resorted to giving "prizes" to children who came to school. I brought food down from the farm: pies that had broken and could not be sold; honey-cakes and small tarts. I also provided some sort of a plain meal for any of them who came for an entire morning. The age-range and numbers of my children expanded. They began to learn.

Other people in the village could grow vegetables and milk cows.

Only Rev. Tripp and I were in a position to teach Cantle children. But the Rev. Tripp preached the gospel of service to the one on high, and he did not always mean God.

I dreamed of teaching enlightenment. And I began to feel that I had indeed found work that I not only enjoyed and felt satisfied in doing, but work that was purposeful, important.

> *Dear Judeth*
>
> *I hope that you have not abandoned your writing. An account of how the Cantle school got started would make interesting reading.*
>
> *I wish that I could write well, for what is happening in the new manufacturing towns should be recorded.*
>
> *Good roads are being made everywhere. Great machines are at work. People, people, people. They come daily looking for the promised land and the fortunes that they believe are here for the asking. Some will make fortunes and many will go under in the squalor that is becoming daily worse in some towns. But we are making some progress.*
>
> *I hope that I shall one day meet your Rob Netherfield. He is right, of course. It is easier to get unity when large numbers of workers living in one area are attached to one type of manufacture, with one employer. On the other hand, if that one employer fails, then huge numbers of workers fail also. An entire city could fail, and I believe that there could be destitution on such a scale as we have never imagined. One thing that we are determined to get employers to agree to is a fund that will be a safeguard against such. It will be one of the most difficult aims to achieve, for They will not like a single penny going from their profits.*
>
> *Why don't you make a book, Judeth? Write it very personally. Relive it and put it down. Write what you felt, even the parts that are painful, and make it into a book. Every letter that you write is like a chapter and I always look forward to receiving the next. Try. I shall buy it directly upon publication.*

I had been writing detailed notes for about two years. At the back of my mind I did think that one day I might attempt to write something: perhaps a fictionalised autobiography or a history. Will's letter prompted me to begin this book.

During these busy months I still went as often as I could to Ham Ford. It was always a stressful day. I usually took John Toose with me, partly because it was only from him that I found out anything at all about Hanna, and partly because seeing John was the only pleasure in my niece's life. She was now almost as tall as Jaen and me, and if she took after the Estover women, then at this age she was nearly at the height at which she would stay. It seemed to me that, although she was no longer chubby and rosy-faced, she was becoming very beautiful; but then I saw her through the eyes of someone who loved her fiercely, albeit unexpressed.

Jaen often receded into a world of her own where it was almost impossible to meet her. Not always: sometimes she was bright and she would greet me with, "Oh, Ju, I'm that glad you've come over. I been thinking about that time when ..." and she would start talking about some incident in our childhood, going over every detail, correcting me as to whether it was self-heal or hyssop that we had rubbed on to our faces to make our skin violet-coloured, or whether it was on Tradden or Winchester where we found two stones that was alike as twins.

"Have Mother still got them?"

When I said, yes, they were still on the dresser shelf, she asked most earnestly that I should bring them over next time.

"I should love to see them again, Ju. You can't think how I'd like to see them. They was twin stones. Remember what we said?"

"We was their keepers and they'd been given to us so that they wouldn't never be parted."

She had looked so very pleased. "Ju, I'm glad you remembered. If you'd a forgot, it would a been bad. I can talk to you, Ju. Dan only thinks me silly and fanciful. It suddenly came to me that them stones was me and you: that's why it was us who found them. I'm glad Mother never throwed them out. I tried to talk to Hanna about all them stories we used to tell, but she's like her father there, she can't see no magic in anything. She can't see no pictures in the fire even."

I asked Jaen if she didn't think that it might be our mother that Hanna took after, and not the Hazelhursts.

She thought before she answered. "Perhaps after all then, Ju, you and me an't so much like the Estovers except in our looks. Perhaps we'm like him. I remember him you know. Not just his blue coat. I can remember his face sometimes. He had a beautiful face. I wish he hadn't gone off like that. If he hadn't a gone off like that we'd a had a father, and then Mother wouldn't a had to be father and all, and we'd a had a mother too."

Gradually she withdrew more and more into herself. If Dan was

[323]

there she made an effort to answer, but she was seldom the initiator of a conversation. When she and I were alone, I think she felt that she could withdraw without criticism, that she did not have to make an effort, that she could be at ease. There were times when she seemed to be like a frail old lady. She would pat my hand and say, "It's only you understands me, Ju."

B EN HANNABLE was quite generous to his "Foundation". I went with Fred to see him in his Blackbrook house. I never knew him in his early days as the eliman, dealing in dribs and drabs of lamp oil and tallow, but Mother knew how poor the Hannables were. Quite different now. Hannables were the largest dealers in oil and Hannables was Ben Hannable. He was little changed from the man who had asked to marry me when I was seventeen. A woman's touch was everywhere in his home, but now that Rose Hannable was dead, it was overlaid with careless masculinity: boots and dogs on the hearth; fowling guns leaning against walls; tobacco smoke on the air.

"Well, Missie, Warren says you want some money."

"Not exactly me, Mr Hannable ..."

"Ben," he interrupted, "Ben, seeing as you might ha' been Mrs Hannable. Then you wouldn't a had to come cap in hand, Missie. You could a had all this lot."

He made an expansive gesture towards the crystal spirit bottles and glasses, oil paintings, swathed velvet and brocade curtains and plump chairs with embroidered seats.

"What do you think, Warren, eh? Her mother wouldn't have me when we was young. Then Missie here wouldn't have me neither. She'd a had a better deal than Bella, too. I was only just starting out when I asked Bella Estover. Be the time Missie here was of age I'd got a tidy long stocking. You should a had me, Missie. I always had a fancy for red hair."

On the surface, his manner implied that it had not mattered one jot that he had not been able to satisfy his fancy for red hair, but I suspected that he had resented, even if he did not now, his attentions being rejected by a farm girl. He was pot-bellied, almost toothless and quite graceless. His pride in his own achievement, in getting from

starveling eliman's son to wealthy Blackbrook businessman made him
a slightly more likeable benefactor than Sir Henry Goodenstone.

The outcome of the visit was a promise from him that he would
keep the school going for two years, provided I taught numbers.

"It's how I got where I am today. Inches in a foot. Yards in a mile.
Two pints, one quart; four quarts, one gallon. Rods, poles and perches.
Six eights is forty-eight. Twelve twelves is a hundred and forty-four.
Hundred and forty-four is twelve dozen. Twelve dozen to the gross.
Twelve pence to the shillin'. One percent discount if you takes four
gallons. That's how I got where I am today! Teach'm that, Missie, and
you taught'm summit worth knowing."

I had swallowed my pride often in the last months, what with the
Goodenstones and then having to "return to the fold" to placate Rev.
Tripp, who was prepared to bring in the full force of the Church to
close me down. So this last was no difficulty. I would do anything to
keep the school going; anything so long as I kept my own self-respect.
Ben Hannable's condition on providing some money; Rev. Tripp's
spiteful threat; the Goodenstone's capriciousness: all this concerned
their self-respect – not mine.

With the onset of winter, several more children came, so we had to
rearrange the boxes, planks and stools to give them all a fair
distribution of the warmth from the fire. That was the one good thing
that the Goodenstones did for us. I had asked Sir Henry if the Estate
would supply logs and a sack of wheat, and surprisingly he had given
his Agent instructions which were never cancelled. So whatever else
my little classroom lacked, it never went without fire or fermity.

At the end of the day, each child in turn was given the task of
setting the wheat in an iron pot over the embers, and each morning
another doled out spoonfuls into the collection of dishes and bowls
that we had begged, borrowed and stolen. When our house-cow was
milking well, I brought some milk. They bolted the fermity with the
speed of the hungry children that they were, and a couple of hours
later the scraping of slates was accompanied by the sound of windy
bellies and giggles.

Slowly, slowly, one or two of the children began haltingly and
laboriously to read a few words and work simple addition. There were
no set times for anything. Whatever went on in my classroom
depended, as everything else in the Cantle valley, upon the weather,
the season, the condition of the crops and nature.

When it was ploughing time, the ten- and eleven-year-old boys came in for only the fifteen minutes that qualified them for the fermity; when the seed had been sown the very littlest children were sent out with tins and boards to scare off the crows and starlings. Girls came and went throughout the day when mothers were laid up in child-bed, and at harvest time I closed up for several weeks, since every child was needed in the fields. I had to admit that bending the brain to understand the difference between two-plus-four and two-times-four would not compete with getting in the harvest.

John Toose, now a seventeen-year-old with a long jaw and the beginnings of a good beard, loved to come into the classroom. He could now read and write well. He had overcome his shyness on the market and was a very good trader. People liked his quiet, broad way of dealing. Fred took the boy under his wing and helped him get papers and booklets on horticultural methods, which John studied and put into practice on the plot that mother had handed over to him some years before. He was very popular in the classroom, where the young children called him Mister Toose.

At Croud Cantle, things were working out very well, for although there was so much poverty and distress amongst the cottagers and land-workers all over the south of England, the people to whom we sold our goods on the market were not much affected by the low wages paid to agricultural workers. We could sell all the vegetables, pies, salads, eggs, cream, fruit, honey and butter that we produced, and now clumps of John Toose's herbs and herbaceous plants were selling well.

Dicken died in November whilst hacking and cursing a vegetable clamp that had become hard and frozen. According to Bob Pointer, he fell over in mid-kick and stopped living. At nearly sixty years of age, he had outlived almost all of his Cantle contemporaries. He had never been outside the Cantle valley, and had come from his cottage next to the Dragon and Fount, up Howgaite to Croud Cantle every day for most of his life. Yet neither Mother nor I could truthfully say, "We shall miss old Dicken." There had always been a feeling that he ran with the hare and the hounds. In the middle of saying something, Mother would hush, "Watch out – here's Dicken," or, "Mind Dicken don't hear you," and gossip filtering back would show that Dicken would tell anybody anything about what went on under the Nugent's roof, and was not above fancifulness if it made a good story. And I had never fathomed out whether his referring to us as Master and Master Jude was a jibe at there not being a proper Master, or because the proper Master had run off, or that neither of us was his master. Dicken was a good worker, but Bob Pointer was better, and you had the feeling that Bob truly was a loyal Croud Cantle man.

Fred told me that Ben Hannable had said he would look us over when he was Cantle way, so I was not surprised when he walked into the classroom just before Christmas. In fact I had prepared the children by teaching them some 'timeses' by rote. To the children he was a figure of authority, and those whose planks barred his way into the room hastily dismantled their seating and drew back against the wall. He seated himself beside the fire and hands on knees asked, "Well, then, what's Missie here been teaching you?"

Of course there was silence. Generations of training told them not to be the one to step forward, not the one to be noticed, leave it for somebody else. When the gentry entered their territory it nearly always meant trouble: melt into the landscape, edge away from the front of a crowd, don't meet their eyes. Eventually I got them to face me and, as we had practised for Ben Hannable's sake, recite a timeses table. I was proud of their achievement – not in the recitation, but in persuading him that they enjoyed it, so that he would believe that he was important, influential, and would continue putting oil money into his Foundation.

"That's summit like!" he said when they had finished. "A penny each for the big boys, a ha'penny for the girls and a farden for the little 'ns." The class immediately found its voice, particularly the little 'ns, trying to prove that there were big.

"And now you can all clear off home and tell your mothers and fathers that it's Mister Benjamin Hannable they got to thank. And you can tell them that it's Mister Hannable what the Lord Chancellor have made a Justice of the Peace."

He looked triumphantly at me through the scramble for the door, as the class got quickly away before anybody remembered the rule that everything had to be clean and tidy and the fermity put on before they went.

"I should congratulate you then," I said, as I began to tidy the room.

"Yes, Missie. Magistrate for the County of Hampshire sitting at Blackbrook. You have to own land worth a hundred a year. I had land

[328]

worth a hundred a year a long time, but they thought I didn't have the way of talking for a JP. But I tell you, Missie, in the end it's money that talks and it can talk like a eliman's son if there's enough of it." He sat back, his thumbs in his waistcoat pockets, patting his bow-window with his fingers.

"You must feel very ... gratified," I said.

"That's right, Missie, gratified. And I shall feel even more – gratified – when it comes to the county quarter sessions and they haves to accept me as one of they. They a get used to me: they an't got no choice. Magistrates is there for life. Stop fiddling about with them things and come and sit here." He patted the bench beside him. I took the stool on the opposite side of the fireplace.

"And that an't all, Missie. I set myself up a long time ago to have the king touch my shoulder. Know what I mean, Missie? Sir Benjamin Hannable, JP – Sir Benjamin. And I shall have it. There an't nothing you can't have if you got enough money."

He reached across and patted my knee. I rose and began pouring the fermity wheat into the iron pot. He rose and came very close to me. "Don't that spark you up, Missie?" He began fingering my hair as though examining fabric. I made a move to side-step him. As I did so he pulled at my hair, undoing the knot. He placed himself in my way. He grabbed my wrist and pulled me towards him. "Don't nothing spark you up, Missie? Are you too special to turn your nose up at being Lady Hannable?" I had been right. He still harboured resentment about my not accepting him when he had thought that he was doing me an honour in offering marriage. It had become worse than resentment: I could see hatred and vindictiveness in him.

"Let me be!" The skin on my wrist burnt as I wrenched it from his grasp.

"Let her be!"

Rob Netherfield was through the door and across the room before Ben Hannable could take a step back. He thrust my attacker's arm high up behind his back and propelled him towards the door, knocking over everything in their path. At the door, Rob gave a push and the Lord Chancellor's new representative tumbled like a tipped milk-churn into Annie Bassett's filthy yard.

He picked himself up and, his face distorted with malevolence, said, "You've had the last penny out of me for your high and mighty scheme, Miss. If you wants a journeyman's hand up your skirt then it

[329]

looks like you got somebody to oblige." He went on in this vein as he mounted his horse. I was too full of white fury even to blush that Rob should hear. "And you!" he flicked a short riding whip at Rob, who jumped back. "I don't know who you are, but by God you'd better not find yourself half an inch the wrong side of the law where I am. One pheasant in your pocket and I'll have you in Austrailee and your feet won't touch the ground."

THE SUNDAY before Christmas, I went over to Newton Clare to try to persuade Jaen and Dan to let Hanna come for a few days.

My mother seemed unwell: not so much physically, except for the rheumatics that made her knuckles swell and the bones in her neck crackle. But she no longer did any spinning or spill-making in the evenings. Instead she sat absorbed in the furtive picking and hiding of morsels that she had begun a few months earlier. And the listening. She always appeared to have her head cocked. Sometimes I asked her, "Can you hear somebody coming?" and she would answer as though not wholly in the real world, yet not in a fantasy.

"I thought for a minute it was Will. Or it was Lovey. I thought I heard her calling the banties in. But it might a been a horse. Or perhaps it's just they old pigeons again. Rob a have to do summit about they, getting in under the eaves. You can't hear nothing proper when they'm up there rattlin' off."

Then she would eye me suspiciously, as though she was not quite sure whether there was something going on that she did not know about.

"You haven't seen Will lately, have you?"

"No, he's still up the north."

"He would come and see me if he came this way?"

I assured her that she would be the first person Will would come to if he ever came south.

"He a come."

She was pining for her Little Lovey, and I thought that a few days in her company would make her feel better.

Jaen would not have minded.

"No," was Dan's reply. "What she want to go all over there for when she got us and her own brothers here."

"Mother's not very bright. She's getting on, and it'd do her good to have Hanna for a few days."

"If she an't well, then it's up to you to nurse her. If you wasn't playing games pretending you'm summit you an't, you'd have enough time to see to your mother without wanting my girl."

I was so surprised at his purposely misinterpreting me that I did not answer.

"She got enough fancy ideas, without her getting no more from stopping with you. You done enough damage to her already."

I just could not stand his implied criticisms of both Hanna and ourselves. "Damage! Fancy ideas? You've said things like that before today. What fancy ideas has Hanna got? She works like a little horse. D'you call it fancy ideas when she's up to her armpits in soap and soda, or up to her knees in muck? When she was at our place she didn't have fancy ideas. She learnt to do nearly every job on the farm, and there isn't any fancy jobs at Croud Cantle."

"You was learning her to read. I caught her time and again with bits o' chalk, writing letters on things. I an't having none of that nonsense, filling her head. She's going to grow up to be a proper woman, decent wife and mother. What kind of a woman is it who spends her time reading? Not no farmer's wife. Not no woman in this house!"

The hostility in his voice brought to mind that same resentment that had been in Ben Hannable's when he had told Fred, "Missie here wouldn't have me."

Of all the tongue-holding I had done over the last year, this was the one time when I should never have let myself go. But I did let go. I told Dan Hazelhurst that he was a beast for the number of children he had fathered upon my sister; that he was a brute and a slave-driver for the way he forced his own daughter to work like a skivvy; that he was a body without a brain and – what infuriated him most – that he was a poor farmer, who had no better sense than to put everything he had into one crop, and that if it was not for what would happen to Jaen and the children, I hoped that he would lose every foot of land and every penny he owned.

Whilst I was pouring out my tirade, I was pinning on my shawl ready to leave. I started to bend to kiss Jaen but he pushed me away. "I don't want to see you nowhere here never again."

The one person I needed to placate. The one time I should have bitten my tongue through rather than say what I thought. I felt cold and sick to my stomach. Fortunately none of the children were in the house, but I left Jaen looking wild-eyed as a rabbit at the moment before it flees from a terrier.

I had reached the Cantle side of Tradden before I realised that I had come so far, and I calmed down ... I caught her time and again writing with bits of chalk ... The significance of his words came suddenly back to me. Hanna had not given up at the first opportunity.

A sudden cold storm blew up and was over in ten minutes, making the clear part of the sky appear unusually bright with the Christmas star above the rim of the downs. I have never been one for omens and the like, but I have to admit that when a fragment of rainbow was visible for a few minutes close to the Christmas star, I hoped that it might be saying something favourable, for things had not gone well of late. My aims and ambitions did not falter, but it did seem as though for every two steps I took forward I had to take one back.

From Tradden I could see Park Manor, where the only lights that showed were dim and high up in the servants' quarters. Smoke rose from the trees so that it was possible to pin-point where every cottage was, even though hidden from view. For every trail of smoke there was a hearth; about every hearth were the people of Cantle.

Most of them large families, living close in the warmth and smell of one another. Women of my age with milky babies and children greasy with bacon fat; their men, sinewy and hard, with faces the colour of red clay and bodies white as rendered pig fat; some who would as soon hit out at wives and children as at plough horses, yet working themselves into the ground to keep their family alive. Close by would be their parents, puzzled that the Bible should give them the expectation of three score years and ten, when they know that after two score years and five you are doing better than many of your neighbours. Some would be old people, perhaps with a son living at home; pleased at their good luck that something is still coming into the house. Around those hearths were rickets, consumption, painful, swollen joints, lungs irritated by chaff from the threshing, thin blood, and legs like Jaen's.

At that moment I wanted Will Vickery more than at any other time. I needed, just then – just for the time when I was looking down upon the place that I loved passionately, yet knew that I was apart from – I needed to be part of something, belong to someone.

[333]

I wished that my father had not gone away.

Maisie Carterage came to meet me as soon as I went in at the gate.

"Your mother, Miss Jude. She've been took very queer."

Between the two of us we got her upstairs, into a nightgown and into bed. One side of her face appeared to have collapsed. Her eye dragged down, showing the inner rim; her cheek sagged and her mouth sagged unable to control the flow of saliva.

"She've had a convulsion, I reckon, Miss Jude."

All through those first days of Bella's illness, Maisie was as loving a nurse as though she was caring for her own mother, constantly seeing that the patient was warm and dry, feeding her milk sops like a baby.

Slowly Bella improved until, by the end of February, Maisie and I were able to get her back downstairs and make a permanent bed for her in the house-place. Rob partitioned off the eating end and put a door in and built another chimney up the outside wall, making a separate kitchen and eating room. I didn't know why we had not made the alteration before, as it made the house much more comfortable.

Each day, Maisie would wash and dry the red tiles, talking to the stricken woman all the while, even though Bella could do little better than produce a long, nasal "aahh" by way of answer. Whilst she was in bed, she had stopped her secret picking and hiding, but when she was in her chair again she started flicking out her good hand and plucking at anything near.

I hated seeing her like that. But however bad it felt to look on, it could not compare to Bella's distress at having to rely on somebody else to be kept alive. Bella Estover, Bella Nugent, independent for almost all of her life, slumped, dumb and drooling.

I would have given anything to see her stumping about the yard, yoked to the clanging pails.

It is hard to see how the school stumbled on during that time. But yes, it was mostly with the support of Fred Warren, who rode over several times a week to work there, and Rob Netherfield, who was always willing to put in hours at Croud Cantle if he was needed. Early as it always was when I awoke, there were mornings when Rob was about the place first.

"Thought I'd just have a look at the well-rope," or, "I remembered that there tile had come off the barn." Many of the jobs

that I had always done Rob took over, but he would never take a
penny more than the rate for the job: although as far as money was
concerned we were not so poor as we used to be, for as Blackbrook
grew in size, so the customers for Croud Cantle produce grew in
number.

A T CHRISTMAS Fred had announced the engagement of Peg to James Carter. James had gone into his father's business and seemed to be settled enough early in life to set up in a house his father bought for him. The wedding was to be in Blackbrook Abbey on Easter Saturday.

"I want your Mother to come, Judeth. Now, it will be all right," he said, as I was about to say that it was not possible. "I shall send a wagon over early in the day and you can bring Mrs Carterage. That will leave you free to enjoy yourself at the breakfast."

And so it was arranged. Although Fred had to see to many of the arrangements that his wife would have been so pleased to do, he still made sure that my mother was attended to and comfortable.

She had regained a little of her speech, and Johnny and Maisie as well as I could understand her. When I had told her about the wedding, she had pulled her brows together, signalling a question, and said, "Will? Will?"

"No. He won't come. It'd take him too long."

She shook her head and said, "Will."

I found Mother's pretty jacket, steamed and aired it, and took out my green dress, which had not seen the light of day for more than three years, and set off early in the day in the back of one of White's light, covered wagons.

There was a large crowd outside the abbey and as Maisie and I helped Mother make her shuffling way inside someone said, loud enough for us to hear, "Oh my eye – that's never Bella Nugent!"

Only Maisie and I knew how much effort went into the straightening of Mother's back and the slow, deliberate attempt at a normal walk.

It was the prettiest that Peg had ever been or would ever be again. She was happy to be exchanging the overseeing of her father's kitchen and dining-room for the overseeing of her husband's. At the placing of the ring, I looked idly at my own hand. As I did so, I suddenly had a feeling that Will was there, that he had come. I turned slightly to where I could see the porch of the west door and saw that he stood there. I wanted to immediately get up and go to him. He raised a hand and nodded.

"Mother. Will," I whispered.

Mother pulled her shoulders round so that she could see, then she nodded and grimaced her smile. As at all weddings, people were dabbing their eyes, but the tears that trickled down my mother's face were not for the bridal white Peg but for her favourite.

On the following day, Easter Sunday, Will must have started out soon after sun-up from Fred's home where he was staying, for he was at Croud Cantle very early. I was expecting him and had bacon and bread ready when he came into the kitchen. Yesterday, briefly, we had held hands in greeting, but now he exuberantly hugged me to him and stood rocking, with his face buried beside my ear. Then we stood apart, holding hands and looking at one another, each of us smiling and shaking our heads.

"You've made some changes." He indicated the alterations to the rooms.

"Mother stays in there."

"Will?" Mother's distorted call.

He went into the other room and sat embracing her.

"Ma. Ah, all that chatter yesterday, never a chance did we have to talk. Now just what have you been and done to yourself." He held her dropped cheek and smoothed her useless hand. I could see them through the little round window in the kitchen door. Where was there another man in the world like him? My passionate radical who had given up a good, safe living to work for nothing except what might be collected at meetings; to go and try to set up schemes for better working conditions for people who, in the end, probably wouldn't thank you for it; a man fired with a dream of a better, fairer world; a man who did not dismiss Bella Nugent because she had lost half a body, but treated her like the woman she had always been – the woman she still was, apart from the stricken muscles and nerves.

Is my stuffy schoolroom and those handful of half-starved children a fair exchange for living, eating, talking and sleeping for a lifetime with him? Again the doubt, the temptation. If a woman could only be

[337]

free to love, just to love, without having to fear the consequences of her own passion. A fair exchange ...?

Nothing is ever fair.

He stayed until the sun began to drop down behind Beacon Hill. Before he left, we went to look at the classroom. Will listened intently to everything I told him: about the difficulty of teaching children when they came irregularly; about trying to look after Mother and manage the farm, as well as my work with the children.

"But I shan't give it up, Will. I want to do this. I think it is important and I'm sure it is what I'm best suited to do. I get such satisfaction every time a child looks at a bundle of letters and recognises it as a word."

"You're right to do it, Judeth."

"I thought you might be going to ask me again ... to go with you."

"I believe I've accepted that you never will, and if I can't have that, then I would rather you were doing this than anything else. 'Ignorance is the ally of our oppressors'."

"Who said that?"

"Will Vickery."

"Oh, Will," I laughed, "you're beginning to sound like a ha'penny tract."

"When did I not?"

We sat in the little classroom and he told me something about his work: about what the new towns and cities were like, about the enormous buildings that were going up to house the dozens of machines and thousands of workers.

"We must start things going down here. I thought if I spoke to your Rob Netherfield ..."

"Is what you do illegal?"

"No."

"Then why should people like Rob be afraid to be seen at meetings?"

"Because people like Rob have no say in their own lives, and those who do have long and corrupt arms that can reach out and punish. People like Rob are going to have to be strong enough not to mind being seen."

"And risk losing the bread from their mouths."

"Yes."

"And their children's?"

"If necessary," Will said.

Rob came with us on a walk up Bellpitt Lane, where both men talked animatedly about reform, enfranchisement and unity. And I remember Ben Hannable's face as he said, "I'll have you in Austrailee so fast your feet won't touch the ground."

The following day Will had to go back North again. He left Mother with promises that he would come back soon.

Gradually, Mother's speech became a bit easier to understand, and she began to find ways of dragging herself about using her one good leg and arm. She did not get so many words wrong lately, and now that she could articulate her needs she became more demanding and fretful, often unnecessarily calling me back, or looking reproachful when I came to say that I was going down to Annie Bassett's.

"I don't like ... on my own," or, "It ... long day you'm gone. Long time."

"Maisie looks after you all right, don't she? She keeps looking in? She's got her other work to do, but I could tell her to come in more often. You've got the bell if you need her."

"Maisie – not – daughter. Not Maisie – duty."

When she was like this I had to make myself walk away. She was trying and difficult: the work could not stop because her convulsion had left her with one side of her body not working properly. Once I returned home to find her face bruised and grazed.

"Oh, Miss Jude," Maisie said, anxious and twisting the ends of her bodice-ties. "Missis tried to get down to the fields by her own, and she went and fell against that old flinty wall. She might a done herself a real mischief."

When I told Mother that it was not fair to Maisie if she went off like that, she said, "Stay here," and I guessed that it was her intention to make me feel guilty and neglectful. There were two more similar incidents and on each occasion, although she had only minor injuries, both Maisie and I were worried.

"What if she'd a been by the well, Miss Jude?"

I did not need to be told. There were a dozen places on the farm where my mother could do herself serious injury. The Dunnock ran close beside Croud Cantle, steeply banked in some places. It was even possible for her to get as far as Chard Lepe Pond, a few dragging steps at a time, if she were determined enough. I was sure that she was pushing me to give up the schoolroom, so when my mother got her third lot of cuts and bruises, I knew that we must fight a battle of wills – and I must win.

"I shall not give it up, Mother."

She clamped together the one side of her mouth that she could control. In spite of her altered face, I easily recognised her old belligerent expression.

"You ought to realise that if Will couldn't persuade me to give up my schoolroom, then you throwing yourself about isn't likely to. So you might as well save yourself the sore places, because you shan't make me give up the children."

There were times when Mother got very frustrated that her speech let her down. It seemed that the more she needed her words, the less able she was to control them.

She pointed to herself. "Children? Duty ... Mother."

I knew exactly what my mother was implying. "You think more of them children who an't nothing to you than you think of your own mother."

"No, Mother. I'm not choosing them instead of you. I'm choosing to do the work I think I ought to be doing; the work I want to do. I'll look after you when I'm here. I'll always see you have Maisie or somebody else about when I'm not, but you won't make me give up my work."

I spoke forcefully, strongly. I had won the battle of wills.

The dreams continued to distress me. Although I still went on facing them, I often felt strange and tired the following day, particularly after a night had been filled with the dream about the world cracking.

This dream developed and changed so that even the people in it appeared covered with marks like those of an empty egg-shell when it has been crushed in the hand. The sky, too, took on these markings. Eventually nothing that appeared in the dream could be trusted not to break up if touched or pressed or walked upon. Nothing could be relied upon not to break up in that nightmare world. Only the hovering, two-headed silver fish remained intact: sometimes menacing, sometimes sinister, it always caused me to awake sweating, trembling and bewildered that the most substantial creation of my dream world should appear two-faced and treacherous. Often Hanna was in this dream. I would be running away from Ham Farm with her when she would break up in my hands, leaving me looking down upon a small heap of what appeared to be crumbs from a crusty loaf, but were really recognisable pieces of Hanna.

After a particularly bad night, the best treatment was to walk out over the chalkhills, as I had done all my life, and this I did one hot Sunday afternoon in August.

I had not been up Bellpitt Lane and on to the Tump for months, and I chose to sit as I had on another Sunday. What years ago it seemed since Mrs Trowell and I had sat there. I took deep breaths, filling my lungs with the hot, sweet air that rose from the hills.

I relaxed into playing a game about the colours of August. Purple geranium, loose-strife, hyssop, self-heal, scabious, flax.

Two figures came into view; tiny, climbing Bellpitt Lane. Viper's grass? Not in August ... Sunday afternoon. Few people had occasion to climb Winchester Hill on Sundays ... Yellow flax, rest-harrow, wandering sailor, golden rod. Did golden rod count? Yes, accept golden rod, for it did grow on the lower slope ...

Two women. No, one was a child, but tall, as tall as the woman. She kept running after something – butterflies perhaps – then skipping, then coming back to the woman, who kept up her steady walk up Bellpitt Lane. Curious as to who was as queer as myself, walking up Winchester unnecessarily on a hot afternoon, I watched their progress.

They each wore the everyday dress of country women and stout boots. The girl's wide, straw hat was hanging down her back, and her tight brown curls tumbled about. The woman wore a deep-brimmed bonnet, tied round with a scarf hiding her face. As they came close, I lay back against the rim of the dish of Bell Tump and listened to the arguments of the rooks in Park Manor.

As the two came close, I could hear the woman. I thought it was someone that I knew.

"No, Rosie. Careful. Not there, Rosie." The woman's voice was raised and strained, pronouncing each word separately, distinctly, carefully.

Not a Cantle voice. Blackbrook? It was a town voice, but difficult to place because of the way the woman was using it. A town voice, yet the bonnet was old-fashioned, like those worn by old women for gleaning in the hot sun. The calling stopped as they came closer to where I lay.

[341]

"Miss Nugent." The woman spoke my name as though she could not believe who it was.

I raised my head, but what with the deep bonnet and the sun behind the women's back, I could not see who it was. I certainly did not know the girl who was looking warily at me from behind the woman.

"Judeth. Isn't it strange that we should meet on the same spot we last met."

"Mrs Trowell!" I leapt to my feet. "I ..." I had been about to say that I did not recognise her, that she looked so different; but I checked tongue in time, for the difference in her appearance was extreme, and she must be conscious of it. The pretty pink and white girl was gone and was replaced by a woman. Charlotte Trowell and Young Harry's Lotte had been superseded by a mature woman with lines in her brow; hard-wearing skirts and boots. But not just that – her youthful, lovely face was destroyed: the line of a puckered scar ran diagonally from her brow, over the eye-lid and down to the ear lobe.

"I was just wondering who it could be walking up here on a hot Sunday. I should have known. I don't think I've ever met anyone else," I said.

"May we sit with you?"

"Of course. I am so pleased to see you again."

She took the girl by the hand and drew her forward, so that I could see that she was not a child, but a young woman.

"Judeth. This is Rosalynd – Rosie."

I said hello to Rosie, who returned my greeting with almost a smile and a glance at Mrs Trowell to see if she approved. Mrs Trowell patted Rosie's hand and looked the girl directly in the face. "Rosie, this is Judeth." Rosie watched Mrs Trowell's mouth and tried to say my name.

"Rosie can hardly hear at all and can't speak, but she's learning." As she said this she nodded and smiled at the girl whose eyes flicked quickly from one to the other of us.

We sat on Bell Tump.

"Is your sister ...? Is Mary ...?" When there is such an obvious change in a person, you have to tread a bit warily, to speculate about other changes.

"Mary's dead. Smallpox. Not long after we left ... that place."

"I'm sorry."

"I still miss her, but in another way it is better. She always persuaded me it was best for Rosie to live away from all that ... all that sort of life we were in. On my own I have to make my own mind up. I hadn't ever done that before."

There was a short silence, then Mrs Trowell said, "You know who Rosie is, Judeth?"

I did indeed know who Rosie was, even though until now I had never suspected her existence, and I was pleased, pleased and moved by the strange girl.

"Rosie's my sister."

Mrs Trowell covered her face with both hands, stifling tears. Rosie looked at her mother with great concern. Mrs Trowell recovered immediately, smiled at Rosie and patted her reassuringly.

"It's all right, Rosie. All right."

It was an extraordinary meeting.

A thousand fragments of thoughts ran through my mind. Why were they climbing Winchester; the face; the scar; Mother, Jaen, Rosie. Rosie.

"I'm sorry, I didn't mean to upset you."

"Sorry? Why, child, it's only that you said the most unexpected thing."

She called me "child", and corrected the balance of our relationship. That had been tilted while she was Young Harry's Lotte.

"Isn't she my sister, then?"

"Yes, yes, of course, but of all the things you might have said. 'Your daughter', 'Harry's child', 'my father's bastard'; but you said, 'my sister'."

"Not Harry Goodenstone's, never! And no ... not bastard, it's a word I can't abide; it's always the child that gets the harm of it. I can't tell why, but I was sure that she must be my sister."

"You are much the same age. Though Rosie is ... It is hard when you can't hear, it means that you can't speak. She isn't ... I don't find it easy to put into words."

"You mean that Rosie is like me and you?"

"Yes, except that we were lucky enough to learn things the easy way, by being told. Just because she can't speak does not mean that she has anything else wrong with her."

Mrs Trowell nodded and smiled at Rosie, and again mouthed, "Judeth". "She understands what I say. She just cannot say words herself."

Again we sat quietly for a minute. It seemed that there were so many things to be said, but we said none of them.

"I've been to Harry's. I didn't know what had happened, about him marrying and all that. I wouldn't have come anywhere near, but I didn't know which way to turn. I wrote to him time and time again, but he didn't answer. I told him all I wanted was the papers. I spent nearly the last penny coming here. There's a house: it's mine; it's what Harry settled on me when I went to live with him – you know, on a permanent kind of basis – years ago. The house is entirely mine, except that Harry has got the papers. I shall have to sell it. I really haven't got a penny. And Harry's got the papers. The place is empty. It's not doing it any good standing empty and I can't sell it without the papers. And I wouldn't have asked, except that I don't know what else to do."

"They've shut up the Big House. I believe they have gone on one of the trading ships belonging to her family. They reckon it might be four years or more before they come home."

"That's what she said." She tightened her mouth and swallowed her hurt. "Mrs Cutts. Oh, like a fool I went round to the side door. I had sense enough not to go up to the main door, but the side door was too good for us. She made us stand at the scullery door like tinkers. She needn't have done that. I didn't want anything except my papers. It was humiliating. You've no idea."

But I had. I knew the Mrs Cutts and the Ol Blackwells who were, in their way, as bad as – perhaps worse than – the gentry. Because the Cutts and Blackwells, in aping the self-esteem of their employers, humiliated their own kind. To me they were odious.

"What will you do?"

"I don't know. I just do not know."

"You could come home."

"Home?"

"With me. To the farm."

"No!"

She seemed horrified at the idea.

"Why not?"

"Because ... Everything! Your mother. We couldn't. You couldn't just ... I could never walk back there more than twenty years after."

"It's Rosie's home, isn't it?"

[344]

We sat silently. My words melted as a question, then reformed as a statement of fact, and hung in the air with us. If my father's daughter's home was not at Croud Cantle, then where was it?

"It isn't possible."

"You have nowhere else to go."

"Mrs Nugent. It would be wrong to expect her to accept such a thing."

"You would find her very changed." I told her about the convulsion and what it had done to her.

"Then we could not possibly go there. It would make her worse. No, I shall go on to Blackbrook. We shall manage."

"Would you let Rosie come, if I can find you a place to sleep? Just for now. It will give you time to see the Agent who is looking after the estate."

In the end she gave in to my suggestion and I took her into the village, where Rob Netherfield's parents gave Mrs Trowell a place in with Rob's children. I told Rob the bare bones and he said, "It seems only right, don't it? The girl can't help what her father did."

Rosie did not mind coming with me. Mrs Trowell placed Rosie's hand between the two palms of mine and said, "Rosie-go-with-Judeth." Rosie nodded and came with me up Howgaite Path. She kept her hand in mine all the way, looking about her, interested, intelligent, smiling and nodding at me from time to time, approvingly, I thought.

I had no time, nor did I attempt, to try to think what I would say to Mother. I was sure that taking Rosie home was right and that was all that seemed to matter for the time being.

We reached home and found that Maisie had brought my mother's chair out so that she could sit under the tree, as I once had that time I hurt my leg. She heard the gate latch and looked up at us. With Rosie still holding my hand like a child I took her to my mother. At that moment I realised the implications of my spontaneous action. I suddenly felt apprehensive, but stopped any tremors so that Rosie would not feel them. However much I felt the rights of my action, the stress might be too much.

"Mother, I've brought somebody to stop for a few days."

My mother peered at Rosie.

"Her name is Rosie. She can't hear what anybody says, but she can tell things from people's lips if you look straight at her. I'll get us all

[345]

something to eat and then I want to talk to you about Rosie."

I knew that I was putting off telling her, but I thought that if she had a chance to be with Rosie a little while, see what a gentle nature Rosie had, then she might accept the situation a bit better. I was trying to tell Rosie to stay with my mother, when Mother darted out her good hand and held on tightly to Rosie, drawing her close, peering into her face. Then Mother's head dropped and tears streamed down her face.

"Tomas. Her father. Tomas," she said, in her slack-jawed speech.

I was astounded. She could not possibly have known. Mrs Trowell had told me that apart from her sister and the woman who had cared for Rosie for twenty years, there was no one who knew who Rosie was.

Rosie, when she saw Mother's tears, took the scarf from her hat and began to wipe them away, making concerned motions, as if to say, don't, don't cry; as though she could not bear to see anyone cry.

If the moment when I had realised that Rosie was my sister was overwhelming, then my mother's action was the more so. She drew Rosie's hand up to her face and brushed it with as near a kiss as she could make.

"Yes, she's Rosie Nugent, but you couldn't have known that, Mother."

In her difficult way of speaking she said, "She's Tomas over again. Beautiful. Like Tomas, beautiful. Same hair, face is alike, just like. You and Jaen all Estover – no Tomas in you. She is all Nugent. No ..." she halted, looking all round her, up at me, back at Rosie, quite perturbed for a moment. "No Holly in her. No Holly." And I supposed that must be true, for I could see nothing of the pink and white of Mrs Trowell.

At that time, I had no idea what it was that had given Rosie her particular quality. She had a kind of innocence, yet she was not childish; had quietness but not silence; she could not speak or hear, yet appeared to understand what was important. She had not heard what my mother and I were saying but she had seen Mother crying and it had concerned her: never mind what made the tears, give comfort, care.

[346]

H AD I KNOWN my mother better, perhaps I would not
have been surprised that she not merely accepted Rosie,
but opened up to her in the way she had to Hanna but had never done
to me. She allowed affection to be given to her, and she gave.

I said nothing much to Mother about Mrs Trowell on the evening
that Rosie arrived, except that the Netherfields had taken her in.
Maisie came back from visiting someone in Motte and did not look for
an explanation for Rosie's sudden appearance. She was a bit ill at ease
at first, having to use ways of communicating that were strange, but
Rosie's smiles and nods soon won Maisie over. Rosie was settled in
Mother's old room and I went to help my mother get out of her day
clothes.

I was always careful not to let her know that I knew about her little
hordes of secret pickings. Fluff, moss, feathers picked from her quilt,
shaped into nests exactly like those of the goldcrest. It was strange
behaviour which I could not understand, except as a sign that there
was something not right in her head, but it was not important and it
did no harm. On that evening though, when I went to her, I saw that
she had been crushing up nests and had apparently been throwing
them into the fire. She seemed more co-operative about getting her
bodice and skirt off and I thought that her speech seemed not so
slurred. I had the impression that she had squared her shoulders and
might almost have stumped off into the yard.

"No room at Netherfields," she said.

"It is only for a night."

"Rosie can stay."

"We can't talk about it tonight. Tomorrow."

"She must not come here. Rosie can stay."

Early next morning Rob Netherfield came into the house. I had said that I would go down to the schoolroom early and meet Charlotte there.

"Well, young Jude? You have some queer ideas, I'll be bound."

"There wasn't anything else we could do."

"I don't care, but they won't like it down there." He nodded in the direction of Cantle. "Nor will old Tripp. Give him a chance to drag out his old sermon about The Sins of the Fathers visited on the children."

"They'll have to lump it then."

"Jude, you a have to be sensible. They'd make her life a misery, let alone yourn."

"I know. I only asked you to keep her there for the night."

"It's not my place, is it? It's the old people's, and they'm only there on sufferance because my Dad still turns out a good pack of hounds for the Estate – old as he is."

Rob was right. It was a queer idea to think that we could deal with the result of my long-dead father's actions in such a simple way as "they can lump it".

We needed to talk to someone outside the tangle, so I got Rob to ride over Blackbrook with a note asking Fred if he would come.

I put Rosie's hand between Maisie's as Mrs Trowell had done with mine and said to her, "Maisie". She pressed her lips together as though to say an "M", then smiled and nodded that she understood. When I left them to go down to the schoolroom, she had taken off my mother's cap and was brushing and fluffing out her hair, which was now creamy-white about her head, but with a still-red knot at the back.

It being the height of a hot, dry harvest season, the schoolroom was empty and it was there that Fred Warren came. Mrs Trowell and I had been together there talking for a couple of hours. She had said, "I thought you might call me by my name – I isn't really Mrs Trowell. It's a name Mary thought up and I've been it so long I don't even think of myself as really being a Holly any more."

I said, "Charlotte?" and she smiled and said, "It's a rare long time since anybody called me that."

We sat with a small meal of bread and bacon dripping and talked. She told me how she had come by the scar on her face.

"It was done in a second. I don't think Harry even realised it had touched me. It had a kind of a hair whisk on it – the crop – it was that

that did it. It was like a burn. The hair had been made stiff with some kind of glue, and perhaps that got into the cut, or it could have been the powder and rouge. It festered up and was bad for a long time. Anyway, it's better now." She smiled wryly. "But there an't much call for a one-eyed Ophelia, nor many parts for a messenger-boy with a scar."

She was trying to make light of it. She was not one-eyed, although the lid was badly puckered, but I did think that the scar left on her memory must have been worse.

"I don't really care about it any more. I always think when people see me first on my good side, then sees the other, they act as though they've bit into an apple and found half a maggot in it. That's why I keep my hair so low and wear that old bonnet. I got used to it – the cut – but it's always new to people who don't know me." She smiled again. "And since I left the theatre, that means most people."

By the time that Fred arrived, Charlotte had told much of what had happened to her since she had fled from Park Manor to Portsmouth. Harry's violent jealousy, Mary's death, then finding herself with not much to live on and being cheated or held over a barrel each time she sold a piece of jewellery.

Rosie had lived in the country ever since she was a baby, and had been brought up by a woman who had an idiot child. They had all thought that there had been something wrong with Rosie's brain, but it was only her hearing. As soon as the woman had realised, she had taught Rosie by showing her.

"Constance worked marvels. She had that much patience with those two babies. She taught Rosie everything by pointing and saying things with her lips."

"Is that how she seems to know what's being said?"

"Only when you are facing her direct. She tells by the shape of your mouth."

I thought that was amazing.

"It's with Constance being on the stage. We uses our lips a lot more in acting than when we're speaking ordinary, and Constance realised after a while that when she was raising her voice to Rosie, Rosie wasn't hearing anything: she was just learning from the shape of Constance's mouth. Constance used to say what a lot of satisfaction she got out of Rosie learning something. I dare say you can understand that from what you do here."

[349]

I did. But to succeed with one of my children so that they compared with the success of Constance with Rosie, I should have to get them to a high standard of education.

"Constance's own little Eileen died, so she had a lot of time to spend with Rosie. I used to go down as often as I could. It wasn't easy with Harry – he never knew about her, of course. He was always so jealous of everybody. Anyway, a year or two ago, Constance got the offer of marriage from a man who was left with children, but he wouldn't have Rosie. Constance wouldn't ever have abandoned her. I should have had Rosie back anyway, sooner or later, but it came about at the same time as Mary dying and all that, so I went and got her back."

Charlotte had been concentrating on combing a tassel of her shawl with her fingernails whilst she had been telling me all this. Then she stopped and looked at me earnestly.

"You like her, Judeth, don't you?" The question was so forceful. "You don't think she's simple? Not simple-minded? You'd say she was normal, wouldn't you, except for being deaf?"

"She seems something above normal."

She was silent for a little while.

"It's what's always worried me. I won't live for ever. It's what will happen to her if she's not all there."

Several times she took a breath in, as though about to say something. At last: "Little Eileen – Constance's girl. She didn't have no brain at all. She couldn't do anything hardly herself, not like Rosie. It was lucky in a way that she ate all the nightshades and lords-and-ladies' berries that she did. You couldn't have blamed Constance if she had seen her eating them ... Anybody might do the same. I might have done the same if Rosie ..."

"Rosie will be all right."

"She will. I'm sure she will. It's just that I sometimes wonder if I see her the same as everybody else does."

"She's beautiful and intelligent, she's my sister and she can stay with me for ever if she wants."

I had not intended saying that. It came spontaneously, sincerely: it was the truth.

We were both quiet for a little while, then Charlotte said, "It's queer how things turn out, isn't it?"

I thought about the twenty years of bitterness and resentment which had started that morning when Mary Holly had come to the back door to say that she thought the Master had run off with her sister, and my mother had retched at her feet. Then I thought of the scene I had left earlier: Rosie brushing my mother's hair.

If Charlotte had experienced many people's distaste on seeing her scar, she did not do so when she met Fred. He was understanding and practical and immediately offered a temporary solution to Charlotte's predicament. She could go with Fred to Blackbrook and collect her belongings, then take over as temporary housekeeper to the Warren household.

"I hope you're good at knocking the heads of boys together. Since their mother died, they are for ever squabbling."

Charlotte responded to Fred well. "I never had much to do with boys, but I reckon I might learn. And if knocking their heads together don't work, then I shall subdue them by making them listen to long bits of boring plays."

"What about your daughter?"

"Let her stop on the farm," I suggested, and went on to argue that it wasn't fair to keep moving her from place to place; that she could keep in touch with Charlotte by going to Blackbrook on market days; that she was used to living in the country. But my pleas were mostly that Judeth Nugent could not bear the thought that the fresh air and light that Rosie had brought the day before into our lack-lustre, faint lives in the Croud Cantle cottage would go so soon.

They agreed that it seemed sense. Nobody knew how long it might be before Charlotte could get the papers on her London house sorted out, and until then it was a good idea not to make too many changes.

For about six months or so after Rosie came to Croud Cantle, Mother rallied in her speech. She and Rosie would sit together for hours, each patient with the other's difficulty in communicating. Mother taught Rosie combing and spinning, and Rosie took over the job of caring for Mother and helping her with her food.

She had learned to handle bees from Constance Sylver, a skill that pleased everybody at Croud Cantle; for since Mother's illness, none of us was very pleased to have that job. When it came to the honey taking, Rosie did not let the traveller take the entire contents of the hives – honey, combs, bees and all – as we usually did at the end of the season. She kept a few hives going over the winter on some of their own honey and some sugar, which she pounded, mixed with water and fed to them. This seemed to be a great extravagance, but in the end it proved not to be and, more importantly, it pleased Mother. She had never liked the bee-killing. She would always have it that "bees is different from other creatures, and next to human".

Sometimes, when the two of them were sitting over quiet work, such as wool-combing, Mother would talk on and on in her slurred way. It did not seem to matter that Rosie heard nothing. Words had little to do with their relationship. Communication was physical: nods, touches, the guiding of hands and little pats of approval. The first time I heard her speak of my father to Rosie was whilst she was rambling on, watching her with the bees. I do not know whether she was talking to Rosie or to the bees, for she was talking low and confidential, as she always did when working round the hives.

"Don't take after him. Tomas was afraid, wasn't he? Couldn't stand the hives, nor his father. No good with bees, Nugents. Must never be afraid. The bees a know if you'm afraid. It's why Nugents gets bad stings: bees go for them that's afraid."

[352]

She tapped Rosie and mimed a bee stinging her arm, then puffed out her cheeks and held her hands to the side to indicate a swelling body, then held her throat and made a choking sound. Rosie responded by holding her finger where a bee would crawl on to it.

"Not Nugent. Not nobody – only Rosie. Just Rosie. Not Nugent, not Tomas."

After a while, though, Mother began to behave strangely again. Sometimes she seemed not to remember who we were, or confused names. For three days she had thought that Johnny-twoey was Will and insisted that he sit with her.

"It's all right, Miss Jude," he said, "it's better if I humours her. It don't matter who she thinks I am, so long as it makes her happy."

As with the last two winters, the classroom was often quite full. Harry Goodenstone's order to supply us with fuel and wheat was still not revoked, so the teaching of Cantle children went ahead; not so much by the carrot method I had told Fred that I would use, but by bribery with a dish of fermity and a blazing log. Several of the children could now read, and a few could write.

Of course Ben Hannable had long since withdrawn his support, so that we now had no help in keeping the school going. Except for Fred, who helped out again and again with paying the small rent, providing slates and, as a carrot for those who succeeded in their efforts to write, precious pencils and paper. There was now no question of the "professionalism" that Fred had at first insisted that I observe. I worked with the children because I had a passion to do so: I had no more fervent ambition than to sit in that little room and try to capture the imagination of succeeding generations of Cantle children.

From time to time, Reverend Tripp tried to persuade, cajole or threaten me to take Church money and teach the children religion and their place in "God's great scheme for us".

At one time he had tried to persuade me that what I was doing was against God; that the "entire principles on which our nation is founded – those of agriculture and trade – will be undermined if cottagers' children grow up to become literate idlers. They will never be content to follow the plough nor reap or thresh", and that they would eventually "turn away from the drudgeries for which they were born". Which, of course, made me even more determined that the Church should never get its hands upon my schoolroom.

Perhaps, had he been a younger man, Reverend Tripp might have

[353]

tried harder to stop what I was doing, for it would not have been difficult. He need only to have announced from the pulpit that the children were in moral danger, or some such thing, and with it now being well known who Rosie was, he could easily have made some mud stick. But, as it was, he either forgot or ignored what went on in Annie Bassett's back room.

THE FOLLOWING AUGUST, almost a year to the day when Charlotte had gone to the Big House to get her papers, the Goodenstone's Agent delivered a letter which had been sent to her from Bristol, just before the Eames-Coates vessel sailed for the East. The gist of it was that the property in Dublin Square, London, "erroneously referred to as in Trust for Mrs Charlotte Trowell", was part of the estate of Sir Henry Goodenstone, as could be verified by various documents listed and attached.

By that time, Charlotte's need to prove that the house belonged to her had gone.

In July of that year, almost five years to the day when Molly Warren had died, she and Fred had been married. Only Rosie, Fred's children, his son-in-law and I had attended the service, and we had later joined in a family celebration at the house.

By that time, Mother was seldom able to move further than from the cottage to the orchard. There she sat, mumbling away at the hives, her jerky and trembling hands occasionally making motions, reaching out, as though the hives were people she was talking to. Once, her jerky hand knocked off a hackle, and she sat there, still as the churchyard cross until the swarm settled. She never got a sting. She grew heavy and was sometimes incontinent, so on the day of the wedding I left her in Maisie's care and Rosie and I went to Blackbrook together.

In preparation, I got out my 'Blackbrook' dress again, but found that since it had last seen the light of day at Peg's wedding, my hips had thickened a bit as a result of the hours I spent sitting down in Annie Bassett's schoolroom. It fitted Rosie perfectly, and she went about showing everybody with unaffected delight. I had a very green skirt made, and a light bodice. The skirt gave me great pleasure, particularly when I sat down: it was like having a lapful of moss from the damp, north bank of Chard Lepe Pond.

Mother watched us closely when we had a try-out of our wedding-day clothes. It was one of her bad-speaking days, so it took me a lot of patience to understand that she wanted me to get out her pretty jacket. At first I thought that she was saying that she too wanted to dress up, but she indicated the jacket and me and Rosie.

"Try it on," I mimed to Rosie.

Rosie was not so full-bosomed as Mother. She pointed to me, indicating that my figure was generous there. True, it fitted me perfectly.

I should give a lot to know what went on in my mother's head sometimes. On her bad-speaking days, she acquiesced or approved of things by rocking her body back and forth – which she did, on and on, when she saw me in the jacket.

At such times, when Rosie and Mother and I were together, I had fleeting daydreams when Jaen and Hanna would be there, too, and my father would come upon us.

All the Nugent women living together – not all, for there was no doubt that Charlotte would have to be included. But I should have liked him to see. As Charlotte had said, it's queer how things turn out.

And I should have liked him to see that after all the havoc he had wreaked by his self-centred nature, we could do very well without him. Very well.

By the time Charlotte became Mrs Fred Warren, Rosie had settled down in Croud Cantle as though she had never lived elsewhere. After the wedding, Charlotte and Fred had her to stop for a week in Blackbrook, so that she might get used to her new home.

I had taken her with me from time to time when I had gone to do the market. Then she had moved about Fred's house, smiling; smoothing Molly Warren's plush, brocade and silky furnishings; looking into mirrored-glass and getting a lot of enjoyment at seeing her own reflection clearly for the first time. After two days of staying in Blackbrook, she indicated to her mother that she wanted to return to the farm.

Charlotte was disappointed.

"Give her time," Fred said, "she can come whenever she wants. Judeth will still bring her."

"I don't want to make her do anything she don't want in that way,

Judeth," Charlotte said. "She was twenty years with Constance, then all of a sudden she had to come with me, then with you. It must be hard for her."

So Rosie came back to Croud Cantle, where she slipped back into her place: comforting, soothing and tending to my mother, who got about the yard by holding on to walls and fences, but was sometimes feeble-minded and unpredictable.

I was pleased when she came back. The place without her seemed quiet and lonely. I had grown to love her: not as I loved Jaen, because Rosie and I had no childhood secrets; nor as I loved Hanna, who I had helped to bring up; but I loved Rosie for the way she filled the house with her enjoyment of life. Sometimes we walked over the hills together, silently, sharing the chalky skeleton of Old Marl, the dips and mounds of Tradden. We would sit staring out over the valley. When I first noticed that she, too, smoothed and scratched her fingers into the rough grass of Tradden, as though petting a donkey, I felt sure that she understood the hills. I wished there was a way of telling her that as a lark flies it fills the sky with clear, joyous song; whilst a butterfly flitters silently. Rosie could no more understand silence than she could that we were sisters. The understanding between us grew from our regard for one another.

At about this same time Maisie, too, married again. She married Rob Netherfield, and moved into the cottage that adjoined that of Rob's parents. There she became a second mother to Rob's children, as well as to the old couple. When it came to reforming society, Maisie was as placid as Rob was hot-blooded. It was a good match and I was pleased, except that we would lose Maisie.

[357]

Part Three

MATRIARCH

January 1796

In this Journal, I have recorded as faithfully as I am able as much of the history of the Estover-Nugent family as I know to be true. It is the history of a family that is as old as any that can boast noble arms and blue blood; the history of a common family that few historians will consider of interest to posterity. I often look at my first entry written at Easter 1782, fourteen years ago, wherein I wrote, "Went to Jaens. Jaen will have a new baby it will come November. Hana will stop with muther and me." Being unsure which was correct I wrote "I" as well, for even then I did not want to be looked down upon for being illiterate.

No other person has read this history, for it is intended to be read by future generations of my family. Indeed, if it were to be read by anyone alive now, then I should be reluctant to record so freely. I have started other writings and I have written part of a book based upon some of the events of the Estover-Nugents. Whether it will ever be completed, only the future knows — perhaps in time I shall be able to look dispassionately on our lives. This Journal, however, I will keep in all circumstances.

Whenever I have had stressful events to record, I am always given to write a preamble such as this. One could say that I am working myself up to committing to paper things so painful that to write them is to relive them. Even now, almost twelve months since the first of the events occurred, I am disturbed by the distress I felt then, and it is only now that a year has passed that I record them.

In the July before last, the year being 1794, after her mother had married Fred Warren, Rosie came back to Croud Cantle, and has lived here ever since. They had hoped that Rosie would live with them and the Warren boys. I continued teaching the village children whenever they came, and put in as much time as I could at the farm and the market. On a Thursday in 1795, John Toose and I returned from Blackbrook to find Mrs Hazelhurst there. It was the start of the most terrible episode in the life of this family.

[361]

NANCE HAZELHURST did not wait until John had gone away before she began angrily shouting at Jude.

"Until I seen it for myself, I wouldn't a believed it. I rue the day our poor Dan got mixed up with you lot. It was me who said he ought to marry her. I shall never forgive myself. He should a left her where she belonged, on this midden, along with the rest of her rotten tribe. She deserved everything she got." The woman was beside herself with rage.

Jude immediately thought that there was some trouble with Jaen.

"What's happened? Has she miscarried another child?"

"Miscarry? A pity she hadn't a miscarried the first cause of it all, then none of it wouldn't never have happened."

"Mrs Hazelhurst. Keep your voice down, and tell me why you're here and what's happened."

At that moment Rosie came from the house, wide-eyed and puzzled, looking from Jude to Nance Hazelhurst and back over her shoulder, pointing her finger and moving it in the way that indicated something was urgent. She tried to say something with her voice but, as always, only animal sounds came out.

Nance Hazelhurst looked at Rosie with disgust.

"My God! It's true what I heard what was going on here, but I wouldn't a believed it if I hadn't a seen it with my own eyes. When I think that our family is linked to the likes of it!"

With one movement, Jude stepped close to the little, brown wiry old woman and slapped her hard across the mouth. Rosie stood watching with tears waiting to fall over. Jude drew her close and held her, trying to reassure her, but all that Rosie could see was violence and anger on the faces of Jude and the old woman.

"Ah, that's it, that's it, a bit more of the Nugent coming out!"

"Don't you ever say one word against Rosie, or anybody else of this family. Before that animal of a son of yours got a child into my sister when she hardly knew what was happening to her she was a happy, ordinary girl, and what is she now? Nothing but a ruined body. She's so full of misery that she don't know any more whether she's coming or going."

"Like all the rest of your lot, then. Your mother in there, gone soft in the head; you'm as queer as they makes them. Wouldn't have our Eddie, would you? High and mighty miss! And there's her! Your own father's by-blow living under the same roof, and none of you ashamed of his sin."

She was making fists and her face was distorted. She looked Rosie up and down, as though at filth.

Violent emotions welled up in Jude, but she swallowed them down.

"I hit you once and I'm sorry for that because you're old, not because you don't deserve it. But if you don't clear off this minute I shall throw you out, and if you ever step foot on this land again I shall be waiting with a hay fork."

"Oh, a hay fork, is it? Not a cleaver?"

The episode was becoming more and more of a nightmare. They were both screaming at one another, yet Jude had no idea what for.

"Why have you come? Did you come all that way just to shout at me and frighten Rosie? Is it Hanna? For God's sake, woman, what's happened?"

"Find out for yourself!"

The whole episode was over in a minute.

The old woman spat at Jude's feet, got into the small cart that had been left at the yard gate and drove away, leaving Jude shaking with anger and bewilderment. For the first time in fourteen years Nance Hazelhurst had come to Croud Cantle. She stood staring into space, until she realised that she still had her arm around Rosie and held her tight by her trembling shoulders.

Then Rosie again began making agitated signs, pulling Jude into the cottage. Bella was slumped in her chair before the hearth, staring into the flames as she often did these days. Jude went to pull her into a more comfortable position so that she would not stop the circulation of blood to her fingers, as she sometimes did when she withdrew into herself. Rosie shook her head at Jude, pointing her finger and jerking it towards the stairs; agitated and pulling at Jude's sleeve.

On Rosie's bed, a figure lay curled close in upon herself, sleeping heavily.

"Hanna!"

Jude was confused and bewildered.

"What, Rosie? What happened?"

Rosie pointed, shook her head, and waved her hand before her face, disturbed and frustrated that she could not make herself understood.

"It's all right, Rosie. All right."

The small apothecary's measure that was used for medicines was beside the bed. Rosie gave it to Jude to smell, pointing at Hanna. She had given her opium tincture and looked relieved and pleased when Jude said that she had done the right thing.

I doubt that I shall ever be able to record the full story of what happened at Ham Ford that day. Hanna will never speak of it; Jaen is dead; and Dan Hazelhurst is in a penal colony thousands of miles from here. What I know of Hanna's part in the tragedy did not come out at the trial.

It was made clear to me that the barrister the Hazelhursts took on to save the murderer from the gallows would have mixed up such a pot of filth from the Nugent history – of my father and Charlotte, Jaen's condition on marriage, Rosie living at Croud Cantle, and the influence upon Hanna of living in such a place – that the scandal would have been printed by the thousand and sold for a penny in every city in the country.

So Hanna was saved the ordeal of having to tell the story of the death of her mother at the hand of her father. What I know of that part is what was told to me by John Toose, who was Hanna's only confidant.

At his trial at the Winchester Assize, Daniel Francis Hazelhurst pleaded guilty to a charge of Manslaughter. Man-slaughter! It was my sweet Jaen who was slaughtered. Womanslaughter. Wifeslaughter. It was only after suffering fourteen years of subjugation that she tried to claim some rights over her own body, but they were not hers to claim, the rights were the husband's – conjugal rights – and when she tried to refuse him those rights, he took them. I sat in the public gallery throughout the entire proceedings, stiff and cold with grief, watching him, hating him with such intensity that I had no feeling except where the misery and hatred lay.

By chance, Will had come south and was in Southampton at the time, and came to Winchester each day with me: guiding me, giving me food, caring for me. But I came and went as though dead, and I could not even tell him that if it had not been for him I might have lost my reason. And, had he asked me then, I might have married him.

Daniel Hazelhurst cried distractedly when he told how his wife had fought him like a fury, attacking him with a cleaver. He had been wounded badly in his back and had lost a lot of blood. He had been forced to protect himself and in doing so had pushed her a bit too hard, and she had fallen, hitting her head against an oak chest.

Nobody asked the enormous man whether it was true that his wife was only five foot tall? Whether she had bad legs that would hardly support her? Whether her body was so ruined by constant child-bearing that she would not have had the strength to attack a dog?

He was found guilty of Manslaughter and sentenced to be transported.

FOR THE FIRST week after Hanna was brought back to Croud Cantle, three of the four of those living there were silent. Apart from Rosie's normal silence, Bella had withdrawn into herself completely and Hanna never spoke one word.

It was Bob Pointer who helped Jude piece together something of what happened that day.

Nance Hazelhurst, in the horse-driven light cart, had come into the yard and started shouting.

"I never knew what it was all about, Miss Jude. It never made no sense. She kep' on about bringing back shit to its own midden. Then I saw the girl. I thought she'd a had a accident, her clothes was covered in blood. Miz Nugent come out and took one look at she and fell down in a dead faint. Miss Rosie come out and the old lady started shouting at her, but a course she didn't understand what was going on. The old lady asks me where you was and I told her it was market day, so first off makes the girl get down and drives out a the yard.

"Lord, Miss Jude, she went off like a twenty-year-old, whipping up the horse. Lord, I thought, she a have that cart over on all they ruts down Howgaite. She was gone for about an hour, then she come back. Be that time I'd a got Miz Nugent into her chair, and me and Miss Rosie got the girl upstairs. Miss Rosie wanted me to do something, but I couldn't understand what it was. Anyway, all I could think of was to get some water because of all the blood, and that's what I did. Be the time I got back, Miss Rosie had got the girl wrapped up in a blanket and she was nodding and pointing. What I think she meant was that the girl wasn't hurt, it was just her clothes where the blood was.

"After that, I stayed in the house till you come back, then I cleared off round the back where I was handy if you wanted me."

Whilst all the shouting was going on, Johnny-twoey had gone unobtrusively into the oathouses with the donkeys, where Bob Pointer was standing as though ready for action.

"It's summat to do with Miz Nugent's grandchild. The old lady brought her back. Wait here with me and just see they'm all right. The old lady's gone off her head, but it an't nothing to do with us what's going on. Just wait."

And Johnny-twoey had waited, still and silent, until the old lady went off. After she had gone, he went into the kitchen and there too waited still and silent for Jude to come.

"Miss Jude? Is it Hanny?" His face pale against the dark beard which made him look more than his twenty years.

Jude laid a hand on his arm for a moment and nodded. "But she's all right. She's not hurt, but something's happened that we don't know about."

"Miss Jude? Can I see her? I won't say nothing, just see her."

"She's asleep, but come with me. Then you can see she's all right."

Enigmatically as always, he looked down at Hanny. "She a be all right, Miss Jude."

When he spoke, Hanna moved and made a sound.

"Miss Jude? Do you think she knows it's me here?"

1st January 1800

An old saying, "Time heals". I do not know that I agree, but it does at least allow scar tissue to grow over wounds. What the passage of time does do is remove the importance, the impact that an incident has on those who live through it.

I am able, at last, to record the final piece of the history of your antecedent, Tomas Nugent.

It should have been written long ago, but as it was so close to the terrible tragedy of Jaen, I have continually avoided doing so — it gives, perhaps, the impression of a history of violence, which would be a wrong impression. It is a history of moments of uncontrolled passion.

Also, over the last few years, I have found it almost impossible to string words together. I abandoned writing the book I had begun, and entries in this Journal have been few. However, from here on I intend to bring our history up to date.

Judeth Nugent

At first, Hanna suffered fits of shaking and sweating, then gradually returned to health. She still held Jude at arm's length, not forgiving her the day when she was left at Ham Ford and Jude returned to Croud Cantle without her.

Like everyone else, Hanna responded to Rosie. Jude was displaced in her role of Aunt and Hanna slipped back into the routine of the work she had done when she was a child. The two of them worked together as Bella and Jaen had once worked, as Jaen and Jude, as Jude and Bella had.

John Toose had everything at his fingertips. Given enough hours in the day, he could have done every job on the farm. Anyone who had known Bella in the days when she stumped about the place would recognise her in Hanna, but there was something less sharp about Hanna. She and John spent a lot of their time together, and it was he who drew the nightmares out of her by getting her to talk.

The only person Jude had left for support now was Will. Although Fred was still a good friend, since he had become enmeshed in the Nugent family by marrying Rosie's mother, Jude never felt able to talk to him about the family. At times of her lowest ebb, when she fully realised that Jaen was not still somewhere the other side of Tradden, she wrote to Will.

Dear Will,

I still find it really hard to accept. I ought to have known that grief, like all the other strong emotions, will leap out when least expected.

I expect her to be on Tradden; I expect her by Chard Lepe pond, or where the Dunnock runs close by the farm; but I am unprepared for her in a phrase in the mouth of one of the children in the classroom, or reflected in a window in Blackbrook.

What can I do about it? That is not a question – there is nothing to be done. When I stand outside myself I can see that I am becoming a silent and sombre woman. But I have Hanna and Rosie and mother, who keeps going – what a strong constitution: she survives everything.

I sometimes catch a glimpse of us from outside. The four of us, making our lives together. Quite unexpectedly successful, in a strange way.

Rosie, Hanna and John Toose now run the market stand, so that my contribution is now that of manager and labourer, mostly done in the early and late hours of the day, leaving me time for my schoolroom.

I am in the schoolroom now, with just one child. A girl who is a second John Toose for learning. I often pay her father what the girl would earn gleaning just to keep her here, where she so obviously loves to be. She is another who absorbs knowledge like a parched field. As I write, she is answering a list of questions I have set for her. She smiles at the "prize" of using paper and pen. I almost hold my breath for her future.

Your voice comes through in your letters. Always write to me,

Judeth

HOT, HOT AUGUST. John and Bob Pointer are not at Croud Cantle, but have gone for a day's harvesting on The Estate. Jude is in her schoolroom, and the village is deserted for the harvest fields.

Jude hears the heavy tread of boots coming down Bellpitt Lane, the sound of a man's voice and occasionally a woman answering in monosyllables. Quietly, so as not to disturb the engrossed, small girl, sucking her knuckle as she thinks, Jude stands so that she can see through the small side-window.

A tall youth, a woman and a man are passing. They are strangers to Cantle – a common enough sight these days, when it sometimes seems that half the farm-workers in England are out on the roads looking for work. The woman and the boy walk together about half a pace behind the man. Idly, Jude watches them. It is the man who attracts her attention because he limps a little, as she does herself. He is quite old, probably about fifty, with a great mane of white hair and a full white beard. Above his eyebrow and running into his hairline is a deep furrow. It reminds her of the indentation in the top of a loaf when it is put down to prove.

Had it been a day when Fred Warren was visiting the schoolroom, he would at once recognise 'Jonah' Smith, the innkeeper from Garlick on the old Roman Road, and his wife Bess, and Andrew, whom he had said was his son "as far as any man knew his own son". But seeing the boy now, fully fifteen years old, anyone can see that this is father and son passing through Cantle.

Andrew Smith, the youth, has grown to be beautiful – a strange description for a boy. Women will say, though, as they did of his father, that beautiful is the right word.

After nearly thirty years, Tomas Nugent is returning to his birthplace, to Croud Cantle – his birthright.

At Croud Cantle, Rosie and Hanna are at work in the bottom fields. Bella is sitting in Johnny-twoey's herb garden. She is watching her bees, busy at the feverfew and marigolds; a constant stream of industry coming and going.

Bella likes it with her bees. Since her convulsion it is too much effort to make anybody understand, but the bees ... you don't have to talk out loud to them.

"I always been good to you, an't I? Always told you everything what was going on.

"Do you remember when Hanna came? That was a night! There wan't many of you here then. Only one old queen I tucked up in the skep with a bit of a comb I left her. Even though it was snowing, I come and told her, 'We got Jaen's baby staying with us.'

"And I told you about Will Vickery. He was the best pair of feet ever came through the yard gate. If I'd a had a son to follow on here, I should a wanted one like him. I thought I should a had him at one time, but there, nothing ever seems to go the way it ought to.

"Nothing haven't never gone on here without I told you, right from the first day I come. I told you – I'm Bella Estover come to nurse your Master into his grave. I've only come to do good to this house.

"And you always let me come close.

"I only ever had four stings in my whole life, and that wasn't from any of you. That was them Rectory bees, attacking bees: they feeds off pollen from the yew-tree with its roots in graveyard bones. I never liked the Rectory bees. They always been vicious: not like you, who flies in the pink apple-blossoms and the spicy sage up here in the clean parts where there an't no dust motes.

"Jaen was stung once: that frightened me. She was only a baby, but she swelled up till her cheeks was level with her nose. I thought she was going to die. I'd a seen that once before in him. In Tomas. I an't hardly let that name pass my lips in twenty-five years. She must have got that from him. You remember him? Tomas, what was your Master – still is your Master by rights, I suppose, for nothing of this can be mine. I wasn't never sensitive to your stings. Jaen must a got it from him.

"He was like that for bee-stings, do you remember? Lord how you went for him when I sent him to tell you his father was dead. I never seen nothing like it. For a couple of days I thought we should a had two corpses to a buried, father and son.

"He wouldn't never come near you no more. If he seen one a you he'd as soon as have a fit as not. Somebody else in their family was killed like that, so I've heard. An uncle of his ... his name was Tomas as well. One bee stung him and he was gone like he had been give deadly poison.

"He never handed that on to Rosie, thank the Lord. You and she gets on all right. I'm glad. Jude nor Hanna never seemed to get the knack of taking your honey right. I don't think they ever trusted you. Rosie trusts you."

The bees hum Bella to an August afternoon light sleep again, where sorting out the past from the present does not matter: it's all one and the same there.

The droning has stopped. There is the sound of boots crunching; limping boots, like Jude's, only heavier. Bella rouses, opens her eyes, yet is still asleep. Tomas walks up. Tomas, white-haired and with a great white beard. He has a terrible dent in his beautiful forehead.

"Hello, Bella," he says. "Did I wake you up?"

Bella hears him. It is Tomas's voice. "Hello Bella." She listens for the bees to start up again, but they are still silent.

"I thought you'd a been dead by now," says Tomas. He turns to Andrew. "Do you reckon she can hear?"

The youth says nothing. He watches his father and the shaking, mumbling old woman.

"Listen bees."

They will not hum.

"Here's some news. Your master is here and he have brought us a son at last. You see him, bees, a boy. An't he beautiful? Spit and image of your old Master."

They do not dance.

Bella lifts off the hackle so that they can hear her.

Tomas runs, flailing his arms at the buzzing.

Bess Smith and Andrew stand stiff with fear.

The bees do not notice them – only Tomas, whose flailing arms are a threat.

1st January 1801

Logically, there is no reason to choose this day to assemble facts and dates, but the first day of a new century does have an appropriateness that appeals to me.

[371]

TOMAS BERTRAM CHESTER NUGENT, b 1744; d 1795
Also known as Jonah Smith of Garlick, Hampshire. Buried in Cantle graveyard after an attack by bees.
ISABELL NUGENT *née* ESTOVER, b 1742; *of Croud Cantle, Hampshire.*
JAEN HAZELHURST *née* NUGENT, b 1762; d 1795.
Elder daughter of Tomas and Bella. m 1780.
Of Ham Ford, Newton Clare, Hampshire.
Buried in Cantle graveyard after a fall.
Mother to Hanna.
Also mother to Daniel, Baxter, Francis, Richard, Gregory, George. All surname HAZELHURST, *believed to be in the care of Up Teg Farm, Newton Clare, Hampshire.*
JUDETH NUGENT, b 1768
Younger daughter of Tomas and Bella.
ROSALINDA HOLLY
Only child of Tomas Nugent and Charlotte Holly.
HANNA TOOSE *née Hazelhurst,* b 1780
m JOHN TOOSE (b 1775)
ANDREW SMITH, b 1780
Only child of Tomas Nugent and Elizabeth Smith of Garlick, Hampshire. Recently of Croud Cantle, Hampshire.

In my first Journal I recorded the first of many facts I have discovered in the Parish Register. Anyone who looks back to that date in 1781 may wonder at the implications of that simple entry which reads: NUGENT, *Tomas Chester Bertram,* b 1744. *Father, George Chester Nugent, A Farmer; Mother, Alice Mary.*

Today, as will be seen from the above entries, Hanna married John Amos Toose in Saint Peter's Church, Cantle, Hampshire. Witnessed only by Rosie, Andrew and myself.

As I watched the ceremony, I saw that in those two serious and hard-working young people lies the only hope that Croud Cantle will not go the way of all else in the Cantle Valley – into the maw of the Goodenstones.

John Toose is an able and good horticulturalist with modern ideas. Hanna Toose, his wife, is as capable and efficient a market trader on Blackbrook market as ever Bella was, and much better than myself.

You who read this in the next century will know whether my hope is fulfilled.

J.N.

JUDE TIED HER wedding bonnet to a juniper and hitched up her new skirt, freeing her to move, to climb Tradden, and be on her own after the quiet wedding and the breakfast. She unpinned the knot at the back of her head and her pale red hair streamed out in the wind. She breathed deeply. The air was dry and sharp and satisfying. Coarse, whitish grasses and empty heather bells, scoured by the winter weather, whisked and rustled.

Cantle, and the church she had come from just now, were far below. In the clear air and pale January sun of the new century, the village looked deceptively solid in the valley. Only the church, the rectory and the Big House were built with sufficiently decent materials to be still standing at the turn of another century, unless the Estate and the Church did something about the more humble, damp and crumbling property which they owned.

Jude wondered what the place would look like then. But the pattern of cottages spread along Bellpitt Lane as far as the ford; the silver line of the Dunnock and the tracks of Howgaite, Raike Bottom and Church Farm Lane were so familiar a part of the scene that Jude could not eradicate them and imagine something else in their place.

For the first time, Jude had noticed the steepness of the last part of Tradden. The knee joint of the leg that had been damaged played her up these days and she was sometimes aware of her thiry-two years, but today she felt more youthful than she had for ages.

Perhaps the worst part of her life was over. Certainly, whatever happened from now on could not be worse than the past.

Bella would die, but that would mean only the death of her body. At nearly sixty she had outlived most of her contemporaries. Well-fed and cared for, and always free of the fevers or consumption that carried off the majority of her kind by the time they were fifty, she appeared to be indestructible. She lived in a world of her own. Was it living? Possibly her mind was as blank as her face. She was no longer difficult: getting up, moving, eating, drinking, doing as she was told; and for the rest of the time, sitting gazing into the hearth when the weather was cold, or into the orchard grass when the sun shone.

Something might happen to Rosie. That would be hard. That would get through the scars. Not quite as hard as losing Jaen, though.

Hanna? Yes, it would hurt to lose Hanna again. She had been lost to Jude before: lost and found again, lost and found. In a way Jude had lost her again this morning, but this time more happily. And not entirely lost, for they would be living in the two new rooms that had been built on to the farmhouse.

From where she stood, facing west across the valley, Jude could see how the shape of Croud Cantle had changed since she was a girl. There was a second chimney and now the new part. It used to be L-shaped, but it now seemed to sprawl.

Hanna and Johnny were going to be all right. Conventional, serious, no unwilling and hasty marriage as Jaen's had been. Nothing about them to hide. Not now. Not since Nance Hazelhurst had died. Now the only people who knew the truth about what happened on the day Jaen was killed were John, Hanna and her transported father.

Over the years, Jude had learned some of it – from John, not Hanna – Hanna had never got back on the old footing with Jude. All Jude knew about that morning was that Hanna had heard Jaen crying and pleading with Dan to leave her alone. Hanna, who had been in the scullery, hacking off pigs' feet, trying not to listen to her parents quarrelling, apparently heard a blow and a cry. She had run and hacked at her father's back to make him stop.

In the clear air, the line of stone that spoilt the curve of Winchester Hill stood out clearly. It was ages since Jude had been up there, except to pass by on the way to market.

She followed the outline of the enclosing hills with her eyes. From the stones, down the steep slope where the Dunnock cut between Winchester and Old Marl; up again along the ridge and around to the west to Tradden; along the curve to her right, east to where the Dunnock ran south out of the valley; up, up to the top of Beacon and round to where, later, the sun would drop down, touching the little windows of Croud Cantle which lay directly facing. Down to the centre of the valley and the cluster of cottages.

Annie Bassett was in the graveyard and her house was now

occupied by one of John Toose's many brothers. The school had
finished on the day when Bella had withdrawn completely: the day
Tomas died from the attack by the bees that followed him as he ran.

Bella was Jude's duty. A senile mother was a responsibility that no
daughter could avoid. Perhaps there might come a day ... Probably
not, for there were still other responsibilities: Rosie, Bess Smith, who
had stayed on doing such chores as she had done throughout her life.
The responsibility of making the farm pay to keep them all. But now
that Hanna and Johnny were there to help run the place, perhaps ...
Perhaps with Andrew and Rosie and Bess, Jude could again make a bit
of a go of the school.

Perhaps ... When Bella was gone – not till then. Bella was
nobody's responsiblity but Jude's.

It would mean a new lot of children. One or two of the girls from
Jude's first class were already married. Occasionally a young person
would come to her on the market, "Remember me, Miss Jude? You
learnt me to read."

That had been the dream, the ambition, which made it
worthwhile. Would it all be too much to fight for again? It was
something you did when you were young, before you had all the
stuffing knocked out of you.

But you couldn't give up on children like Tillie Martin – it had
been Tillie Martin who had been in the schoolroom on that hot, hot
August day. Tillie Martin was ten now, and could read and write as
well as Jude herself. Five years come next August since that day. It was
queer that: she had watched him walk back into the village he had left
twenty years before; left Mother, Jaen, herself.

Watched her father come home. It was queer when you came to
think of it.

A white-haired stranger who had a limp like her own and a dent in
his skull. He had seemed so insignificant. Even with his dead face, all
disfigured from the bee poison, he seemed insignificant.

What would it all have been like if she'd married Will? Will. The
last letter she had received had been written from him in Leeds gaol.
Will, a thorn in the side of authority. He had held a meeting outside a
factory and been bound over to keep the peace in the sum of five
pounds. Then he had held another meeting, and when it came to
forfeit the five pounds he could not pay; neither could the rest of his
associates. Jude sent five pounds for "The Funds". In every letter he

wrote, "I am still waiting for you to change your mind, Judeth."

Round the bend of the raike, something moving drew Jude's attention back from the enclosed valley. Rosie. Jude smiled to herself. Rosie.

You had to be up here looking down to really see them as other people did – that lot up a Croud Cantle, was what the villagers called them. Bella, Bess, Jude, Rosie, Hanna and John and Andrew. She smiled again: that would have been a bag of bones for Dicken to have rattled in the Dragon and Fount.

Rosie pointed to the juniper bush. She had tied her bonnet beside Jude's. Green ribbons flicked and fluttered with yellow ribbons. Rosie always seemed to find something to be glad about. Smiling and waving she climbed up to where Jude was. Rosie, at thirty-two, was as youthful as her pink and white mother had been. She came close to Jude, held her arm and pointed in her urgent way at Croud Cantle.

A wagon was drawing in at the yard gate. It was impossible to see from here, but the sisters knew it to be beribboned and wreathed for the bridal couple.

Jude nodded at Rosie – Rosie smiled at Jude.